THE OLD MAJOR.

The Works of E. P. Roe

VOLUME THIRTEEN

HIS SOMBRE RIVALS

ILLUSTRATED

NEW YORK
P. F. COLLIER & SON

PREFACE

The following story has been taking form in my mind for several years, and at last I have been able to write it out. With a regret akin to sadness, I take my leave, this August day, of people who have become very real to me, whose joys and sorrows I have made my own. Although a Northern man, I think my Southern readers will feel that I have sought to do justice to their motives. At this distance from the late Civil War, it is time that passion and prejudice sank below the horizon, and among the surviving soldiers who were arrayed against each other I think they have practically disappeared. Stern and prolonged conflict taught mutual respect. The men of the Northern armies were convinced, beyond the shadow of a doubt, that they had fought men and Americans —men whose patriotism and devotion to a cause sacred to them was as pure and lofty as their own. It is time that sane men and women should be large-minded enough to recognize that, whatever may have been the original motives of political leaders, the people on both sides were sincere and honest; that around the camp-fires at their hearths and in their places of worship they looked for God's blessing on their efforts with equal freedom from hypocrisy.

I have endeavored to portray the battle of Bull Run as it could appear to a civilian spectator: to give a suggestive picture and not a general description. The following war-scenes are imaginary, and colored by personal reminiscence. I was in the service nearly four years, two of which were spent with the cavalry. Nevertheless, justly distrustful of my knowledge of military affairs, I have submitted my proofs to my friend Colonel H. C. Hasbrouck, Commandant of Cadets at West Point, and therefore have confidence that as mere sketches of battles and skirmishes they are not technically defective.

The title of the story will naturally lead the reader to expect that deep shadows rest upon many of its pages. I know it is scarcely the fashion of the present time to portray men and women who feel very deeply about anything, but there certainly was deep feeling at the time of which I write, as, in truth, there is to-day. The heart of humanity is like the ocean. There are depths to be stirred when the causes are adequate.   E. P. R.

CORNWALL-ON-THE-HUDSON,
    August 21, 1883.

CONTENTS

CHAPTER X

CHAPTER XXXVI

CHAPTER XXXVII

CHAPTER XXXVIII

CHAPTER XXXIX

CHAPTER XL

CHAPTER XLI

HIS SOMBRE RIVALS

HIS SOMBRE RIVALS

CHAPTER I

AN EMBODIMENT OF MAY

"BEYOND that revolving light lies my home. And yet why should I use such a term when the best I can say is that a continent is my home? Home suggests a loved familiar nook in the great world. There is no such niche for me, nor can I recall any place around which my memory lingers with especial pleasure."

In a gloomy and somewhat bitter mood, Alford Graham thus soliloquized as he paced the deck of an in-coming steamer. In explanation it may be briefly said that he had been orphaned early in life, and that the residences of his guardians had never been made homelike to him. While scarcely more than a child he had been placed at boarding-schools where the system and routine made the youth's life little better than that of a soldier in his barrack. Many boys would have grown hardy, aggressive, callous, and very possibly vicious from being thrown out on the world so early. Young Graham became reticent and to superficial observers shy. Those who cared to observe him closely, however, discovered that it was not diffidence, but indifference toward others that characterized his manner. In the most impressible period of his life he had received instruction, advice and discipline in abundance, but love and sympathy had been denied. Unconsciously his heart had become chilled, benumbed and overshadowed by his intellect. The actual world gave him little and seemed to promise less, and, as a result not at all unnatural, he became something of a recluse and bookworm even before he had left behind him the years of boyhood.

Both comrades and teachers eventually learned that the retiring and solitary youth was not to be trifled with. He looked his instructor steadily in the eye when he recited, and while his manner was respectful, it was never deferential, nor could he be induced to yield a point, when believing himself in the right, to mere arbitrary assertion; and sometimes he brought confusion to his teacher by quoting in support of his own view some unimpeachable authority.

At the beginning of each school term there were usually rough fellows who thought the quiet boy could be made the subject of practical jokes and petty annoyances without much danger of retaliation. Graham would usually remain patient up to a certain point, and then, in dismay and astonishment, the offender would suddenly find himself receiving a punishment which he seemed powerless to resist. Blows would fall like hail, or if the combatants closed in the struggle, the aggressor appeared to find in Graham's slight form sinew and fury only. It seemed as if the lad's spirit broke forth in such a flame of indignation that no one could withstand him. It was also remembered that while he was not noted for prowess on the playground, few could surpass him in the gymnasium, and that he took long solitary rambles. Such of his classmates, therefore, as were inclined to quarrel with him because of his unpopular ways soon learned that he kept up his muscle with the best of them, and that, when at last roused, his anger struck like lightning from a cloud.

During the latter part of his college course he gradually formed a strong friendship for a young man of a different type, an ardent sunny-natured youth, who proved an antidote to his morbid tendencies. They went abroad together and studied for two years at a German university, and then Warren Hilland, Graham's friend, having inherited large wealth, returned to his home. Graham, left to himself, delved more and more deeply in certain phases of sceptical philosophy. It appeared to him that in the past men had believed almost everything, and that the heavier the drafts made on credulity the more largely had they been honored. The two friends had long since resolved that the actual and the proved should be the base from which they would advance into the unknown, and they discarded with equal indifference unsubstantiated theories of science and what they were pleased to term the illusions of faith. "From the verge of the known explore the unknown," was their motto, and it had been their hope to spend their lives in extending the outposts of accurate knowledge, in some one or two directions, a little beyond the points already reached. Since the scalpel and microscope revealed no soul in the human mechanism they regarded all theories and beliefs concerning a separate spiritual existence as mere assumption. They accepted the materialistic view. To them each generation was a link in an endless chain, and man himself wholly the product of an evolution which had no relations to a creative mind, for they had no belief in the existence of such a mind. They held that one had only to live wisely and well, and thus transmit the principle of life, not only unvitiated, but strengthened and enlarged. Sins against body and mind were sins against the race, and it was their creed that the stronger, fuller and more nearly complete they made their lives the richer and fuller would be the life that succeeded them. They scouted as utterly unproved and irrational the idea that they could live after death, excepting as the plant lives by adding to the material life and well-being of other plants. But at that time the spring and vigor of youth were in their heart and brain, and it seemed to them a glorious thing to live and do their part in the advancement of the race toward a stage of perfection not dreamed of by the unthinking masses.

Alas for their visions of future achievement! An avalanche of wealth had overwhelmed Hilland. His letters to his friend had grown more and more infrequent, and they contained many traces of the business cares and the distractions inseparable from his possessions and new relations. And now for causes just the reverse Graham also was forsaking his

studies. His modest inheritance, invested chiefly in real estate, had so far depreciated that apparently it could not much
longer provide for even his frugal life abroad.

"I must give up my chosen career for a life of bread-win-
ning," he had concluded sadly, and he was ready to avail
himself of any good opening that offered. Therefore he knew
not where his lot would be cast on the broad continent beyond the revolving light that loomed every moment more distinctly in the west.

A few days later found him at the residence of Mrs. Mayburn, a pretty cottage in a suburb of an eastern city. This
lady was his aunt by marriage, and had long been a widow.
She had never manifested much interest in her nephew, but
since she was his nearest relative he felt that he could not do
less than call upon her. To his agreeable surprise he found
that time had mellowed her spirit and softened her angulari-
ties. After the death of her husband she had developed unusual ability to take care of herself, and had shown little disposition to take care of any one else. Her thrift and economy had greatly enhanced her resources, and her investments
had been profitable, while the sense of increasing abundance
had had a happy effect on her character. Within the past
year she had purchased the dwelling in which she now re-
sided, and to which she welcomed Graham with unexpected
warmth. So far from permitting him to make simply a formal call, she insisted on an extended visit, and he, divorced
from his studies and therefore feeling his isolation more
keenly than ever before, assented.

"My home is accessible," she said, "and from this point
you can make inquiries and look around for business opportunities quite as well as from a city hotel."

She was so cordial, so perfectly sincere, that for the first
time in his life he felt what it was to have kindred and a place
in the world that was not purchased.

He had found his financial affairs in a much beter condition than he had expected. Some improvements were on
foot which promised to advance the value of his real estate so

largely as to make him independent, and he was much inclined to return to Germany and resume his studies.

"I will rest and vegetate for a time," he concluded. "I
will wait till my friend Hilland returns from the West, and
then, when the impulse of work takes possession of me again,
I will decide upon my course."

He had come over the ocean to meet his fate, and not the
faintest shadow of a presentiment of this truth crossed his
mind as he looked tranquilly from his aunt's parlor window
at the beautiful May sunset. The cherry blossoms were on
the wane, and the light puffs of wind brought the white petals
down like flurries of snow; the plum-trees looked as if the
snow had clung to every branch and spray, and they were as
white as they could have been after some breathless, large-
flaked December storm; but the great apple-tree that stood
well down the path was the crowning product of May. A
more exquisite bloom of pink and white against an emerald
foil of tender young leaves could not have existed even in
Eden, nor could the breath of Eve have been more sweet than
the fragrance exhaled. The air was soft with summer-like
mildness, and the breeze that fanned Graham's cheek brought
no sense of chilliness. The sunset hour, with its spring
beauty, the song of innumerable birds, and especially the
strains of a wood-thrush, that, like a *prima donna*, trilled her
melody, clear, sweet and distinct above the feathered chorus,
penetrated his soul with subtle and delicious influences. A
vague longing for something he had never known or felt, for
something that books had never taught, or experimental
science revealed, throbbed in his heart. He felt that his life
was incomplete, and a deeper sense of isolation came over him
than he had ever experienced in foreign cities where every
face was strange. Unconsciously he was passing under the
most subtle and powerful of all spells, that of spring, when
the impulse to mate comes not to the birds alone.

It so happened that he was in just the condition to succumb to this influence. His mental tension was relaxed.
He had sat down by the wayside of life to rest awhile. He

had found that there was no need that he should bestir himself in money-getting, and his mind refused to return immediately to the deep abstractions of science. It pleaded weariness of the world and of the pros and cons of conflicting theories and questions. He admitted the plea and said:—

"My mind *shall* rest, and for a few days, possibly weeks, it shall be passively receptive of just such influences as nature and circumstances chance to bring to it. Who knows but that I may gain a deeper insight into the hidden mysteries than if I were delving among the dusty tomes of a university library? For some reason I feel to-night as if I could look at that radiant, fragrant apple-tree and listen to the lullaby of the birds forever. And yet their songs suggest a thought that awakens an odd pain and dissatisfaction. Each one is singing to his mate. Each one is giving expression to an overflowing fulness and completeness of life; and never before have I felt my life so incomplete and isolated.

"I wish Hilland was here. He is such a true friend that his silence is companionship, and his words never jar discordantly. It seems to me that I miss him more to-night than I did during the first days after his departure. It's odd that I should. I wonder if the friendship, the love of a woman could be more to me than that of Hilland. What was that paragraph from Emerson that once struck me so forcibly? My aunt is a woman of solid reading; she must have Emerson. Yes, here in her bookcase, meagre only in the number of volumes it contains, is what I want," and he turned the leaves rapidly until his eyes lighted on the following passage:—

"No man ever forgot the visitations of that power to his heart and brain which created all things new; which was the dawn in him of music, poetry, and art; which made the face of nature radiant with purple light, the morning and the night varied enchantments; when a single tone of one voice could make the heart bound, and the most trivial circumstance associated with one form was put in the amber of memory;

when he became all eye when one was present, and all memory when one was gone."

"Emerson never learned that at a university, German or otherwise. He writes as if it were a common human experience, and yet I know no more about it than of the sensations of a man who has lost an arm. I suppose losing one's heart is much the same. As long as a man's limbs are intact he is scarcely conscious of them, but when one is gone it troubles him all the time, although it isn't there. Now when Hilland left me I felt guilty at the ease with which I could forget him in the library and laboratory. I did not become all memory. I knew he was my best, my only friend; he is still; but he is not essential to my life. Clearly, according to Emerson, I am as ignorant as a child of one of the deepest experiences of life, and very probably had better remain so, and yet the hour is playing strange tricks with my fancy."

Thus it may be perceived that Alford Graham was peculiarly open on this deceitful May evening, which promised peace and security, to the impending stroke of fate. Its harbinger first appeared in the form of a white Spitz dog, barking vivaciously under the apple-tree, where a path from a neighboring residence intersected the walk leading from Mrs. Mayburn's cottage to the street. Evidently some one was playing with the little creature, and was pretending to be kept at bay by its belligerent attitude. Suddenly there was a rush and a flutter of white draperies, and the dog retreated toward Graham, barking with still greater excitement. Then the young man saw coming up the path with quick, lithe tread, sudden pauses, and little impetuous dashes at her canine playmate, a being that might have been an emanation from the radiant apple-tree, or, rather, the human embodiment of the blossoming period of the year. Her low wide brow and her neck were snowy white, and no pink petal on the trees above her could surpass the bloom on her cheeks. Her large, dark, lustrous eyes were brimming over with fun, and unconscious of observation, she moved with the natural, unstudied grace of a child.

Graham thought, "No scene of nature is complete without the human element, and now the very genius of the hour and season has appeared;" and he hastily concealed himself behind the curtains, unwilling to lose one glimpse of a picture that made every nerve tingle with pleasure. His first glance had revealed that the fair vision was not a child, but a tall, graceful girl, who happily had not yet passed beyond the sportive impulses of childhood.

Every moment she came nearer, until at last she stood opposite the window. He could see the blue veins branching across her temples, the quick rise and fall of her bosom, caused by rather violent exertion, the wavy outlines of light brown hair that was gathered in a Greek coil at the back of the shapely head. She had the rare combination of dark eyes and light hair which made the lustre of her eyes all the more striking. He never forgot that moment as she stood panting before him on the gravel walk, her girlhood's grace blending so harmoniously with her budding womanhood. For a moment the thought crossed his mind that under the spell of the spring evening his own fancy had created her, and that if he looked away and turned again he would see nothing but the pink and white blossoms, and hear only the jubilant song of the birds.

The Spitz dog, however, could not possibly have any such unsubstantial origin, and this small Cerberus had now entered the room, and was barking furiously at him as an unrecognized stranger. A moment later his vision under the window stood in the doorway. The sportive girl was transformed at once into a well-bred young woman who remarked quietly, "I beg your pardon. I expected to find Mrs. Mayburn here;" and she departed to search for that lady through the house with a prompt freedom which suggested relations of the most friendly intimacy.

CHAPTER II

MERE FANCIES

GRAHAM'S disposition to make his aunt a visit was not at all chilled by the discovery that she had so fair a neighbor. He was conscious of little more than an impulse to form the acquaintance of one who might give a peculiar charm and piquancy to his May-day vacation, and enrich him with an experience that had been wholly wanting in his secluded and studious life. With a smile he permitted the fancy—for he was in a mood for all sorts of fancies on this evening—that if this girl could teach him to interpret Emerson's words, he would make no crabbed resistance. And yet the remote possibility of such an event gave him a sense of security, and prompted him all the more to yield himself for the first time to whatever impressions a young and pretty woman might be able to make upon him. His very disposition toward experiment and analysis inclined him to experiment with himself. Thus it would seem that even the perfect evening, and the vision that had emerged from under the apple-boughs, could not wholly banish a tendency to give a scientific cast to the mood and fancies of the hour.

His aunt now summoned him to the supper-room, where he was formally introduced to Miss Grace St. John, with whom his first meal under his relative's roof was destined to be taken.

As may naturally be supposed, Graham was not well furnished with small talk, and while he had not the proverbial shyness and awkwardness of the student, he was somewhat silent because he knew not what to say. The young guest was entirely at her ease, and her familiarity with the hostess enabled her to chat freely and naturally on topics of mutual interest, thus giving Graham time for those observations to which all are inclined when meeting one who has taken a sudden and strong hold upon the attention.

He speedily concluded that she could not be less than nineteen or twenty years of age, and that she was not what he would term a society girl—a type that he had learned to recognize from not a few representatives of his countrywomen whom he had seen abroad, rather than from much personal acquaintance. It should not be understood that he had shunned society altogether, and his position had ever entitled him to enter the best; but the young women whom it had been his fortune to meet had failed to interest him as completely as he had proved himself a bore to them. Their worlds were too widely separated for mutual sympathy; and after brief excursions among the drawing-rooms to which Hilland had usually dragged him, he returned to his books with a deeper satisfaction and content. Would his acquaintance with Miss St. John lead to a like result? He was watching and waiting to see, and she had the advantage—if it was an advantage—of making a good first impression.

Every moment increased this predisposition in her favor. She must have known that she was very attractive, for few girls reach her age without attaining such knowledge; but her observer, and in a certain sense her critic, could not detect the faintest trace of affectation or self-consciousness. Her manner, her words, and even their accent seemed unstudied, unpracticed, and unmodelled after any received type. Her glance was peculiarly open and direct, and from the first she gave Graham the feeling that she was one who might be trusted absolutely. That she had tact and kindliness also was evidenced by the fact that she did not misunderstand or resent his comparative silence. At first, after learning that he had lived much abroad, her manner toward him had been a little shy and wary, indicating that she may have surmised that his reticence was the result of a certain kind of superiority which travelled men—especially young men—often assume when meeting those whose lives are supposed to have a narrow horizon; but she quickly discovered that Graham had no foreign-bred pre-eminence to parade— that he wanted to talk with her if he could only find some common subject of interest. This she supplied by taking him to ground with which he was perfectly familiar, for she asked him to tell her something about university life in Germany. On such a theme he could converse well, and before long a fire of eager questions proved that he had not only a deeply interested listener but also a very intelligent one.

Mrs. Mayburn smiled complacently, for she had some natural desire that her nephew should make a favorable impression. In regard to Miss St. John she had long ceased to have any misgivings, and the approval that she saw in Graham's eyes was expected as a matter of course. This approval she soon developed into positive admiration by leading her favorite to speak of her own past.

"Grace, you must know, Alford, is the daughter of an army officer, and has seen some odd phases of life at the various military stations where her father has been on duty."

These words piqued Graham's curiosity at once, and he became the questioner. His own frank effort to entertain was now rewarded, and the young girl, possessing easy and natural powers of description, gave sketches of life at military posts which to Graham had more than the charm of novelty. Unconsciously she was accounting for herself. In the refined yet unconventional society of officers and their wives she had acquired the frank manner so peculiarly her own. But the characteristic which won Graham's interest most strongly was her abounding mirthfulness. It ran through all her words like a golden thread. The instinctive craving of every nature is for that which supplements itself, and Graham found something so genial in Miss St. John's ready smile and laughing eyes, which suggested an over-full

fountain of joyousness within, that his heart, chilled and
repressed from childhood, began to give signs of its existence,
even during the first hour of their acquaintance. It is true,
as we have seen, that he was in a very receptive condition, but
then a smile, a glance that is like warm sunshine, is never
devoid of power.

The long May twilight had faded, and they were still
lingering over the supper-table, when a middle-aged colored
woman in a flaming red turban appeared in the doorway and
said, "Pardon, Mis' Mayburn; I'se a-hopin' you'll 'scuse me.
I jes step over to tell Miss Grace dat de major's po'ful oneasy,
—'spected you back afo'."

The girl arose with alacrity, saying, "Mr. Graham, you
have brought me into danger, and must now extricate me.
Papa is an inveterate whist-player, and you have put my
errand here quite out of my mind. I didn't come for the
sake of your delicious muffins altogether"—with a nod
at her hostess; "our game has been broken up, you know,
Mrs. Mayburn, by the departure of Mrs. Weeks and her
daughter. You have often played a good hand with us, and
papa thought you would come over this evening, and that
you, from your better acquaintance with our neighbors,
might know of some one who enjoyed the game sufficiently
to join us quite often. Mr. Graham, you must be the one I
am seeking. A gentleman versed in the lore of two con-
tinents certainly understands whist, or, at least, can penetrate
its mysteries at a single sitting."

"Suppose I punish the irony of your concluding words,"
Graham replied, "by saying that I know just enough about
the game to be aware how much skill is required to play with
such a veteran as your father?"

"If you did you would punish papa also, who is innocent."

"That cannot be thought of, although, in truth, I play
but an indifferent game. If you will make amends by teaching me I will try to perpetrate as few blunders as possible."

"Indeed, sir, you forget. You are to make amends for

keeping me talking here, forgetful of filial duty, by giving me a chance to teach you. You are to be led meekly in as a trophy by which I am to propitiate my stern parent, who has military ideas of promptness and obedience."

"What if he should place me under arrest?"

"Then Mrs. Mayburn and I will become your jailers, and we shall keep you here until you are one of the most accomplished whist-players in the land."

"If you will promise to stand guard over me some of the time I will submit to any conditions."

"You are already making one condition, and may think of a dozen more. It will be better to parole you with the understanding that you are to put in an appearance at the hour for whist;" and with similar light talk they went down the walk under the apple-boughs, whence in Graham's fancy the fair girl had had her origin. As they passed under the shadow he saw the dusky outline of a rustic seat leaning against the bole of the tree, and he wondered if he should ever induce his present guide through the darkened paths to come there some moonlight evening, and listen to the fancies which her unexpected appearance had occasioned. The possibility of such an event in contrast with its far greater improbability caused him to sigh, and then he smiled broadly at himself in the darkness.

When they had passed a clump of evergreens, a lighted cottage presented itself, and Miss St. John sprang lightly up the steps, pushed open the hall door, and cried through the open entrance to a cosey apartment, "No occasion for hostilities, papa. I have made a capture that gives the promise of whist not only this evening but also for several more to come."

As Graham and Mrs. Mayburn entered, a tall, white-haired man lifted his foot from off a cushion, and rose with some little difficulty, but having gained his feet, his bearing was erect and soldier-like, and his courtesy perfect, although toward Mrs. Mayburn it was tinged with the gallantry of a former generation. Some brief explanations followed, and then Major St. John turned upon Graham the dark eyes

which his daughter had inherited, and which seemed all the
more brilliant in contrast with his frosty eyebrows, and said
genially, "It is very kind of you to be willing to aid in beguiling an old man's tedium." Turning to his daughter he
added a litle querulously, "There must be a storm brewing,
Grace," and he drew in his breath as if in pain.

"Does your wound trouble you to-night, papa ?" she asked
gently.

"Yes, just as it always does before a storm."

"It is perfectly clear without," she resumed. "Perhaps
the room has become a little cold. The evenings are still
damp and chilly;" and she threw two or three billets of wood
on the open fire, kindling a blaze that sprang cheerily up the
chimney.

The room seemed to be a combination of parlor and library, and it satisfied Graham's ideal of a living apartment.
Easy-chairs of various patterns stood here and there and
looked as if constructed by the very genius of comfort. A
secretary in the corner near a window was open, suggesting
absent friends and the pleasure of writing to them amid such
agreeable surroundings. Again Graham queried, prompted
by the peculiar influences that had gained the mastery on this
tranquil but eventful evening, "Will Miss St. John ever sit
there penning words straight from her heart to me ?"

He was brought back to prose and reality by the major.
Mrs Mayburn had been condoling with him, and he now
turned and said, "I hope, my dear sir, that you may never
carry around such a barometer as I am afflicted with. A
man with an infirmity grows a little egotistical, if not
worse."

"You have much consolation, sir, in remembering how
you came by your infirmity," Graham replied. "Men bearing such proofs of service to their country are not plentiful in
our money-getting land."

His daughter's laugh rang out musically as she cried,
"That was meant to be a fine stroke of diplomacy. Papa,
you will now have to pardon a score of blunders."

"I have as yet no proof that any will be made," the major remarked, and in fact Graham had underrated his acquaintance with the game. He was quite equal to his aunt in proficiency, and with Miss St. John for his partner he was on his mettle. He found her skilful indeed, quick, penetrating, and possessed of an excellent memory. They held their own so well that the major's spirits rose hourly. He forgot his wound in the complete absorption of his favorite recreation.

As opportunity occurred Graham could not keep his eyes from wandering here and there about the apartment that had so taken his fancy, especially toward the large, well-filled bookcase and the pictures, which, if not very expensive, had evidently been the choice of a cultivated taste.

They were brought to a consciousness of the flight of time by a clock chiming out the hour of eleven, and the old soldier with a sigh of regret saw Mrs. Mayburn rise. Miss St. John touched a silver bell, and a moment later the same negress who had reminded her of her father's impatience early in the evening entered with a tray bearing a decanter of wine, glasses, and some wafer-like cakes.

"Have I earned the indulgence of a glance at your books?" Graham asked.

"Yes, indeed," Miss St. John replied; "your martyr-like submission shall be further rewarded by permission to borrow any of them while in town. I doubt, however, if you will find them profound enough for your taste."

"I shall take all point from your irony by asking if you think one can relish nothing but intellectual roast beef. I am enjoying one of your delicate cakes. You must have an excellent cook."

"Papa says he has, in the line of cake and pastry; but then he is partial."

"What! did you make them?"

"Why not?"

"Oh, I'm not objecting. Did my manners permit, I'd empty the plate. Still, I was under the impression that young ladies were not adepts in this sort of thing."

"You have been abroad so long that you may have to revise many of your impressions. Of course retired army officers are naturally in a condition to import *chefs de cuisine,* but then we like to keep up the idea of republican simplicity."

"Could you be so very kind as to induce your father to ask me to make one of your evening quartette as often as possible?"

"The relevancy of that request is striking. Was it suggested by the flavor of the cakes? I sometimes forget to make them."

"Their absence would not prevent my taste from being gratified if you will permit me to come. Here is a marked volume of Emerson's works. May I take it for a day or two?"

She blushed slightly, hesitated perceptibly, and then said, "Yes."

"Alford," broke in his aunt, "you students have the name of being great owls, but for an old woman of my regular habits it's getting late."

"My daughter informs me," the major remarked to Graham in parting, "that we may be able to induce you to take a hand with us quite often. If you should ever become as old and crippled as I am you will know how to appreciate such kindness.'"

"Indeed, sir, Miss St. John must testify that I asked to share your game as a privilege. I can scarcely remember to have passed so pleasant an evening."

"Mrs. Mayburn, do try to keep him in this amiable frame of mind," cried the girl.

"I think I shall need your aid," said that lady, with a smile. "Come, Alford, it is next to impossible to get you away."

"Papa's unfortunate barometer will prove correct, I fear," said Miss St. John, following them out on the piazza, for a thin scud was already veiling the stars, and there was an ominous moan of the wind.

"To-morrow will be a stormy day," remarked Mrs. Mayburn, who prided herself on her weather wisdom.

"I'm sorry," Miss St. John continued, "for it will spoil our fairy world of blossoms, and I am still more sorry for papa's sake."

"Should the day prove a long, dismal, rainy one," Graham ventured, "may I not come over and help entertain your father?"

"Yes," said the girl, earnestly. "It cannot seem strange to you that time should often hang heavily on his hands, and I am grateful to any one who helps me to enliven his hours."

Before Graham repassed under the apple-tree boughs he had fully decided to win at least Miss St. John's gratitude.

CHAPTER III

THE VERDICT OF A SAGE

WHEN Graham reached his room he was in no mood
for sleep. At first he lapsed into a long revery
over the events of the evening, trivial in themselves, and yet for some reason holding a controlling influence over his thoughts. Miss St. John was a new revelation
of womanhood to him, and for the first time in his life his
heart had been stirred by a woman's tones and glances. A
deep chord in his nature vibrated when she spoke and smiled.
What did it mean? He had followed his impulse to permit
this stranger to make any impression within her power, and
he found that she had decidedly interested him. As he tried
to analyze her power he concluded that it lay chiefly in the
mirthfulness, the joyousness of her spirit. She quickened
his cool, deliberate pulse. Her smile was not an affair of
facial muscles, but had a vivifying warmth. It made him
suspect that his life was becoming cold and self-centred, that
he was missing the deepest and best experiences of an existence that was brief indeed at best, and, as he believed, soon
ceased forever. The love of study and ambition had sufficed
thus far, but actuated by his own materialistic creed he was
bound to make the most of life while it lasted. According
to Emerson he was as yet but in the earlier stages of evolution, and his highest manhood wholly undeveloped. Had
not "music, poetry, and art" dawned in his mind? Was nature but a mechanism after whose laws he had been groping
like an anatomist who finds in the godlike form bone and
tissue merely? As he had sat watching the sunset a few

hours previous, the element of beauty had been present to him
as never before. Could this sense of beauty become so enlarged that the world would be transfigured, "radiant with
purple light"? Morning had often brought to him weariness
from sleepless hours during which he had racked his brain
over problems too deep for him, and evening had found him
still baffled, disappointed, and disposed to ask in view of his
toil, *Cui bono?* What ground had Emerson for saying that
these same mornings and evenings might be filled with "varied
enchantments"? The reason, the cause of these unknown
conditions of life, was given unmistakably. The Concord
sage had virtually asserted that he, Alford Graham, would
never truly exist until his one-sided masculine nature had
been supplemented by the feminine soul which alone could
give to his being completeness and the power to attain his
full development.

"Well," he soliloquized, laughing, "I have not been aware
that hitherto I have been only a mollusk, a polyp of a man.
I am inclined to think that Emerson's 'Pegasus' took the bit
—got the better of him on one occasion; but if there is any
truth in what he writes it might not be a bad idea to try a
little of the kind of evolution that he suggests and see what
comes of it. I am already confident that I could see infinitely more than I do if I could look at the world through
Miss St. John's eyes as well as my own, but I run no slight
risk in obtaining that vision. Her eyes are stars that must
have drawn worshippers, not only from the east, but from
every point of the compass. I should be in a sorry plight
if I should become 'all memory,' and from my fair divinity
receive as sole response, 'Please forget.' If the philosopher
could guarantee that she also would be 'all eye and all memory,' one might indeed covet Miss St. John as the teacher of
the higher mysteries. Life is not very exhilarating at best,
but for a man to set his heart on such a woman as this girl
promises to be, and then be denied—why, he had better remain a polyp. Come, come, Alford Graham, you have had
your hour of sentiment—out of deference to Mr. Emerson I

won't call it weakness—and it's time you remembered that
you are a comparatively poor man, that Miss St. John has
already been the choice of a score at least, and probably has
made her own choice. I shall therefore permit no delusions
and the growth of no false hopes."

Having reached this prudent conclusion, Graham yawned,
smiled at the unwonted mood in which he had indulged, and
with the philosophic purpose of finding an opiate in the pages
that had contained one paragraph rather too exciting, he
took up the copy of Emerson that he had borrowed. The
book fell open, indicating that some one had often turned to
the pages before him. One passage was strongly marked on
either side and underscored. With a laugh he saw that it
was the one he had been dwelling upon—"No man ever
forgot," etc.

"Now I know why she blushed slightly and hesitated to
lend me this volume," he thought. "I suppose I may read in
this instance, 'No woman ever forgot.' Of course, it would
be strange if she had not learned to understand these words.
What else has she marked?"

Here and there were many delicate marginal lines indicating approval and interest, but they were so delicate as to
suggest that the strong scoring of the significant passage was
not the work of Miss St. John, but rather of some heavy
masculine hand. This seemed to restore the original reading, "No *man* ever forgot," and some man had apparently
tried to inform her by his emphatic lines that he did not
intend to forget.

"Well, suppose he does not and cannot," Graham mused.
"That fact places her under no obligations to be 'all eye and
memory' for him. And yet her blush and hesitancy and the
way the book falls open at this passage look favorable for
him. I can win her gratitude by amusing the old major,
and with that, no doubt, I shall have to be content."

This limitation of his chances caused Graham so little
solicitude that he was soon sleeping soundly.

CHAPTER IV

WARNING OR INCENTIVE?

THE next morning proved that the wound which Major St. John had received in the Mexican War was a correct barometer. From a leaden, lowering sky the rain fell steadily, and a chilly wind was fast dismantling the trees of their blossoms. The birds had suspended their nest-building, and but few had the heart to sing.

"You seem to take a very complacent view of the dreary prospect without," Mrs. Mayburn remarked, as Graham came smilingly into the breakfast-room and greeted her with a cheerful note in his tones. "Such a day as this means rheumatism for me and an aching leg for Major St. John."

"I am very sorry, aunt," he replied, "but I cannot help remembering also that it is not altogether an ill wind, for it will blow me over into a cosey parlor and very charming society—that is, if Miss St. John will give me a little aid in entertaining her father."

"So we old people don't count for anything."

"That doesn't follow at all. I would do anything in my power to banish your rheumatism and the major's twinges, but how was it with you both at my age? I can answer for the major. If at that time he knew another major with such a daughter as blesses his home, his devotion to the preceding veteran was a little mixed."

"Are you so taken by Miss St. John?"

"I have not the slightest hope of being taken by her."

"You know what I mean?"

"Yes, but I wished to suggest my modest hopes and expectations so that you may have no anxieties if I avail my-self, during my visit, of the chance of seeing what I can of an unusually fine girl. Acquaintance with such society is the part of my education most sadly neglected. Nevertheless, you will find me devotedly at your service whenever you will express your wishes."

"Do not imagine that I am disposed to find fault. Grace is a great favorite of mine. She is a good old-fashioned girl, not one of your vain, heartless, selfish creatures with only a veneer of good breeding. I see her almost every day, either here or in her own home, and I know her well. You have seen that she is fitted to shine anywhere, but it is for her home qualities that I love and admire her most. Her father is crippled and querulous; indeed he is often exceedingly irritable. Everything must please him or else he is inclined to storm as he did in his regiment, and occasionally he emphasizes his words without much regard to the third commandment. But his gusts of anger are over quickly, and a kinderhearted and more upright man never lived. Of course American servants won't stand harsh words. They want to do all the fault-finding, and the poor old gentleman would have a hard time of it were it not for Grace. She knows how to manage both him and them, and that colored woman you saw wouldn't leave him if he beat and swore at her every day. She was a slave in the family of Grace's mother, who was a Southern lady, and the major gave the poor creature her liberty when he brought his wife to the North. Grace is sunshine embodied. She makes her old, irritable, and sometimes gouty father happy in spite of himself. It was just like her to accept of your offer last evening, for to banish all dullness from her father's life seems her constant thought. So if you wish to grow in the young lady's favor don't be so attentive to her as to neglect the old gentleman."

Graham listened to this good-natured gossip with decided interest, feeling that it contained valuable suggestions. The response seemed scarcely relevant. "When is she to be married?" he asked.

"Married!"

"Yes. It is a wonder that such a paragon has escaped thus long."

"You have lived abroad too much," said his aunt satirically. "American girls are not married out of hand at a certain age. They marry when they please or not at all if they please. Grace easily escapes marriage."

"Not from want of suitors, I'm sure."

"You are right there."

"How then?"

"By saying, 'No, I thank you.' You can easily learn how very effectual such a quiet negative is, if you choose."

"Indeed! Am I such a very undesirable party?" said Graham, laughing, for he heartily enjoyed his aunt's brusque way of talking, having learned already the kindliness it masked.

"Not in my eyes. I can't speak for Grace. She'd marry you if she loved you, and were you the Czar of all the Russias you wouldn't have the ghost of a chance unless she did. I know that she has refused more than one fortune. She seems perfectly content to live with her father, until the one prince having the power to awaken her appears. When he comes rest assured she'll follow him, and also be assured that she'll take her father with her, and to a selfish, exacting Turk of a husband he might prove an old man of the sea. And yet I doubt it. Grace would manage any one. Not that she has much management either. She simply laughs, smiles, and talks every one into good humor. Her mirthfulness, her own happiness, is so genuine that it is contagious. Suppose you exchange duties and ask her to come over and enliven me while you entertain her father," concluded the old lady mischievously.

"I would not dare to face such a fiery veteran as you have described alone."

"I knew you would have some excuse. Well, be on your guard. Grace will make no effort to capture you, and therefore you will be in all the more danger of being captured. If you lose your heart in vain to her you will need more than German philosophy to sustain you."

"I have already made to myself in substance your last remark."

"I know you are not a lady's man, and perhaps for that very reason you are all the more liable to an acute attack."

Graham laughed as he rose from the table, and asked, "Should I ever venture to lay siege to Miss St. John, would I not have your blessing?"

"Yes, and more than my blessing."

"What do you mean by more than your blessing?"

"I shall not commit myself until you commit yourself, and I do not wish you to take even the first step without appreciating the risk of the venture."

"Why, bless you, aunt," said Graham, now laughing heartily, "how seriously you take it! I have spent but one evening with the girl."

The old lady nodded her head significantly as she replied, "I have not lived to my time of life without learning a thing or two. My memory also has not failed as yet. There were young men who looked at me once just as you looked at Grace last evening, and I know what came of it in more than one instance. You are safe now, and you may be invulnerable, although it does not look like it; but if you can see much of Grace St. John and remain untouched you are unlike most men."

"I have always had the name of being that, you know. But as the peril is so great had I not better fly at once?"

"Yes, I think we both have had the name of being a little peculiar, and my brusque, direct way of coming right to the point is one of my peculiarities. I am very intimate with the St. Johns, and am almost as fond of Grace as if she were my own child. So of course you can see a great deal of her if you wish, and this arrangement about whist will add to your opportunities. I know what young men are, and I know too what often happens when their faces express as much admiration and interest as yours did last night. What's more," continued the energetic old lady with an emphatic tap on the floor with her foot, and a decided nod of her head, "if I were a young man, Grace would have to marry some one else to get rid of me. Now I've had my say, and my con-science is clear, whatever happens. As to flight, why, you must settle that question, but I am sincere and cordial in my request that you make your home with me until you decide upon your future course."

Graham was touched, and he took his aunt's hand as he said, "I thank you for your kindness, and more than all for your downright sincerity. When I came here it was to make but a formal call. With the exception of one friend, I believed that I stood utterly alone in the world—that no one cared about what I did or what became of me. I was accustomed to isolation and thought I was content with it, but I find it more pleasant than I can make you un-derstand to know there is one place in the world to which I can come, not as a stranger to an inn, but as one that is re-ceived for other than business considerations. Since you have been so frank with me I will be equally outspoken;" and he told her just how he was situated, and what were his plans and hopes. "Now that I know there is no necessity of earning my livelihood," he concluded, "I shall yield to my impulse to rest awhile, and then quite probably resume my studies here or abroad until I can obtain a position suited to my plans and taste. I thank you for your note of alarm in regard to Miss St. John, although I must say that to my mind there is more of incentive than of warning in your words. I think I can at least venture on a few reconnoissances, as the major might say, before I beat a retreat. Is it too early to make one now?"

Mrs. Mayburn smiled. "No," she said, laconically.

"I see that you think my reconnoissance will lead to a siege," Graham added. "Well, I can at least promise that there shall be no rash movements."

CHAPTER V

IMPRESSIONS

GRAHAM, smiling at his aunt and still more amused
at himself, started to pay his morning visit. "Yesterday afternoon," he thought, "I expected to make
but a brief call on an aunt who was almost a stranger to me,
and now I am domiciled under her roof indefinitely. She
has introduced me to a charming girl, and in an ostensible
warning shrewdly inserted the strongest incentives to venture
everything, hinting at the same time that if I succeeded she
would give me more than her blessing. What a vista of
possibilities has opened since I crossed her threshold! A
brief time since I was buried in German libraries, unaware
of the existence of Miss St. John, and forgetting that of my
aunt. Apparently I have crossed the ocean to meet them
both, for had I remained abroad a few days longer, letters on
the way would have prevented my returning. Of course it
is all chance, but a curious chance. I don't wonder that people are often superstitious; and yet a moment's reasoning
proves the absurdity of this sort of thing. Nothing truly
strange often happens, and only our egotism invests events
of personal interest with a trace of the marvellous. My business man neglected to advise me of my improved finances as
soon as he might have done. My aunt receives me, not as
I expected, but as one would naturally hope to be met by a
relative. She has a fair young neighbor with whom she is
intimate, and whom I meet as a matter of course, and as a
matter of course I can continue to meet her as long as I choose
without becoming 'all eye and all memory.' Surely a man

can enjoy the society of any woman without the danger my aunt suggests and—as I half believe—would like to bring about. What signify my fancies of last evening? We often enjoy imagining what might be without ever intending it shall be. At any rate, I shall not sigh for Miss St. John or any other woman until satisfied that I should not sigh in vain. The probabilities are therefore that I shall never sigh at all."

As he approached Major St. John's dwelling he saw the object of his thoughts standing by the window and reading a letter. A syringa shrub partially concealed him and his umbrella, and he could not forbear pausing a moment to note what a pretty picture she made. A sprig of white flowers was in her light wavy hair, and another fastened by her breastpin drooped over her bosom. Her morning wrapper was of the hue of the sky that lay back of the leaden clouds. A heightened color mantled her cheeks, her lips were parted with a smile, and her whole face was full of delighted interest.

"By Jove!" muttered Graham. "Aunt Mayburn is half right, I believe. A man must have the pulse of an anchorite to look often at such a vision as that and remain untouched. One might easily create a divinity out of such a creature, and then find it difficult not to worship. I could go away now and make her my ideal, endowing her with all impossible attributes of perfection. Very probably fuller acquaintance will prove that she is made of clay not differing materially from that of other womankind. I envy her correspondent, however, and would be glad if I could write a letter that would bring such an expression to her face. Well, I am reconnoitring true enough, and had better not be detected in the act;" and he stepped rapidly forward.

She recognized him with a piquant little nod and smile. The letter was folded instantly, and a moment later she opened the door for him herself, saying, "Since I have seen you and you have come on so kind an errand I have dispensed with the formality of sending a servant to admit you."

"Won't you shake hands as a further reward?" he asked. "You will find me very mercenary."

"Oh, certainly. Pardon the oversight. I should have done so without prompting since it is so long since we have met."

"And having known each other so long also," he added in the same light vein, conscious meantime that he held a hand that was as full of vitality as it was shapely and white.

"Indeed," she replied; "did last evening seem an age to you?"

"I tried to prolong it, for you must remember that my aunt said that she could not get me away; and this morning I was indiscreet enough to welcome the rain, at which she reminded me of her rheumatism and your father's wound."

"And at which I also hope you had a twinge or two of conscience. Papa," she added, leading the way into the parlor, "here is Mr. Graham. It was his fascinating talk about life in Germany that so delayed me last evening."

The old gentleman started out of a doze, and his manner proved that he welcomed any break in the monotony of the day. "You will pardon my not rising," he said; "this confounded weather is playing the deuce with my leg."

Graham was observant as he joined in a general condemnation of the weather; and the manner in which Miss St. John rearranged the cushion on which her father's foot rested, coaxed the fire into a more cheerful blaze, and bestowed other little attentions, proved beyond a doubt that all effort in behalf of the suffering veteran would be appreciated. Nor was he so devoid of a kindly good-nature himself as to anticipate an irksome task, and he did his utmost to discover the best methods of entertaining his host. The effort soon became remunerative, for the major had seen much of life, and enjoyed reference to his experiences. Graham found that he could be induced to fight his battles over again, but always with very modest allusion to himself. In the course of their talk it also became evident that he was a man of somewhat extensive reading, and the daily paper must have been almost literally devoured to account for his acquaintance with contemporary affairs. The daughter was often not a little amused at Graham's blank looks as her father broached topics of American interest which to the student from abroad were as little known or understood as the questions which might have been agitating the inhabitants of Jupiter. Most ladies would have been politely oblivious of her guest's blunders and infelicitous remarks, but Miss St. John had a frank, merry way of recognizing them, and yet malice and ridicule were so entirely absent from her words and ways that Graham soon positively enjoyed being laughed at, and much preferred her delicate open raillery, which gave him a chance to defend himself, to a smiling mask that would leave him in uncertainty as to the fitness of his replies. There was a subtle flattery also in this course, for she treated him as one capable of holding his own, and not in need of social charity and protection. With pleasure he recognized that she was adopting toward him something of the same sportive manner which characterized her relations with his aunt, and which also indicated that as Mrs. Mayburn's nephew he had met with a reception which would not have been accorded to one less favorably introduced.

How vividly in after years Graham remembered that rainy May morning! He could always call up before him, like a vivid picture, the old major with his bushy white eyebrows and piercing black eyes, the smoke from his meerschaum creating a sort of halo around his gray head, the fine, venerable face often drawn by pain which led to half-muttered imprecations that courtesy to his guest and daughter could not wholly suppress. How often he saw again the fire curling softly from the hearth with a contented crackle, as if pleased to be once more an essential to the home from which the advancing summer would soon banish it! He could recall every article of the furniture with which he afterward became so familiar. But that which was engraven on his memory forever was a fair young girl sitting by the window with a background of early spring greenery swaying to and fro in the storm. Long afterward, when watching on the perilous picket line or standing in his place on the battle-field, he would close his eyes that he might recall more vividly the little white hands deftly crocheting on some feminine mystery, and the mirthful eyes that often glanced from it to him as the quiet flow of their talk rippled on. A rill, had it conscious life, would never forget the pebble that deflected its course from one ocean to another; human life as it flows onward cannot fail to recognize events, trivial in themselves, which nevertheless gave direction to all the future.

Graham admitted to himself that he had found a charm at this fireside which he had never enjoyed elsewhere in so-ciety—the pleasure of being perfectly at ease. There was a genial frankness and simplicity in his entertainers which banished restraint, and gave him a sense of security. He felt instinctively that there were no adverse currents of men-tal criticism and detraction, that they were loyal to him as their invited guest, notwithstanding jest, banter, and good-natured satire.

The hours had vanished so swiftly that he was at a loss to account for them. Miss St. John was a natural foe to dul-ness of all kinds, and this too without any apparent effort. Indeed, we are rarely entertained by evident and deliberate exertion. Pleasurable exhilaration in society is obtained from those who impart, like warmth, their own spontaneous vivacity. Miss St. John's smile was an antidote for a rainy day, and he was loath to pass from its genial power out under the dripping clouds. Following an impulse, he said to the girl, "You are more than a match for the weather."

These words were spoken in the hall after he had bidden adieu to the major.

"If you meant a compliment it is a very doubtful one," she replied, laughing. "Do you mean that I am worse than the weather which gives papa the horrors, and Mrs. Mayburn the rheumatism?"

"And me one of the most delightful mornings I ever en-joyed," he added, interrupting her. "You were in league with your wood fire. The garish sunshine of a warm day robs a house of all cosiness and snugness. Instead of being depressed by the storm and permitting others to be dull, you have the art of making the clouds your foil."

"Possibly I may appear to some advantage against such a dismal background," she admitted.

"My meaning is interpreted by my unconscionably long visit. I now must reluctantly retreat into the dismal background."

"A rather well-covered retreat, as papa might say, but you will need your umbrella all the same;" for he, in looking back at the archly smiling girl, had neglected to open it.

"I am glad it is not a final retreat," he called back. "I shall return this evening reinforced by my aunt."

"Well," exclaimed that lady when he appeared before her, "lunch has been waiting ten minutes or more."

"I feared as much," he replied, shaking his head ruefully.

"What kept you?"

"Miss St. John."

"Not the major? I thought you went to entertain him?"

"So I did, but man proposes—"

"Oh, not yet, I hope," cried the old lady with assumed dismay. "I thought you promised to do nothing rash."

"You are more precipitate than I have been. All that I propose is to enjoy my vacation and the society of your charming friend."

"The major?" she suggested.

"A natural error on your part, for I perceived he was very gallant to you. After your remarks, however, you cannot think it strange that I found the daughter more interesting—so interesting indeed that I have kept you waiting for lunch. I'll not repeat the offence any oftener than I can help. At the same time I find that I have not lost my appetite, or anything else that I am aware of."

"How did Grace appear?" his aunt asked as they sat down to lunch.

"Like myself."

"Then not like any one else you know?"

"We agree here perfectly."

"You have no fear?"

"No, nor any hopes that I am conscious of. Can I not admire your paragon to your heart's content without insisting that she bestow upon me the treasures of her life? Miss St. John has a frank, cordial manner all her own, and I think also that for your sake she has received me rather graciously, but I should be blind indeed did I not recognize that it would require a siege to win her; and that would be useless, as you said, unless her own heart prompted the surrender. I have heard and read that many women are capable of passing fancies of which adroit suitors can take advantage, and they are engaged or married before fully comprehending what it all means. Were Miss St. John of this class I should still hesitate to venture, for nothing in my training has fitted me to take an advantage of a lady's mood. I don't think your favorite is given to fancies. She is too well poised. Her serene, laughing confidence, her more than content, comes either from a heart already happily given, or else from a nature so sound and healthful that life in itself is an unalloyed joy. She impresses me as the happiest being I ever met, and as such it is a delight to be in her presence; but if I should approach her as a lover, something tells me that I should find her like a snowy peak, warm and rose-tinted in the sunlight, as seen in the distance, but growing cold as you draw near. There may be subterranean fires, but they would manifest themselves from some inward impulse. At least I do not feel conscious of any power to awaken them."

Mrs. Mayburn shook her head ominously.

"You are growing very fanciful," she said, "which is a sign, if not a bad one. Your metaphors, too, are so far-fetched and extravagant as to indicate the earliest stages of the divine madness. Do you mean to suggest that Grace will break forth like a volcano on some fortuitous man? If that be your theory you would stand as good a chance as any one. She might break forth on you."

"I have indeed been unfortunate in my illustration, since you can so twist my words even in jest. Here's plain enough prose for you. No amount of wooing would make the slightest difference unless by some law or impulse of her own nature Miss St. John was compelled to respond."

"Isn't that true of every woman?"

"I don't think it is."

"How is it that you are so versed in the mysteries of the feminine soul?"

"I have not lived altogether the life of a monk, and the history of the world is the history of women as well as of men. I am merely giving the impression that has been made upon me."

CHAPTER VI

PHILOSOPHY AT FAULT

IF Mrs. Mayburn had fears that her nephew's peace would be affected by his exposure to the fascinations of Miss St. John, they were quite allayed by his course for the next two or three weeks. If she had indulged the hope that he would speedily be carried away by the charms which seemed to her irresistible, and so give the chance of a closer relationship with her favorite, she saw little to encourage such a hope beyond Graham's evident enjoyment in the young girl's society, and his readiness to seek it on all fitting occasions. He played whist assiduously, and appeared to enjoy the game. He often spent two or three hours with the major during the day, and occasionally beguiled the time by reading aloud to him, but the element of gallantry toward the daughter seemed wanting, and the aunt concluded, "No woman can rival a book in Alford's heart—that is, if he has one—and he is simply studying Grace as if she were a book. There is one symptom, however, that needs explanation—he is not so ready to talk about her as at first, and I don't believe that indifference is the cause."

She was right: indifference was not the cause. Graham's interest in Miss St. John was growing deeper every day, but the stronger the hold she gained upon his thoughts, the less inclined was he to speak of her. He was the last man in the world to be carried away by a Romeo-like gust of passion, and no amount of beauty could hold his attention an hour, did not the mind ray through it with a sparkle and power essentially its own.

Miss St. John had soon convinced him that she could do more than look sweetly and chatter. She could not only talk to a university-bred man, but also tell him much that was new. He found his peer, not in his lines of thought, but in her own, and he was so little of an egotist that he admired her all the more because she knew what he did not, and could never become an echo of himself. In her world she had been an intelligent observer and thinker, and she interpreted that world to him as naturally and unassumingly as a flower blooms and exhales its fragrance. For the first time in his life he gave himself up to the charm of a cultivated woman's society, and to do this in his present leisure seemed the most sensible thing possible.

"One can see a rare flower," he had reasoned, "without wishing to pluck it, or hear a wood-thrush sing without straightway thinking of a cage. Miss St. John's affections may be already engaged, or I may be the last person in the world to secure them. Idle fancies of what she might become to me are harmless enough. Any man is prone to indulge in these when seeing a woman who pleases his taste and kindles his imagination. When it comes to practical action one may expect and desire nothing more than the brightening of one's wits and the securing of agreeable pastime. I do not see why I should not be entirely content with these motives, until my brief visit is over, notwithstanding my aunt's ominous warnings;" and so without any misgivings he had at first yielded himself to all the spells that Miss St. John might unconsciously weave.

As time passed, however, he began to doubt whether he could maintain his cool, philosophic attitude of enjoyment. He found himself growing more and more eager for the hours to return when he could seek her society, and the intervening time was becoming dull and heavy-paced. The impulse to go back to Germany and to resume his studies was slow in coming. Indeed, he was at last obliged to admit to himself that a game of whist with the old major had more attractions than the latest scientific treatise. Not that he doted on the irascible veteran, but because he thus secured a fair partner whose dark eyes were beaming with mirth and intelligence, whose ever-springing fountain of happiness was so full that even in the solemnity of the game it found expression in little piquant gestures, brief words, and smiles that were like glints of sunshine. Her very presence lifted him to a higher plane, and gave a greater capacity for enjoyment, and sometimes simply an arch smile or an unexpected tone set his nerves vibrating in a manner as delightful as it was unexplainable by any past experience that he could recall. She was a good walker and horsewoman, and as their acquaintance ripened he began to ask permission to join her in her rides and rambles. She assented without the slightest hesitancy, but he soon found that she gave him no exclusive monopoly of these excursions, and that he must share them with other young men. Her absences from home were always comparatively brief, however, and that which charmed him most was her sunny devotion to her invalid and often very irritable father. She was the antidote to his age and to his infirmities of body and temper. While she was away the world in general, and his own little sphere in particular, tended toward a hopeless snarl. Jinny, the colored servant, was subserviency itself, but her very obsequiousness irritated him, although her drollery was at times diverting. It was usually true, however, that but one touch and one voice could soothe the jangling nerves. As Graham saw this womanly magic, which apparently cost no more effort than the wood fire put forth in banishing chilliness and discomfort, the thought would come, "Blessed will be the man who can win her as the light and life of his home!"

When days passed, and no one seemed to have a greater place in her thoughts and interest than himself, was it unnatural that the hope should dawn that she might create a home for him? If she had a favored suitor his aunt would be apt to know of it. She did not seem ambitious, or disposed to invest her heart so that it might bring fortune and social eminence. Never by word or sign had she appeared to chafe at her father's modest competency, but with tact and skill, taught undoubtedly by army experience, she made their slender income yield the essentials of comfort and refinement, and seemed quite indifferent to non-essentials. Graham could never hope to possess wealth, but he found in Miss St. John a woman who could impart to his home the crowning grace of wealth—simple, unostentatious elegance. His aunt had said that the young girl had already refused more than one fortune, and the accompanying assurance that she would marry the man she loved, whatever might be his circumstances, seemed verified by his own observation. Therefore why might he not hope? Few men are so modest as not to indulge the hope to which their heart prompts them. Graham was slow to recognize the existence of this hope, and then he watched its growth warily. Not for the world would he lose control of himself, not for the world would he reveal it to any one, least of all to his aunt or to her who had inspired it, unless he had some reason to believe she would not disappoint it. He was prompted to concealment, not only by his pride, which was great, but more by a characteristic trait, an instinctive desire to hide his deeper feelings, his inner personality from all others. He would not admit that he had fallen in love. The very phrase was excessively distasteful. To his friend Hilland he might have given his confidence, and he would have accounted for himself in some such way as this:—

"I have found a child and a woman; a child in frankness and joyousness, a woman in beauty, strength, mental maturity, and unselfishness. She interested me from the first, and every day I know better the reason why—because she *is* interesting. My reason has kept pace with my fancy and my deeper feeling, and impels me to seek this girl quite as much as does my heart. I do not think a man meets such a woman or such a chance for happiness twice in a lifetime. I did not believe there was such a woman in the world. You may laugh and say that is the way all lovers talk. I answer emphatically, No. I have not yet lost my poise, and I never was a predestined lover. I might easily have gone through life and never given to these subjects an hour's thought. Even now I could quietly decide to go away and take up my old life as I left it. But why should I? Here is an opportunity to enrich existence immeasurably, and to add to all my chances of success and power. So far from being a drag upon one, a woman like Miss St. John would incite and inspire a man to his best efforts. She would sympathize with him because she could understand his aims and keep pace with his mental advance. Granted that my prospects of winning her are doubtful indeed, still as far as I can see there *is* a chance. I would not care a straw for a woman that I could have for the asking—who would take me as a *dernier ressort*. Any woman that I would marry, many others would gladly marry also, and I must take my chance of winning her from them. Such would be my lot under any circumstances, and if I give way to a faint heart now I may as well give up altogether and content myself with a library as a bride."

Since he felt that he might have taken Hilland into his confidence, he had, in terms substantially the same as those given, imagined his explanation, and he smiled as he portrayed to himself his friend's jocular response, which would have nevertheless its substratum of true sympathy. "Hilland would say," he thought, " 'That is just like you, Graham. You can't smoke a cigar or make love to a girl without analyzing and philosophizing and arranging all the wisdom of Solomon in favor of your course. Now I would make love to a girl because I loved her, and that would be the end on't.' "

Graham was mistaken in this case. Not in laughing sympathy, but in pale dismay, would Hilland have received this revelation, for *he* was making love to Grace St. John because he loved her with all his heart and soul. There had been a time when Graham might have obtained a hint of this had circumstances been different, and it had occurred quite early in his acquaintance with Miss St. John. After a day that had been unusually delightful and satisfactory he was accompanying the young girl home from his aunt's cottage in the twilight. Out of the complacency of his heart he remarked, half to himself, "If Hilland were only here, my vacation would be complete."

In the obscurity he could not see her sudden burning flush, and since her hand was not on his arm he had no knowledge of her startled tremor. All that he knew was that she was silent for a moment or two, and then she asked quietly, "Is Mr. Warren Hilland an acquaintance of yours?"

"Indeed he is not," was the emphatic and hearty response. "He is the best friend I have in the world, and the best fellow in the world."

Oh, fatal obscurity of the deepening twilight! Miss St. John's face was crimson and radiant with pleasure, and could Graham have seen her at that moment he could not have failed to surmise the truth.

The young girl was as jealous of her secret as Graham soon became of his, and she only remarked demurely, "I have met Mr. Hilland in society," and then she changed the subject, for they were approaching the piazza steps, and she felt that if Hilland should continue the theme of conversation under the light of the chandelier, a telltale face and manner would betray her, in spite of all effort at control. A fragrant blossom from the shrubbery bordering the walk brushed against Graham's face, and he plucked it, saying, "Beyond that it is fragrant I don't know what this flower is. Will you take it from me?"

"Yes," she said, hesitatingly, for at that moment her absent lover had been brought so vividly to her consciousness that her heart recoiled from even the slightest hint of gallantry from another. A moment later the thought occurred, "Mr. Graham is *his* dearest friend; therefore he is my friend, although I cannot yet be as frank with him as I would like to be."

She paused a few moments on the piazza, to cool her hot face and quiet her fluttering nerves, and Graham saw with much pleasure that she fastened the flower to her breastpin.

When at last she entered she puzzled him a little by leaving him rather abruptly at the parlor door and hastening up the stairs.

She found that his words had stirred such deep, full fountains that she could not yet trust herself under his observant eyes. It is a woman's delight to hear her lover praised by other men, and Graham's words had been so hearty that they had set her pulses bounding, for they assured her that she had not been deceived by love's partial eyes.

"It's true, it's true," she murmured, softly, standing with dewy eyes before her mirror. "He is the best fellow in the world, and I was blind that I did not see it from the first. But all will yet be well;" and she drew a letter from her bosom and kissed it.

Happy would Hilland have been had he seen the vision reflected by that mirror—beauty, rich and rare in itself, but enhanced, illumined, and made divine by the deepest, strongest, purest emotions of the soul.

CHAPTER VII

WARREN HILLAND

THE closing scenes of the preceding chapter demand some explanation. Major St. John had spent part of the preceding summer at a seaside resort, and his daughter had inevitably attracted not a little attention. Among those that sought her favor was Warren Hilland, and in accordance with his nature he had been rather precipitate. He was ardent, impulsive, and, indulged from earliest childhood, he had been spoiled in only one respect— when he wanted anything he wanted it with all his heart and immediately. Miss St. John had seemed to him from the first a pearl among women. As with Graham, circumstances gave him the opportunity of seeing her daily, and he speedily succumbed to the "visitation of that power" to which the strongest must yield. Almost before the young girl suspected the existence of his passion, he declared it. She refused him, but he would take no refusal. Having won from her the admission that he had no favored rival, he lifted his handsome head with a resolution which she secretly admired, and declared that only when convinced that he had become hateful to her would he give up his suit.

He was not a man to become hateful to any woman. His frank nature was so in accord with hers that she responded in somewhat the same spirit, and said, half laughingly and half tearfully, "Well, if you will, you will, but I can offer no encouragement."

And yet his downright earnestness had agitated her deeply, disturbing her maiden serenity, and awaking for

the first time the woman within her heart. Hitherto her
girlhood's fancies had been like summer zephyrs, disturbing
but briefly the still, clear waters of her soul; but now she
became an enigma to herself as she slowly grew conscious of
her own heart and the law of her woman's nature to love
and give herself to another. But she had too much of the
doughty old major's fire and spirit, and was too fond of
her freedom, to surrender easily. Both Graham and Mrs.
Mayburn were right in their estimate—she would never yield
her heart unless compelled to by influences unexpected, at
first unwelcomed, but in the end overmastering.

The first and chief effect of Hilland's impetuous wooing
was, as we have seen, to destroy her sense of maidenly security, and to bring her face to face with her destiny. Then his
openly avowed siege speedily compelled her to withdraw her
thoughts from man in the abstract to himself. She could
not brush him aside by a quiet negative, as she had already
done in the case of several others. Clinging to her old life,
however, and fearing to embark on this unknown sea of new
experiences, she hesitated, and would not commit herself until
the force that impelled was greater than that which restrained. He at last had the tact to understand her and to
recognize that he had spoken to a girl, indeed almost a child,
and that he must wait for the woman to develop. Hopeful,
almost confident, for success and prosperity had seemingly
made a league with him in all things, he was content to wait.
The major had sanctioned his addresses from the first, and he
sought to attain his object by careful and skilful approaches.
He had shown himself such an impetuous wooer that she
might well doubt his persistence; now he would prove himself so patient and considerate that she could not doubt him.

When they parted at the seaside Hilland was called to
the far West by important business interests. In response to
his earnest pleas, in which he movingly portrayed his loneli-
ness in a rude mining village, she said he might write to her
occasionally, and he had written so quietly and sensibly, so
nearly as a friend might address a friend, that she felt there

could be no harm in a correspondence of this character.
During the winter season their letters had grown more frequent, and he with consummate skill had gradually tinged
his words with a warmer hue. She smiled at his artifice.
There was no longer any need of it, for by the wood fire, when
all the house was still and wrapped in sleep, she had become
fully revealed unto herself. She found that she had a
woman's heart, and that she had given it irrevocably to
Warren Hilland.

She did not tell him so—far from it. The secret seemed
so strange, so wonderful, so exquisite in its blending of pain
and pleasure, that she did not tell any one. Hers was not
the nature that could babble of the heart's deepest mysteries
to half a score of confidants. To him first she would make
the supreme avowal that she had become his by a sweet compulsion that had at last proved irresistible, and even he must
again seek that acknowledgment directly, earnestly. He
was left to gather what hope he could from the fact that she
did not resent his warmer expressions, and this leniency from
a girl like Grace St. John meant so much to him that he did
gather hope daily. Her letters were not nearly so frequent
as his, but when they did come he fairly gloated over them.
They were so fresh, crisp and inspiring that they reminded
him of the seaside breezes that had quickened his pulses with
health and pleasure during the past summer. She wrote in
an easy, gossiping style of the books she was reading; of the
good things in the art and literary journals, and of such questions of the day as would naturally interest her, and he so
gratefully assured her that by this course she kept him
within the pale of civilization, that she was induced to
write oftener. In her effort to gather material that would
interest him, life gained a new and richer zest, and she
learned how the kindling flame within her heart could illu-
mine even common things. Each day brought such a wealth
of joy that it was like a new and glad surprise. The page
she read had not only the interest imparted to it by the
author, but also the far greater charm of suggesting thoughts

of him or for him; and so began an interchange of books and periodicals, with pencillings, queries, marks of approval and disapproval. "I will show him," she had resolved, "that I am not a doll to be petted, but a woman who can be his friend and companion."

And she proved this quite as truly by her questions, her intelligent interest in his mining pursuits and the wild region of his sojourn, as by her words concerning that with which she was familiar.

It was hard for Hilland to maintain his reticence or submit to the necessity of his long absence. She had revealed the rich jewel of her mind so fully that his love had increased with time and separation, and he longed to obtain the complete assurance of his happiness. And yet not for the world would he again endanger his hopes by rashness. He ventured, however, to send the copy of Emerson with the quotation already given strongly underscored. Since she made no allusion to this in her subsequent letter, he again grew more wary, but as spring advanced the tide of feeling became too strong to be wholly repressed, and words indicating his passion would slip into his letters in spite of himself. She saw what was coming as truly as she saw all around her the increasing evidences of the approach of summer, and no bird sang with a fuller or more joyous note than did her heart at the prospect.

Graham witnessed this culminating happiness, and it would have been well for him had he known its source. Her joyousness had seemed to him a characteristic trait, and so it was, but he could not know how greatly it was enhanced by a cause that would have led to very different action on his part.

Hilland had decided that he would not write to his friend concerning his suit until his fate was decided in one way or the other. In fact, his letters had grown rather infrequent, not from waning friendship, but rather because their mutual interests had drifted apart. Their relations were too firmly established to need the aid of correspondence, and each knew

that when they met again they would resume their old ways.
In the sympathetic magnetism of personal presence confidences would be given that they would naturally hesitate to
write out in cool blood.

Thus Graham was left to drift and philosophize at first.
But his aunt was right: he could not daily see one who so
fully satisfied the cravings of his nature and coolly consider
the pros and cons. He was one who would kindle slowly, but
it would be an anthracite flame that would burn on while life
lasted.

He felt that he had no reason for discouragement, for she
seemed to grow more kind and friendly every day. This was
true of her manner, for, looking upon him as Hilland's best
friend, she gave him a genuine regard, but it was an esteem
which, like reflected light, was devoid of the warmth of affection that comes direct from the heart.

She did not suspect the feeling that at last began to deepen
rapidly, nor had he any adequate idea of its strength. When
a grain of corn is planted it is the hidden root that first develops, and the controlling influence of his life was taking
root in Graham's heart. If he did not fully comprehend this
at an early day it is not strange that she did not. She had
no disposition to fall in love with every interesting man she
met, and it seemed equally absurd to credit the gentlemen of
her acquaintance with any such tendency. Her manner,
therefore, toward the other sex was characterized by a frank,
pleasant friendliness which could be mistaken for coquetry
by only the most obtuse or the most conceited of men. With
all his faults Graham was neither stupid nor vain. He understood her regard, and doubted whether he could ever
change its character. He only hoped that he might, and until he saw a better chance for this he determined not to reveal
himself, fearing that if he did so it might terminate their
acquaintance.

"My best course," he reasoned, "is to see her as often as
possible, and thus give her the opportunity to know me well.
If I shall ever have any power to win her love, she, by some-

thing in her manner or tone, will unconsciously reveal the
truth to me. Then I will not be slow to act. Why should I
lose the pleasure of these golden hours by seeking openly that
which as yet she has not the slightest disposition to give ?"

This appeared to him a safe and judicious policy, and yet
it may well be doubted whether it would ever have been successful with Grace St. John, even had she been as fancy free
as when Hilland first met her. She was a soldier's daughter,
and could best be won by Hilland's soldier-like wooing. Not
that she could have been won any more readily by direct and
impetuous advances had not her heart been touched, but the
probabilities are that her heart never would have been touched
by Graham's army-of-observation tactics. It would scarcely
have occurred to her to think seriously of a man who did not
follow her with an eager quest.

On the other hand, as his aunt had suggested from the
first, poor Graham was greatly endangering his peace by this
close study of a woman lovely in herself, and, as he fully believed, peculiarly adapted to satisfy every requirement of
his nature. A man who knows nothing of a hidden treasure
goes unconcernedly on his way; if he discovers it and then
loses it he feels impoverished.

CHAPTER VIII

SUPREME MOMENTS

GRAHAM'S visit was at last lengthened to a month, and yet the impulse of work or of departure had not seized him. Indeed, there seemed less prospect of anything of the kind than ever. A strong mutual attachment was growing between himself and his aunt. The brusque, quick-witted old lady interested him, while her genuine kindness and hearty welcome gave to him, for the first time in his life, the sense of being at home. She was a woman of strong likes and dislikes. She had taken a fancy to Graham from the first, and this interest fast deepened into affection. She did not know how lonely she was in her isolated life, and she found it so pleasant to have some one to look after and think about that she would have been glad to have kept him with her always.

Moreover, she had a lurking hope, daily gaining confirmation, that her nephew was not so indifferent to her favorite as he seemed. In her old age she was beginning to long for kindred and closer ties, and she felt that she could in effect adopt Grace, and could even endure the invalid major for the sake of one who was so congenial. She thought it politic however to let matters take their own course, for her strong good sense led her to believe that meddling rarely accomplishes anything except mischief. She was not averse to a little indirect diplomacy, however, and did all in her power to make it easy and natural for Graham to see the young girl as often as possible, and one lovely day, early in June, she planned a little excursion, which, according to the experience of her early days, promised well for her aims.

One breathless June morning that was warm, but not sultry, she went over to the St. Johns', and suggested a drive to the brow of a hill from which there was a superb view of the surrounding country. The plan struck the major pleasantly, and Grace was delighted. She had the craving for out-of-door life common to all healthful natures, but there was another reason why she longed for a day under the open sky with her thoughts partially and pleasantly distracted from one great truth to which she felt she must grow accustomed by degrees. It was arranged that they should take their lunch and spend the larger part of the afternoon, thus giving the affair something of the aspect of a quiet little picnic.

Although Graham tried to take the proposition quietly, he could not repress a flush of pleasure and a certain alacrity of movement eminently satisfactory to his aunt. Indeed, his spirits rose to a degree that made him a marvel to himself, and he wonderingly queried, "Can I be the same man who but a few weeks since watched the dark line of my native country loom up in the night, and with prospects as vague and dark as that outline?"

Miss St. John seemed perfectly radiant that morning, her eyes vying with the June sunlight, and her cheeks emulating the roses everywhere in bloom. What was the cause of her unaffected delight? Was it merely the prospect of a day of pleasure in the woods? Could he hope that his presence added to her zest for the occasion? Such were the questions with which Graham's mind was busy as he aided the ladies in their preparations. She certainly was more kind and friendly than usual—yes, more familiar. He was compelled to admit, however, that her manner was such as would be natural toward an old and trusted friend, but he hoped—never before had he realized how dear this hope was becoming—that some day she would awaken to the consciousness that he might be more than a friend. In the meantime he would

be patient, and, with the best skill he could master, endeavor
to win her favor, instead of putting her on the defensive by
seeking her love.

"Two elements cannot pass into combination until there
is mutual readiness," reasoned the scientist. "Contact is
not combination. My province is to watch until in some un-
guarded moment she gives the hope that she would listen with
her heart. To speak before that, either by word or action,
would be pain to her and humiliation to me."

The gulf between them was wide indeed, although she
smiled so genially upon him. In tying up a bundle their
hands touched. He felt an electric thrill in all his nerves;
she only noticed the circumstance by saying, "Who is it that
is so awkward, you or I ?"

"You are Grace," he replied. "It was I."

"I should be graceless indeed were I to find fault with
anything to-day," she said impulsively, and raising her head
she looked away into the west as if her thoughts had followed
her eyes.

"It certainly is a very fine day," Graham remarked sententiously.

She turned suddenly, and saw that he was watching her
keenly. Conscious of her secret she blushed under his detected scrutiny, but laughed lightly, saying, "You are a
happy man, Mr. Graham, for you suggest that perfect
weather leaves nothing else to be desired."

"Many have to be content with little else," he replied,
"and days like this are few and far between."

"Not few and far between for me," she murmured to herself as she moved away.

She *was* kinder and more friendly to Graham than ever
before, but the cause was a letter received that morning,
against which her heart now throbbed. She had written to
Hilland of Graham, and of her enjoyment of his society,
dwelling slightly on his disposition to make himself agreeable
without tendencies toward sentiment and gallantry.

Love is quick to take alarm, and although Graham was

his nearest friend, Hilland could not endure the thought of leaving the field open to him or to any one a day longer. He knew that Graham was deliberate and by no means susceptible. And yet, to him, the fact conveyed by the letter, that his recluse friend had found the society of Grace so satisfactory that he had lingered on week after week, spoke volumes. It was not like his studious and solitary companion of old. Moreover, he understood Graham sufficiently well to know that Grace would have peculiar attractions for him, and that upon a girl of her mind he would make an impression very different from that which had led society butterflies to shun him as a bore. Her letter already indicated this truth. The natural uneasiness that he had felt all along lest some master spirit should appear was intensified. Although Graham was so quiet and undemonstrative, Hilland knew him to be possessed of an indomitable energy of will when once it was aroused and directed toward an object. Thus far from Grace's letter he believed that his friend was only interested in the girl of his heart, and he determined to forestall trouble, if possible, and secure the fruits of his patient waiting and wooing, if any were to be gathered. At the same time he resolved to be loyal to his friend, as far as he could admit his claims, and he wrote a glowing eulogy of Graham, unmarred by a phrase or word of detraction. Then, as frankly, he admitted his fears, in regard not only to Graham, but to others, and followed these words with a strong and impassioned plea in his own behalf, assuring her that time and absence, so far from diminishing her mastery over him, had rendered it complete. He entreated for permission to come to her, saying that his business interests, vast as they were, counted as less than nothing compared with the possession of her love—that he would have pressed his suit by personal presence long before had not obligations to others detained him. These obligations he now could and would delegate, for all the wealth of the mines on the continent would only be a burden unless she could share it with him. He also informed her that a ring made of gold, which he himself had mined deep in the mountain's heart, was on the way to her—that his own hands had helped to fashion the rude circlet—and that it was significant of the truth that he sought her not from the vantage ground of wealth, but because of a manly devotion that would lead him to delve in a mine or work in a shop for her, rather than live a life of luxury with any one else in the world.

For the loving girl what a treasure was such a letter! The joy it brought was so overwhelming that she was glad of the distractions which Mrs. Mayburn's little excursion promised. She wished to quiet the tumult at her heart, so that she could write as an earnest woman to an earnest man, which she could not do on this bright June morning, with her heart keeping tune with every bird that sang. Such a response as she then might have made would have been the one he would have welcomed most, but she did not think so. "I would not for the world have him know how my head is turned," she had laughingly assured herself, not dreaming that such an admission would disturb his equilibrium to a far greater degree.

"After a day," she thought, "out of doors with Mrs. Mayburn's genial common-sense and Mr. Graham's cool, half-cynical philosophy to steady me, I shall be sane enough to answer."

They were soon bowling away in a strong, three-seated rockaway, well suited to country roads, Graham driving, with the object of his thoughts and hopes beside him. Mrs. Mayburn and the major occupied the back seat, while Jinny, with a capacious hamper, was in the middle seat, and in the estimation of the diplomatic aunt made a good screen and division.

All seemed to promise well for her schemes, for the young people appeared to be getting on wonderfully together. There was a constant succession of jest and repartee. Grace was cordiality itself; and in Graham's eyes that morning there was coming an expression of which he may not have been fully aware, or which at last he would permit to be seen. Indeed, he was yielding rapidly to the spell of her beauty and the charm of her mind and manner. He was conscious of a strange, exquisite exhilaration. Every nerve in his body seemed alive to her presence, while the refined and delicate curves of her cheek and throat gave a pleasure which no statue in the galleries of Europe had ever imparted.

He wondered at all this, for to him it was indeed a new experience. His past with its hopes and ambitions seemed to have floated away to an indefinite distance, and he to have awakened to a new life—a new phase of existence. In the exaltation of the hour he felt that, whatever might be the result, he had received a revelation of capabilities in his nature of which he had not dreamed, and which at the time promised to compensate for any consequent reaction. He exulted in his human organism as a master in music might rejoice over the discovery of an instrument fitted to respond perfectly to his genius. Indeed, the thought crossed his mind more than once that day that the marvel of marvels was that mere clay could be so highly organized. It was not his thrilling nerves alone which suggested this thought, or the pure mobile face of the young girl, so far removed from any suggestion of earthliness, but a new feeling, developing in his heart, that seemed so deep and strong as to be deathless.

They reached their destination in safety. The June sunlight would have made any place attractive, but the brow of the swelling hill with its wide outlook, its background of grove and intervening vistas, left nothing to be desired. The horses were soon contentedly munching their oats, and yet their stamping feet and switching tails indicated that even for the brute creation there is ever some alloy. Graham, however, thought that fortune had at last given him one perfect day. There was no perceptible cloud. The present was so eminently satisfactory that it banished the past, or, if remembered, it served as a foil. The future promised a chance for happiness that seemed immeasurable, although the horizon of his brief existence was so near; for he felt that with her as his own, human life with all its limitations

was a richer gift than he had ever imagined possible. And
yet, like a slight and scarcely heard discord, the thought
would come occasionally, "Since so much is possible, more
ought to be possible. With such immense capability for life
as I am conscious of to-day, how is it that this life is but a
passing and perishing manifestation?"

Such impressions took no definite form, however, but
merely passed through the dim background of his consciousness, while he gave his whole soul to the effort to make the
day one that from its unalloyed pleasure could not fail to recall him to the memory of Miss St. John. He believed himself to be successful, for he felt as if inspired. He was ready
with a quick reply to all her mirthful sallies, and he had the
tact to veil his delicate flattery under a manner and mode of
speech that suggested rather than revealed his admiration.
She was honestly delighted with him and his regard, as she
understood it, and she congratulated herself again and again
that Hilland's friend was a man that she also would find unusually agreeable. His kindness to her father had warmed
her heart toward him, and now his kindness and interest were
genuine, although at first somewhat hollow and assumed.

Graham had become a decided favorite with the old gentleman, for he had proved the most efficient ally that Grace
had ever gained in quickening the pace of heavy-footed Time.
Even the veteran's chilled blood seemed to feel the influences
of the day, and his gallantry toward Mrs. Mayburn was more
pronounced than usual. "We, too, will be young people once
more," he remarked, "for the opportunity may not come to
us again."

They discussed their lunch with zest, they smiled into one
another's face, and indulged in little pleasantries that were
as light and passing as the zephyrs that occasionally flut-
tered the leaves above their heads; but deep in each heart
were memories, tides of thought, hopes, fears, joys, that form
the tragic background of all human life. The old major
gave some reminiscences of his youthful campaigning. In
his cheerful mood his presentation of them was in harmony

with the sunny afternoon. The bright sides of his experiences were toward his auditors, but what dark shadows of wounds, agony, and death were on the further side! And of these he could never be quite unconscious, even while awakening laughter at the comic episodes of war.

Mrs. Mayburn seemed her plain-spoken, cheery self, intent only on making the most of this genial hour in the autumn of her life, and yet she was watching over a hope that she felt might make her last days her best days. She was almost praying that the fair girl whom she had so learned to love might become the solace of her age, and fill, in her childless heart, a place that had ever been an aching void. Miss St. John was too preoccupied to see any lover but one, and he was ever present, though thousands of miles away. But she saw in Graham his friend, and had already accepted him also as her most agreeable friend, liking him all the better for his apparent disposition to appeal only to her fancy and reason, instead of her heart. She saw well enough that he liked her exceedingly, but Hilland's impetuous wooing and impassioned words had made her feel that there was an infinite difference between liking and loving; and she pictured to herself the pleasure they would both enjoy when finding that their seemingly chance acquaintance was but preparation for the closer ties which their several relations to Hilland could not fail to occasion.

The object of this kindly but most temperate regard smiled into her eyes, chatted easily on any topic suggested, and appeared entirely satisfied; but was all the while conscious of a growing need which, denied, would impoverish his life, making it, brief even as he deemed it to be, an intolerable burden. But on this summer afternoon hope was in the ascendant, and he saw no reason why the craving of all that was best and noblest in his nature should not be met. When a supreme affection first masters the heart it often carries with it a certain assurance that there must be a response, that when so much is given by a subtle, irresistible, unexpected impulse, the one receiving should, sooner or later, by some law of correspondence, be inclined to return a similar regard. All living things in nature, when not interfered with, at the right time and in the right way, sought and found what was essential to the completion of their life, and he was a part of nature. According to the law of his own individuality he had yielded to Miss St. John's power. His reason had kept pace with his heart. He had advanced to his present attitude toward her like a man, and had not been driven to it by the passion of an animal. Therefore he was hopeful, self-complacent, and resolute. He not only proposed to win the girl he loved, cost what it might in time and effort, but in the exalted mood of the hour felt that he could and must win her.

She, all unconscious, smiled genially, and indeed seemed the very embodiment of mirth. Her talk was brilliant, yet interspersed with strange lapses that began to puzzle him. Meanwhile she scarcely saw him, gave him but the passing attention with which one looks up from an absorbing story, and all the time the letter against which her heart pressed seemed alive and endowed with the power to make each throb more glad and full of deep content.

How isolated and inscrutable is the mystery of each human life! Here were four people strongly interested in each other and most friendly, between whom was a constant interchange of word and glance, and yet their thought and feeling were flowing in strong diverse currents, unseen and unsuspected.

As the day declined they all grew more silent and abstracted. Deeper shadows crept into the vistas of memory with the old, and those who had become but memories were with them again as they had been on like June days half a century before. With the young the future, outlined by hope, took forms so absorbing that the present was forgotten. Ostensibly they were looking off at the wide and diversified landscape; in reality they were contemplating the more varied experiences, actual and possible, of life.

At last the major complained querulously that he was

growing chilly. The shadow in which he shivered was not caused by the sinking sun.

The hint was taken at once, and in a few moments they were on their way homeward. The old sportive humor of the morning did not return. The major was the aged invalid again. Mrs. Mayburn and Graham were perplexed, for Grace had seemingly become remote from them all. She was as kind as ever; indeed her manner was characterized by an unusual gentleness; but they could not but see that her thoughts were not with them. The first tumultuous torrent of her joy had passed, and with it her girlhood. Now, as an earnest woman, she was approaching the hour of her betrothal, when she would write words that would bind her to another and give direction to all her destiny. Her form was at Graham's side; the woman was not there. Whither and to whom had she gone? The question caused him to turn pale with fear.

"Miss Grace," he said at last, and there was a tinge of reproach in his voice, "where are you? You left us some time since," and he turned and tried to look searchingly into her eyes.

She met his without confusion or rise in color. Her feelings had become so deep and earnest, so truly those of a woman standing on the assured ground of fealty to another, that she was beyond her former girlish sensitiveness and its quick, involuntary manifestations. She said gently, "Pardon me, Mr. Graham, for my unsocial abstraction. You deserve better treatment for all your efforts for our enjoyment to-day."

"Please do not come back on compulsion," he said. "I do not think I am a natural Paul Pry, but I would like to know where you have been."

"I will tell you some day," she said, with a smile that was so friendly that his heart sprang up in renewed hope. Then, as if remembering what was due to him and the others, she buried her thoughts deep in her heart until she could be alone with them and their object. And yet her secret joy, like a hidden fire, tinged all her words with a kindly warmth. Graham and his aunt were not only pleased but also perplexed, for both were conscious of something in Grace's manner which they could not understand. Mrs. Mayburn was sanguine that her June-day strategy was bringing forth the much-desired results; her nephew only hoped. They all parted with cordial words, which gave slight hint of that which was supreme in each mind.

CHAPTER IX

THE REVELATION

G RAHAM found letters which required nis absence for a day or two, and it seemed to him eminently fitting that he should go over in the evening and say good-by to Miss St. John. Indeed he was disposed to say more, if the opportunity offered. His hopes sank as he saw that the first floor was darkened, and in answer to his summons Jinny informed him that the major and Miss Grace were "po'ful tired" and had withdrawn to their rooms.

He trembled to find how deep was his disappointment, and understood as never before that his old self had ceased to exist. A month since no one was essential to him; now his being had become complex. Then he could have crossed the ocean with a few easily spoken farewells; now he could not go away for a few hours without feeling that he must see one who was then a stranger. The meaning of this was all too plain, and as he walked away in the June starlight he admitted it fully. Another life had become essential to his own. And still he clung to his old philosophy, muttering, "If this be true, why will not my life become as needful to her?" His theory, like many another, was a product of wishes rather than an induction from facts.

When he returned after a long ramble, the light still burning in Miss St. John's window did not harmonize with the story of the young girl's fatigue. The faint rays, however, could reveal nothing, although they had illumined page after page traced full of words of such vital import to him.

Mrs. Mayburn shared his early breakfast, and before he took his leave he tried to say in an easy, natural manner:

"Please make my adieus to Miss St. John, and say I called to present them in person, but it seemed she had retired with the birds. The colored divinity informed me that she was 'po'ful tired,' and I hope you will express my regret that the day proved so exceedingly wearisome." Mrs. Mayburn lifted her keen gray eyes to her nephew's face, and a slow rising flush appeared under her scrutiny. Then she said gently, "That's a long speech, Alford, but I don't think it expresses your meaning. If I give your cordial good-by to Grace and tell her that you hope soon to see her again, shall I not better carry out your wishes?"

"Yes," was the grave and candid reply.

"I believe you are in earnest now."

"I am, indeed," he replied, almost solemnly, and with these vague yet significant words they came to an understanding.

Three days elapsed, and still Graham's business was not completed. In his impatience he left it unfinished and returned. How his heart bounded as he saw the familiar cottage! With hasty steps he passed up the path from the street. It was just such another evening as that which had smiled upon his first coming to his aunt's residence, only now there was summer warmth in the air, and the richer, fuller promise of the year. The fragrance that filled the air, if less delicate, was more penetrating, and came from flowers that had absorbed the sun's strengthening rays. If there was less of spring's ecstasy in the song of the birds, there was now in their notes that which was in truer accord with Graham's mood.

At a turn of the path he stopped short, for on the rustic seat beneath the apple-tree he saw Miss St. John reading a letter; then he went forward to greet her, almost impetuously, with a glow in his face and a light in his eyes which no one had ever seen before. She rose to meet him, and there was an answering gladness in her face which made her seem divine to him.

"You are welcome," she said cordially. "We have all

missed you more than we dare tell you;" and she gave his hand a warm, strong pressure.

The cool, even-pulsed man, who as a boy had learned to hide his feelings, was for a moment unable to speak. His own intense emotion, his all-absorbing hcpe, blinded him to the character of her greeting, and led him to give it a meaning it did not possess. She, equally preoccupied with her one thought, looked at him for a moment in surprise, and then cried, "He has told you—has written?"

"He! who?" Graham exclaimed with a blanching face.

"Why, Warren Hilland, your friend. I told you I would tell you, but I could not before I told him," she faltered.

He took an uncertain step or two to the tree, and leaned against it for support.

The young girl dropped the letter and clasped her hands in her distress. "It was on the drive—our return, you remember," she began incoherently. "You asked where my thoughts were, and I said I would tell you soon. Oh! we have both been blind. I am so—so sorry."

Graham's face and manner had indeed been an unmistakable revelation, and the frank, generous girl waited for no conventional acknowledgment before uttering what was uppermost in her heart.

By an effort which evidently taxed every atom of his manhood, Graham gained self-control, and said quietly, "Miss St. John, I think better of myself for having loved you. If I had known! But you are not to blame. It is I who have been blind, for you have never shown other than the kindly regard which was most natural, knowing that I was Hilland's friend. I have not been frank either, or I should have learned the truth long ago. I disguised the growing interest I felt in you from the first, fearing I should lose my chance if you understood me too early. I am Hilland's friend. No one living now knows him better than I do, and from the depths of my heart I congratulate you. He is the best and truest man that ever lived."

"Will you not be my friend, also?" she faltered.

He looked at her earnestly as he replied, "Yes, for life."

"You will feel differently soon," said the young girl, trying to smile reassuringly. "You will see that it has all been a mistake, a misunderstanding; and when your friend returns we will have the merriest, happiest times together."

"Could you soon feel differently?" he asked.

"Oh! why did you say that?" she moaned, burying her face in her hands. "If you will suffer even in a small degree as I should!"

Her distress was so evident and deep that he stood erect and stepped toward her. "Why are you so moved, Miss St. John?" he asked. "I have merely paid you the highest compliment within my power."

Her hands dropped from her face, and she turned away, but not so quickly as to hide the tears that dimmed her lustrous eyes. His lip quivered for a moment at the sight of them, but she did not see this.

"You have merely paid me a compliment," she repeated in a low tone.

The lines of his mouth were firm now, his face grave and composed, and in his gray eyes only a close observer might have seen that an indomitable will was resuming sway. "Certainly," he continued, "and such compliments you have received before and would often again were you free to receive them. I cannot help remembering that there is nothing unique in this episode."

She turned and looked at him doubtingly, as she said with hesitation, "You then regard your—your—"

"My vacation experience," he supplied.

Her eyes widened in what resembled indignant surprise, and her tones grew a little cold and constrained as she again repeated his words.

"You then regard your experience as a vacation episode."

"Do not for a moment think I have been insincere," he said, with strong emphasis, "or that I should not have esteemed it the chief honor of my life had I been successful—"

D—Roe—XIII

"As to that," she interrupted, "there are so many other honors that a man can win."

"Assuredly. Pardon me, Miss St. John, but I am sure you have had to inflict similar disappointments before. Did not the men survive?"

The girl broke out into a laugh in which there was a trace of bitterness. "Survive!" she cried. "Indeed they did. One is already married, and another I happen to know is engaged. I'm sure I'm glad, however. Your logic is plain and forcible, Mr. Graham, and you relieve my mind greatly. Men must be different from women."

"Undoubtedly."

"What did you mean by asking me, 'Could you soon feel differently?'"

He hesitated a moment and flushed slightly, then queried with a smile, "What did you mean by saying that I should soon learn to feel differently, and that when Hilland returned we should have the merriest times together?"

It was her turn now to be confused now; and she saw that her words were hollow, though spoken from a kindly impulse.

He relieved her by continuing: "You probably spoke from an instinctive estimate of me. You remembered what a cool and wary suitor I had been. Your father would say that I had adopted an-army-of-observation tactics, and I might have remembered that such armies rarely accomplish much. I waited for you to show some sign of weakness, and now you see that I am deservedly punished. It is ever best to face the facts as they are."

"You appear frank, Mr. Graham, and you certainly have not studied philosophy in vain."

"Why should I not take a philosophical view of the affair? In my policy, which I thought so safe and astute, I blundered. If from the first I had manifested the feeling" —the young girl smiled slightly at the word—"which you inspired, you would soon have taught me the wisdom of repressing its growth. Thus you see that you have not the slightest reason for self-censure; and I can go on my way, at least a wiser man."

She bowed gracefully, as she said with a laugh, "I am now beginning to understand that Mr. Graham can scarcely regret anything which adds to his stores of wisdom, and certainly not so slight an 'affair' as a 'vacation episode.' Now that we have talked over this little misunderstanding so frankly and rationally, will you not join us at whist to-night?"

"Certainly. My aunt and I will come over as usual."

Her brow contracted in perplexity as she looked searchingly at him for a moment; but his face was simply calm, grave, and kindly in its expression, and yet there was something about the man which impressed her and even awed her—something unseen, but felt by her woman's intuition. It must be admitted that it was felt but vaguely at the time; for Grace after all was a woman, and Graham's apparent philosophy was not altogether satisfactory. It had seemed to her as the interview progressed that she had been surprised into showing a distress and sympathy for which there was no occasion—that she had interpreted a cool, self-poised man by her own passionate heart and boundless love. In brief, she feared she had been sentimental over an occasion which Graham, as he had suggested, was able to view philosophically. She had put a higher estimate on his disappointment than he, apparently; and she had too much of her father's spirit, and too much womanly pride not to resent this, even though she was partially disarmed by this very disappointment, and still more so by his self-accusation and his tribute to Hilland. But that which impressed her most was something of which she saw no trace in the calm, self-controlled man before her. As a rule, the soul's life is hidden, except as it chooses to reveal itself; but there are times when the excess of joy or suffering cannot be wholly concealed, even though every muscle is rigid and the face marble. Therefore, although there were no outward signals of distress, Graham's agony was not without its influence on the woman before him, and it led her to say, gently and hesitatingly, "But you promised to be my friend, Mr. Graham."

His iron will almost failed him, for he saw how far removed she was from those women who see and know nothing save that which strikes their senses. He had meant to pique her pride as far as he could without offence, even though he sank low in her estimation; but such was the delicacy of her perceptions that she half divined the trouble he sedulously strove to hide. He felt as if he could sit down and cry like a child over his immeasurable loss, and for a second feared he would give way. There was in his eyes a flash of anger at his weakness, but it passed so quickly that she could scarcely note, much less interpret it.

Then he stepped forward in a friendly, hearty way, and took her hand as he said: "Yes, Miss St. John, and I will keep my promise. I will be your friend for life. If you knew my relations to Hilland, you could not think otherwise. I shall tell him when we meet of my first and characteristic siege of a woman's heart, of the extreme and prudent caution with which I opened my distant parallels, and how, at last, when I came within telescopic sight of the prize, I found that he had already captured it. My course has been so perfectly absurd that I must laugh in spite of myself;" and he did laugh so naturally and genially that Grace was constrained to join him, although the trouble and perplexity did not wholly vanish from her eyes.

"And now," he concluded, "that I have experienced my first natural surprise, I will do more than sensibly accept the situation. I congratulate you upon it as no one else can. Had I a sister I would rather that she married Hilland than any other man in the world. We thus start on the right basis for friendship, and there need be no awkward restraint on either side. I must now pay my respects to my aunt, or I shall lose not only her good graces but my supper also;" and with a smiling bow he turned and walked rapidly up the path, and disappeared within Mrs. Mayburn's open door.

Grace looked after him, and the perplexed contraction of her brow deepened. She picked up Hilland's letter, and slowly and musingly folded it. Suddenly she pressed a fervent kiss upon it, and murmured: "Thank God, the writer of this has blood in his veins; and yet—and yet—he looked at first as if he had received a mortal wound, and—and—all the time I felt that he suffered. But very possibly I am crediting him with that which would be inevitable were my case his."

With bowed head she returned slowly and thoughtfully through the twilight to her home.

CHAPTER X

THE KINSHIP OF SUFFERING

WHEN Graham felt that he had reached the refuge of his aunt's cottage, his self-control failed him, and he almost staggered into the dusky parlor and sank into a chair. Burying his face in his hands, he muttered: "Fool, fool, fool!" and a long, shuddering sigh swept through his frame.

How long he remained in this attitude he did not know, so overwhelmed was he by his sense of loss. At last he felt a hand laid upon his shoulder; he looked up and saw that the lamp was lighted and that his aunt was standing beside him. His face was so altered and haggard that she uttered an exclamation of distress.

Graham hastily arose and turned down the light. "I cannot bear that you should look upon my weakness," he said, hoarsely.

"I should not be ashamed of having loved Grace St. John," said the old lady, quietly.

"Nor am I. As I told her, I think far better of myself for having done so. A man who has seen her as I have would be less than a man had he not loved her. But oh, the future, the future! How am I to support the truth that my love is useless, hopeless?"

"Alford, I scarcely need tell you that my disappointment is bitter also. I had set my heart on this thing."

"You know all, then?"

"Yes, I know she is engaged to your friend, Warren Hilland. She came over in the dusk of last evening, and, sitting just where you are, told me all. I kept up. It was not for me to reveal your secret. I let the happy girl talk on, kissed her, and wished her all the happiness she deserves. Grace is unlike other girls, or I should have known about it long ago. I don't think she even told her father until she had first written to him her full acknowledgment. Your friend, however, had gained her father's consent to his addresses long since. She told me that."

"Oh, my awful future!" he groaned.

"Alford," Mrs. Mayburn said, gently but firmly, "think of *her* future. Grace is so good and kind that she would be very unhappy if she saw and heard you now. I hope you did not give way thus in her presence."

He sprang to his feet and paced the room rapidly at first, then more and more slowly. Soon he turned up the light, and Mrs. Mayburn was surprised at the change in his appearance.

"You are a strong, sensible woman," he began.

"Well, I will admit the premise for the sake of learning what is to follow."

"Miss St. John must never know of my sense of loss—my present despair," he said, in low, rapid speech. "Some zest in life may come back to me in time; but, be that as it may, I shall meet my trouble like a man. To make her suffer now—to cloud her well-merited happiness and that of my friend—would be to add a bitterness beyond that of death. Aunt, you first thought me cold and incapable of strong attachments, and a few weeks since I could not have said that your estimate was far astray, although I'm sure my friendship for Hilland was as strong as the love of most men. Until I met you and Grace it was the only evidence I possessed that I had a heart. Can you wonder? He was the first one that ever showed me any real kindness. I was orphaned in bitter truth, and from childhood my nature was chilled and benumbed by neglect and isolation. Growth and change are not so much questions of time as of conditions. From the first moment that I saw Grace St. John,

she interested me deeply; and, self-complacent, self-confident
fool that I was, I thought I could deal with the supreme
question of life as I had dealt with those which half the
world never think about at all.   I remember your warning,
aunt; and yet, as I said to myself at the time, there was
more of incentive than warning in your words.   How self-
confidently I smiled over them!   How perfectly sure I was
that I could enjoy this rare girl's society as I would look
at a painting or listen to a symphony!   Almost before I was
aware, I found a craving in my heart which I now know
all the world cannot satisfy.   That June day which you
arranged so kindly in my behalf made all as clear as the
cloudless sun that shone upon us.   That day I was revealed
fully unto myself, but my hope was strong, for I felt that
by the very law and correspondence of nature I could not
have such an immeasurable need without having that need
supplied.   In my impatience I left my business unfinished
and returned this evening, for I could not endure another
hour of delay.   She seemed to answer my glad looks when
we met; she gave her hand in cordial welcome.   I, blinded
by feeling, and thinking that its very intensity must awaken
a like return, stood speechless, almost overwhelmed by my
transcendent hope.   She interpreted my manner naturally
by what was uppermost in her mind, and exclaimed: 'He
has told you—he has written.'   In a moment I knew the
truth, and I scarcely think that a knife piercing my heart
could inflict a deeper pang.   I could not rally for a moment
or two.   When shall I forget the sympathy—the tears that
dimmed her dear eyes!   I have a religion at last, and I worship the divine nature of that complete woman.   The thought
that I made her suffer aroused my manhood; and from that
moment I strove to make light of the affair—to give the impression that she was taking it more seriously than I did.
I even tried to pique her pride—I could not wound her
vanity, for she has none—and I partially succeeded.   My
task, however, was and will be a difficult one, for her
organization is so delicate and fine that she feels what she

cannot see. But I made her laugh in spite of herself at my prudent, wary wooing. I removed, I think, all constraint, and we can meet as if nothing had happened. Not that we can meet often—that would tax me beyond my strength—but often enough to banish solicitude from her mind and from Hilland's. Now you know the facts sufficiently to become a shrewd and efficient ally. By all your regard for me—what is far more, by all your love for her—I entreat you let me bring no cloud across her bright sky. We are going over to whist as usual to-night. Let all be as usual."

"Heaven bless you, Alford!" faltered his aunt, with tearful eyes.

"Heaven! what a mockery! Even the lichen, the insect, lives a complete life, while we, with all our reason, so often blunder, fail, and miss that which is essential to existence."

Mrs. Mayburn shook her head slowly and thoughtfully, and then said: "This very fact should teach us that our philosophy of life is false. We are both materialists—I from the habit of living for this world only; you, I suppose, from mistaken reasoning; but in hours like these the mist is swept aside, and I feel, I know, that this life cannot, must not, be all in all."

"Oh, hush!" cried Graham, desperately. "To cease to exist and therefore to suffer, may become the best one can hope for. Were it not cowardly, I would soon end it all."

"You may well use the word 'cowardly,'" said his aunt in strong emphasis; "and brave Grace St. John would revolt at and despise such cowardice by every law of her nature."

"Do not fear. I hope never to do anything to forfeit her respect, except it is for the sake of her own happiness, as when to-day I tried to make her think my veins were filled with ice-water instead of blood. Come, I have kept you far too long. Let us go through the formality of supper; and then I will prove to you that if I have been weak here I can be strong for her sake. I do not remember my mother; but nature is strong, and I suppose there comes a time in every one's life when he must speak to some one as he would to a mother. You have been very kind, dear aunt, and I shall never forget that you have wished and schemed for my happiness.''

The old lady came and put her arm around the young man's neck and looked into his face with a strange wistfulness as she said, slowly: "There is no blood relationship between us, Alford, but we are nearer akin than such ties could make us. You do not remember your mother; I never had a child. But, as you say, nature is strong; and although I have tried to satisfy myself with a hundred things, the mother in my heart has never been content. I hoped, I prayed, that you and Grace might become my children. Alford, I have been learning of late that I am a lonely, unhappy old woman. Will you not be my boy? I would rather share your sorrow than be alone in the world again.''

Graham was deeply touched. He bowed his head upon her shoulder as if he were her son, and a few hot tears fell from his eyes. "Yes, aunt," he said, in a low tone, "you have won the right to ask anything that I can give. Fate, in denying us both what our hearts most craved, has indeed made us near akin; and there can be an unspoken sympathy between us that may have a sustaining power that we cannot now know. You have already taken the bitterness, the despair out of my sorrow; and should I go to the ends of the earth I shall be the better for having you to think of and care for.''

"And you feel that you cannot remain here, Alford?''

"No, aunt, that is now impossible; that is, for the present.''

"Yes, I suppose it is," she admitted, sadly.

"Come, aunty dear, I promised Miss St. John that we

would go over as usual to-night, and I would not for the world break my word."

"Then we shall go at once. We shall have a nice little supper on our return. Neither of us is in the mood for it now."

After a hasty toilet Graham joined his aunt. She looked at him, and had no fears.

CHAPTER XI

THE ORDEAL

GRACE met them at the door. "It is very kind of you," she said, "to come over this evening after a fatiguing journey."

"Very," he replied, laughingly; "a ride of fifty miles in the cars should entitle one to a week's rest."

"I hope you are going to take it."

"Oh, no; my business man in New York has at last aroused me to heroic action. With only the respite of a few hours' sleep I shall venture upon the cars again and plunge into all the perils and excitements of a real estate speculation. My property is going up, and 'there's a tide,' you know, 'which, taken at its flood—' "

"Leads away from your friends. I see that it is useless for us to protest, for when did a man ever give up a chance for speculation?"

"Then it is not the fault of man: we merely obey a general law."

"That is the way with you scientists," she said with a piquant nod and smile. "You do just as you please, but you are always obeying some profound law that we poor mortals know nothing about. We don't fall back upon the arrangements of the universe for our motives, do we, Mrs. Mayburn?"

"Indeed we don't," was the brusque response. " 'When she will, she will, and when she won't, she won't,' answers for us."

"Grace! Mrs. Mayburn!" called the major from the

parlor; "if you don't come soon I'll order out the guard and have you brought in. Mr. Graham," he continued, as the young man hastened to greet him, "you are as welcome as a leave of absence. We have had no whist since you left us, and we are nearly an hour behind time to-night. Mrs. Mayburn, your humble servant. Excuse me for not rising. Why the deuce my gout should trouble me again just now I can't see. I've not seen you since that juvenile picnic which seemed to break up all our regular habits. I never thought that you would desert me. I suppose Mr. Graham carries a roving commission and can't be disciplined. I propose, however, that we set to at once and put the hour we've lost at the other end of the evening."

It was evident that the major was in high spirits, in spite of his catalogue of ills; and in fact his daughter's engagement had been extremely satisfactory to him. Conscious of increasing age and infirmity, he was delighted that Grace had chosen one so abundantly able to take care of her and of him also. For the last few days he had been in an amiable mood, for he felt that fortune had dealt kindly by him. His love for his only child was the supreme affection of his heart, and she by her choice had fulfilled his best hopes. Her future was provided for and safe. Then from the force of long habit he thought next of himself. If his tastes were not luxurious, he had at least a strong liking for certain luxuries, and to these he would gladly add a few more did his means permit. He was a connoisseur in wines and the pleasures of the table—not that he had any tendencies toward excess, but he delighted to sip the great wines of the world, to expatiate on their age, character, and origin. Sometimes he would laughingly say, "Never dilate on the treasures bequeathed to us by the old poets, sages, and artists, but for inspiration and consolation give me a bottle of old, old wine—wine made from grapes that ripened before I was born."

He was too upright a man, however, to gratify these tastes beyond his means; but Grace was an indulgent and

skilful housekeeper, and made their slender income minister to her father's pleasure in a way that surprised even
her practical friend, Mrs. Mayburn. In explanation she
would laughingly say, "I regard housekeeping as a fine
art. The more limited your materials the greater the
genius required for producing certain results. Now, I'm
a genius, Mrs. Mayburn. You wouldn't dream it, would
you ? Papa sometimes has a faint consciousness of the fact
when he finds on his table wines and dishes of which he
knows the usual cost. 'My dear,' he will say severely, 'is
this paid for?' 'Yes,' I reply, meekly. 'How did you
manage it?' Then I stand upon my dignity, and reply
with offended majesty, 'Papa, I am housekeeper. You are
too good a soldier to question the acts of your superior officer.' Then he makes me a most profound bow and apology, and rewards me amply by his almost childlike enjoyment of what after all has only cost me a little undetected
economy and skill in cookery."

But the major was not so blind as he appeared to be.
He knew more of her "undetected" economies, which usually came out of her allowance, than she supposed, and his
conscience often reproached him for permitting them; but
since they appeared to give her as much pleasure as they
afforded him, he had let them pass. It is hard for a petted
and weary invalid to grow in self-denial. While the old
gentleman would have starved rather than angle for Hilland or plead his cause by a word—he had given his consent
to the young man's addresses with the mien of a major-general—he nevertheless foresaw that wealth as the ally of his
daughter's affection would make him one of the most dis-
criminating and fastidious *gourmands* in the land.

In spite of his age and infirmity the old soldier was exceedingly fond of travel and of hotel life. He missed the
varied associations of the army. Pain he had to endure
much of the time, and from it there was no escape. Change
of place, scene, and companionship diverted his mind, and
he partially forgot his sufferings. As we have shown, he

was a devourer of newspapers, but he enjoyed the world's gossip far more when he could talk it over with others, and maintain on the questions of the day half a dozen good-natured controversies. When at the seashore the previous summer he had fought scores of battles for his favorite measures with other ancient devotees of the newspaper. Grace had made Graham laugh many a time by her inimitable descriptions of the quaint tilts and chaffings of these graybeards, as each urged the views of his favorite journals; and then she would say, "You ought to see them sit down to whist. Such prolonged and solemn sittings upset my gravity more than all their *bric-à-brac* jokes." And then she had sighed and said, "I wish we could have remained longer, for papa improved so much and was so happy."

The time was coming when he could stay longer—as long as he pleased—for whatever pleased her father would please Grace, and would have to please her husband. Her mother when dying had committed the old man to her care, and a sacred obligation had been impressed upon her childish mind which every year had strengthened.

As we have seen, Grace had given her heart to Hilland by a compulsion which she scarcely understood herself. No thrifty calculations had had the slightest influence in bringing the mysterious change of feeling that had been a daily surprise to the young girl. She had turned to Hilland as the flower turns to the sun, with scarcely more than the difference that she was conscious that she was turning. When at last she ceased to wonder at the truth that her life had become blended with that of another—for, as her love developed, this union seemed the most natural and inevitable thing in the world—she began to think of Hilland more than of herself, and of the changes which her new relations would involve. It became one of the purest sources of her happiness that she would eventually have the means of gratifying every taste and whim of her father, and could surround him with all the comforts which his age and infirmities permitted him to enjoy.

Thus the engagement ring on Miss St. John's finger had its heights and depths of meaning to both father and daughter; and its bright golden hue pervaded all the prospects and possibilities—the least as well as the greatest—of the future. It was but a plain, heavy circlet of gold, and looked like a wedding-ring. Such to Graham it seemed to be, as its sheen flashed upon his eyes during their play, which continued for two hours or more, with scarcely a remark or an interruption beyond the requirements of the game. The old major loved this complete and scientific absorption, and Grace loved to humor him. Moreover, she smiled more than once at Graham's intentness. Never had he played so well, and her father had to put forth all his veteran skill and experience to hold his own. "To think that I shed tears over his disappointment, when a game of whist can console him!" she thought. "How different he is from his friend! I suppose that is the reason that they are such friends—they are so unlike. The idea of Warren playing with that quiet, steady hand and composed face under like circumstances! And yet, why is he so pale?"

Mrs. Mayburn understood this pallor too well, and she felt that the ordeal had lasted long enough. She, too, had acted her part admirably, but now she pleaded fatigue, saying that she had not been very well for the last day or two. She was inscrutable to Grace, and caused no misgivings. It is easier for a woman than for a man to hide emotions from a woman, and Mrs. Mayburn's gray eyes and strong features rarely revealed anything that she meant to conceal. The major acquiesced good-naturedly, saying, "You are quite right to stop, Mrs. Mayburn, and I surely have no cause to complain. We have had more play in two hours than most people have in two weeks.. I congratulate you, Mr. Graham; you are becoming a foeman worthy of any man's steel."

Graham rose with the relief which a man would feel on leaving the rack, and said, smilingly, "Your enthusiasm is contagious. Any man would soon be on his mettle who played often with you."

"Is enthusiasm one of your traits?" Grace asked, with an arch smile over her shoulder, as she went to ring the bell.

"What! Have you not remarked it?"

"Grace has been too preoccupied to remark anything— sly puss!" said the major, laughing heartily. "My dear Mrs. Mayburn, I shall ask for your congratulations to-night. I know we shall have yours, Mr. Graham, for Grace has informed me that Hilland is your best and nearest friend. This little girl of mine has been playing blindman's-buff with her old father. She thought she had the handkerchief tight over my eyes, but I always keep one corner raised a little. Well, Mr. Graham, this dashing friend of yours, who thinks he can carry all the world by storm, asked me last summer if he could lay siege to Grace. I felt like wringing his neck for his audacity and selfishness. The idea of any one taking Grace from me!"

"And no one shall, papa," said Grace, hiding her blushing face behind his white shock of hair. "But I scarcely think these details will interest—"

"What!" cried the bluff, frank old soldier—"not interest Mrs. Mayburn, the best and kindest of neighbors? not interest Hilland's *alter ego?*"

"I assure you," said Graham, laughing, "that I am deeply interested; and I promise you, Miss Grace, that I shall give Hilland a severer curtain lecture than he will ever receive from you, because he has left me in the dark so long."

"Stop pinching my arm," cried the major, who was in one of his jovial moods, and often immensely enjoyed teasing his daughter. "You may well hide behind me. Mrs. Mayburn, I'm going to expose a rank case of filial deception that was not in the least successful. This 'I came, I saw, I conquered' friend of yours, Mr. Graham, soon discovered that he was dealing with a race that was not in the habit of surrendering. But your friend, like Wellington, never knew when he was beaten. He wouldn't retreat an inch, but drawing his lines as close as he dared, sat down to a regular siege."

Graham again laughed outright, and with a comical glance at the young girl, asked, "Are you sure, sir, that Miss St. John was aware of these siege operations?"

"Indeed she was. Your friend raised his flag at once, and nailed it to the staff. And this little minx thought that she could deceive an old soldier like myself by play-ing the rôle of disinterested friend to a lonely young man condemned to the miseries of a mining town. I was often tempted to ask her why she did not extend her sympathy to scores of young fellows in the service who are in danger of being scalped every day. But the joke of it was that I knew she was undermined and must surrender long before Hilland did."

"Now, papa, it's too bad of you to expose me in this style. I appeal to Mrs. Mayburn if I did not keep my flag flying so defiantly to the last that even she did not suspect me."

"Yes," said the old lady, dryly; "I can testify to that."

"Which is only another proof of my penetration," chuckled the major. "Well, well, it is so seldom I can get ahead of Grace in anything that I like to make the most of my rare good fortune; and it seems, Mr. Graham, as if you and your aunt had already become a part of our present and prospective home circle. I have seen a letter in which Warren speaks of you in a way that reminds me of a friend who was shot almost at my side in a fight with the Indians. That was nearly half a century ago, and yet no one has taken his place. With men, friendships mean something, and last."

"Come, come," cried Mrs. Mayburn, bristling up, "nei-ther Grace nor I will permit such an implied slur upon our sex."

"My friendship for Hilland will last," said Graham, with quiet emphasis. "Most young men are drawn together by a mutual liking—by something congenial in their natures.

I owe him a debt of gratitude that can never be repaid. He found me a lonely, neglected boy, who had scarcely ever known kindness, much less affection, and his ardent, generous nature became an antidote to my gloomy tendencies. From the first he has been a constant and faithful friend. He has not one unworthy trait. But there is nothing negative about him, for he abounds in the best and most manly qualities; and I think," he concluded, speaking slowly and deliberately, as if he were making an inward vow, "that I shall prove worthy of his trust and regard."

Grace looked at him earnestly and gratefully, and the thought again asserted itself that she had not yet gauged his character or his feeling toward herself. To her surprise she also noted that Mrs. Mayburn's eyes were filled with tears, but the old lady was equal to the occasion, and misled her by saying, "I feel condemned, Alford, that you should have been so lonely and neglected in early life, but I know it was so."

"Oh, well, aunt, you know I was not an interesting boy, and had I been imposed upon you in my hobbledehoy period, our present relations might never have existed. I must ask your congratulations also," he continued, turning toward the major and his daughter. "My aunt and I have in a sense adopted each other. I came hither to pay her a formal call, and have made another very dear friend."

"Have you made only one friend since you became our neighbor?" asked Grace, with an accent of reproach in her voice.

"I would very gladly claim you and your father as such," he replied, smilingly.

The old major arose with an alacrity quite surprising in view of his lameness, and pouring out two glasses of the wine that Jinny had brought in answer to Grace's touch of the bell, he gave one of the glasses to Graham, and with the other in his left hand, he said, "And here I pledge you the word of a soldier that I acknowledge the claim in full, not only for Hilland's sake, but your own. You have generously sought to beguile the tedium of a crotchety and irritable old man; but such as he is he gives you his hand as a true, stanch friend; and Grace knows this means a great deal with me.''

"Yes, indeed," she cried. "I declare, papa, you almost make me jealous. You treated Warren as if you were the Great Mogul, and he but a presuming subject. Mr. Graham, if so many new friends are not an embarrassment of riches, will you give me a little niche among them?''

"I cannot give you that which is yours already," he replied; "nor have I a little niche for you. You have become identified with Hilland, you know, and therefore require a large space.''

"Now, see here, my good friends, you are making too free with my own peculiar property. You are already rich in each other, not counting Mr. Hilland, who, according to Alford, seems to embody all human excellence. I have only this philosophical nephew, and even with him shall find a rival in every book he can lay hands upon. I shall therefore carry him off at once, especially as he is to be absent several days.''

The major protested against his absence, and was cordiality itself in his parting words.

Grace followed them out on the moonlit piazza. "Mr. Graham," she said, hesitatingly, "you will not be absent very long, I trust.''

"Oh, no," he replied, lightly; "only two or three weeks. In addition to my affairs in the city, I have some business in Vermont, and while there shall follow down some well-remembered trout-streams.''

She turned slightly away, and buried her face in a spray of roses from the bush that festooned the porch. He saw that a tinge of color was in her cheeks, as she said in a low tone, "You should not be absent long; I think your friend will soon visit us, and you should be here to welcome him,'' and she glanced hastily toward him. Was it the moonlight that made him look so very pale ? His eyes held hers.

Mrs. Mayburn had walked slowly on, and seemingly he had forgotten her. The young girl's eyes soon fell before his fixed gaze, and her face grew troubled. He started, and said lightly, "I beg your pardon, Miss Grace, but you have no idea what a picture you make with the aid of those roses. The human face in clear moonlight reveals character, it is said, and I again congratulate my friend without a shadow of doubt. Unversed as I am in such matters, I am quite satisfied that Hilland will need no other welcome than yours, and that he will be wholly content with it for some time to come. Moreover, when I find myself among the trout, there's no telling when I shall get out of the woods."

"Is fishing, then, one of your ruling passions?" the young girl asked, with an attempt to resume her old piquant style of talk with him.

"Yes," he replied, laughing, so that his aunt might hear him; "but when one's passions are of so mild a type one may be excused for having a half-dozen. Good-by!"

She stepped forward and held out her hand. "You have promised to be my friend," she said, gently.

His hand trembled in her grasp as he said quietly and firmly, "I will keep my promise."

She looked after him wistfully, as she thought, "I'm not sure about him. I hope it's only a passing disappointment, for we should not like to think that our happiness had brought him wretchedness."

CHAPTER XII

FLIGHT TO NATURE

GRAHAM found his aunt waiting for him on the rustic seat beneath the apple-tree. Here, a few hours before, his heart elate with hope, he had hastened forward to meet Grace St. John. Ages seemed to have passed since that moment of bitter disappointment, teaching him how relative a thing is time.

The old lady joined him without a word, and they passed on silently to the house. As they entered, she said, trying to infuse into the commonplace words something of her sympathy and affection, "Now we will have a cosey little supper."

Graham placed his hand upon her arm, and detained her, as he replied, "No, aunt; please get nothing for me. I must hide myself for a few hours from even your kind eyes. Do not think me weak or unmanly. I shall soon get the reins well in hand, and shall then be quiet enough."

"I think your self-control has been admirable this evening."

"It was the self-control of sheer, desperate force, and only partial at that. I know I must have been almost ghostly in my pallor. I have felt pale—as if I were bleeding to death. I did not mean to take her hand in parting, for I could not trust myself; but she held it out so kindly that I had to give mine, which, in spite of my whole will power, trembled. I troubled and perplexed her. I have infused an element of sorrow and bitterness into her happy love; for in the degree in which it gives her joy she will fear that it brings the heartache to me, and she is too good and kind not to care. I must go away and not return until my face is bronzed and my nerves are steel. Oh, aunt! you cannot understand me; I scarcely understand myself. It seems as if all the love that I might have given to many in the past, had my life been like that of others, had been accumulating for this hopeless, useless waste—this worse than waste, since it only wounds and pains its object.''

"And do I count for so little, Alford?"

"You count for more now than all others save one; and if you knew how contrary this utter unreserve is to my nature and habit, you would understand how perfect is my confidence in you and how deep is my affection. But I am learning with a sort of dull, dreary astonishment that there are heights and depths of experience of which I once had not the faintest conception. This is a kind of battle that one must fight out alone. I must go away and accustom myself to a new condition of life. But do not worry about me. I shall come back a vertebrate;'' and he tried to summon a reassuring smile, as he kissed her in parting.

That night Graham faced his trouble, and decided upon his future course.

After an early breakfast the next morning, the young man bade his aunt good-by. With moist eyes, she said, "Alford, I am losing you, just as I find how much you are and can be to me.''

"No, aunty dear; my course will prove best for us both,'' he replied, gently. "You would not be happy if you saw me growing more sad and despairing every day through inaction, and—and—well, I could never become strong and calm with that cottage there just beyond the trees. You have not lost me, for I shall try to prove a good correspondent.''

Graham kept his word. His "real estate speculation'' did not detain him long in the city, for his business agent was better able to manage such interests than the inexperienced student; and soon a letter dated among the mountains

and the trout streams of Vermont assured Mrs. Mayburn
that he had carried out his intentions. Not long after, a
box with a score of superb fish followed the letter, and
Major St. John's name was pinned on some of the largest
and finest. During the next fortnight these trophies of his
sport continued to arrive at brief intervals, and they were
accompanied by letters, giving in almost journal form
graphic descriptions of the streams he had fished, their
surrounding scenery, and the amusing peculiarities of the
natives. There was not a word that suggested the cause
that had driven him so suddenly into the wilderness, but
on every page were evidences of tireless activity.

The major was delighted with the trout, and enjoyed
a high feast almost every day. Mrs. Mayburn, imagining
that she had divined Graham's wish, read from his letters
glowing extracts which apparently revealed an enthusiastic
sportsman.

After his departure Grace had resumed her frequent visits to her congenial old friend, and confidence having now
been given in respect to her absent lover, the young girl
spoke of him out of the abundance of her heart. Mrs. Mayburn tried to be all interest and sympathy, but Grace was
puzzled by something in her manner—something not absent
when she was reading Graham's letters. One afternoon she
said: "Tell your father that he may soon expect something
extraordinarily fine, for Alford has written me of a twenty-
mile tramp through the mountains to a stream almost unknown and inaccessible."

"Won't you read the description to us this evening?
You have no idea how much pleasure papa takes in Mr.
Graham's letters. He says they increase the gamy flavor
of the fish he enjoys so much; and I half believe that Mr.
Graham in this indirect and delicate way is still seeking to
amuse my father, and so compensate him for his absence.
Warren will soon be here, however, and then we can resume
our whist parties. Do you know that I am almost jealous?
Papa talks more of Vermont woods than of Western mines.

You ought to hear him expatiate upon the trout. He seems to follow Mr. Graham up and down every stream; and he explains to me with the utmost minuteness just how the flies are cast and just where they were probably thrown to snare the speckled beauties. By the way, Mr. Graham puzzles me. He seems to be the most indefatigable sportsman I ever heard of. But I should never have suspected it from the tranquil weeks he spent with us. He seemed above all things a student of the most quiet and intellectual tastes, one who could find more pleasure in a library and laboratory than in all the rest of the world together. Suddenly he develops into the most ardent disciple of Izaak Walton. Indeed, he is too ardent, too full of restless activity, to be a true follower of the gentle, placid Izaak. At his present rate he will soon overrun all Vermont;'' and she looked searchingly at her friend.

A faint color stole into the old lady's cheeks, but she replied, quietly: "I have learned to know Alford well enough to love him dearly; and yet you must remember that but a few weeks ago he was a comparative stranger to me. He certainly is giving us ample proof of his sportsmanship, and now that I recall it, I remember hearing of his fondness for solitary rambles in the woods when a boy.''

"His descriptions certainly prove that he is familiar with them,'' was the young girl's answer to Mrs. Mayburn's words. Her inward comment on the slight flush that accompanied them was: "She knows. He has told her; or she, less blind than I, has seen.'' But she felt that the admission of his love into which Graham had been surprised was not a topic for her to introduce, although she longed to be assured that she had not seriously disturbed the peace of her lover's friend. A day or two later Hilland arrived, and her happiness was too deep, too complete, to permit many thoughts of the sportsman in the Vermont forests. Nor did Hilland's brief but hearty expressions of regret at Graham's temporary absence impose upon her. She saw that the former was indeed more than content with her welcome; that while his friendship was a fixed star of the first magnitude, it paled and almost disappeared before the brightness and fulness of her presence. "Nature," indeed, became "radiant" to both "with purple light, the morning and the night varied enchantments."

Grace waited for Graham to give his own confidence to his friend if he chose to do so, for she feared that if she spoke of it estrangement might ensue. The unsuspecting major was enthusiastic in his praises of the successful fisherman, and Hilland indorsed with emphasis all he said. Graham's absence and Grace's reception had banished even the thought that he might possibly find a rival in his friend, and his happiness was unalloyed.

One sultry summer evening in early July Graham returned to his aunt's residence, and was informed that she was, as usual, at her neighbor's. He went immediately to his room to remove the dust and stains of travel. On his table still lay the marked copy of Emerson that Grace had lent him, and he smiled bitterly as he recalled his complacent, careless surmises over the underscored passage, now so well understood and explained. Having finished his toilet, he gazed steadily at his reflection in the mirror, as a soldier might have done to see if his equipment was complete. It was evident he had not gone in vain to nature for help. His face was bronzed, and no telltale flush or pallor could now be easily recognized. His expression was calm and resolute, indicating nerves braced and firm. Then he turned away with the look of a man going into battle, and without a moment's hesitancy he sought the ordeal. The windows and doors of Major St. John's cottage were open, and as he mounted the piazza the group around the whist-table was in full view—the major contracting his bushy eyebrows over his hand as if not altogether satisfied, Mrs. Mayburn looking at hers with an interest so faint as to suggest that her thoughts were wandering, and Hilland with his laughing blue eyes glancing often from his cards to the fair face of his partner, as if he saw there a story that would deepen in its inthralling interest through life. There was no shadow, no doubt on his wide, white brow. It was the genial, frank, merry face of the boy who had thawed the reserve and banished the gathering gloom of a solitary youth at college, only now it was marked by the stronger lines of early manhood. His fine, short upper lip was clean shaven, and its tremulous curves indicated a nature quick, sensitive, and ready to respond to every passing influence, while a full, tawny beard and broad shoulders banished all suggestion of effeminacy. He appeared to be, what in truth he was, an unspoiled favorite of fortune, now supremely happy in her best and latest gift. "If I could but have known the truth at first," sighed Graham, "I would not have lingered here until my very soul was enslaved; for he is the man above all others to win and hold a woman's heart."

That he held the heart of the fair girl opposite him was revealed by every glance, and Graham's heart ached with a pain hard to endure, as he watched for a moment the exquisite outlines of her face, her wide, low brow with its halo of light-colored hair that was in such marked contrast with the dark and lustrous eyes, now veiled by silken lashes as she looked downward intent on the game, now beaming with the very spirit of mirth and mischief as she looked at her opponents, and again softening in obedience to the controlling law of her life as she glanced half shyly from time to time at the great bearded man on the other side of the table.

"Was not the world wide enough for me to escape seeing that face?" he groaned. "A few months since I was content with my life and lot. Why did I come thousands of miles to meet such a fate? I feared I should have to face poverty and privation for a time. Now they are my lot for life, an impoverishment that wealth would only enhance. I cannot stay here, I will not remain a day longer than is essential to make the impression I wish to leave;" and with a firm step he crossed the piazza, rapped lightly in announcement of his presence, and entered without ceremony.

Hilland sprang forward joyously to meet him, and gave him just such a greeting as accorded with his ardent spirit. "Why, Graham!" he cried, with a crushing grasp, and resting a hand on his shoulder at the same time, "you come unexpectedly, like all the best things in the world. We looked for a letter that would give us a chance to celebrate your arrival as that of the greatest fisherman of the age."

"Having taken so many unwary trout, it was quite in keeping to take us unawares," said Grace, pressing forward with outstretched hand, for she had determined to show in the most emphatic way that Hilland's friend was also hers.

Graham took the proffered hand and held it, while, with a humorous glance at his friend, he said: "See here, Hilland, I hold an indisputable proof that it's time you appeared on the confines of civilization and gave an account of yourself."

"I own up, old fellow. You have me on the hip. I have kept one secret from you. If we had been together the thing would have come out, but somehow I couldn't write, even to you, until I knew my fate."

"Mr. Graham," broke in the major, "if we were in the service, I should place you in charge of the commissary department, and give you a roving commission. I have lived like a lord for the past two weeks;" and he shook Graham's hand so cordially as to prove his heart had sympathized with an adjacent organ that had been highly gratified.

"I have missed you, Alford," was his aunt's quiet greeting, and she kissed him as if he were her son, causing a sudden pang as he remembered how soon he would bid her farewell again.

"Why, Graham, how you have improved! You have gained a splendid color in the woods. The only trouble is that you are as attenuated as some of the theories we used to discuss."

"And you, giddy boy, begin to look quite like a man. Miss Grace, you will never know how greatly you are indebted to me for my restraining influence. There never was a fellow who needed to be sat down upon so often as Hilland. I have curbed and pruned him; indeed, I have almost brought him up."

"He does you credit," was her reply, spoken with mirthful impressiveness, and with a very contented glance at the laughing subject of discussion.

"Yes, Graham," he remarked, "you were a trifle heavy at times, and were better at bringing a fellow down than up. It took all the leverage of my jolly good nature to bring you up occasionally. But I am glad to see and hear that you have changed so happily. Grace and the major say you have become the best of company, taking a human interest in other questions than those which keep the scientists by the ears."

"That is because I have broken my shell and come out into the world. One soon discovers that there are other questions, and some of them conundrums that the scientists may as well give up at the start. I say, Hilland, how young we were over there in Germany when we thought ourselves growing hourly into *savants !*"

"Indeed we were, and as sublimely complacent as we were young. Would you believe it, Mrs. Mayburn, your nephew and I at one time thought we were on the trail of some of the most elusive secrets of the universe, and that we should soon drag them from cover. I have learned since that this little girl could teach me more than all the universities."

Graham shot a swift glance at his aunt, which Grace thought she detected; but he turned to the latter, and said genially: "I congratulate you on excelling all the German doctors. I know he's right, and he'll remember the lore obtained from you long after he has forgotten the deep, guttural abstractions that droned on his ears abroad. It will do him more good, too."

"I fear I am becoming a subject of irony to you both," said Grace.

"They are both becoming too deep for us, are they not,

Mrs. Mayburn?" put in the major. "You obtained your best knowledge, Mr. Graham, when you trampled the woods as a boy, and though you gathered so much of it by hook it's like the fish you killed, rare to find. If we were in the service and I had the power, I'd have you brevetted at once, and get some fellow knocked on the head to make a vacancy. You have been contributing royally to our mess, and now you must take a soldier's luck with us to-night. Grace, couldn't you improvise a nice little supper?"

"Please do not let me cause any such trouble this hot evening," Graham began; "I dined late in town, and—"

"No insubordination," interrupted Grace, rising with alacrity. "Certainly I can, papa," and as she paused near Graham, she murmured: "Don't object; it will please papa."

She showed what a provident housekeeper she was, for they all soon sat down to an inviting repast, of which fruit was the staple article, with cake so light and delicate that it would never disturb a man's conscience after he retired. Then with genial words and smiles that masked all heart-ache, Graham and his aunt said good-night and departed, Hilland accompanying his friend, that he might pour out the long-delayed confidence. Graham shivered as he thought of the ordeal, as a man might tremble who was on his way to the torture-chamber, but outwardly he was quietly cordial

CHAPTER XIII

THE FRIENDS

AFTER accompanying Mrs. Mayburn to her cottage door, the friends strolled away together, the sultry evening rendering them reluctant to enter the house. When they reached the rustic seat under the apple-tree, Hilland remarked: "Here's a good place for our—"

"Not here," interrupted Graham, in a tone that was almost sharp in its tension.

"Why not?" asked his friend, in the accent of surprise.

"Oh, well," was the confused answer, "some one may be passing—servants may be out in the grounds. Suppose we walk slowly."

"Graham, you seem possessed by the very demon of restlessness. The idea of walking this hot night!"

"Oh, well, it doesn't matter," Graham replied, carelessly, although his face was rigid with the effort; and he threw himself down on the rustic seat. "We are not conspirators that we need steal away in the darkness. Why should I not be restless after sitting in the hot cars all day, and with the habit of tramping fresh upon me?"

"What evil spirit drove you into the wilderness and made you the champion tramp of the country? It seems to me you must have some remarkable confidences also."

"No evil spirit, I assure you; far from it. My tramp has done me good; indeed, I never derived more benefit from an outing in the woods in my life. You will remember that when we were boys at college no fellow took longer

walks than I. I am simply returning to the impulses of my
youth. The fact is, I've been living too idly, and of course
there would be a reaction in one of my temperament and
habits. The vital force which had been accumulating under
my aunt's high feeding and the inspiration resulting from
the society of two such charming people as Major and Miss
St. John had to be expended in some way. Somehow I've
lost much of my old faith in books and laboratories. I've
been thinking a great deal about it, and seeing you again has
given a strong impulse to a forming purpose. I felt a sincere commiseration when you gave up your life of a student.
I was a fool to do so. I have studied your face and manner
this evening, and can see that you have developed more
manhood out in those Western mines, in your contact with
men and things and the large material interests of the world,
than you could have acquired by delving a thousand years
among dusty tomes.''

"That little girl over there has done more for me than
Western mines and material interests."

"That goes without saying; and yet she could have done
little for you, had you been a dawdler. Indeed, in that case
she would have had nothing to do with you. She recognized
that you were like the gold you are mining—worth taking
and fashioning; and I tell you she is not a girl to be imposed upon.''

"Flatterer!"

"No; friend."

"You admire Grace very much."

"I do indeed, and I respect her still more. You know
I never was a lady's man; indeed, the society of most young
women was a weariness to me. Don't imagine I am assert-
ing any superiority. You enjoyed their conversation, and
you are as clever as I am.''

"I understand," said Hilland, laughing; "you had nothing in common. You talked to a girl as if she were a mile
off, and often broached topics that were cycles away. Now,
a girl likes a fellow to come reasonably close—metaphoric-

ally, if not actually—when he chats with her. Moreover, many that you met, if they had brains, had never cultivated them. They were as shallow as a duck-pond, and with their small deceits, subterfuges, and affectations were about as transparent. Some might imagine them deep. They puzzled and nonplussed you, and you slunk away. Now I, while rating them at their worth, was able from previous associations to talk a little congenial nonsense, and pass on. They amused me, too. You know I have a sort of laughing philosophy, and everything and everybody amuses me. The fellows would call these creatures angels, and they would flap their little butterfly wings as if they thought they were. How happened it that you so soon were *en rapport* with Grace?"

"Ah, wily wretch!" Graham laughed gayly, while the night hid his lowering brows; "praise of your mistress is sweeter than flattery to yourself. Why, simply because she is Grace St. John. I imagine that it is her army life that has so blended unconventionality with perfect good breeding. She is her bluff, honest, high-spirited old father over again, only idealized, refined, and womanly. Then she must have inherited some rare qualities from her Southern mother: you see my aunt has told me all about them. I once met a Southern lady abroad, and although she was middle-aged, she fascinated me more than any girl I had ever met. In the first place, there was an indescribable accent that I never heard in Europe—slight, indeed, but very pleasing to the ear. I sometimes detect traces of it in Miss St. John's speech. Then this lady had a frankness and sincerity of manner which put you at your ease at once; and yet with it all there was a fine reserve. You no more feared that she would blurt out something unsanctioned by good taste than that she would dance a hornpipe. She was singularly gentle and retiring in her manner; and yet one instinctively felt he would rather insult a Southern fire-eater than offend her. She gave the impression that she had been accustomed to a chivalric deference from men, rather than mere society attentions; and one unconsciously infused a subtle homage in his very accent when speaking to her. Now, I imagine that Miss St. John's mother must have been closely akin to this woman in character. You know my weakness for analyzing everything. You used to say I couldn't smoke a cigar without going into the philosophy of it. I had not spent one evening in the society of Miss St. John before I saw that she was a *rara avis*. Then her devotion to her invalid father is superb. She enlisted me in his service the first day of my arrival. Although old, crippled, often racked with pain, and afflicted with a temper which arbitrary command has not improved, she beguiles him out of himself, smiles away his gloom—in brief, creates so genial an atmosphere about him that every breath is balm, and does it all, too, without apparent effort. You see no machinery at work. Now, this was all a new and very interesting study of life to me, and I studied it. There, too, is my aunt, who is quite as interesting in her way. Such women make general or wholesale cynicism impossible, or else hypocritical;" and he was about to launch out into as extended an analysis of the old lady's peculiarities, when Hilland interrupted him with a slap on the shoulder and a ringing laugh.

"Graham, you haven't changed a mite. You discourse just as of old, when in our den at the university we befogged ourselves in the tobacco-smoke and the denser obscurities of German metaphysics, only your theme is infinitely more interesting. Now, when I met my paragon, Grace, whom you have limned with the feeling of an artist rather than of an analyst, although with a blending of both, I fell in love with her."

"Yes, Hilland, it's just like you to fall in love. My fear has ever been that you would fall in love with a face some day, and not with a woman. But I now congratulate you from the depths of my soul."

"How comes it that *you* did not fall in love with one whom you admire so much? You were not aware of my suit."

"I suppose it is not according to my nature to 'fall in love,' as you term it. The very phrase is repugnant to me. When a man is falling in any sense of the word, his reason is rather apt to be muddled and confused, and he cannot be very sure where he will land. If you had not appeared on the scene my reason would have approved of my marriage with Miss St. John—that is, if I had seen the slightest chance of acceptance, which, of course, I never have. I should be an egregious fool were it otherwise."

"How about your heart?"

"The heart often leads to the sheerest folly," was the sharp rejoinder.

Hilland laughed in his good-humored way. His friend's reply seemed the result of irritation at the thought that the heart should have much to say when reason demurred. "Well, Graham," he said, kindly and earnestly, "if I did not know you so well, I should say you were the most cold-blooded, frog-like fellow in existence. You certainly are an enigma to me on the woman question. I must admit that my heart went headlong from the first; but when at last reason caught up, and had time to get her breath and look the case over, she said it was 'all right'—far better than she had expected. To one of my temperament, however, it seems very droll that reason should lead the way to love, and the heart come limping after."

"Many a one has taken the amatory tumble who would be glad to reason his way up and back. But we need not discuss this matter in the abstract, for we have too much that is personal to say to each other. You are safe; your wonted good fortune has served you better than ever. All the wisdom of Solomon could not have enabled you to fall in love more judiciously. Indeed, when I come to think of it, the wisdom of Solomon, according to history, was rather at fault in these matters. Tell me how it all came about" (for he knew the story must come); "only outline the tale to-night. I've been speculating and analyzing so long that it is late; and the major, hearing voices in the grounds, may bring some of his old army ordnance to bear on us."

But Hilland, out of the abundance of his heart, found much to say; and his friend sat cold, shivering in the sultry night, his heart growing more despairing as he saw the heaven of successful wooing that he could never enter. At last Hilland closed with the words, "I say, Graham, are you asleep?"

"Oh, no," in a husky voice.

"You are taking cold."

"I believe I am."

"I'm a brute to keep you up in this style. As I live, I believe there is the tinge of dawn in the east."

"May every dawn bring a happy day to you, Warren," was said so gently and earnestly that Hilland rested his arm on his friend's shoulder as he replied, "You've a queer heart, Alford, but such as it is I would not exchange it for that of any man living." Then abruptly, "Do you hold to our old views that this life ends all?"

A thrill of something like exultation shot through Graham's frame as he replied, "Certainly."

Hilland sprang up and paced the walk a moment, then said, "Well, I don't know. A woman like Grace St. John shakes my faith in our old belief. It seems profanation to assert that she is mere clay."

The lurid gleam of light which the thought of ceasing to exist and to suffer had brought to Graham faded. It did seem like profanation. At any rate, at that moment it was a hideous truth that such a creature might by the chance of any accident resolve into mere dust. And yet it seemed a truth which must apply to her as well as to the grossest of her sisterhood. He could only falter, "She is very highly organized."

They both felt that it was a lame and impotent conclusion.

But the spring of happiness was in Hilland's heart. The present was too rich for him to permit such dreary speculations, and he remarked cordially and laughingly, "Well, Graham, we have made amends for our long separation and silence. We have talked all the summer night. I am rich, indeed, in such a friend and such a sweetheart; and the latter must truly approach perfection when my dear old philosopher of the stoic school could think it safe and wise to marry her, were all the conditions favorable. You don't wish that I was at the bottom of one of my mines, do you, Alford?"

Graham felt that the interview must end at once, so he rose and said, "No, I do not. My reason approves of your choice. If you wish more, my 'queer heart, such as it is,' approves of it also. If I had the power to change everything this moment I would not do so. You have fairly won your love, and may all the forces of nature conspire to prosper you both. But come," he added in a lighter vein, "Miss St. John may be watching and waiting for your return, and even imagining that I, with my purely intellectual bent, may regard you as a disturbing element in the problem, and so be led to eliminate you in a quiet, scientific manner."

"Well, then, good night, or morning, rather. Forgive a lover's garrulousness."

"I was more garrulous than you, without half your excuse. No, I'll see you safely home. I wish to walk a little to get up a circulation. With your divine flame burning so brightly, I suppose you could sit through a zero night; but you must remember that such a modicum of philosophy as I possess will not keep me warm. There, good-by, old fellow. Sleep the sleep of the just, and, what is better in this chance-medley world, of the happy. Don't be imagining that you have any occasion to worry about me."

Hilland went to his room in a complacent mood, and more in love than ever. Had not his keen-eyed, analytical friend, after weeks of careful observation, testified to the exceeding worth of the girl of his heart? He had been in love, and he had ever heard that love is blind. It seemed to him that his friend could never love as he understood the

word; and yet the peerless maiden had so satisfied the exac-
tions of Graham's taste and reason, and had proved herself
so generally admirable, that he felt it would be wise and advantageous to marry her.

"It's a queer way of looking at these things," he concluded, with a shrug, "but then it is Graham's way."

Soon he was smiling in his repose, for the great joy of
his waking hours threw its light far down into the obscurity
of sleep.

Graham turned slowly away, and walked with downcast
face to the rustic seat. He stood by it a moment, and then
sank into it like a man who has reached the final limit of
human endurance. He uttered no sound, but at brief intervals a shiver ran through his frame. His head sank into
his hands, and he looked and felt like one utterly crushed
by a fate from which there was no escape. His ever-recur-
ring thought was, "I have but one life, and it's lost, worse
than lost. Why should I stagger on beneath the burden of
an intolerable existence, which will only grow heavier as the
forces of life fail?"

At last in his agony he uttered the words aloud. A
hand was laid upon his shoulder, and a husky, broken
voice said, "Here is one reason."

He started up, and saw that his aunt stood beside
him.

The dawn was gray, but the face of the aged woman
was grayer and more pallid. She did not entreat—her feeling seemed too deep for words—but with clasped hands she
lifted her tear-dimmed eyes to his. Her withered bosom rose
and fell in short, convulsive sobs, and it was evident that she
could scarcely stand.

His eyes sank, and a sudden sense of guilt and shame at
his forgetfulness of her overcame him. Then yielding to an
impulse, all the stronger because mastering one who had
few impulses, he took her in his arms, kissed her repeat-
edly, and supported her tenderly to the cottage. When at
last they reached the quaint little parlor he placed her ten-

derly in her chair, and, taking her hand, he kissed it, and said solemnly, "No, aunty, I will not die. I will live out my days for your sake, and do my best."

"Thank God!" she murmured—"thank God!" and for a moment she leaned her head upon his breast as he knelt beside her. Suddenly she lifted herself, with a return of her old energy; and he rose and stood beside her. She looked at him intently as if she would read his thoughts, and then shook her finger impressively as she said, "Mark my words, Alford, mark my words: good will come of that promise."

"It has come already," he gently replied, "in that you, my best friend, are comforted. Now go and rest and sleep. Have no fear, for your touch of love has broken all evil spells."

Graham went to his room, calmed by an inflexible resolution. It was no longer a question of happiness or unhappiness, or even of despair; it was simply a question of honor, of keeping his word. He sat down and read once more the paragraph in the marked copy of Emerson, "No man ever forgot—" He gave the words a long, wistful look, and then closed the volume as if he were closing a chapter of his life.

"Well," he sighed, "I did my best last night not to dispel their enchantment, for of course Hilland will tell her the substance of our talk. Now, it must be my task for a brief time to maintain and deepen the impression that I have made."

Having no desire for sleep, he softly paced his room, but it was not in nervous excitement. His pulse was quiet and regular, and his mind reverted easily to a plan of extended travel upon which he had been dwelling while in the woods. At last he threw himself upon his couch, and slept for an hour or two. On awaking he found that it was past the usual breakfast hour, and after a hasty toilet he went in search of his aunt, but was informed that she was still sleeping.

"Do not disturb her," he said to the servant.   "Let her sleep as long as she will."

He then wrote a note, saying that he had decided to go to town to attend to some business which had been neglected in his absence, and was soon on his way to the train.

CHAPTER XIV

NOBLE DECEPTION

IN the course of the forenoon Hilland called on his friend, and was informed that Graham had gone to the city on business, but would return in the evening. He also learned that Mrs. Mayburn was indisposed, and had not yet risen. At these tidings Grace ran over to see her old friend, hoping to do something for her comfort, and the young girl was almost shocked when she saw Mrs. Mayburn's pinched and pallid face upon her pillow. She seemed to have aged in a night.

"You are seriously ill!" she exclaimed, "and you did not let me know. Mr. Graham should not have left you."

"He did not know," said the old lady, sharply, for the slightest imputation against Graham touched her keenly. "He is kindness itself to me. He only heard this morning that I was sleeping, and he left word that I should not be disturbed. He also wrote a note explaining the business which had been neglected in his absence. Oh, I assure you, no one could be more considerate."

"Dear, loyal Mrs. Mayburn, you won't hear a word against those you love. I think Mr. Graham wonderfully considerate for a man. You know we should not expect much of men. I have to manage two, and it keeps me busy, but never so busy that I cannot do all in my power for my dear old friend. I'll get your breakfast myself, and bring it to you with my own hands, and force it upon you with the inexorable firmness of Sairy Gamp;" and she vanished to the kitchen.

The old lady turned her face to the wall and moaned, "Oh, if it could only have been! Why is it that we so often set our hearts on that which is denied? After a long, dull sleep of years it seemed as if my heart had wakened in my old age only to find how poor and lonely I am. Alford cannot stay with me—I could not expect it—neither can Grace; and so I must go on alone to the end. I'm punished, punished that years ago I did not make some one love me; but I was self-sufficient then."

Her regret was deepened when Grace returned with a dainty breakfast, and waited on her with a daughter's gentleness and tenderness, making her smile in spite of herself at her funny speeches, and beguiling her into enjoyment of the present moment with a witchery that none could resist.

Presently Mrs. Mayburn sighed, "It's a fearfully hot day for Alford to be in town."

"For a student," cried Grace, "he is the most indefatigable man I ever heard of. Warren told me that they sat out there under the apple-tree and poured out their hearts till dawn. Talk about schoolgirls babbling all night. My comment on Warren's folly was a dose of quinine. It's astonishing how these *savants*, these intellectual giants, need taking care of like babies. Woman's mission will never cease as long as there are learned men in the world. They will sit in a draught and discuss some obscure law concerning the moons of Jupiter; but when the law resulting in influenza manifests itself, then they learn our worth."

"Oh, dear!" groaned Mrs. Mayburn, "I didn't give Alford any quinine. You were more provident than I."

"How could you, when you were asleep?"

"Ah, true!" was the confused reply. "But then I should have been awake. I should have remembered that he did not come in when I did last night."

The faint color that stole into the face that had been so pale gave some surprise to the young girl. When once her mind was directed to a subject her intuitions were exceedingly keen.

From the time the secret of his regard for her had been
surprised from him, Graham had been a puzzle to her. Was
he the cool, philosophical lover that he would have her
think? Hilland was so frank in nature and so wholly
under her influence that it was next to impossible for him
not to share with her his every thought. She had, therefore, learned substantially the particulars of last night's
interview, and she could not fully accept his belief that
Graham's intellect alone had been captivated. She remembered how he had leaned against the tree for support; how
pale he had been during the evening that followed; and
how his hand had trembled in parting. She remembered
his sudden flight to the mountains, his tireless energy there,
as if driven on by an aching wound that permitted no rest.
True, he had borne himself strongly and well in her presence the evening before; and he had given the friend who
knew him so well the impression that it was merely an instance of the quiet weighing of the pros and cons, in which,
after much deliberation, the pros had won. There had been
much in his course, too, to give color to this view of the
case; but her woman's instinct suggested that there was
something more—something she did not know about; and
she would have been less or more than woman had she not
wished to learn the whole truth in a matter of this nature.
She hoped that her lover was right, and that Graham's
heart, in accordance with his development theory, was so
inchoate as to be incapable of much suffering. She was not
sure, however. There was something she surmised rather
than detected. She felt it now in Mrs. Mayburn's presence,
and caught a glimpse of it in the flush that was fading from
her cheeks. Had the nephew given his aunt his confidence?
or had she with her ripe experience and keen insight discovered the ultimate truth?

It was evident that while Mrs. Mayburn still loved her
dearly, and probably was much disappointed that things
had turned out as they had, she had given her loyalty to
Graham, and would voluntarily neither do nor say anything

that would compromise him. The slight flush suggested to
Grace that the aunt had awaited the nephew's return in the
early dawn, and that they had spoken freely together before
separating; but she was the last one in the world to attempt
to surprise a secret from another.

Still she wished to know the truth, for she felt a little
guilty over her reticence in regard to her relations with Hilland. She, perhaps, had made too much of the luxury of
keeping her secret until it could shine forth as the sun
of her life; and Graham had been left in an ignorance that
had not been fair to him. With a growing perception of
his character, now that she had given thought to the subject, she saw that if he had learned to love her at all, it
must have been in accordance with his nature, quietly, deliberately, even analytically. He was the last man to fall
tumultuously in love. But when he had given it in his
own way, could she be sure it was a cool, easily managed
preference that he might at his leisure transfer to another
who satisfied his reason and taste even more fully than herself? If this were true, her mind would be at rest; and she
could like Hilland's friend heartily, as one of the most
agreeable human oddities it had been her fortune to meet.
She had serious misgivings, however, which Mrs. Mayburn's sudden indisposition, and the marks of suffering
upon her face, did not tend to banish.

Whatever the truth might be, she felt that he had shown
much thoughtfulness for her in his frankness with Hilland.
He had rendered it unnecessary for her to conceal her knowledge of his regard. She need have no secrets, so far as he
was concerned. The only question was as to the nature of
this regard. If the impression he sought to give her lover
was correct, neither of them had cause for much solicitude.
If to save them pain he was seeking to hide a deeper wound,
it was a noble deception, and dictated by a noble, unselfish
nature. If the latter supposition should prove true, she felt
that she would discover it without any direct effort. But she
also felt that her lover should be left, if possible, under the

impression his friend had sought to make, and that Graham should have the solace of thinking he had concealed his feelings from them both.

As the long evening shadows stretched eastward across the sloping lawn in front of the St. John cottage, the family gathered on the piazza to enjoy the welcome respite from the scorching heat of the day.

The old major looked weary and overcome. A July sun was the only fire before which he had ever flinched. Hilland still appeared a little heavy from his long hot afternoon nap, his amends for the vigils of the previous night. Grace was enchanting in her light clinging draperies, which made her lovely form tenfold more beautiful, because clothed in perfect taste. The heat had deepened the flush upon her cheeks, and brought a soft languor into her eyes, and as she stood under an arch of the American woodbine, that mantled the supports of the piazza roof, she might easily have fulfilled an artist's dream of summer. Hilland's eyes kindled as he looked upon her, as she stood with averted face, conscious meanwhile of his admiration, and exulting in it. What sweeter incense is ever offered to a woman ?

"Grace," he whispered, "you would create a pulse in a marble statue to-night. You never looked more lovely."

"There is a glamour on your eyes, Warren," she replied; and yet the quick flash of joy that came into her face proved the power of his words, which still had all the exquisite charm of novelty.

"It's the glamour that will last while I do," he responded, earnestly. "Are not this scene and hour perfect? and you are the gem of it all. I don't see how a man could ask or wish for more than I have to-night, except that it might last forever." A shadow passed over his face, and he added, presently, "To think that after a few weeks I must return to those blasted mines! One thing is settled, however. I shall close out my interests there as speedily as possible; and were it not for my obligations to others,

I'd never go near them again. I have money enough twice over, and am a fool to miss one hour with you."

"You will be all the happier, Warren, if you close up your interests in the West in a manly, business-like way. I always wish to be as proud of you as I am now. What's more, I don't believe in idle men, no matter how rich they are. I should be worried at once if you had nothing to do but sit around and make fine speeches. You'd soon weary of the sugar-plum business, and so should I. I have read somewhere that the true way to keep a man a lover is to give him plenty of work."

"Will you choose my work for me?"

"No; anything you like, so it is not speculation."

"I think I'll come and be your father's gardener."

"If you do," she replied, with a decisive little nod, "you will have to rake and hoe so many hours a day before you can have any dinner."

"But you, fair Eve, would bring your fancy-work, and sit with me in the shade."

"The idea of a gardener sitting in the shade, with weeds growing on every side."

"But you would, my Eve."

"Possibly, after I had seen that you had earned your bread by the 'perspiration of your brow,' as a very nice maiden lady, a neighbor of ours, always phrases it."

"That shall be my calling as soon as I can get East again. Major, I apply for the situation of gardener as soon as I can sell out my interests in the mines."

"I have nothing to do with it," was the reply. "Grace commands this post, and while here you are under her orders."

"And you'll find out, too, what a martinet I am," she added. "There's no telling how often I'll put you under arrest and mount guard over you myself. So!"

"What numberless breaches of discipline there will be!"

Lovers' converse consists largely in tone and glance, and

these cannot be written; and were this possible, it could have but the slenderest interest to the reader.

After a transient pause Hilland remarked: "Think of poor Graham in the fiery furnace of New York to-day. I can imagine what a wilted and dilapidated-looking specimen he will be if he escapes alive— By Jove, there he is!" and the subject of his speech came as briskly up the walk as if the thermometer had been in the seventies instead of the nineties. His dress was quiet and elegant, and his form erect and step elastic.

As he approached the piazza and doffed his hat, Hilland cried: "Graham, you are the coolest fellow I ever saw. I was just commiserating you, and expecting you to look like a cabbage—no, rose—leaf that had been out in the sun; and you appear just as if you had stepped from a refrigerator."

"All a matter of temperament and will, my dear fellow. I decided I would not be hot to-day; and I've been very comfortable."

"Why did you not decide not to be cold last night?"

"I was so occupied with your interminable yarns that I forgot to think about it. Miss Grace, for your sake and on this evening, I might wish that there was a coolness between us, but from your kind greeting I see there is not. Good-evening, major; I have brought with me a slight proof that I do not forget my friends;" and he handed him a large package of newspapers, several of them being finely illustrated foreign prints.

"I promote you on the spot," cried the delighted veteran. "I felt that fate owed me some amends for this long, horrid day. My paper did not come this morning, and I had too much regard for the lives of my household to send any one up the hot streets after one."

"Oh, papa!" cried Grace, "forgive me that I did not discover the fact. I'm sure I saw you reading a paper."

"It was an old one. I read it through again, advertisements and all. Oh, I know you. You'd have turned out the whole garrison at twelve M., had you found it out.''

Graham dropped carelessly into an easy-chair, and they all noted the pleasure with which the old gentleman adjusted his glasses, and scanned the pictures of the world's current history. Like many whose sight is failing, and to whom the tastes and memories of childhood are returning, the poor old man found increasing delight in a picture which suggested a great deal, and aided him to imagine more; and he would often beguile his tedium by the hour with the illustrated journals.

"Mr. Graham," said Grace, after a pause in their talk, "have you seen your aunt since your return?"

"No," he replied, turning hastily toward her.

"She is not very well; I've been to see her twice."

He gave her a momentary but searching glance, rose instantly, and said: "Please excuse me, then. I feel guilty that I have delayed a moment, but this piazza was so inviting!" and he hastened away.

"Does he look and act like a man who 'hid a secret sorrow'?" whispered Hilland, confidently. "I never saw him appear so well before."

Grace smiled, but kept her thoughts to herself. To her also Graham had never appeared so well. There was decision in his step and slightest movement. The old easy saunter of leisure was gone; the old half-dreamy and slightly cynical eyes of the student showed a purpose which was neither slight nor indefinite; and that brief, searching glance—what else could it be than a query as to the confidences his aunt may have bestowed during the day? Moreover, why did he avoid looking at her unless there was distinct occasion for his glance?

She would have known too well had she heard poor Graham mutter: "My will must be made of Bessemer steel if I can see her often as she looked to-night and live."

In the evening Hilland walked over to call on his friend and make inquiries. Through the parlor windows he saw

Graham reading to his aunt, who reclined on a lounge; and he stole away again without disturbing them.

The next few days passed uneventfully away, and Graham's armor was almost proof against even the penetration of Grace. He did not assume any mask of gayety. He seemed to be merely his old self, with a subtle difference, and a very unobtrusive air of decision in all his movements. He was with his friend a great deal; and she heard them talking over their old life with much apparent zest. He was as good company for the major as ever, and when at whist played so good a game as to show that he was giving it careful attention. There was a gentleness toward his aunt that rather belied his character of stoic philosopher. Indeed, he seemed to have dropped this phase also, and was simply a well-bred man of the world, avoiding reference to himself, and his past or present views, as far as possible.

To a question of Hilland's one day he replied: "No; I shall not go back to my studies at present. As I told you the other night, my excursion into the world has shown me the advantage of studying it more fully. While I shall never be a Crœsus like yourself, I am modestly independent; and I mean to see the world we live in, and then shall know better what I am studying about."

When Hilland told Grace of this purpose, she felt it was in keeping with all the rest. It might mean what was on the surface; it might mean more. It might be a part of the possible impulse that had driven him into the Vermont woods, or the natural and rational step he would have taken had he never seen her. At any rate, she felt that he was daily growing more remote, and that by a nice gradation of effort he was consciously withdrawing himself. And yet she could scarcely dwell on a single word or act, and say: "This proves it." His manner toward her was most cordial. When they conversed he looked at her steadily and directly, and would respond in kind to her mirthful words and Hilland's broad raillery; but she never detected one of the furtive, lingering glances that she now remembered with compunction were once frequent. It was quite proper that this should be so, but it was unnatural. If hitherto she had only pleased his taste and satisfied his reason, it would be a safe and harmless pastime for him to linger near her still in thought and reality. If he was struggling with a passion that had struck its root deep, then there was good reason for that steady withdrawal from her society which he managed so naturally that no one observed it but herself. Hilland had no misgivings, and she suggested none; but whenever she was in the presence of Graham or Mrs. Mayburn, although their courtesy and kind manner were unexceptionable, she felt there was "something in the air."

CHAPTER XV

"I WISH HE HAD KNOWN"

THE heat continued so oppressive that the major gave signs of prostration, and Grace decided to take him to his old haunt by the seashore. The seclusion of their cottage was, of course, more agreeable to Hilland and herself under the circumstances; but Grace never hesitated when her father was concerned. Shortly after the decision was reached, Hilland met his friend, and promptly urged that he and Mrs. Mayburn should accompany them.

"Certainly," was the quiet reply, "if my aunt wishes to go."

But for some cause, if not for the reasons given, the old lady was inexorable that evening, even though the major with much gallantry urged her compliance. She did not like the seashore. It did not agree with her; and, what was worse, she detested hotels. She was better in her own quiet nook, etc. Alford might go, if he chose.

But Graham when appealed to said it was both his duty and his pleasure to remain with his aunt, especially as he was going abroad as soon as he could arrange his affairs. "Don't put on that injured air," he added, laughingly, to Hilland. "As if you needed me at present! You two are sufficient for yourselves; and why should I tramp after you like the multitude I should be?"

"What do you know about our being sufficient for ourselves, I'd like to ask?" was the bantering response.

"I have the best authority for saying what I do—written authority, and that of a sage, too. Here it is, heavily under-

scored by a hand that I imagine is as heavy as your own.
Ah! Miss Grace's conscious looks prove that I am right,"
he added, as he laid the open volume of Emerson, which
he had returned, before her. "I remember reading that
paragraph the first evening I came to my aunt's house; and
I thought it a very curious statement. It made me feel as
if I were a sort of polyp or mollusk, instead of a man."

"Let me see the book," cried Hilland. "Oh, yes," he
continued, laughing; "I remember it all well—the hopes,
the misgivings with which I sent the volume eastward on
its mission—the hopes and fears that rose when the book
was acknowledged with no chidings or coldness, and also
with no allusions to the marked passage—the endless surmises as to what this gentle reader would think of the
sentiments within these black lines. Ha! ha! Graham.
No doubt but this is Sanscrit; and all the professors of
all the universities could not interpret it to you."

"That's what I said in substance on the evening referred
to—that Emerson never learned this at a university. I confess that it's an experience that is and ever will be beyond
me. But it's surely good authority for remaining here with
my aunt, who needs me more than you do."

"How is it, then, Mr. Graham, that you can leave your
aunt for months of travel?" Grace asked.

"Why, Grace," spoke up Mrs. Mayburn, quickly, "you
cannot expect Alford to transform himself into an old lady's
life-long attendant. He will enjoy his travel and come back
to me."

The young girl made no answer, but thought: "Their
defensive alliance is a strong one."

"Besides," continued the old lady, after a moment, "I
think it's very kind of him to remain with me, instead of
going to the beach for his own pleasure and the marring
of yours."

"Now, that's putting it much too strong," cried Hilland.
"Graham never marred our pleasure."

"And I hope he never will," was the low, earnest response. To Grace's ear it sounded more like a vow or the expression of a controlling purpose than like a mere friendly remark.

The next day the St. John cottage was alive with the bustle of preparation for departure. Graham made no officious offers of assistance, which, of course, would be futile, but quietly devoted himself to the major. Whenever Grace appeared from the upper regions, she found her father amused or interested, and she smiled her gratitude. In the evening she found a chance to say in a low aside: "Mr. Graham, you are keeping your word to be my friend. If the sea-breezes prove as beneficial to papa as your society to-day, I shall be glad indeed. You don't know how much you have aided me by entertaining him so kindly."

Both her tone and glance were very gentle as she spoke these words, and for a moment his silence and manner perplexed her. Then he replied lightly: "You are mistaken, Miss Grace. Your father has been entertaining me."

They were interrupted at this point, and Graham seemed to grow more remote than ever.

Hilland was parting from his friend with evident and sincere regret. He had made himself very useful in packing, strapping trunks, and in a general eagerness to save his betrothed from all fatigue; but whenever occasion offered he would sally forth upon Graham, who, with the major, followed the shade on the piazza. Some jocular speech usually accompanied his appearance, and he always received the same in kind with such liberal interest that he remarked to Grace more than once, "You are the only being in the world for whom I'd leave Graham during his brief stay in this land."

"Oh, return to him by all means," she had said archly upon one occasion. "We did very well alone last year before we were aware of your existence."

"*You* may not care," was his merry response, "but it is written in one of the oldest books of the world, 'It is not good for *man* to be alone.' Oh, Grace, what an infinite difference there is between love for a woman like you and the strongest friendship between man and man! Graham just suits me as a friend. After a separation of years I find him just the same even-pulsed, half-cynical, yet genial good fellow he always was. It's hard to get within his shell; but when you do, you find the kernel sweet and sound to the core, even if it is rather dry. From the time we struck hands as boys there has never been an unpleasant jar in our relations. We supplement each other marvellously; but how infinitely more and beyond all this is your love! How it absorbs and swallows up every other consideration, so that one hour with you is more to me than an age with all the men of wit and wisdom that ever lived! No; I'm not a false friend when I say that I am more than content to go and remain with you; and if Graham had a hundredth part as much heart as brains he would understand me. Indeed, his very intellect serves in the place of a heart after a fashion; for he took Emerson on trust so intelligently as to comprehend that I should not be inconsolable."

"Mr. Graham puzzles me," Grace had remarked, as she absently inspected the buttons on one of her father's vests. "I never met just such a man before."

"And probably never will again. He has been isolated and peculiar from childhood. I know him well, and he has changed but little in essentials since I left him over two years ago."

"I wish I had your complacent belief about him," was her mental conclusion. "I sometimes think you are right, and again I feel as if some one in almost mortal pain is near me, and that I am to blame in part."

Whist was dispensed with the last night they were together, for the evening was close, and all were weary. Grace thought Graham looked positively haggard; but, whether by design or chance, he kept in the shadows of the piazza most of the time. Still she had to admit that he was the life of the party. Mrs. Mayburn was apparently so overcome by the heat as to be comparatively silent; and

Hilland openly admitted that the July day and his exertions had used him up. Therefore the last gathering at the St. Johns' cottage came to a speedy end; and Graham not only said good-night, but also good-by; for, as he explained, business called him to town early the following morning. He parted fraternally with Hilland, giving a promise to spend a day with him before he sailed for Europe. Then he broke away, giving Grace as a farewell only a strong, warm pressure of the hand, and hastened after his aunt, who had walked on slowly before. The major, after many friendly expressions, had retired quite early in the evening.

Grace saw the dark outline of Graham's form disappear like a shadow, and every day thereafter he grew more shadowy to her. To a degree she did not imagine possible he had baffled her scrutiny and left her in doubt. Either he had quietly and philosophically accepted the situation, or he wished her to think so. In either case there was nothing to be done. Once away with father and lover she had *her* world with her; and life grew richer and more full of content every day.

Lassitude and almost desperate weariness were in Graham's step as he came up the path the following evening, for there was no further reason to keep up the part he was acting. When he greeted his aunt he tried to appear cheerful, but she said gently, "Put on no mask before me, Alford. Make no further effort. You have baffled even Grace, and thoroughly satisfied your friend that all is well. Let the strain cease now; and let my home be a refuge while you remain. Your wound is one that time only can heal. You have made an heroic struggle not to mar their happiness, and I am proud of you for it. But don't try to deceive me or put the spur any longer to your jaded spirit. Reaction into new hopes and a new life will come all the sooner if you give way for the present to your mood."

The wise old woman would have been right in dealing with most natures. But Graham would not give way to his bitter disappointment, and for him there would come no reaction. He quietly read to her the evening papers, and after she had retired stole out and gazed for hours on the St. John cottage, the casket that had contained for him the jewel of the world. Then, compressing his lips, he returned to his room with the final decision, "I will be her friend for life; but it must be an absent friend. I think my will is strong; but half the width of the world must be between us."

For the next two weeks he sought to prepare his aunt for a long separation. He did not hide his feeling; indeed, he spoke of it with a calmness which, while it surprised, also convinced her that it would dominate his life. She was made to see clearly the necessity of his departure, if he would keep his promise to live and do his best. He promised to be a faithful and voluminous correspondent, and she knew she would live upon his letters. After the lapse of three weeks he had arranged his affairs so as to permit a long absence, and then parted with his aunt as if he had been her son.

"Alford," she said, "all that I have is yours, as you will find in my will."

"Dear aunty," was his reply, "in giving me your love you have given me all that I crave. I have more than enough for my wants. Forgive me that I cannot stay; but I cannot. I have learned the limit of my power of endurance. I know that I cannot escape myself or my memories, but new scenes divert my thoughts. Here, I believe, I should go mad, or else do something wild and desperate. Forgive me, and do not judge me harshly because I leave you. Perhaps some day this fever of unrest will pass away. When it does, rest assured you shall see me again."

He then went to the seaside resort where Hilland with the major and his daughter was sojourning, and never had they seen a man who appeared so far removed from the lackadaisical, disconsolate lover. His dress was elegant, although very quiet, his step firm and prompt, and his manner that of a man who is thoroughly master of the situation. The major was ill from an indiscretion at the table during the preceding day, and Grace could not leave him very long. He sent to his favorite companion and antagonist at whist many feeling messages and sincere good wishes, and they lost nothing in hearty warmth as they came from Grace's lips; and for some reason, which she could scarcely explain to herself, tears came into her eyes as she gave him her hand in parting.

He had been laughing and jesting vivaciously a moment before; but as he looked into her face, so full of kindly feeling which she could not wholly repress, his own seemed to grow rigid, and the hand she held was so cold and tense as to remind her of a steel gauntlet. In the supreme effort of his spiritual nature he belied his creed. His physical being was powerless in the grasp of the dominant soul. No martyr at the stake ever suffered more than he at that moment, but he merely said with quiet emphasis, "Good-by, Grace St. John. I shall not forget my promise, nor can there come a day on which I shall not wish you all the happiness you deserve."

He then bowed gravely and turned away. She hastily sought her room, and then burst into an irrepressible passion of tears. "It's all in vain," she sobbed. "I felt it. I know it. He suffers as I should suffer, and his iron will cannot disguise the truth."

The friends strolled away up the beach for their final talk, and at length Hilland came back in a somewhat pensive but very complacent mood. Grace looked at him anxiously, but his first sentences reassured her.

"Well," he exclaimed, "if Graham is odd, he's certainly the best and most sensible fellow that ever lived, and the most steadfast of friends. Here we've been separated for years, and yet, for any change in his attitude toward me, we might have parted overnight at the university. He was as badly smitten by the girl I love as a man of his temperament could be; but on learning the facts he recognizes the situation with a quiet good taste which leaves nothing to be desired. He made it perfectly clear to me that travel for the present was only a broader and more effective way of continuing his career as a student, and that when tired of wandering he can go back to books with a larger knowledge of how to use them. One thing he has made clearer still— if we do not see each other for ten years, he will come back the same stanch friend."

"I think you are right, Warren. He certainly has won my entire respect."

"I'm glad he didn't win anything more, sweetheart."

"That ceased to be possible long before he came, but I —I wish he had known it," was her hesitating response, as she pushed Hilland's hair back from his heated brow.

"Nonsense, you romantic little woman! You imagine he has gone away with a great gaping wound in his heart. Graham is the last man in the world for that kind of thing, and no one would smile more broadly than he, did he know of your gentle solicitude."

Grace was silent a moment, and then stole away to her father's side.

The next tidings they had of Graham was a letter dated among the fiords and mountains of Norway.

At times no snowy peak in that wintry land seemed more shadowy or remote to Grace than he. Again, while passing to and fro between their own and Mrs. Mayburn's cottage in the autumn, she would see him, with almost the vividness of life, deathly pale as when he leaned against the apple-tree at their well-remembered interview.

CHAPTER XVI

THE CLOUD IN THE SOUTH

THE summer heat passed speedily, and the major returned to his cottage invigorated and very complacent over his daughter's prospects. Hilland had proved himself as manly and devoted a lover as he had been an ardent and eventually patient suitor. The bubbling, overflowing stream of happiness in Grace's heart deepened into a wide current, bearing her on from day to day toward a future that promised to satisfy every longing of her woman's heart. There was, of course, natural regret that Hilland was constrained to spend several months in the West in order to settle up his large interests with a due regard to the rights of others, and yet she would not have it otherwise. She was happy in his almost unbounded devotion; she would have been less happy had this devotion kept him at her side when his man's part in the world required his presence elsewhere. Therefore she bade him farewell with a heart that was not so very heavy, even though tears gemmed her eyes.

The autumn and early winter months lapsed quietly and uneventfully, and the inmates of the two cottages ever remembered that period of their lives as the era of letters—Graham's from over the sea abounding in vivid descriptions of scenes that to Mrs. Mayburn's interested eyes were like glimpses of another world, and Hilland's, even more voluminous and infinitely more interesting to one fair reader, to whom they were sacred except as she doled out occasional paragraphs which related sufficiently to the general order of things to be read aloud.

Graham's letters, however, had a deep interest to Grace, who sought to trace in them the working of his mind in regard to herself. She found it difficult, for his letters were exceedingly impersonal, while the men and things he saw often stood out upon his page with vivid realism. It seemed to her that he grew more shadowy, and that he was wandering rather than travelling, drifting whithersoever his fancy or circumstances pointed the way. It was certain he avoided the beaten paths, and freely indulged his taste for regions remote and comparatively unknown. His excuse was that life was far more picturesque and unhackneyed, with a chance for an occasional adventure, in lands where one was not jostled by people with guide-books—that he saw men and women as the influences of the ages had been fashioning them, and not conventionalized by the mode of the hour. "Chief of all," he concluded, jestingly, "I can send to my dear aunt descriptions of people and scenery that she will not find better set forth in half a dozen books within her reach."

After a month in Norway, he crossed the mountains into Sweden, and as winter approached drifted rapidly to the south and east. One of his letters was dated at the entrance of the Himalayas in India, and expressed his purpose to explore one of the grandest mountain systems in the world.

Mrs. Mayburn gloated over the letters, and Grace laughingly told her she had learned more about geography since her nephew had gone abroad than in all her life before. The major, also, was deeply interested in them, especially as Graham took pains in his behalf to give some account of the military organizations with which he came in contact. They had little of the nature of a scientific report. The soldier, his life and weapons, were sketched with a free hand merely, and so became even to the ladies a picturesque figure rather than a military abstraction. From time to time a letter appeared in Mrs. Mayburn's favorite journal signed by the initials of the traveller; and these epistles she cut out and pasted most carefully in a book which Grace jestingly called her "family Bible."

But as time passed, Graham occupied less and less space in the thoughts of all except his aunt. The major's newspaper became more absorbing than ever, for the clouds gathering in the political skies threatened evils that seemed to him without remedy. Strongly Southern and conservative in feeling, he was deeply incensed at what he termed "Northern fanaticism." Only less hateful to him was a class in the South known in the parlance of the times as "fire-eaters."

All through the winter and spring of 1860 he had his "daily growl," as Grace termed it; and she assured him it was growing steadily deeper and louder. Yet it was evidently a source of so much comfort to him that she always smiled in secret over his invective—noting, also, that while he deplored much that was said and done by the leaders of the day, the prelude of the great drama interested him so deeply that he half forgot his infirmities. In fact, she had more trouble with Hilland, who had returned, and was urging an early date for their marriage. Her lover was an ardent Republican, and hated slavery with New England enthusiasm. The arrogance and blindness of the South had their counterpart at the North, and Hilland had not escaped the infection. He was much inclined to belittle the resources of the former section, to scoff at its threats, and to demand that the North should peremptorily and imperiously check all further aggressions of slavery. At first it required not a little tact on the part of Grace to preserve political harmony between father and lover; but the latter speedily recognized that the major's age and infirmities, together with his early associations, gave him almost unlimited privilege to think and say what he pleased. Hilland soon came to hear with good-natured nonchalance his Northern allies berated, and considered himself well repaid by one mirthful, grateful glance from Grace.

After all, what was any political squabble compared with the fact that Grace had promised to marry him in June? The settlement of the difference between the North and South was only a question of time, and that, too, in his belief, not far remote.

"Why should I worry about it?" he said to Grace. "When the North gets angry enough to put its foot down, all this bluster about State-rights, and these efforts to foist slavery on a people who are disgusted with it, will cease."

"Take care," she replied, archly. "I'm a Southern girl. Think what might happen if I put my foot down."

"Oh, when it comes to you," was his quick response, "I'm the Democratic party. I will get down on my knees at any time; I'll yield anything and stand everything."

"I hope you will be in just such a frame of mind ten years hence."

It was well that the future was hidden from her.

Hilland wrote to his friend, asking, indeed almost insisting, that he should return in time for the wedding. Graham did not come, and intimated that he was gathering materials which might result in a book. He sent a letter, however, addressed to them both, and full of a spirit of such loyal good-will that Hilland said it was like a brother's grip. "Well, well," he concluded, "if Graham has the book-making fever upon him, we shall have to give him up indefinitely."

Grace was at first inclined to take the same view, feeling that, even if he had been sorely wounded, his present life and the prospects it gave of authorship had gained so great a fascination that he would come back eventually with only a memory of what he had suffered. Her misgivings, how-ever, returned when, on seeing the letter, Mrs. Mayburn's eyes became suddenly dimmed with tears. She turned away abruptly and seemed vexed with herself for having shown the emotion, but only said quietly, "I once thought Alford had no heart; but that letter was not written 'out of his head,' as we used to say when children."

She gave Grace no reason to complain of any lack of affectionate interest in her preparations; and when the wedding day came she assured the blushing girl that "no one had ever looked upon a lovelier bride."

Ever mindful of her father, Grace would take no wedding journey, although her old friend offered to come and care for him. She knew well how essential her voice and hand were to his comfort; and she would not permit him to entertain, even for a moment, the thought that in any sense he had lost her. So they merely returned to his favorite haunt by the sea, and Hilland was loyal to the only condition in their engagement—that she should be permitted to keep her promise to her dying mother, and never leave her father to the care of others, unless under circumstances entirely beyond her control.

Later in the season Mrs. Mayburn joined them at the beach, for she found her life at the cottage too lonely to be endured.

It was a summer of unalloyed happiness to Hilland and his wife, and the major promised to renew his youth in the warm sunlight of his prosperity. The exciting presidential canvass afforded abundant theme for the daily discussions in his favorite corner of the piazza, where, surrounded by some veteran cronies whom he had known in former years, he joined them in predictions and ominous head-shakings over the monstrous evils that would follow the election of Mr. Lincoln. Hilland, sitting in the background with Grace, would listen and stroke his tawny beard as he glanced humorously at his wife, who knew that he was working, quietly out of deference to his father-in-law, but most effectively, in the Republican campaign. Although Southern born she had the sense to grant to men full liberty of personal opinion—a quality that it would be well for many of her sisterhood to imitate. Indeed, she would have despised a man who had not sufficient force to think for himself; and she loved her husband all the more because in some of his views he differed radically with her father and herself.

Meantime the cloud gathering in the South grew darker
and more portentous; and after the election of President
Lincoln the lightning of hate and passion began to strike
from it directly at the nation's life. The old major was
both wrong and right in regard to the most prominent leaders of the day. Many whom he deemed the worst fanatics
in the land were merely exponents of a public opinion that
was rising like an irresistible tide from causes beyond human
control—from the God-created conscience illumined by His
own truth. In regard to the instigators of the Rebellion,
he was right. Instead of representing their people, they
deceived and misled them; and, with an astute understanding of the chivalrous, hasty Southern temper, they so
wrought upon their pride of section by the false presentation of fancied and prospective wrongs, that loyalty to
the old flag, which at heart they loved, was swept away
by the madness which precedes destruction. Above all and
directing all was the God of nations; and He had decreed
that slavery, the gangrene in the body politic, must be cut
out, even though it should be with the sword. The surgery
was heroic, indeed; but as its result the slave, and especially
the master and his posterity, will grow into a large, healthful, and prosperous life; and the evidences of such life are
increasing daily.

At the time of which I am writing, however, the future
was not dreamed of by the sagacious Lincoln even, or his
cabinet, much less was it foreseen by the humbler characters
of my story. Hilland after reading his daily journal would
sit silent for a long time with contracted brow. The white
heat of anger was slowly kindling in his heart and in that of
the loyal North; and the cloud in the South began to throw
its shadow over the hearth of the happy wife.

Although Hilland hated slavery it incensed him beyond
measure that the South could be made to believe that the
North would break through or infringe upon the constitutional safeguards thrown around the institution. At the
same time he knew, and it seemed to him every intelligent

man should understand, that if a sufficient majority should
decide to forbid the extension of the slave system to new
territory, that should end the question, or else the Constitution was not worth the paper on which it was written.
"Law and order," was his motto; and "All changes and
reforms under the sanction of law, and at the command
of the majority," his political creed.

The major held the Southern view. "Slaves are property," he said; "and the government is bound to permit a
man to take his property where he pleases, and protect him
in all his rights." The point where the veteran drew the
line was in disloyalty to the flag which he had sworn to
defend, and for which he had become a cripple for life.
As the Secession spirit became more rampant and open in
South Carolina, the weight of his invective fell more heavily
upon the leaders there than upon the hitherto more detested
abolitionists.

When he read the address of Alexander H. Stephens,
delivered to the same people on the following evening,
wherein that remarkable man said, "My object is not to
stir up strife, but to allay it; not to appeal to your passions, but to your reason. Shall the people of the South
secede from the Union in consequence of the election of
Mr. Lincoln? My countrymen, I tell you frankly, can-
didly, and earnestly, that I do not think they ought. In
my judgment the election of no man, constitutionally
chosen, is sufficient cause for any State to separate from
the Union. It ought to stand by and aid still in maintain-
ing the Constitution of the country. We are pledged to
maintain the Constitution. Many of us are sworn to support it"—when the veteran came to these words, he sprang
to his feet without a thought of his crutch, and cried in a
tone with which he would order a charge, "There is the
man who ought to be President. Read that speech."

Hilland did read it aloud, and then said thoughtfully,
"Yes; if the leaders on both sides were of the stamp of Mr.
Stephens and would stand firm all questions at issue could

be settled amicably under the Constitution. But I fear the passion of the South, fired by the unscrupulous misrepresentations of a few ambitious men, will carry the Cotton States into such violent disloyalty that the North in its indignation will give them a lesson never to be forgotten."

"Well!" shouted the major, "if they ever fire on the old flag, I'll shoulder my crutch and march against them myself —I would, by heaven! though my own brother fired the gun."

Grace's merry laugh rang out—for she never lost a chance to throw oil on the troubled waters—and she cried, "Warren, if this thing goes on, you and papa will stand shoulder to shoulder."

But the time for that had not yet come. Indeed, there would ever remain wide differences of opinion between the two men. The major believed that if Congress conceded promptly all that the slave power demanded, "the demagogues of the South would soon be without occupation;" while Hilland asserted that the whole thing originated in bluster to frighten the North into submission, and that the danger was that the unceasing inflammatory talk might so kindle the masses that they would believe the lies, daily iterated, and pass beyond the control of their leaders.

When at last South Carolina seceded, and it became evident that other States would follow, the major often said with bitter emphasis that the North would have to pay dearly for its sentiment in regard to the negro. In Hilland's case strong exultation became a growing element in his anger, for he believed that slavery was destined to receive heavier blows from the mad zeal of its friends than Northern abolitionists could have inflicted in a century.

"If the South casts aside constitutional protection," he reasoned, "she must take the consequences. After a certain point is passed, the North will make sharp, quick work with anything that interferes with her peace and prosperity."

"The work will be sharp enough, young man," replied the major testily; "but don't be sure about its being quick.

If the South once gets to fighting, I know her people well enough to assure you that the Republican party can reach its ends only through seas of blood, if they are ever attained.''

Hilland made no reply—he never contradicted the old gentleman—but he wrote Graham a rather strong letter intimating that it was time for Americans to come home.

Graham would not have come, however, had not Grace, who had just returned from Mrs. Mayburn's cottage, caused a postscript to be added, giving the information that his aunt was seriously ill, and that her physician thought it might be a long time before she recovered, even if life was spared.

This decided him at once; and as he thought he might never see his kind old friend again, he bitterly regretted that he had remained away so long. And yet he felt he could scarcely have done otherwise; for in bitter disappointment he found that his passion, so far from being conquered, had, by some uncontrollable law of his nature, simply grown with time and become interwoven with every fibre of his nature. Hitherto he had acted on the principle that he must and would conquer it; but now that duty called him to the presence of the one whose love and kindness formed an indisputable claim upon him, he began to reason that further absence was futile, that he might as well go back, and—as he promised his aunt—''do the best he could.''

It must be admitted that Hilland's broad hint, that in the coming emergency Americans should be at home, had little weight with him. From natural bent he had ever been averse to politics. In accordance with his theory of evolution, he believed the negro was better off in his present condition than he could be in any other. He was the last man to cherish an enthusiasm for an inferior race. Indeed, he would have much preferred it should die out altogether and make room for better material. The truth was that his prolonged residence abroad had made the questions of American politics exceedingly vague and inconsequential. He believed them to be ephemeral to the last degree—in the main, mere struggles of parties and partisans for power and spoils; and for their hopes, schemes, and stratagems to gain temporary success, he cared nothing.

He had not been an idler in his prolonged absence. In the first place, he had striven with the whole force of a powerful will to subdue a useless passion, and had striven in vain. He had not, however, yielded for a day to a dreamy melancholy, but, in accordance with his promise "to do his best," had been tireless in mental and physical activity. The tendency to wander somewhat aimlessly had ceased, and he had adopted the plan of studying modern life at the old centres of civilization and power.

Hilland's letter found him in Egypt, and only a few weeks had elapsed after its reception when, with deep anxiety, he rang the bell at his aunt's cottage door. He had not stopped to ask for letters in London, for he had learned that by pushing right on he could catch a fast out-going steamer and save some days.

The servant who admitted him uttered a cry of joy; and a moment later his aunt rose feebly from the lounge in her sitting-room, and greeted him as her son.

CHAPTER XVII

PREPARATION

GRAHAM learned with deep satisfaction that the dangerous symptoms of his aunt's illness had passed away, and that she was now well advanced in convalescence. They gave to each other an hour or two of unreserved confidence; and the old lady's eyes filled with tears more than once as she saw how vain had been her nephew's struggle. It was equally clear, however, that he had gained strength and a nobler manhood in the effort; and so she told him.

"If supper is ready," he replied, "I'll prove to you that I am in very fair condition."

An hour later he left her, cheerful and comparatively happy, for the St. Johns' cottage. From the piazza he saw through the lighted windows a home-scene that he had once dreamed might bless his life. Hilland, evidently, was reading the evening paper aloud, and his back was toward his friend. The major was nervously drumming on the table with his fingers, and contracting his frosty eyebrows, as if perturbed by the news. But it was on the young wife that Graham's eyes dwelt longest. She sat with some sewing on the further side of the open fire, and her face was toward him. Had she changed? Yes; but for the better. The slight matronly air and fuller form that had come with wifehood became her better than even her girlish grace. As she glanced up to her husband from time to time, Graham saw serene loving trust and content.

"It is all well with them," he thought; "and so may it ever be."

A servant who was passing out opened the door, and thus he was admitted without being announced, for he cautioned the maid to say nothing. Then pushing open the parlor door, which was ajar, he entered, and said quietly: "I've come over for a game of whist."

But the quietness of his greeting was not reciprocated. All rose hastily, even to the major, and stared at him. Then Hilland half crushed the proffered hand, and the major grasped the other, and there came a fire of exclamations and questions that for a moment or two left no space for answer.

Grace cried: "Come, Warren, give Mr. Graham a chance to get his breath and shake hands with me. I propose to count for something in this welcome."

"Give him a kiss, sweetheart," said her delighted husband.

Grace hesitated, and a slight flush suffused her face. Graham quickly bent over her hand, which he now held, and kissed it, saying: "I've been among the Orientals so long that I've learned some of their customs of paying homage. I know that you are queen here as of old, and that Hilland is by this time the meekest of men."

"Indeed, was I so imperious in old times?" she asked, as he threw himself, quite at home, into one of the easy-chairs.

"You are of those who are born to rule. You have a way of your own, however, which some other rulers might imitate to advantage."

"Well, my first command is that you give an account of yourself. So extensive a traveller never sat down at our quiet fireside before. Open your budget of wonders. Only remember we have some slight acquaintance with Baron Munchausen."

"The real wonders of the world are more wonderful than his inventions. Beyond that I hastened home by the shortest possible route after receiving Hilland's letter, I have little to say."

"I thought my letter would stir you up."

"In sincerity, I must say it did not. The postscript did, however."

"Then, in a certain sense, it was I who brought you home, Mr. Graham," said Grace. "I had just returned from a call on Mrs. Mayburn, and I made Warren open the letter and add the postscript. I assure you we were exceedingly anxious about her for weeks."

"And from what she has told me I am almost convinced that she owes her life more to you than to her physician. Drugs go but a little way, especially at her time of life; but the delicacies and nourishing food you saw she was provided with so regularly rallied her strength. Yes; it was your postscript that led to my immediate return, and not Hilland's political blast."

"Why, Graham! Don't you realize what's going on here?"

"Not very seriously."

"You may have to fight, old fellow."

"I've no objections after I have decided which side to take."

"Good heavens, Graham! you will be mobbed if you talk that way here in New England. This comes of a man's living abroad so much that he loses all love for his native land."

"Squabbling politicians are not one's native land. I am not a hater of slavery as you are; and if it produces types of men and women like that Southern lady of whom I told you, it must be an excellent institution."

"Oh, yes," cried Hilland laughing. "By the way, Grace, my cool, cynical friend was once madly in love—at first sight, too—and with a lady old enough to be his mother. I never heard a woman's character sketched more tenderly; and his climax was that your mother must have closely resembled her."

"Mr. Graham is right," said the major impressively. "The South produces the finest women in the world; and when the North comes to meet its men, as I fear it must, it will find they are their mothers' sons."

"Poor Warren!" cried Grace; "here are all three of us against you—all pro-slavery and Southern in our sympathies."

"I admit at once that the South has produced *the* finest woman in the world, " said Hilland, taking his wife's hand. "But I must add that many of her present productions are not at all to my taste; nor will they be to yours, Graham, after you have been here long enough to understand what is going on—that is, if anything at home can enlist your interest."

"I assure you I am deeply interested. It's exhilarating to breathe American air now, especially so after just coming from regions where everything has been dead for centuries; for the people living there now are scarcely alive. Of course I obtained from the papers in Egypt very vague ideas of what was going on; and after receiving your letter my mind was too preoccupied with my aunt's illness to dwell on much besides. If the flag which gave me protection abroad, and under which I was born, is assailed, I shall certainly fight for it, even though I may not be in sympathy with the causes which led to the quarrel. What I said about being undecided as to which side I would take was a half-jocular way of admitting that I need a great deal of information; and between you and the major I am in a fair way to hear both sides. I cannot believe, however, that a civil war will break out in this land of all others. The very idea seems preposterous, and I am not beyond the belief that the whole thing is political excitement. I have learned this much, that the old teachings of Calhoun have borne their legitimate fruit, and that the Cotton States by some hocus-pocus legislation declare themselves out of the Union. But then the rational, and to my mind inevitable, course will be, that the representative men of both sides will realize at last to what straits their partisanship is bringing them, and so come together and adjust their real or fancied grievances. Meanwhile, the excitement will die out; and a good many will have a dim consciousness that they have made fools of themselves, and go quietly about their own business the rest of their days."

"Graham, you don't know anything about the true state of affairs," said Hilland; and before the evening was over he proved his words true to his friend, who listened attentively to the history of his native land for the past few months. In conclusion, Hilland said, "At one time—not very long ago, either—I held your opinion that it was the old game of bluster and threatening on the part of Southern politicians. But they are going too far; they have already gone too far. In seizing the United States forts and other property, they have practically waged war against the government. My opinions have changed from week to week under the stern logic of events, and I now believe that the leading spirits in the South mean actual and final separation. I've no doubt that they hope to effect their purpose peaceably, and that the whole thing will soon be a matter of diplomacy between two distinct governments. But they are preparing for war, and they will have it, too, to their hearts' content. President Buchanan is a muff. He sits and wrings his hands like an old woman, and declares he can do nothing. But the new administration will soon be in power, and it will voice the demand of the North that this nonsense be stopped; and if no heed is given, it will stop it briefly, decisively."

"My son Warren," said the major, "you told your friend some time since that he knew nothing about this affair. You must permit me to say the same to you. I fear that both sides have gone too far, much too far; and what the end will be, and when it will come, God only knows."

Before many weeks passed Graham shared the same view.

Events crowded upon each other; pages of history were made daily, and often hourly. In every home, as well as in the cottages wherein dwelt the people of my story, the daily journals were snatched and read at the earliest possible mo-

ment.   Many were stern and exultant like Hilland; more
were dazed and perplexed, feeling that something ought to
be done to stem the torrent, and at the same time were astonished and troubled to find that perhaps a 'next-door
neighbor sympathized with the rebellion and predicted its
entire success.   The social atmosphere was thick with doubt,
heavy with despondency, and often lurid with anger.

Graham became a curious study to both Grace and his
aunt; and sometimes his friend and the major were inclined
to get out of patience with him.   He grew reticent on the
subject concerning which all were talking, but he read with
avidity, not only the history of the day, but of the past as it
related to the questions at issue.

One of his earliest acts had been the purchase of a horse
noted in town as being so powerful, spirited, and even vicious, that few dared to drive or ride him.   He had finally
brought his ill-repute to a climax by running away, wreck-
ing the carriage, and breaking his owner's ribs.   He had
since stood fuming in idleness; and when Graham wished
him brought to the unused stable behind his aunt's cottage,
no one would risk the danger.   Then the young man went
after the horse himself.

"I've only one man in my employ who dares clean and
take care of him," remarked the proprietor of the livery
stable where he was kept; "and he declares that he won't
risk his life much longer unless the brute is used and tamed
down somewhat.   There's your property and I'd like to
have it removed as soon as possible."

"I'll remove it at once," said Graham, quietly; and
paying no heed to the crowd that began to gather when it
was bruited that "Firebrand"—for such was the horse's
name—was to be brought out, he took a bridle and went
into the stall, first speaking gently, then stroking the animal with an assured touch.   The horse permitted himself
to be bridled and led out; but there was an evil fire in his
eye, and he gave more than one ominous snort of defiance.
The proprietor, smitten by a sudden compunction, rushed

forward and cried, "Look here, sir; you are taking your life in your hand."

"I say, Graham," cried Hilland's voice, "what scrape are you in, that you have drawn such a crowd?"

"No scrape at all," said Graham, looking around and recognizing his friend and Grace mounted and passing homeward from their ride. "I've had the presumption to think that you would permit me to join you occasionally, and so have bought a good horse. Isn't he a beauty?"

"What, Firebrand?"

"That's his present name. I shall rechristen him."

"Oh, come, Graham! if you don't value your neck, others do. You've been imposed upon."

"I've warned him—" began the keeper of the livery stable; but here the horse reared and tried to break from Graham's grasp.

"Clear the way," the young man cried; and as the brute came down he seized his mane and vaulted upon his bare back. The action was so sudden and evidently so unexpected that the horse stood still and quivered for a moment, then gave a few prodigious bounds; but the rider kept his seat so perfectly that he seemed a part of the horse. The beast next began to rear, and at one time it seemed as if he would fall over backward, and his master sprang lightly to the ground. But the horse was scarcely on all fours before Graham was on his back again. The brute had the bit in his teeth, and paid no attention to it. Graham now drew a flexible rawhide from his pocket, and gave his steed a severe cut across the flanks. The result was another bound into the air, such as experts present declared was never seen before; and then the enraged animal sped away at a tremendous pace There was a shout of applause; and Hilland and Grace galloped after, but soon lost sight of Graham. Two hours later he trotted quietly up to their door, his coal-black horse white with foam, quivering in every muscle, but perfectly subdued.

"I merely wished to assure you that my neck was safe,

and that I have a horse fit to go to the war that you predict so confidently," he said to Hilland, who with Grace
rushed out on the piazza.

"I say, Graham, where did you learn to ride?" asked
his friend.

"Oh, the horses were nobler animals than the men in
some of the lands where I have been, and I studied them.
This creature will be a faithful friend in a short time. You
have no idea how much intelligence such a horse as this has
if he is treated intelligently. I don't believe he has ever
known genuine kindness. I'll guarantee that I can fire a
pistol between his ears within two weeks, and that he won't
flinch. Good-by. I shall be my own hostler for a short
time, and must work an hour over him after the run he's
had."

"Well," exclaimed Hilland, as he passed into the house
with his wife, "I admit that Graham has changed. He was
always great on tramps, but I never knew him to care for a
horse before."

Grace felt that he had changed ever since he had leaned
for support against the apple-tree by which he was now passing down the frozen walk, but she only said, "I never saw
such superb horsemanship."

She had not thought Graham exactly fine-looking in former days; but in his absence his slight figure had filled out,
and his every movement was instinct with reserved force.
The experiences through which he had passed removed
him, as she was conscious, beyond the sphere of ordinary
men. Even his marked reticence about himself and his
views was stimulating to the imagination. Whether he had
conquered his old regard for her she could not tell. He certainly no longer avoided her, and he treated her with the
frank courtesy he would naturally extend to his friend's
wife. But he spent far more time with his aunt than with
them; and it became daily more and more evident that he
accepted the major's view, and was preparing for what he
believed would be a long and doubtful conflict. Since it

must come, he welcomed the inevitable, for in his condition of mind it was essential that he should be intensely occupied. Although his aunt had to admit that he was a little peculiar, his manner was simple and quiet; and when he joined his friends on their drives or at their fireside, he was usually as genial as they could desire, and his tenderness for his aunt daily increased the respect which he had already won from Grace.

CHAPTER XVIII

THE CALL TO ARMS

ON the 4th of March, 1861, was inaugurated as President the best friend the South ever had. He would
never have deceived or misled her. In all the bloody
struggle that followed, although hated, scoffed at, and ma-
ligned as the vilest monster of earth, he never by word or
act manifested a vindictive spirit toward her.   Firm and
sagacious, Lincoln would have protected the South in her
constitutional rights, though every man at the North had
become an abolitionist. Slavery, however, had long been
doomed, like other relics of barbarism, by the spirit of the
age; and his wisdom and that of men like him, with the
logic of events and the irresistible force of the world's
opinion, would have found some peaceful, gradual remedy
for an evil which wrought even more injury to the master
than to the bondman.   In his inaugural address he repeated
that he had "no purpose, directly or indirectly, to interfere
with slavery in the States where it existed."

An unanswerable argument against disunion, and an
earnest appeal to reason and lawful remedy, he followed
by a most impressive declaration of peace and good-will:
"In your hands, my dissatisfied fellow-countrymen, and
not mine, is the momentous issue of civil war. The government will not assail you. You can have no conflict
without being yourselves the aggressors. You have no
oath registered in heaven to destroy the government; while
I shall have the most solemn one to preserve, protect, and
defend it."

These were noble words, and to all minds not confused
by the turmoil, passion, and prejudices of the hour, they
presented the issue squarely. If the leaders of the South
desired peaceful negotiation, the way was opened, the opportunity offered; if they were resolved on the destruction
of the Union, Lincoln's oath meant countless men and
countless treasure to defend it.

Men almost held their breath in suspense. The air became thick with rumors of compromise and peace. Even
late in March, Mr. Seward, the President's chief adviser,
"believed and argued that the revolution throughout the
South had spent its force and was on the wane; and that
the evacuation of Sumter and the manifestation of kindness
and confidence to the Rebel and Border States would un-
dermine the conspiracy, strengthen the Union sentiment
and Union majorities, and restore allegiance and healthy
political action without resort to civil war."

To Graham, who, in common with millions in their
homes, was studying the problem, this course seemed so
rational and so advantageous to all concerned, that he accepted it as the outline of the future. The old major shook
his head and growled, "You don't know the South; it's too
late; their blood is up."

Hilland added exultantly, "Neither do you know the
North, Graham. There will come a tidal wave soon that
will carry Mr. Seward and the hesitating President to the
boundaries of Mexico."

The President was not hesitating, in the weak sense of
the word. Equally removed from Mr. Buchanan's timidity
and Mr. Seward's optimistic confidence, he was feeling his
way, gathering the reins into his hands, and seeking to
comprehend an issue then too obscure and vast for mortal
mind to grasp. What is plain to-day was not plain then.

It speedily became evident, however, that all talk of
compromise on the part of the Southern leaders was de-
ceptive—that they were relentlessly pursuing the course
marked out from the first, hoping, undoubtedly, that the

government would be paralyzed by their allies at the North, and that their purposes would be effected by negotiation and foreign intervention.

And so the skies grew darker and the political and social atmosphere so thick with doubt and discordant counsels that the horizon narrowed about even those on the mountain-top of power. All breathed heavily and felt the oppression that precedes some convulsion of nature.

At length, on the morning of the 12th of April, as the darkness which foreruns the dawn was lifting from Charleston Harbor, and Sumter lay like a shadow on the waves, a gun was fired whose echoes repeated themselves around the world. They were heard in every home North and South, and their meaning was unmistakable. The flash of that mortar gun and of the others that followed was as the lightning burning its way across the vault of heaven, revealing everything with intense vividness, and rending and consuming all noxious vapors. The clouds rolled speedily away, and from the North came the sound of "a rushing, mighty wind."

The crisis and the leader came together. The news reached Washington on Saturday. On Sunday Mr. Lincoln drafted his memorable call to arms, and on Monday it was telegraphed throughout the land. The response to that call forms one of the sublimest chapters of history.

In the St. John cottage, as in nearly all other homes, differences of opinion on minor questions melted into nothingness.

Graham read the electric words aloud, and his friend's only excited comment was:

"Graham, you will go."

"Not yet," was the quiet response· "and I sincerely hope you will not."

"How can a man do otherwise?"

"Because he is a man, and not an infuriated animal. I've been very chary in giving my opinion on this subject, as you know. You also know that I have read and thought about it almost constantly since my return. I share fully in Major St. John's views that this affair is not to be settled by a mad rush southward of undisciplined Northern men. I have traced the history of Southern regiments and officers in the Revolution and in our later wars, and I assure you that we are on the eve of a gigantic conflict. In that degree that we believe the government right, we, as rational men, should seek to render it effective service. The government does not need a mob: it needs soldiers, and such are neither you nor I. I have informed myself somewhat on the militia system of the country, and there are plenty of organized regiments of somewhat disciplined men who can go at an hour's notice. If you went now, you—a millionaire—would not count for as much as an Irishman who had spent a few months in a drill-room. The time may come when you can equip a regiment if you choose. Moreover, you have a controlling voice in large business interests; and this struggle is doomed from the start if not sustained financially."

"Mr. Graham is right," said Grace, emphatically. "Even my woman's reason makes so much clear to me."

"Your woman's reason would serve most men better than their own," was his smiling reply. Then, as he looked into her lovely face, pale at the bare thought that her husband was going into danger, he placed his hand on Hilland's shoulder and continued, "Warren, there are other sacred claims besides those of patriotism. The cause should grow desperate indeed before you leave that wife."

"Mr. Graham," Grace began, with an indignant flush mantling the face that had been so pale, "I am a soldier's daughter; and if Warren believed it to be his duty—" Then she faltered, and burst into a passion of tears, as she moaned, "O God! it's—it's true. The bullet that struck him would inflict a deadlier wound on me;" and she hid her face on Hilland's breast and sobbed piteously.

"It is also true," said Graham, in tones that were as grave and solemn as they were gentle, "that your father's spirit—nay, your own—would control you. Under its influence you might not only permit but urge your husband's departure, though your heart broke a thousand times. Therefore, Hilland, I appeal to your manhood. You would be unworthy of yourself and of this true woman were you guided by passion or excitement. As a loyal man you are bound to render your country your best service. To rush to the fray now would be the poorest aid you could give."

"Graham talks sense," said the major, speaking with the authority of a veteran. "If I had to meet the enemy at once, I'd rather have a regiment of *canaille*, and cowards at that, who could obey orders like a machine, than one of hot-headed millionaires who might not understand the command 'Halt!' Mr. Graham is right again when he says that Grace will not prevent a man from doing his duty any more than her mother did."

"What do *you* propose to do?" asked Hilland, breathing heavily. It was evident that a tremendous struggle was going on in his breast, for it had been his daily and nightly dream to join the grand onset that should sweep slavery and rebellion out of existence.

"Simply what I advise—watch, wait, and act when I can be of the most service."

"I yield," said Hilland, slowly, "for I suppose you are right. You all know well, and you best of all, sweetheart" —taking his wife's face in his hands and looking down into her tearful eyes—"that here is the treasure of my life. But you also know that in all the past there have come times when a man must give up everything at the need of his country."

"And when that time comes," sobbed his wife, "I—I— will not—" But she could not finish the sentence.

Graham stole away, awed, and yet with a peace in his heart that he had not known for years. He had saved his friend from the first wild mêlée of the war—the war that promised rest and nothingness to him, even while he kept his promise to "live and do his best."

CHAPTER XIX

THE BLOOD-RED SKY

DAYS and weeks of intense excitement followed the terrific Union reverses which at one time threatened the loss of the national capital; and the North began to put forth the power of which it was only half conscious, like a giant taken unawares; for to all, except men of Hilland's hopeful confidence, it soon became evident that the opponent was a giant also. It is not my purpose to dwell upon this, however, except as it influenced the actors of my story.

Hilland, having given up his plans, was contentedly carrying out the line of action suggested by his friend. By all the means within his power he was furthering the Union cause, and learned from experience how much more he could accomplish as a business man than by shouldering a musket, or misleading a regiment in his ignorance. He made frequent trips to New York, and occasionally went to Washington. Graham often accompanied him, and also came and went on affairs of his own. Ostensibly he was acting as correspondent for the journal to which he had written when abroad. In reality, he was studying the great drama with an interest that was not wholly patriotic or scientific. He had found an antidote. The war, dreaded so unspeakably by many, was a boon to him; and the fierce excitement of the hour a counter-irritant to the pain at heart which he believed had become his life-long heritage.

He had feared the sorrowful reproaches of his aunt, as

he gave himself almost wholly up to its influences, and became an actor in the great struggle.   In this he was agree-
ably mistaken, for the spirited old lady, while averse to
politics as such, had become scarcely less belligerent than
the major since the fall of Sumter.   She cheerfully let him
come and go at his will; and in his loving gratitude it must
be admitted that his letters to her were more frequent and
interesting than those to the journal whose badge was his
passport to all parts of our lines.   He spent every hour he
could with her, also; and she saw with pleasure that his
activity did him good.   Grace thought he found few opportunities to pass an evening with them.   She was exceedingly grateful—first, that he had interpreted her so nobly,
but chiefly because it was his influence and reasoning that
had led her husband into his present large, useful, happy
action; and she could not help showing it.

Graham's position of correspondent gave him far better
opportunities for observation than he could have had in any
arm of the service.   Of late he was following the command
of General Patterson, believing from his sanguinary vapor-
ing that in his army would be seen the first real work of the
war.'   He soon became convinced, however, that the veteran of the Mexican War, like the renowned King of France,
would march his "twenty thousand men" up the hill only to
march them down again.   Hearing that McDowell proposed
to move against the enemy at Manassas, he hastily repaired
to Washington, hoping to find a general that dared to come
within cannon-range of the foe.

A sultry day late in the month of July was drawing to
a close.   Hilland and his wife, with Mrs. Mayburn, were
seated under the apple-tree, at which point the walk intersected with the main one leading to the street.   The young
man, with a heavy frown, was reading from an "extra" a
lurid outline of General McDowell's overwhelming defeat
and the mad panic that ensued.   Grace was listening with

---

¹ Patterson wrote to the Secretary of War: "You have the means; place
them at my disposal, and shoot me if I do not use them to advantage."

deep solicitude, her work lying idle in her lap. It had been a long, hard day for her. Of late her father had been deeply excited, and now was sleeping from sheer reaction. Mrs. Mayburn, looking as grim as fate, sat bolt upright and knitted furiously. One felt instinctively that in no emergency of life could she give way to a panic.

"Well," cried Hilland, springing to his feet and dashing the paper to the ground with something like an oath, "one battle has been fought in America at which I thank the immortal gods I was not present. Why did not McDowell drive a flock of sheep against the enemy, and furnish his division commanders with shepherds' crooks? Oh, the burning, indelible disgrace of it all! And yet—and the possibility of it makes me feel that I would destroy myself had it happened—I might have run like the blackest sheep of them all. I once read up a little on the subject of panics; and there's a mysterious, awful contagion about them impossible to comprehend. These men were Americans; they had been fighting bravely; what the devil got into them that they had to destroy themselves and everything in an insane rush for life?"

"Oh, Warren, see the sky!" cried his wife, the deep solicitude of her expression giving place to a look of awe.

They all turned to the west, and saw a sunset that from the excitable condition of their minds seemed to reflect the scenes recently enacted, and to portend those in prospect now for years to come. Lines of light and broken columns of cloud had ranged themselves across the western arch of the sky, and almost from the horizon to the zenith they were blood-red. So deep, uniform, and ensanguined was the crimson, that the sense of beauty was subordinated to the thought of the national tragedy reflected in the heavens. Hilland's face grew stern as he looked, and Grace hid hers on his breast.

After a moment, he said, lightly, "What superstitious fools we are! It's all an accidental effect of light and cloud."

A cry from Mrs. Mayburn caused them to turn hastily, and they saw her rushing down the path to the street entrance. Two men were helping some one from a carriage. As their obscuring forms stood aside, Graham was seen balancing himself on crutches.

Hilland placed his wife hastily but tenderly on the seat, and was at the gateway in almost a single bound.

"You had better let us carry you," Grace heard one of the men say in gruff kindness.

"Nonsense!" was the hearty reply. "I have not retreated thus far so masterfully only to give my aunt the hysterics at last."

"Alford," said his aunt, sternly, "if it's wise for you to be carried, be carried. Any man here is as liable to hysterics as I am."

"Graham, what does this mean?" cried his friend, in deep excitement. "You look as if half cut to pieces."

"It's chiefly my clothes; I am a fitter subject for a tailor than for a surgeon. Come, good people, there is no occasion for melodrama. With aunty's care I shall soon be as sound as ever. Very well, carry me, then. Perhaps I ought not to use my arm yet;" for Hilland, taking in his friend's disabled condition more fully, was about to lift him in his arms without permission or apology. It ended in his making what is termed a "chair" with one of the men, and Graham was borne speedily up the path.

Grace stood at the intersection with hands clasped in the deepest anxiety; but Graham smiled reassuringly, as he said, "Isn't this an heroic style of returning from the wars? Not quite like Walter Scott's knights; but we've fallen on prosaic times. Don't look so worried. I assure you I'm not seriously hurt."

"Mrs. Mayburn," said Hilland, excitedly, "let us take him to our cottage. We can all take better care of him there."

"Oh, do! please do!" echoed Grace. "You are alone; and Warren and I could do so much—"

"No," said the old lady quietly and decisively; for the moment the proposition was broached Graham's eyes had sought hers in imperative warning. "You both can help me as far as it is needful."

Grace detected the glance and noted the result, but Hilland began impetuously: "Oh, come, dear Mrs. Mayburn, I insist upon it. Graham is making light of it; but I'm sure he'll need more care than you realize—"

"Hilland, I know the friendship that prompts your wish," interrupted Graham, "but my aunt is right. I shall do better in my own room. I need rest more than anything else. You and your wife can do all you wish for me. Indeed, I shall visit you to-morrow and fight the battle over again with the major. Please take me to my room at once," he added in a low tone. "I'm awfully tired."

"Come, Mr. Hilland," said Mrs. Mayburn, in a tone almost authoritative; and she led the way decisively.

Hilland yielded, and in a few moments Graham was in his own room, and after taking a little stimulant, explained.

"My horse was shot and fell on me. I am more bruised, scratched and used up, than hurt;" and so it proved, though his escape had evidently been almost miraculous. One leg and foot had been badly crushed. There were two flesh wounds in his arm; and several bullets had cut his clothing, in some places drawing blood. All over his clothes, from head to foot, were traces of Virginia soil; and he had the general appearance of a man who had passed through a desperate mêlée.

"I tried to repair damages in Washington," he said, "but the confusion was so dire I had to choose between a hospital and home; and as I had some symptoms of fever last night, I determined to push on till under the wing of my good old aunty and your fraternal care. Indeed, I think I was half delirious when I took the train last evening; but it was only from fatigue, lack of sleep, and perhaps loss of blood. Now, please leave me to aunty's care to-night, and I will tell you all about it to-morrow."

Hilland was accordingly constrained to yield to his friend's wishes. He brought the best surgeon in town, however, and gave directions that, after he had dressed Graham's wounds, he should spend the night in Mrs. Mayburn's parlor, and report to him if there was any change for the worse. Fortunately, there was no occasion for his solicitude. Graham slept with scarcely a break till late the next morning; and his pulse became so quiet that when he waked with a good appetite the physician pronounced all danger passed.

In the evening he was bent on visiting the major. He knew they were all eager for his story, and, calculating upon the veteran's influence in restraining Hilland from hasty action, he resolved that his old and invalid friend should hear it with the first. From the character of Hilland he knew the danger to be apprehended was that he would throw himself into the struggle in some way that would paralyze, or at the least curtail, his efficiency. Both his aunt and the physician, who underrated the recuperative power of Graham's fine physical condition, urged quiet until the following day; but he assured them he would suffer more from restlessness than from a moderate degree of effort. He also explained to his aunt that he wished to talk with Hilland, and, if possible, in the presence of his wife and the major.

"Then they must come here," said the old lady, resolutely.

With this compromise he had to be content; and Hilland, who had been coming and going, readily agreed to fetch the major.

CHAPTER XX

TWO BATTLES

IN less than an hour Graham was in the parlor, looking, it is true, somewhat battered, but cheerful and resolute. His friends found him installed in a great armchair, with his bruised foot on a cushion, his arm in a sling, and a few pieces of court-plaster distributed rather promiscuously over his face and head. He greeted Hilland and his wife so heartily, and assured the major so genially that he should now divide with him his honors as a veteran, that they were reassured, and the rather tragic mood in which they had started on the visit was dispelled.

"I must admit, though," he added to his old friend, who was also made comfortable in his chair, which Hilland had brought over, "that in my fall on the field of glory I made a sorry figure. I was held down by my horse and trampled on as if I had been a part of the 'sacred soil.'"

"'Field of glory,' indeed!" exclaimed Hilland, contemptuously.

"I did not know that you had become a soldier," said Grace, with surprise.

"I was about as much of a soldier as the majority, from the generals down," was the laughing reply.

"I don't see how you could have been a worse one, if you had tried," was his friend's rejoinder. "I may do no better; but I should be less than man if I did not make an effort to wipe out the disgrace as soon as possible. No reflection on you, Graham. Your wounds exonerate you; and I know you did not get them in running away.''

"Yes, I did—two of them, at least—these in my arm. As to 'wiping out this disgrace as soon as possible,' I think that is a very secondary matter.''

"Well! I don't understand it at all,'' was Hilland's almost savage answer. "But I can tell you from the start you need not enter on your old prudent counsels that I should serve the government as a stay-at-home quartermaster and general supply agent. In my opinion, what the government needs is men—men who at least won't run away. I now have Grace's permission to go—dear, brave girl!—and go I shall. To stay at home because I am rich seems to me the very snobbishness of wealth; and the kind of work I have been doing graybeards can do just as well, and better.''

Graham turned a grave look of inquiry upon the wife. She answered it by saying with a pallid face: "I had better perish a thousand times than destroy Warren's self-respect.''

"What right have you to preach caution,'' continued Hilland, "when you went far enough to be struck by half a dozen bullets?''

"The right of a retreat which scarcely slackened until I was under my aunt's roof.''

"Come, Graham, you are tantalizing us,'' said Hilland, impatiently. "There, forgive me, old fellow. I fear you are still a little out of your head,'' he added, with a slight return of his old good-humor. "Do give us, then, if you can, some account of your impetuous advance on Washington, instead of Richmond.''

"Yes, Mr. Graham,'' added the major, "if you are able to give me some reason for not blushing that I am a Northern man, I shall be glad to hear it.''

"Mrs. Hilland,'' said Graham, with a smiling glance at the young wife's troubled face, "you have the advantage of us all. You can proudly say, 'I'm a Southerner.' Hilland and I are nothing but 'low-down Yankees.' Come, good friends, I have seen enough tragedy of late; and if I have to describe a little to-night, let us look at matters philosophically. If I received some hard knocks from your kin, Mrs. Hilland—"

"Don't say 'Mrs. Hilland,'" interrupted his friend. "As I've told you before, my wife is 'Grace' to you."

"So be it then. The hard knocks from your kin have materially added to my small stock of sense; and I think the entire North will be wiser as well as sadder before many days pass. We have been taught that taking Richmond and marching through the South will be no holiday picnic. Major St. John has been right from the start. We must encounter brave, determined men; and, whatever may be true of the leaders, the people are as sincere in their patriotism as we are. They don't even dream that they are fighting in a bad cause. The majority will stand up for it as stoutly and conscientiously as your husband for ours. Have I not done justice to your kin, Grace?"

"Yes," she replied, with a faint smile.

"Then forgive me if I say that until four o'clock last Sunday afternoon, and in a fair, stand-up fight between a Northern mob and a Southern mob, we whipped them."

"But I thought the men of the North prided themselves on their 'staying power.'"

"They had no 'staying power' when they found fresh regiments and batteries pouring in on their flank and rear. I believe that retreat was then the proper thing. The wild panic that ensued resulted naturally from the condition of the men and officers, and especially from the presence of a lot of nondescript people that came to see the thing as a spectacle, a sort of gladiatorial combat, upon which they could look at a safe distance. Two most excellent results have been attained: I don't believe we shall ever send out another mob of soldiers; and I am sure that a mob of men and women from Washington will never follow it to see the fun."

"I wish Beauregard had corralled them all—the mob of

sight-seers, I mean," growled the major. "I must say, Mr. Graham, that the hard knocks you and others have received may result in infinite good. I think I take your meaning, and that we shall agree very nearly before you are through. You know that I was ever bitterly opposed to the mad 'On to Richmond' cry; and now the cursed insanity of the thing is clearly proved."

"I agree with you that it was all wrong—that it involved risks that never should have been taken at this stage of the war; and I am told that General Scott and other veteran officers disapproved of the measure. Nevertheless, it came wonderfully near being successful. We should have gained the battle if the attack had been made earlier, or if that old muff, Patterson, had done his duty."

"If you are not too tired, give us the whole movement, just as you saw it," said Hilland, his eyes glowing with excitement.

"Oh, I feel well enough for another retreat to-night. My trouble was chiefly fatigue and lack of sleep."

"Because you make light of wounds, we do not," said Grace.

"Hilland knows that the loss of a little blood as pale and watery as mine would be of small account," was Graham's laughing response.

"Well, to begin at the beginning, I followed Patterson till convinced that his chief impulse was to get away from the enemy. I then hastened to Washington only to learn that McDowell had already had a heavy skirmish which was not particularly to our advantage. This was Saturday morning, and the impression was that a general engagement would be fought almost immediately. The fact that our army had met with little opposition thus far created a false confidence. I did not care to risk my pet horse, Mayburn. You must know, aunty, I've rechristened Firebrand in your honor," said Graham. "I tried to get another mount, but could not obtain one for love or money. Every beast and conveyance in the city seemed already engaged for the coming spectacle. The majority of these civilians did not leave till early on Sunday morning, but I had plenty of company on Saturday, when with my good horse I went in a rather leisurely way to Centerville; for as a correspondent I had fairly accurate information of what was taking place, and had heard that there would be no battle that day.

"I reached Centerville in the evening, and soon learned that the forward movement would take place in the night. Having put my horse in thorough condition for the morrow, and made an enormous supper through the hospitality of some staff-officers, I sought a quiet knoll on which to sleep in soldier fashion under the sky, but found the scene too novel and beautiful for such prosaic oblivion. I was on the highest ground I could find, and beneath and on either side of me were the camp-fires of an army. Around the nearest of these could be seen the forms of the soldiers in every picturesque attitude; some still cooking and making their rude suppers, others executing double-shuffles like war-dances, more discussing earnestly and excitedly the prospects of the coming day, and not a few looking pensively into the flames as if they saw pictures of the homes and friends they might never see again. In the main, however, animation and jollity prevailed; and from far and near came the sound of song, and laughter, and chaffing. Far down the long slope toward the dark, wooded valley of Bull Run, the light of the fires shaded off into such obscurity as the full moon permitted, while beyond the stream in the far distance a long, irregular line of luminous haze marked the encampments of the enemy.

"As the night advanced the army grew quiet; near and distant sounds died away; the canvas tents were like mounds of snow; and by the flickering, dying flames were multitudes of quiet forms. At midnight few scenes could be more calm and beautiful, so tenderly did the light of the moon soften and etherealize everything. Even the parked artillery lost much of its grim aspect, and all nature seemed to breathe peace and rest.

"It was rumored that McDowell wished to make part of the march in the evening, and it would have been well if he had done so. A little past midnight a general stir and bustle ran through the sleeping army. Figures were seen moving hurriedly, men forming into lines, and there was a general commotion. But there was no promptness of action. The soldiers stood around, sat down, and at last lay on their arms and slept again. Mounting my horse, with saddle-bags well stuffed with such rations as I could obtain, I sought the centres of information. It appeared that the division under General Tyler was slow in starting, and blocked the march of the Second and the Third Division. As I picked my way around, only a horse's sagacity kept me from crushing some sleeping fellow's leg or arm, for a horse won't step on a man unless excited.

"Well, Tyler's men got out of the way at last in a haphazard fashion, and the Second and Third Divisions were also steadily moving, but hours behind time. Such marching! It reminded one of countrymen streaming along a road to a Fourth of July celebration.

"My main policy was to keep near the commander-in-chief, for thus I hoped to obtain from the staff some idea of the plan of battle and where its brunt would fall. I confess that I was disgusted at first, for the general was said to be ill, and he followed his columns in a carriage. It seemed an odd way of leading an army. But he came out all right; and he did his duty as a soldier and a general, although every one is cursing him to-day. He was the first man on the real battlefield, and by no means the first to leave it.

"Of course I came and went along the line of march, or of straggling rather, as I pleased; but I kept my eye on the general and his staff. I soon observed that he decided to make his headquarters at the point where a road leading from the great Warrenton Turnpike passed to the north through what is known as the 'Big Woods.' Tyler's command continued westward down the turnpike to what is known as the Stone Bridge, a single substantial arch at which the enemy were said to be in force. It now became clear that the first fighting would be there, and that it was McDowell's plan to send his main force under Hunter and Heintzelman further north through the woods to cross at some point above. I therefore followed Tyler's column, as that must soon become engaged.

"The movements had all been so mortally slow that any chance for surprise was lost. As we approached the bridge it was as lovely a summer morning as you would wish to see. I had ridden ahead with the scouts. Thrushes, robins, and other birds were singing in the trees. Startled rabbits, and a mother-bird with a brood of quails, scurried across the road, and all seemed as still and peaceful as any Sunday that had ever dawned on the scene. It was hard to persuade one's self that in front and rear were the forces of deadly war.

"We soon reached an eminence from which we saw what dispelled at once the illusion of sylvan solitude. The sun had been shining an hour or two, and the bridge before us and the road beyond were defended by *abatis* and other obstructions. On the further bank a line of infantry was in full view with batteries in position prepared to receive us. I confess it sent a thrill through every nerve when I first saw the ranks of the foe we must encounter in no mere pageant of war.

"In a few moments our forces came up, and at first one brigade deployed on the left and another on the right of the pike. At last I witnessed a scene that had the aspect of war. A great thirty-pound Parrot gun unlimbered in the centre of the pike, and looked like a surly mastiff. In a moment an officer, who understood his business, sighted it. There was a flash, bright even in the July sunlight, a grand report awakening the first echoes of a battle whose thunder was heard even in Washington; and a second later we saw the shell explode directly over the line of Confederate infantry. Their ranks broke and melted away as if by magic."

"Good shot, well aimed. Oh heavens! what would I not give to be thirty years younger! Go on, Graham, go on;" for the young man had stopped to take a sip of wine.

"Yes, Graham," cried Hilland, springing to his feet; "what next?"

"I fear we are doing Mr. Graham much wrong," Grace interrupted. "He must be going far beyond his strength."

The young man had addressed his words almost solely to the major, not only out of courtesy, but also for a reason that Grace partially surmised. He now turned and smiled into her flushed, troubled face, and said, "I fear you find these details of war dull and wearisome."

"On the contrary, you are so vivid a *raconteur* that I fear Warren will start for the front before you are through."

"When I am through you will think differently."

"But you *are* going beyond your strength."

"I assure you I am not; though I thank you for your thoughtfulness. I never felt better in my life; and it gives me a kind of pleasure to make you all realize things as I saw them."

"And it gives us great pleasure to listen," cried Hilland. "Even Mrs. Mayburn there is knitting as if her needles were bayonets; and Grace has the flush of a soldier's daughter on her cheeks."

"Oh, stop your chatter, and let Graham go on," said the major—"that is, if it's prudent for him," he added from a severe sense of duty. "What followed that blessed shell?"

"A lame and impotent conclusion in the form of many other shells that evoked no reply; and beyond his feeble demonstration Tyler did nothing. It seemed to me that a determined dash at the bridge would have carried it. I was fretting and fuming about when a staff-officer gave me a hint that nothing was to be done at present—that it was all only a feint, and that the columns that had gone northward through the woods would begin the real work. His words were scarcely spoken before I was making my way to the rear. I soon reached McDowell's carriage at the intersection of the roads, and found it empty. Learning that the general, in his impatience, had taken horse and galloped off to see what had become of his tardy commanders, I followed at full speed.

"It was a wild, rough road, scarcely more than a lane through the woods; but Mayburn was equal to it, and like a bird carried me through its gloomy shades, where 1 observed not a few skulkers cowering in the brush as I sped by. I overtook Heintzelman's command as it was crossing the run at Sudley's Ford; and such a scene of confusion I hope never to witness again. The men were emptying their canteens and refilling them, laving their hands and faces, and refreshing themselves generally. It was really quite a picnic. Officers were storming and ordering 'the boys'— and boys they seemed, indeed—to move on; and by dint of much profanity, and the pressure of those following, regiment after regiment at last straggled up the further bank, went into brigade formation, and shambled forward."

"The cursed mob!" muttered the major.

"Well, poor fellows! they soon won my respect; and yet, as I saw them then, stopping to pick blackberries along the road, I did feel like riding them down. I suppose my horse and I lowered the stream somewhat as we drank, for the day had grown sultry and the sun's rays intensely hot. Then I hastened on to find the general. It seemed as if we should never get out of the woods, as if the army had lost itself in an interminable forest. Wild birds and game fled before us; and I heard one soldier call out to another that it was 'a regular Virginia coon-hunt.' As I reached the head of the column the timber grew thinner, and I was told that McDowell was reconnoitring in advance. Galloping out into the open fields, I saw him far beyond me, already the target of Rebel bullets. His staff and a company of cavalry were with him; and as I approached he seemed rapidly taking in the topographical features of the field. Having apparently satisfied himself, he galloped to the rear; and at the same time Hunter's troops came pouring out of the woods.

"There was now a prospect of warm work and plenty of it. For the life of me I can't tell you how the battle began. Our men came forward in an irregular manner, rushing onward impetuously, halting unnecessarily, with no master mind directing. It seemed at first as if the mere momentum of the march carried us under the enemy's fire; and then there was foolish delay. By the aid of my powerful glass I was convinced that we might have walked right over the first thin Rebel line on the ridge nearest us.

"The artillery exchanged shots awhile. Regiments under the command of General Burnside deployed in the fields to the left of the road down which we had come; skirmishers were thrown out rapidly and began their irregular firing at an absurd distance from the enemy. There was hesitancy, delay; and the awkwardness of troops unaccustomed to act together in large bodies was enhanced by the excitement inseparable from their first experience of real war.

"In spite of all this the battlefield began to present grand and inspiring effects. The troops were debouching rapidly from the woods, their bayonets gleaming here and there through the dust raised by their hurrying feet, and burning in serried lines when they were ranged under the cloudless sun. In every movement made by every soldier the metal points in his accoutrements flashed and scintillated. Again there was something very spirited in the appearance of a battery rushed into position at a gallop—the almost instantaneous unlimbering, the caissons moving to the rear, and the guns at the same moment thundering their defiance, while the smoke, lifting slowly on the heavy air, rises and blends with that of the other side, and hangs like a pall to leeward of the field. The grandest thing of all, however, was the change in the men. The uncouth, coarsely jesting, blackberry-picking fellows that lagged and straggled to the battle became soldiers in their instincts and rising excitement and courage, if not in machine-like discipline and coolness. As I rode here and there I could see that they were erect, eager, and that their eyes began to glow like coals from their dusty, sunburned visages. If there were occasional evidences of fear, there were more of resolution and desire for the fray.

"The aspect of affairs on the ridge, where the enemy awaited us, did not grow encouraging. With my glass I could see re-inforcements coming up rapidly during our delay. New guns were seeking position, which was scarcely taken before there was a puff of smoke and their iron message. Heavens! what a vicious sound those shells had! something between a whiz and a shriek. Even the horses would cringe and shudder when one passed over them, and the men would duck their heads, though the missile was thirty feet in the air. I suppose there was some awfully wild firing on both sides; but I saw several of our men carried to the rear. But all this detail is an old, old story to you, Major."

"Yes, an old story, but one that can never lose its fierce charm. I see it all as you describe it. Go on, and omit nothing you can remember of the scene. Mrs. Mayburn looks as grim as one of your cannon; and Grace, my child, you won't flinch, will you?"

"No, papa."

"That's my brave wife's child. She often said, 'Tell me all. I wish to know just what you have passed through.'"

A brief glance assured Graham that her father's spirit was then supreme, and that she looked with woman's admiration on a scene replete with the manhood woman most admires.

"I cannot describe to you the battle, as such," continued Graham. "I can only outline faintly the picture I saw dimly through dust and smoke from my own standpoint. Being under no one's orders, I could go where I pleased, and I tried to find the vital points. Of course, there was much heavy fighting that I saw nothing of, movements unknown to me or caught but imperfectly. During the preliminary conflict I remained on the right of Burnside's command near the Sudley Road by which our army had reached the field.

"When at last his troops began to press forward, their advance was decided and courageous; but the enemy held their own stubbornly. The fighting was severe and deadly, for we were now within easy musket range. At one time I trembled for Burnside's lines, and I saw one of his aides gallop furiously to the rear for help. It came almost immediately in the form of a fine body of regulars under Major Sykes; and our wavering lines were rendered firm and more aggressive than ever. At the same time it was evident that our forces were going into action off to the right of the Sudley Road, and that another battery had opened on the enemy. I afterward learned that they were Rickett's guns. Under this increasing and relentless pressure the enemy's lines were seen to waver. Wild cheers went up from our ranks; and such is the power of the human voice—the echo direct from the heart—that these shouts rose above the roar of the cannon, the crash of musketry, and thrilled every nerve and fibre. Onward pressed our men; the Rebel lines yielded, broke, and our foes retreated down the hill, but at a dogged, stubborn pace, fighting as they went. Seeing the direction they were taking, I dashed into the Sudley Road near which I had kept as the centre of operations. At the intersection of this road with the Warrenton Turnpike was a stone house, and behind this the enemy rallied as if determined to retreat no further. I had scarcely observed this fact when I saw a body of men forming in the road just above me. In a few moments they were in motion. On they came, a resistless human turrent with a roar of hoarse shouts and cries. I was carried along with them; but before we reached the stone house the enemy broke and fled, and the whole Rebel line was swept back half a mile or more.

"Thus you see that in the first severe conflict of the day,

and when pitted against numbers comparatively equal, we
won a decided victory."

Both the major and Hilland drew a long breath of relief;
and the former said: "I have been hasty and unjust in my
censure. If that raw militia could be made to fight at all,
it can in time be made to fight well. Mr. Graham, you have
deeply gratified an old soldier to-night by describing scenes
that carry me back to the grand era of my life. I believe
I was born to be a soldier; and my old campaigns stand
out in memory like sun-lighted mountain-tops. Forgive
such high-flown talk—I know it's not like me—but I've
had to-night some of my old battle excitement. I never
thought to feel it again. We'll hear the rest of your story
to-morrow. I outrank you all, by age at least; and I now
order 'taps.' "

Graham was not sorry, for in strong reaction a sudden
sense of almost mortal weakness overcame him. Even the
presence of Grace, for whose sake, after all, he had unconsciously told his story, could not sustain him any longer,
and he sank back looking very white.

"You *have* overexerted yourself," she said gently,
coming to his side. "You should have stopped when I
cautioned you; or rather, we should have been more
thoughtful."

"Perhaps I have overrated my strength—it's a fault
of mine," was his smiling reply. "I shall be perfectly
well after a night's rest."

He had looked up at her as he spoke; and in that moment of weakness there was a wistful, hungry look in his
eyes that smote her heart.

A shallow, silly woman, or an intensely selfish one,
would have exulted. Here was a man, cool, strong, and
masterful among other men—a man who had gone to the
other side of the globe to escape her power—one who
within the last few days had witnessed a battle with the
quiet poise that enabled him to study it as an artist or
a tactician; and yet he could not keep his eyes from betray-

ing the truth that there was something within his heart
stronger than himself.

Did Grace Hilland lay this flattering unction to her soul?
No.   She went away inexpressibly sad.   She felt that two
battle scenes had been presented to her mind; and the conflict that had been waged silently, patiently, and unceas-
ingly in a strong man's soul had to her the higher elements
of heroism.   It was another of those wretched problems
offered by this imperfect world for which there seems no
remedy.

When Hilland hastened over to see his friend and add
a few hearty words to those he had already spoken, he was
told that he was sleeping.

CHAPTER XXI

THE LOGIC OF EVENTS

GRAHAM was right in his prediction that another night's rest would carry him far on the road to recovery; and he insisted, when Hilland called in the morning, that the major should remain in his accustomed chair at home, and listen to the remainder of the story. "My habit of life is so active," he said, "that a little change will do me good;" and so it was arranged. By leaning on Hilland's shoulder he was able to limp the short distance between the cottages; and he found that Grace had made every arrangement for his comfort on the piazza, where the major welcomed him with almost the eagerness of a child for whom an absorbing story is to be continued.

"You can't know how you interested us all last night," Grace began. "I never knew papa to be more gratified; and as for Warren, he could not sleep for excitement. Where did you learn to tell stories?"

"I was said to be very good at fiction when a boy, especially when I got into scrapes. But you can't expect in this garish light any such effects as I may have created last evening. It requires the mysterious power of night and other conditions to secure a glamour; and so you must look for the baldest prose to-day."

"Indeed, Graham, we scarcely know what to expect from you any more," Hilland remarked. "From being a quiet cynic philosopher, content to delve in old libraries like the typical bookworm, you become an indefatigable sportsman, horse-tamer, explorer of the remote parts of the earth, and last, and strangest, a newspaper correspondent who doesn't

know that the place to see and write about battles is several
miles in the rear.   What will you do next?''

"My future will be redeemed from the faintest trace of
eccentricity. I shall do what about a million other Americans will do eventually—go into the army.''

"Ah! now you talk sense, and I am with you. I shall be
ready to go as soon as you are well enough.''

"I doubt it.''

"I don't.''

"Grace, what do you say to all this?'' turning a troubled
look upon the wife.

"I foresee that, like my mother, I am to be the wife of
a soldier,'' she replied with a smile, while tears stood in her
eyes. "I did not marry Warren to destroy his sense of
manhood.''

"You see, Graham, how it is. You also perceive what
a knight I must be to be worthy of the lady I leave in
bower.''

"Yes; I see it all too well. But I must misquote Shake-
speare to you, and 'charge you to stand on the *order* of your
going;' and I think the rest of my story will prove that I
have good reason for the charge.''

"I should have been sorry,'' said the major, "to have
had Grace marry a man who would consult only ease and
safety in times like these. It will be awfully hard to have
him go. But the time may soon come when it would be
harder for Grace to have him stay; that is, if she is like
her mother. But what's the use of looking at the gloomy
side? I've been through a dozen battles; and here I am to
plague the world yet. But now for the story. You left off,
Mr. Graham, at the rout of the first Rebel line of battle.''

"And this had not been attained,'' resumed Graham,
"without serious loss to our side. Colonel Hunter, who
commanded the Second Division, you remember, was so
severely wounded by a shell that he had to leave the field
early in the action. Colonel Slocum of one of the Rhode
Island regiments was mortally wounded; and his major had

his leg crushed by a cannon ball which at the same time killed his horse. Many others were wounded and must have had a hard time of it, poor fellows, that hot day. As for the dead that strewed the ground—their troubles were over."

"But not the troubles of those that loved them," said Grace, bitterly.

Graham turned hastily away. When a moment later he resumed his narrative, she noticed that his eyes were moist and his tones husky.

"Our heaviest loss was in the demoralization of some of the regiments engaged. They appeared to have so little cohesion that one feared all the time that they might crumble away into mere human atoms.

"The affair continually took on a larger aspect, as more troops became engaged. We had driven the Confederates down a gentle slope, across a small stream called Young's Branch, and up a hill beyond and to the south. This position was higher and stronger than any they had yet occupied. On the crest of the hill were two houses; and the enemy could be seen forming a line extending from one to the other. They were evidently receiving re-enforcements rapidly. I could see gray columns hastening forward and deploying; and I've no doubt that many of the fugitives were rallied beyond this line. Meanwhile, I was informed that Tyler's Division, left in the morning at Stone Bridge, had crossed the Run, in obedience to McDowell's orders, and were on the field at the left of our line. Such, as far as I could judge, was the position of affairs between twelve and one, although I can give you only my impressions. It appeared to me that our men were fighting well, gradually and steadily advancing, and closing in upon the enemy. Still, I cannot help feeling that if we had followed up our success by the determined charge of one brigade that would hold together, the hill might have been swept, and victory made certain.

"I had taken my position near Rickett's and Griffin's

batteries on the right of our line, and decided to follow them up, not only because they were doing splendid work, but also for the reason that they would naturally be given commanding positions at vital points. By about two o'clock we had occupied the Warrenton Turnpike; and we justly felt that much had been gained. The Confederate lines between the two houses on the hill had given way; and from the sounds we heard, they must have been driven back also by a charge on our extreme left. Indeed, there was scarcely anything to be seen of the foe that thus far had been not only seen but felt.

"From a height near the batteries where I stood, the problem appeared somewhat clear to me. We had driven the enemy up and over a hill of considerable altitude, and across an uneven plateau, and they were undoubtedly in the woods beyond, a splendid position which commanded the entire open space over which we must advance to reach them. They were in cover; we should be in full view in all efforts to dislodge them. Their very reverses had secured for them a position worth half a dozen regiments; and I trembled as I thought of our raw militia advancing under conditions that would try the courage of veterans. You remember that if Washington, in the Revolution, could get his new recruits behind a rail-fence, they thought they were safe.

"Well, there was no help for it. The hill and plateau must be crossed under a pointblank fire, in order to reach the enemy, and that, too, by men who had been under arms since midnight, and the majority wearied by a long march under a blazing sun.

"About half-past two, when the assault began, a strange and ominous quiet rested on the field. As I have said, the enemy had disappeared. The men scarcely knew what to think of it; and in some a false confidence, speedily dispelled, was begotten. Rickett's battery was moved down across the valley to the top of a hill just beyond the residence owned and occupied by a Mrs. Henry. I followed and entered the house, already shattered by shot and shell, curious to know whether it was occupied, and by whom. Pitiful to relate, I found that Mrs. Henry was a widow and a helpless invalid. The poor woman was in mortal terror; and it was my hope to return and carry her to some place of safety, but the swift and deadly tide of war gave me no chance.'

"Ricketts' battery had scarcely unlimbered before death was busy among his cannoneers and even his horses. The enemy had the cover not only of the woods, but of a second growth of pines, which fringed them and completely concealed the Rebel sharpshooters. When a man fell, nothing could be seen but a puff of smoke. These little jets and wreaths of smoke half encircled us, and made but a phantom-like target for our people; and I think it speaks well for officers and men that they not only did their duty, but that Griffin's battery also came up, and that both batteries held their own against a terrific pointblank fire from the Rebel cannon, which certainly exceeded ours in number. The range was exceedingly short, and a more terrific artillery duel it would be hard to imagine. At the same time the more deadly little puffs of smoke continued; and men in every attitude of duty would suddenly throw up their hands and fall. The batteries had no business to be so exposed, and their supports were of no real service.

"I can give you an idea of what occurred at this point only; but, from the sounds I heard, there was very heavy fighting elsewhere, which I fear, however, was too spasmodic and ill-directed to accomplish the required ends. A heavy, persistent, concentrated attack, a swift push with the bayonet through the low pines and woods, would have saved the day. Perhaps our troops were not equal to it; and yet, poor fellows, they did braver things that were utterly useless.

"I still believe, however, all might have gone well, had

---

¹ Mrs. Henry, although confined to her bed, was wounded two or three times, and died soon afterward.

it not been for a horrible mistake. I was not very far from Captain Griffin, and was watching his cool, effective super-intendence of his guns, when suddenly I noticed a regiment in full view on our right advancing toward us. Griffin caught sight of it at the same moment, and seemed amazed. Were they Confederates or National? was the question to be decided instantly. They might be his own support. Doubtful and yet exceedingly apprehensive, he ordered his guns to be loaded with canister and trained upon this dubious force that had come into view like an apparition; but he still hesitated, restrained, doubtless, by the fearful thought of annihilating a Union regiment.

"'Captain,' said Major Barry, chief of artillery, 'they are your battery support.'

"'They are Confederates,' Griffin replied, intensely excited. 'As certain as the world, they are Confederates.'

"'No,' was the answer, 'I know they are your battery support.'

"I had ridden up within ear-shot, and levelled my glass upon them. 'Don't fire,' cried Griffin, and he spurred forward to satisfy himself.

"At the same moment the regiment, now within short range, by a sudden instantaneous act levelled their muskets at us. I saw we were doomed, and yet by some instinct tightened my rein while I dug my spurs into my horse. He reared instantly. I saw a line of fire, and then poor Mayburn fell upon me, quivered, and was dead. The body of a man broke my fall in such a way that I was not hurt. Indeed, at the moment I was chiefly conscious of intense anger and disgust. If Griffin had followed his instinct and destroyed that regiment, as he could have done by one discharge, the result of the whole battle might have been different. As it was, both his and Rickett's batteries were practically annihilated." [1]

___

[1] Since the above was written Colonel Hasbrouck has given me an account of this crisis in the battle. He was sufficiently near to hear the conversation found in the text, and to enable me to supplement it by fuller details. Cap-

The major uttered an imprecation.

"I was pinned to the ground by the weight of my horse, but not so closely but that I could look around. The carnage had been frightful. But few were on their feet, and they in rapid motion to the rear. The horses left alive rushed down the hill with the caissons, spreading dismay, confusion, and disorder through the ascending line of battle. Our supporting regiment in the rear, that had been lying on their arms, sprang to their feet and stood like men paralyzed with horror; meanwhile, the Rebel regiment, re-enforced, was advancing rapidly on the disabled guns—their defenders lay beneath and around them—firing as they came. Our support gave them one ineffectual volley, then turned and fled."

tain Griffin emphatically declared that no Union regiment could possibly come from that quarter, adding, "They are dressed in gray."

Major Barry with equal emphasis asserted that they were National troops, and unfortunately we had regiments in gray uniforms. Seeing that Captain Griffin was not convinced, he said peremptorily, "I command you not to fire on that regiment."

Of course this direct order ended the controversy, and Captain Griffin directed that his guns be shifted again toward the main body of the enemy, while he rode forward a little space to reconnoitre.

During all this fatal delay the Confederate regiment was approaching, marching by the flank, and so passed at one time within pointblank range of the guns that would scarcely have left a man upon his feet. The nature of their advance was foolhardy in the extreme, and at the time that Captain Griffin wished to fire they were practically helpless. A Virginia worm-fence was in their path, and so frightened, nervous, and excited were they that, instead of tearing it down, they began clambering over it until by weight and numbers it was trampled under foot.

They approached so near that the order to "fire low" was distinctly heard by our men as the Confederates went into battle-line formation.

The scene following their volley almost defies description. The horses attached to caissons not only tore down and through the ascending National battle-line, but Colonel—then Lieutenant—Hasbrouck saw several teams dash over the knoll toward the Confederate regiment, that opened ranks to let them pass. So novel were the scenes of war at that time that the Confederates were as much astonished as the members of the batteries left alive, and at first did not advance, although it was evident that there were, at the moment, none to oppose them. The storm of Rebel bullets had ranged so low that Lieutenant Hasbrouck and Captain Griffin owed their safety to the fact that they were mounted. The horses of both officers were wounded. On the way down the northern slope of the hill, with the few Union survivors, Captain Griffin met Major Barry, and in his intense anger and grief reproached him bitterly. The latter gloomily admitted that he had been mistaken.

Captain Ricketts was wounded, and the battle subsequently surged back and forth over his prostrate form, but eventually he was sent as a captive to Richmond.

Again the major relieved his mind in his characteristic way.

"But you, Alford?" cried Grace, leaning forward with clasped hands, while his aunt came and buried her face upon his shoulder. "Are you keeping your promise to live?" she whispered.

"Am I not here safe and sound?" he replied, cheerily. "Nothing much happened to me, Grace. When I saw the enemy was near, I merely doubled myself up under my horse, and was nothing to them but a dead Yankee. I was only somewhat trodden upon, as I told you, when the Confederates tried to turn the guns against our forces.

"I fear I am doing a wrong to the ladies by going into these sanguinary details."

"No," said the major, emphatically; "Mrs. Mayburn would have been a general had she been a man; and Grace has heard about battles all her life. It's a great deal better to understand from the start what this war means."

"I especially wished Hilland to hear the details of this battle as far as I saw them, for I think they contain lessons that may be of great service to him. That he would engage in the war was a foregone conclusion from the first; and with his means and ability he may take a very important part in it. But of this later.

"As I told you, I made the rather close acquaintance of your kin, Grace, and can testify that the 'fa' of their feet' was not 'fairy-like.' Before they could accomplish their purpose of turning the guns on our lines, I heard the rushing tramp of a multitude, with defiant shouts and yells. Rebels fell around me. The living left the guns, sought to form a line, but suddenly gave way in dire confusion, and fled to the cover from which they came. A moment later a body of our men surged like an advancing wave over the spot they had occupied.

"Now was my chance; and I reached up and seized the hand of a tall, burly Irishman.

" What the divil du ye want?" he cried, and in his

mad excitement was about to thrust me through for a Confederate.

" 'Halt!' I thundered. The familiar word of command restrained him long enough for me to secure his attention. 'Would you kill a Union man?' "

" 'Is it Union ye are? What yez doin' here, thin, widut a uniform?'

"I showed him my badge of correspondent, and explained briefly.

"Strange as it may seem to you, he uttered a loud, jolly laugh. 'Faix, an' it's a writer ye are. Ye'll be apt to git some memmyrandums the day that ye'll carry about wid ye till ye die, and that may be in about a minnit. I'll shtop long enough to give yez a lift, or yez hoss, rather;' and he seized poor Mayburn by the head. His excitement seemed to give him the strength of a giant, for in a moment I was released and stood erect.

" 'Give me a musket,' I cried, 'and I'll stand by you.'

" 'Bedad, hilp yersilf,' he replied, pushing forward. 'There's plenty o' fellers lyin' aroun' that has no use for them;' and he was lost in the confused advance.

"All this took place in less time than it takes to describe it, for events at that juncture were almost as swift as bullets. Lame as I was, I hobbled around briskly, and soon secured a good musket with a supply of cartridges. As with the rest, my blood was up—don't smile, Hilland: I had been pretty cool until the murderous discharge that killed my horse—and I was soon in the front line, firing with the rest.

"Excited as I was, I saw that our position was desperate, for a heavy force of Confederates was swarming toward us. I looked around and saw that part of our men were trying to drag off the guns. This seemed the more important work; and discretion also whispered that with my bruised foot I should be captured in five minutes unless I was further to the rear. So I took a pull at a gun; but we had made little progress before there was another great surging wave from the other direction, and our forces were swept down the hill again, I along with the rest. The confusion was fearful; the regiments with which I had been acting went all to pieces, and had no more organization than if they had been mixed up by a whirlwind.

"I was becoming too lame to walk, and found myself in a serious dilemma."

"Ha! ha! ha!" laughed Hilland. "It was just becoming serious, eh?"

"Well, I didn't realize my lameness before; and as retreat was soon to be the order of the day, there was little prospect of my doing my share. As I was trying to extricate myself from the shattered regiments, I saw a riderless horse plunging toward me. To seize his bridle and climb into the saddle was the work of a moment; and I felt that, unlike McDowell, I was still master of the situation. Working my way out of the press and to our right, I saw that another charge for the guns by fresh troops was in progress. It seemed successful at first. The guns were retaken, but soon the same old story was repeated, and a corresponding rush from the other side swept our men back.

"Would you believe it, this capture and recapture occurred several times. A single regiment even would dash forward, and actually drive the Rebels back, only to lose a few moments later what they had gained. Never was there braver fighting, never worse tactics. The repeated successes of small bodies of troops proved that a compact battle line could have swept the ridge, and not only retaken the guns, but made them effective in the conflict. As it was, the two sides worried and tore each other like great dogs, governed merely by the impulse and instinct of fight. The batteries were the bone between them.

"This senseless, wasteful struggle could not go on forever. That it lasted as long as it did speaks volumes in favor of the material of which our future soldiers are to be made. As I rode slowly from the line and scene of actual battle, of which I had had enough, I became disheartened. We had men in plenty—there were thousands on every side

—but in what condition! There was no appearance of fear among the men I saw at about four P.M. (I can only guess the time, for my watch had stopped), but abundant evidence of false confidence and still more of the indifference of men who feel they have done all that should be required of them and are utterly fagged out. Multitudes, both officers and privates, were lying and lounging around waiting for their comrades to finish the ball.

"For instance, I would ask a man to what regiment he belonged, and he would tell me.

"'Where is it?'

"'Hanged if I know. Saw a lot of the boys awhile ago.'

"Said an officer in answer to my inquiries, 'No; I don't know where the colonel is, and I don't care. After one of our charges we all adjourned like a town meeting. I'm played out; have been on my feet since one o'clock last night.'

"These instances were characteristic of the state of affairs in certain parts of the field that I visited. Plucky or conscientious fellows would join their comrades in the fight without caring what regiment they acted with; but the majority of the great disorganized mass did what they pleased, after the manner of a country fair, crowding in all instances around places where water could be obtained. Great numbers had thrown away their canteens and provisions, as too heavy to carry in the heat, or as impediments in action. Officers and men were mixed up promiscuously, hobnobbing and chaffing in a languid way, and talking over their experiences, as if they were neighbors at home. The most wonderful part of it all was that they had no sense of their danger and of the destruction they were inviting by their unsoldierly course.

"I tried to impress these dangers on one or two, but the reply was, 'Oh, hang it! The Rebs are as badly used up as we are. Don't you see things are growing more quiet? Give us a rest!'

"By this time I had worked my way well to my right,

and was on a little eminence watching our line advance,
wondering at the spirit with which the fight was still maintained. Indeed, I grew hopeful once more as I saw the
good work that the regiments still intact were doing.
There was much truth in the remark that the Rebels were
used up also, unless they had reserves of which we knew
nothing. At that time we had no idea that we had been
fighting, not only Beauregard, but also Johnson from the
Shenandoah.

"My hope was exceedingly intensified by the appearance of a long line of troops emerging from the woods on
our flank and rear, for I never dreamed that they could be
other than our own re-enforcements. Suddenly I caught
sight of a flag which I had learned to know too well. The
line halted a moment, muskets were levelled, and I found
myself in a perfect storm of bullets. I assure you I made a
rapid change of base, for when our line turned I should be
between two fires. As it was, I was cut twice in this arm
while galloping away. In a few moments a battery also
opened upon our flank; and it became as certain as day
that a large Confederate force from some quarter had been
hurled upon the flank and rear of our exhausted forces.
The belief that Johnson's army had arrived spread like
wildfire. How absurd and crude it all seems now! We
had been fighting Johnson from the first.

"All aggressive action on our part now ceased; and as if
governed by one common impulse, the army began its retreat.

"Try to realize it. Our retirement was not ordered.
There were thousands to whom no order could be given
unless with a voice like a thunder peal. Indeed, one may
say, the order was given by the thunder of that battery on
our flank. It was heard throughout the field; and the
army, acting as individuals or in detachments, decided to
leave. To show how utterly bereft of guidance, control,
and judgment were our forces, I have merely to say that
each man started back by exactly the same route he had
come, just as a horse would do, while right before them

was the Warrenton Pike, a good, straight road direct to Centerville, which was distant but little over four miles.

"This disorganized, exhausted mob was as truly in just the fatal condition for the awful contagion we call 'panic' as it would have been from improper food and other causes, for some other epidemic. The Greeks, who always had a reason for everything, ascribed the nameless dread, the sudden and unaccountable fear, which bereaves men of manhood and reason, to the presence of a god. It is simply a latent human weakness, which certain conditions rarely fail to develop. They were all present at the close of that fatal day. I tell you frankly that I felt something of it myself, and at a time, too, when I knew I was not in the least immediate danger. To counteract it I turned and rode deliberately toward the enemy, and the emotion passed. I half believe, however, that if I had yielded, it would have carried me away like an attack of the plague. The moral of it all is, that the conditions of the disease should be guarded against.

"When it became evident that the army was uncontrollable and was leaving the field, I pressed my way to the vicinity of McDowell to see what he would do. What could he do? I never saw a man so overwhelmed with astonishment and anger. Almost to the last I believe he expected to win the day. He and his officers commanded, stormed, entreated. He might as well have tried to stop Niagara above the falls as that human tide. He sent orders in all directions for a general concentration at Centerville, and then with certain of his staff galloped away. I tried to follow, but was prevented by the interposing crowd.

"I then joined a detachment of regulars and marines, who marched quietly in prompt obedience of orders; and we made our way through the disorder like a steamer through the surging waves. All the treatises on discipline that were ever written would not have been so convincing as that little oasis of organization. They marched very slowly, and often halted to cover the retreat.

"I had now seen enough on the further bank of Bull Run, and resolved to push ahead as fast as my horse would walk to the eastern side. Moreover, my leg and wounds were becoming painful, and I was exceedingly weary. I naturally followed the route taken by Tyler's command in coming upon and returning from the field, and crossed Bull Run some distance above the Stone Bridge. The way was so impeded by fugitives that my progress was slow, but when I at last reached the Warrenton Turnpike and proceeded toward a wretched little stream called Cub Run, I witnessed a scene that beggars description.

"Throughout the entire day, and especially in the afternoon, vehicles of every description—supply wagons, ambulances, and the carriages of civilians—had been congregating in the Pike vicinity of Stone Bridge. When the news of the defeat reached this point, and the roar of cannon and musketry began to approach instead of recede, a general movement toward Centerville began. This soon degenerated into the wildest panic, and the road was speedily choked by storming, cursing, terror-stricken men, who in their furious haste, defeated their own efforts to escape. It was pitiful, it was shameful, to see ambulances full of the wounded shoved to one side and left by the cowardly thieves who had galloped away on the horses. It was one long scene of wreck and ruin, through which pressed a struggling, sweating, cursing throng. Horses with their traces cut, and carrying two and even three men, were urged on and over everybody that could not get out of the way. Everything was abandoned that would impede progress, and arms and property of all kinds were left as a rich harvest for the pursuing Confederates. Their cavalry, hovering near, like hawks eager for the prey, made dashes here and there, as opportunity offered.

"I picked my way through the woods rather than take my chances in the road, and so my progress was slow. To make matters tenfold worse, I found when I reached the road leading to the north through the 'Big Woods' that the head of the column that had come all the way around by Sudley's Ford, the route of the morning march, was mingling with the masses already thronging the Pike. The confusion, the selfish, remorseless scramble to get ahead, seemed as horrible as it could be; but imagine the condition of affairs when on reaching the vicinity of Cub Run we found that a Rebel battery had opened upon the bridge, our only visible means of crossing. A few moments later, from a little eminence, I saw a shot take effect on a team of horses; and a heavy caisson was overturned directly in the centre of the bridge, barring all advance, while the mass of soldiers, civilians, and nondescript army followers, thus detained under fire, became perfectly wild with terror. The caisson was soon removed, and the throng rushed on.

"I had become so heart-sick, disgusted, and weary of the whole thing, that my one impulse was to reach Centerville, where I supposed we should make a stand. As I was on the north side of the Pike, I skirted up the stream with a number of others until we found a place where we could scramble across, and soon after we passed within a brigade of our troops that were thrown across the road to check the probable pursuit of the enemy.

"On reaching Centerville, we found everything in the direst confusion. Colonel Miles, who com anded the reserves at that point, was unfit for the position, and had given orders that had imperilled the entire army. It was said that the troops which had come around by Sudley's ford had lost all their guns at Cub Run; and the fugitives arriving were demoralized to the last degree. Indeed, a large part of the army, without waiting for orders or paying heed to any one, continued their flight toward Washington. Holding the bridle of my horse, I lay down near headquarters to rest and to learn what would be done. A council of war was held, and as the result we were soon on the retreat again. The retreat, or panic-stricken flight rather, had, in fact, never ceased on the part of most of those who had been in the main battle. That they could keep up this desperate tramp was a remarkable example of human endurance when sustained by excitement, fear, or any strong emotion. The men who marched or fled on Sunday night had already been on their feet twenty-four hours, and the greater part of them had experienced the terrific strain of actual battle.

"My story has already been much too long. From the daily journals you have learned pretty accurately what occurred after we reached Centerville. Richardson's and Blenker's brigades made a quiet and orderly retreat when all danger to the main body was over. The sick and wounded were left behind with spoils enough to equip a good-sized Confederate army. I followed the headquarters escort, and eventually made my way into Washington in the drenching rain of Monday, and found the city crowded with fugitives to whom the loyal people were extending unbounded hospitality. I felt ill and feverish, and yielded to the impulse to reach home; and I never acted more wisely.

"Now you have the history of my first battle; and may I never see one like it again. And yet I believe the battle of Bull Run will become one of the most interesting studies of American history and character. On our side it was not directed by generals, according to the rules of war. It was fought by Northern men after their own fashion and according to their native genius; and I shall ever maintain that it was fought far better than could have been expected of militia who knew less of the practical science of war than of the philosophy of Plato.

"The moral of my story, Hilland, scarcely needs pointing; and it applies to us both. When we go, let us go as soldiers; and if we have only a corporal's command, let us lead soldiers. The grand Northern onset of which you have dreamed so long has been made. You have seen the result. You have the means and ability to equip and command a regiment. Infuse into it your own spirit; and at the same time make it a machine that will hold together as long as you have a man left."

"Graham," said Hilland, slowly and deliberately, "there is no resisting the logic of events. You have convinced me of my error, and I shall follow your advice."

"And, Grace," concluded Graham, "believe me, by so doing he adds tenfold to his chances of living to a good old age."

"Yes," she said, looking at him gratefully through tear-dimmed eyes. "You have convinced me of that also."

"Instead of rushing off to some out-of-the-way place or camp, he must spend months in recruiting and drilling his men; and you can be with him."

"Oh, Alford!" she exclaimed, "is that the heavenly logic of your long, terrible story?"

"It's the rational logic; you could not expect any other kind from me."

"Well, Graham," ejaculated the major, with a long sigh of relief, "I wouldn't have missed your account of the battle for a year's pay. And mark my words, young men, you may not live to see it, or I either, but the North will win in this fight. That's the fact that I'm convinced of in spite of the panic."

"The fact that I'm convinced of," said Mrs. Mayburn brusquely, mopping her eyes meanwhile, "is that Alford needs rest. I'm going to take him home at once." And the young man seconded her in spite of all protestations.

"Dear, vigilant old aunty," said Graham, when they were alone, "you know when I have reached the limit of endurance."

"Ah! Alford, Alford," moaned the poor woman, "I fear you are seeking death in this war."

He looked at her tenderly for a moment, and then said, "Hereafter I will try to take no greater risks than a soldier's duties require."

CHAPTER XXII

SELF—SENTENCED

DAYS, weeks, and months with their changes came
and went. Hilland, with characteristic promptness,
carried out his friend's suggestion; and through his
own means and personal efforts, in great measure, recruited
and equipped a regiment of cavalry. He was eager that his
friend should take a command in it; but Graham firmly
refused.

"Our relations are too intimate for discipline," he said.
"We might be placed in situations wherein our friendship
would embarrass us."

Grace surmised that he had another reason; for, as time
passed, she saw less and less of him. He had promptly obtained a lieutenancy in a regiment that was being recruited
at Washington; and by the time her husband's regiment
reached that city, the more disciplined organization to
which Graham was attached was ordered out on the Virginia picket line beyond Arlington Heights.

Hilland, with characteristic modesty, would not take the
colonelcy of the regiment that he chiefly had raised; but
secured for the place a fine officer of the regular army, and
contented himself with a captaincy. "Efficiency of the
service is what I am aiming at," he said. "I would much
rather rise by merit from the ranks than command a brigade
by favor."

Unlike many men of wealth, he had a noble repugnance
to taking any public advantage of it; and the numerous

officers of the time that had obtained their positions by influence were his detestation.

Graham's predictions in regard to Grace were fulfilled. For long months she saw her husband almost daily, and, had it not been for the cloud that hung over the future, it would have been one of the happiest periods of her life. She saw Hilland engaged in tasks that brought him a deep and growing satisfaction. She saw her father in his very element. There were no more days of dulness and weariness for him. The daily journals teemed with subjects of interest, and with their aid he planned innumerable campaigns. Military men were coming and going, and with these young officers the veteran was an oracle. He gave Hilland much shrewd advice; and even when it was not good, it was listened to with deference, and so the result was just as agreeable to the major.

What sweeter joy is there for the aged than to sit in the seat of judgment and counsel, and feel that the world would go awry were it not for the guidance and aid of their experience! Alas for the poor old major, and those like him! The world does not grow old as they do. It only changes and becomes more vast and complicated. What was wisest and best in their day becomes often as antiquated as the culverin that once defended castellated ramparts.

Happily the major had as yet no suspicion of this; and when he and Grace accompanied Hilland and his regiment to Washington, the measure of his content was full. There he could daily meet other veterans of the regular service; and in listening to their talk, one might imagine that McClellan had only to attend their sittings to learn how to subdue the rebellion within a few months. These veterans were not bitter partisans. General Robert E. Lee was "Bob Lee" to them; and the other chiefs of the Confederacy were spoken of by some familiar *sobriquet*, acquired in many instances when boys at West Point. They would have fought these old friends and acquaintances to the bitter end, according to the tactics of the old school; but after the battle, those that survived would have hobnobbed together over a bottle of wine as sociably as if they had been companions in arms.

Mrs. Mayburn accompanied the major's party to Washington, for, as she said, she was "hungry for a sight of her boy." As often as his duties permitted, Graham rode in from the front to see her. But it began to be noticed that after these visits he ever sought some perilous duty on the picket line, or engaged in some dash at the enemy or guerillas in the vicinity. He could not visit his aunt without seeing Grace, whose tones were now so gentle when she spoke to him, and so full of her heart's deep gratitude, that a renewal of his old fierce fever of unrest was the result. He was already gaining a reputation for extreme daring, combined with unusual coolness and vigilance; and before the campaign of '62 opened he had been promoted to a first lieutenancy.

Time passed; the angry torrent of the war broadened and deepened. Men and measures that had stood out like landmarks were engulfed and forgotten.

It goes without saying that the friends did their duty in camp and field. There were no more panics. The great organizer, McClellan, had made soldiers of the vast army; and had he been retained in the service as the creator of armies for other men to lead, his labors would have been invaluable.

At last, to the deep satisfaction of Graham and Hilland, their regiments were brigaded together, and they frequently met. It was then near the close of the active operations of '62, and the friends now ranked as Captain Graham and Major Hilland. Notwithstanding the reverses suffered by the Union arms, the young men's confidence was unabated as to the final issue. Hilland had passed through several severe conflicts, and his name had been mentioned by reason of his gallantry. Grace began to feel that fate could never be so cruel as to destroy her very life in his life. She saw that her father exulted more over her husband's soldierly qualities than in all his wealth; and although they spent the summer season as usual at the seaside with Mrs. Mayburn, the hearts of all three were following two regiments through the forests and fields of Virginia. Half a score of journals were daily searched for items concerning them, and the arrival of the mails was the event of the day.

There came a letter in the autumn which filled the heart of Grace with immeasurable joy and very, very deep sadness. Mrs. Mayburn was stricken to the heart, and would not be comforted, while the old major swore and blessed God by turns.

The cause was this. The brigade with which the friends were connected was sent on a *reconnoissance*, and they felt the enemy strongly before retiring, which at last they were compelled to do precipitately. It so happened that Hilland commanded the rear-guard. In an advance he ever led; on a retreat he was apt to keep well to the rear. In the present instance the pursuit had been prompt and determined, and he had been compelled to make more than one repelling charge to prevent the retiring column from being pressed too hard. His command had thus lost heavily, and at last overwhelming numbers drove them back at a gallop.

Graham, in the rear of the main column, which had just crossed a small wooden bridge over a wide ditch or little run through the fields, saw the headlong retreat of Hilland's men, and he instantly deployed his company that he might check the close pursuit by a volley. As the Union troopers neared the bridge it was evidently a race for life and liberty, for they were outnumbered ten to one. In a few moments they began to pour over, but Hilland did not lead. They were nearly all across, but their commander was not among them; and Graham was wild with anxiety as he sat on his horse at the right of his line waiting to give the order to fire. Suddenly, in the failing light of the evening, he saw Hilland with his right arm hanging helpless, spurring a horse badly blown; while gaining fast upon him were four savage-looking Confederates, their sabres emitting a steely, deadly sheen, and uplifted to strike the moment they could reach him.

With the rapidity of light, Graham's eye measured the distance between his friend and the bridge, and his instantaneous conviction was that Hilland was doomed, for he could not order a volley without killing him almost to a certainty. At that supreme crisis, the suggestion passed through his mind like a lurid flash, "In a few moments Hilland will be dead, and Grace may yet be mine."

Then, like an avenging demon, the thought confronted him. He saw it in its true aspect, and in an outburst of self-accusing fury he passed the death sentence on himself. Snatching out the long, straight sword he carried, he struck with the spur the noble horse he bestrode, gave him the rein, and made straight for the deep, wide ditch. There was no time to go around by the bridge, which was still impeded by the last of the fugitives.

His men held their breath as they saw his purpose. The feat seemed impossible; but as his steed cleared the chasm by a magnificent bound, a loud cheer rang down the line. The next moment Hilland, who had mentally said farewell to his wife, saw Graham passing him like a thunderbolt. There was an immediate clash of steel, and then the foremost pursuer was down, cleft to the jaw. The next shared the same fate; for Graham, in what he deemed his death struggle, had almost ceased to be human. His spirit, stung to a fury that it had never known and would never know again, blazed in his eyes and flashed in the lightning play of his sword. The two others pursuers reined up their steeds and sought to attack him on either side. He threw his own horse back almost upon his haunches, and was on his guard, meaning to strike home the moment the fence of his opponents permitted. At this instant, however, there were a dozen shots from the swarming Rebels, that were almost upon him, and he and his horse were seen to fall to the ground. Meantime Hilland had instinctively tried to rein in his horse, that he might return to the help of his friend, although from his wound he could render no aid. Some of his own men who had crossed the bridge, and in a sense of safety had regained their wits, saw his purpose, and dashing back, they formed a body-guard around him, and dragged his horse swiftly beyond the line of battle.

A yell of anger accompanied by a volley came from Graham's men that he had left in line, and a dozen Confederate saddles were emptied; but their return fire was so deadly, and their numbers were so overwhelming, that the officer next in command ordered retreat at a gallop. Hilland, in his anguish, would not have left his friend had not his men grasped his rein and carried him off almost by force. Meanwhile the darkness set in so rapidly that the pursuit soon slackened and ceased.

During the remainder of the ride back to their camp, which was reached late at night, the ardent-natured Hilland was almost demented. He wept, raved, and swore. He called himself an accursed coward, that he had left the friend who had saved his life. His broken arm was as nothing to him, and eventually the regimental surgeon had to administer strong opiates to quiet him.

When late the next day he awoke, it all came back to him with a dully heavy ache at heart. Nothing could be done. His mind, now restored to its balance, recognized the fact. The brigade was under orders to move to another point, and he was disabled and compelled to take a leave of absence until fit for duty. The inexorable mechanism of military life moves on, without the slightest regard for the individual; and Graham's act was only one of the many heroic deeds of the war, some seen and more unnoted.

CHAPTER XXIII

AN EARLY DREAM FULFILLED

A FEW days later Grace welcomed her husband with a long, close embrace, but with streaming eyes; while he bowed his head upon her shoulder and groaned in the bitterness of his spirit.

"Next to losing you, Grace," he said, "this is the heaviest blow I could receive; and to think that he gave his life for me! How can I ever face Mrs. Mayburn?"

But his wife comforted him as only she knew how to soothe and bless; and Mrs. Mayburn saw that he was as sincere a mourner as herself. Moreover they would not despair of Graham, for although he had been seen to fall, he might only have been wounded and made a prisoner. Thus the bitterness of their grief was mitigated by hope.

This hope was fulfilled in a most unexpected way, by a cheerful letter from Graham himself; and the explanation of this fact requires that the story should return to him.

He thought that the sentence of death which he had passed upon himself had been carried into effect. He had felt himself falling, and then there had been sudden darkness. Like a dim taper flickering in the night, the spark of life began to kindle again. At first he was conscious of but one truth—that he was not dead. Where he now was, in this world or some other, what he now was, he did not know; but the essential *ego*, Alford Graham, had not ceased to exist. The fact filled him with a dull, wondering awe. Memory slowly revived, and its last impression was that he was to die and had died, and yet he was not dead.

As a man's characteristic traits will first assert themselves, he lay still and feebly tried to comprehend it all.
Suddenly a strange, horrid sound smote upon his senses
and froze his blood with dread. It must be life after death,
for only his mind appeared to have any existence. He could
not move. Again the unearthly sound, which could not be
a human shriek, was repeated; and by half-involuntary and
desperate effort he started up and looked around. The scene
at first was obscure, confused, and awful. His eye could
not explain it, and he instinctively stretched out his hands;
and through the sense of touch all that had happened came
back to his confused brain. He first felt of himself, passed
his hand over his forehead, his body, his limbs: he certainly was in the flesh, and that to his awakening intelligence meant much, since it accorded with his belief that
life and the body were inseparable. Then he felt around
him in the darkness, and his hands touched the grassy
field. This fact righted him speedily. As in the old
fable, when he touched the earth he was strong. He next
noted that his head rested on a smooth rock that rose but
little above the plain, and that he must have fallen upon it.
He sat up and looked around; and as the brain gradually
resumed its action after its terrible shock, the situation became intelligible. The awful sounds that he had heard
came from a wounded horse that was struggling feebly in
the light of the rising moon, now in her last quarter. He
was upon the scene of last evening's conflict, and the obscure objects that lay about him were the bodies of the
dead. Yes, there before him were the two men he had
killed; and their presence brought such a strong sense of
repugnance and horror that he sprang to his feet and recoiled away.

He looked around. There was not a living object in
sight except the dying horse. The night wind moaned
about him, and soughed and sighed as if it were a living
creature mourning over the scene.

It became clear to him that he had been left as dead.

Yes, and he had been robbed, too; for he shivered, and
found that his coat and vest were gone, also his hat, his
money, his watch, and his boots. He walked unsteadily to
the little bridge, and where he had left his line of faithful
men, all was dark and silent. With a great throb of joy he
remembered that Hilland must have sped across that bridge
to safety, while he had expiated his evil thought.

He then returned and circled around the place. He was
evidently alone; but the surmise occurred to him that the
Confederates would return in the morning to bury their
dead, and if he would escape he must act promptly. And
yet he could not travel in his present condition. He must
at least have hat, coat, and boots. His only resource was
to take them from the dead; but the thought of doing so
was horrible to him. Reason about it as he might, he drew
near their silent forms with an uncontrollable repugnance.
He almost gave up his purpose, and took a few hasty steps
away, but a thorn pierced his foot and taught him his folly.
Then his imperious will asserted itself, and with an imprecation on his weakness he returned to the nearest silent form,
and took from it a limp felt hat, a coat, and a pair of boots,
all much the worse for wear; and having arrayed himself in
these, started on the trail of the Union force.

He had not gone over a mile when, on surmounting an
eminence, he saw by dying fires in a grove beneath him
that he was near the bivouac of a body of soldiers. He
hardly hoped they could be a detachment of Union men;
and yet the thought that it was possible led him to approach stealthily within earshot. At last he heard one
patrol speak to another in unmistakable Southern accent,
and he found that the enemy was in his path.

Silently as a ghost he stole away, and sought to make a
wide detour to the left, but soon lost himself hopelessly in
a thick wood. At last, wearied beyond mortal endurance,
he crawled into what seemed the obscurest place he could
find, and lay down and slept.

The sun was above the horizon when he awoke, stiff,

sore, and hungry, but refreshed, rested. A red squirrel was barking at him derisively from a bough near, but no other evidences of life were to be seen. Sitting up, he tried to collect his thoughts and decide upon his course. It at once occurred to him that he would be missed, and that pursuit might be made with hounds. At once he sprang to his feet and made his way toward a valley, which he hoped would be drained by a running stream. The welcome sound of water soon guided him, and pushing through the underbrush he drank long and deeply, bathed the ugly bruise on his head, and then waded up the current.

He had not gone much over half a mile before he saw through an opening a negro gazing wonderingly at him. "Come here, my good fellow," he cried.

The man approached slowly, cautiously.

"I won't hurt you," Graham resumed; "indeed you can see that I'm in your power. Won't you help me?"

"Dunno, mas'r," was the non-committal reply.

"Are you in favor of Lincoln's men or the Confederates?"

"Dunno, mas'r. It 'pends."

"It depends upon what?"

"On whedder you'se a Linkum man or 'Federate."

"Well, then, here's the truth. The Lincoln men are your best friends, if you've sense enough to know it; and I'm one of them. I was in the fight off there yesterday, and am trying to escape."

"Oh golly! I'se sense enough;" and the genial gleam of the man's ivory was an omen of good to Graham. "But," queried the negro, "how you wear 'Federate coat and hat?"

"Because I was left for dead, and mine were stolen. I had to wear something. The Confederates don't wear blue trousers like these."

"Dat's so; an' I knows yer by yer talk and look. I knows a 'Federate well as I does a coon. But dese yere's mighty ticklish times; an' a nigger hab no show ef he's foun' meddlin'. What's yer gwine ter do?"

"Perhaps you can advise me. I'm afraid they'll put hounds on my trail."

"Dat dey will, if dey misses yer."

"Well, that's the reason I'm here in the stream. But I can't keep this up long. I'm tired and hungry. I've heard that you people befriended Lincoln's men. We are going to win, and now's the time for you to make friends with those who will soon own this country."

"Ob corse, you'se a-gwine ter win. Linkum is de Moses we're all a-lookin' ter. At all our meetin's we'se a-prayin' for him and to him. He's de Lord's right han' to lead we alls out ob bondage."

"Well, I swear to you I'm one of his men."

"I knows you is, and I'se a-gwine to help you, houn's or no houn's. Keep up de run a right smart ways, and you'se 'll come ter a big flat stun'. Stan' dar in de water, an I'll be dar wid help." And the man disappeared in a long swinging run.

Graham did as he was directed, and finally reached a flat rock, from which through the thick bordering growth something like a path led away. He waited until his patience was wellnigh exhausted, and then heard far back upon his trail the faint bay of a hound. He was about to push his way on up the stream, when there was a sound of hasty steps, and his late acquaintance with another stalwart fellow appeared.

"Dere's no time ter lose, mas'r. Stan' whar you is," and in a moment he splashed in beside him. "Now get on my back. Jake dar will spell me when I wants him; fer yer feet mustn't touch de groun';" and away they went up the obscure path.

This was a familiar mode of locomotion to Graham, for he had been carried thus by the hour over the mountain passes of Asia. They had not gone far before they met two or three colored women with a basket of clothes.

"Dat's right," said Graham's conveyance; "wash away right smart, and dunno nothin'. Yer see," he continued, "dis yer is Sunday, and we'se not in de fields, an de women folks can help us;" and Graham thought that the old superstition of a Sabbath had served him well for once.

They soon left the path and entered some very heavy timber, through an opening of which he saw the negro quarters and plantation dwellings in the distance.

At last they stopped before an immense tree. Some brush was pushed aside, revealing an aperture through which Graham was directed to crawl, and he found himself within a heart of oak.

"Dar's room enough in dar ter sit down," said his sable friend. "An' you'se 'll find a jug ob milk an' a pone ob corn meal. Luck ter yer. Don't git lonesome like and come out. We'se a-gwine ter look arter yer;" and the opening was hidden by brush again, and Graham was left alone.

From a small aperture above his head a pencil of sunlight traversed the gloom, to which his eyes soon grew accustomed, and he saw a rude seat and the food mentioned. By extending his feet slightly through the opening by which he had entered, he found the seat really comfortable; and the coarse fare was ambrosial to his ravenous appetite. Indeed, he began to enjoy the adventure. His place of concealment was so unexpected and ingenious that it gave him a sense of security. He had ever had a great love for trees, and now it seemed as if one had opened its very heart to hide him.

Then his hosts and defenders interested him exceedingly. By reason of residence in New England and his life abroad, he was not familiar with the negro, especially his Southern type. Their innocent guile and preposterous religious belief amused him. He both smiled and wondered at their faith in "Linkum," whom at that time he regarded as a long-headed, uncouth Western politician, who had done not a little mischief by interfering with the army.

"It is ever so with all kinds of superstition and sentimental belief," he soliloquized. "Some conception of the mind is embodied, or some object is idealized and magnified until the original is lost sight of, and men come to worship a mere fancy of their own. Then some mind, stronger and more imaginative than the average, gives shape and form to this confused image; and so there grows in time a belief, a theology, or rather a mythology. To think that this Lincoln, whom I've seen in attitudes anything but divine, and telling broad, coarse stories—to think that he should be a demigod, antitype of the venerated Hebrew! In truth it leads one to suspect, according to analogy, that Moses was a money-making Jew, and his effort to lead his people to Palestine an extensive land speculation.''

Graham lived to see the day when he acknowledged that the poor negroes of the most remote plantations had a truer conception of the grand proportions of Lincoln's character at that time than the majority of his most cultivated countrymen.

His abstract speculations were speedily brought to a close by the nearer baying of hounds as they surmounted an eminence over which lay his trail. On came the hunt, with its echoes rising and falling with the wind or the inequalities of the ground, until it burst deep-mouthed and hoarse over the brow of the hill that sloped to the stream. Then there were confused sounds, both of the dogs and of men's voices, which gradually approached until there was a pause, caused undoubtedly by a colloquy with Aunt Sheba and her associate washerwomen. It did not last very long; and then, to Graham's dismay, the threatening sounds were renewed, and seemed coming directly toward him. He soon gave up all hope, and felt that he had merely to congratulate himself that, from the nature of his hiding-place, he could not be torn by the dogs, when he perceived that the hunt was coming no nearer—in brief, that it was passing. He then understood that his refuge must be near the bed of the stream, from which his pursuers were seeking on either side his diverging trail. This fact relieved him at once, and quietly he listened to the sounds, dying away as they had come.

As the sun rose higher the ray of light sloped downward until it disappeared; and in the profound gloom and quiet he fell asleep. He was awaked by hearing a voice call, "Mas'r."

Looking down, he saw that the brush had been removed, and that the opening was partially obstructed by a goblin-like head with little horns rising all over it.

"Mas'r," said the apparition, "Aunt Sheba sends you dis, and sez de Lord be wid you."

"Thanks for Aunt Sheba, and you, too, whatever you are," cried Graham; and to gratify his curiosity he sprang down on his knees and peered out in time to see a little negro girl replacing the brush, while what he had mistaken for horns was evidently the child's manner of wearing her hair. He then gave his attention to the material portion of Aunt Sheba's offering, and found a rude sort of platter, or low basket, made of corn husks, and in this another jug of milk, corn bread, and a delicious broiled chicken done to that turn of perfection of which only the colored aunties of the South are capable.

"Well!" ejaculated Graham. "From this day I'm an abolitionist, a Republican of the blackest dye." A little later he added, "Any race that can produce a woman capable of such cookery as this has a future before it."

Indeed, the whole affair was taking such an agreeable turn that he was inclined to be jocular.

After another long sleep in the afternoon, he was much refreshed, and eager to rejoin his command. But Issachar, or Iss, as his associates called him, the negro who had befriended him in the first instance, came and explained that the whole country was full of Confederates; and that it might be several days before it would be safe to seek the Union lines.

"We'se all lookin' out fer yer, mas'r," he continued; "you won't want for nothin'. An' we won't kep yer in dis woodchuck hole arter nine ob de ev'nin'. Don't try ter come out. I'm lookin' t'oder way while I'se a-talkin'.

Mean niggers an' 'Federates may be spyin' aroun'. But
I reckon not; I'se laid in de woods all day, a-watchin'.

"Now I tell yer what 'tis, mas'r, I'se made up my mine
to put out ob heah. I'se gwine ter jine de Linkum men
fust chance I gits. An' if yer'll wait an' trus' me, I'll take
yer slick and clean; fer I know dis yer country and ebery
hole whar ter hide well as a fox. If I gits safe ter de
Linkum folks, yer'll say a good word fer Iss, I reckon."

"Indeed, I will. If you wish, I'll take you into my own
service, and pay you good wages."

"Done, by golly; and when dey cotch us, dey'll cotch
a weasel asleep."

"But haven't you a wife and children?"

"Oh, yah. I'se got a wife, an' I'se got a lot ob chillen
somewhar in de 'Fed'racy; but I'll come wid you uns bime
by, an' gedder up all I can fine. I'se 'll come 'long in de
shank ob de ev'nin', mas'r, and guv yer a shakedown in
my cabin, an' I'll watch while yer sleeps. Den I'll bring
yer back heah befo' light in de mawnin'."

The presence of Confederate forces required these pre-
cautions for several days, and Iss won Graham's whole
heart by his unwearied patience and vigilance. But the
young man soon prevailed on the faithful fellow to sleep
nights while he watched; for after the long inaction of the
day he was almost wild for exercise. Cautious Iss would
have been nearly crazed with anxiety had he known of the
reconnaissances in which his charge indulged while he slept.
Graham succeeded in making himself fully master of the
disposition of the Rebel forces in the vicinity, and eventually learned that the greater part of them had been withdrawn. When he had communicated this intelligence to
Iss, they prepared to start for the Union lines on the following night, which proved dark and stormy.

Iss, prudent man, kept the secret of his flight from even
his wife, and satisfied his marital compunctions by chucking
her ander the chin and calling her "honey" once or twice
while she got supper for him. At eight in the evening he

summoned Graham from his hiding-place, and led him, with almost the unerring instinct of some wild creature of the night, due northeast, the direction in which the Union forces were said to be at that time.   It was a long, desolate tramp, and the dawn found them drenched and weary.   But the glorious sun rose warm and bright, and in a hidden glade of the forest they dried their clothes, rested, and refreshed themselves.   After a long sleep in a dense thicket they were ready to resume their journey at nightfall.   Iss proved an invaluable guide, for, concealing Graham, he would steal away, communicate with the negroes, and bring fresh provisions.

On the second night he learned that there was a Union force not very far distant to the north of their line of march. Graham had good cause to wonder at the sort of freemasonry that existed among the negroes, and the facility with which they obtained and transmitted secret intelligence.   Still more had he reason to bless their almost universal fidelity to the Union cause.

Another negro joined them as guide, and in the gray of the morning they approached the Union pickets.   Graham deemed it wise to wait till they could advance openly and boldly; and by nine o'clock he was received with acclamations by his own regiment as one risen from the dead.

After congratulations and brief explanations were over, his first task was to despatch the two brief letters mentioned, to his aunt and Hilland, in time to catch the daily mail that left their advanced position.   Then he saw his brigade commander, and made it clear to him that with a force of about two regiments he could strike a heavy blow against the Confederates whom he had been reconnoitring; and he offered to act as guide.   His proposition was accepted, and the attacking force started that very night.   By forced marches they succeeded in surprising the Confederate encampment and in capturing a large number of prisoners.   Iss also surprised his wife and Aunt Sheba even more profoundly, and before their exclamations ceased he had bundled them and their meagre belongings into a mule cart, with such of the "chillen" as had been left to him, and was following triumphantly in the wake of the victorious Union column; and not a few of their sable companions kept them company.

The whole affair was regarded as one of the most brilliant episodes of the campaign: and Graham received much credit, not only in the official reports, but in the press. Indeed, the latter, although with no aid from the chief actor, obtained an outline of the whole story, from the rescue of his friend to his guidance of the successful expedition, and it was repeated with many variations and exaggertions. He cared little for these brief echoes of fame; but the letters of his aunt, Hilland, and even the old major, were valued indeed, while a note from the grateful wife became his treasure of treasures.

They had returned some time before to the St. John cottage, and she had at last written him a letter "straight from her heart," on the quaint secretary in the library, as he had dreamed possible on the first evening of their acquaintance.

CHAPTER XXIV

UNCHRONICLED CONFLICTS

GRAHAM'S friends were eager that he should obtain leave of absence, but he said, "No, not until some time in the winter."

His aunt understood him sufficiently well not to urge the matter, and it may be added that Grace did also.

Hilland's arm healed rapidly, and happy as he was in his home life at the cottage he soon began to chafe under inaction. Before very long it became evident that the major had not wholly outlived his influence at Washington, for there came an order assigning Major Hilland to duty in that city; and thither, accompanied by Grace and her father, he soon repaired. The arrangement proved very agreeable to Hilland during the period when his regiment could engage in little service beyond that of dreary picket duty. He could make his labors far more useful to the government in the city, and could also enjoy domestic life with his idolized wife. Mrs. Mayburn promised to join them after the holidays, and the reason for her delay was soon made evident.

One chilly, stormy evening, when nature was in a most uncomfortable mood, a card was brought to the door of Hilland's rooms at their inn just as he, with his wife and the major, was sitting down to one of those exquisite little dinners which only Grace knew how to order. Hilland glanced at the card, and gave such a shout that the waiter nearly fell over backward.

"Where is the gentleman? Take me to him on the double-quick. It's Graham. Hurrah! I'll order another dinner!" and he vanished, chasing the man downstairs and

into the waiting-room, as if he were a detachment of Confederate cavalry. The decorous people in the hotel parlor
were astounded as Hilland nearly ran over the breathless
waiter at the door, dashed in like a whirlwind, and carried
off his friend, laughing, chaffing, and embracing him all the
way up the stairs. It was the old, wild exuberancy of his
college days, only intensified by the deepest and most grateful emotion.

Grace stood within her door blushing, smiling, and with
tears of feeling in her lovely eyes.

"Here he is," cried Hilland—"the very god of war.
Give him his reward, Grace—a kiss that he will feel to the
soles of his boots."

But she needed no prompting, for instead of taking
Graham's proffered hand, she put her hands on his shoulders and kissed him again and again, exclaiming, "You
saved Warren's life; you virtually gave yours for his; and
in saving him you saved me. May God bless you every
hour you live!"

"Grace," he said, gravely and gently, looking down into
her swimming eyes and retaining her hands in a strong,
warm clasp, "I am repaid a thousand-fold. I think this is
the happiest moment of my life;" and then he turned to the
major, who was scarcely less demonstrative in his way than
Hilland had been.

"By Jove!" cried the veteran, "the war is going to be
the making of you young fellows. Why, Graham, you no
more look like the young man that played whist with me
years since than I do. You have grown broad-shouldered
and *distingué*, and you have the true military air in spite of
that quiet civilian's dress."

"Oh, I shall always be comparatively insignificant," replied Graham, laughing. "Wait till Hilland wears the stars,
as he surely will, and then you'll see a soldier."

"We see far more than a soldier in you, Alford," said
Grace, earnestly. "Your men told Warren of your almost
miraculous leap across the ditch; and Warren has again and

again described your appearance as you rushed by him on his pursuers. Oh, I've seen the whole thing in my dreams so often!''

"Yes, Graham; you looked like one possessed. You reminded me of the few occasions when, in old college days, you got into a fury."

A frown as black as night lowered on Graham's brow, for they were recalling the most hateful memory of his life —a thought for which he felt he ought to die; but it passed almost instantly, and in the most prosaic tones he said, "Good friends, I'm hungry. I've splashed through Virginia mud twelve mortal hours to-day. Grace, be prepared for such havoc as only a cavalryman can make. We don't get such fare as this at the front."

She, with the pretty housewifely bustle which he had admired years ago, rang the bell and made preparations for a feast.

"Every fatted calf in Washington should be killed for you," she cried—"prodigal that you are, but only in brave deeds. Where's Iss? I want to see and feast him also."

"I left him well provided for in the lower regions, and astounding the 'cullud bredren' with stories which only the African can swallow. He shall come up by and by, for I have my final orders to give. He leads my horse back to the regiment in the morning, and takes care of him in my absence. I hope to spend a month with aunt."

"And how much time with us?" asked Hilland, eagerly.

"This evening."

"Now, Graham, I protest—"

"Now, Hilland, I'm ravenous, and here's a dinner fit for the Great Mogul."

"Oh, I know you of old. When you employ a certain tone you intend to have your own way; but it isn't fair."

"Don't take it to heart. I'll make another raid on you when I return, and then we shall soon be at the front together again. Aunty's lonely, you know."

"Grace and I don't count, I suppose," said the major.

"I had a thousand questions to ask you;" and he looked so aggrieved that Graham compromised and promised to spend the next day with him.

Then he gave an almost hilarious turn to the rest of the evening, and one would have thought that he was in the high spirits natural to any young officer with a month's leave of absence. He described the "woodchuck hole" which had been his hiding-place, sketched humorously the portraits of Iss, Aunt Sheba, who was now his aunt's cook, and gave funny episodes of his midnight prowlings while waiting for a chance to reach the Union lines. Grace noted how skilfully he kept his own personality in the background unless he appeared in some absurd or comical light; and she also noted that his eyes rested upon her less and less often, until at last, after Iss had had his most flattering reception, he said good-night rather abruptly.

The next day he entertained the major in a way that was exceedingly gratifying and flattering to the veteran. He brought some excellent maps, pointed out the various lines of march, the positions of the opposing armies, and showed clearly what had been done and what might have been. He next became the most patient and absorbed listener, as the old gentleman, by the aid of the same maps, planned a campaign which during the coming year would have annihilated the Confederacy. Grace, sitting near the window, might have imagined herself almost ignored. But she interpreted him differently. She now had the key which explained his conduct, and more than once tears came into her eyes.

Hilland returned early, having hastened through his duties, and was in superb spirits. They spent an afternoon together which stood out in memory like a broad gleam of sunshine in after years; and then Graham took his leave with messages from all to Mrs. Mayburn, who was to return with him.

As they were parting, Grace hesitated a moment, and then stepping forward impulsively she took Graham's hand in both of hers, and said impetuously: "You have seen how very, very happy we all are. Do you think that I forget for a moment that I owe it to you?"

Graham's iron nerves gave way. His hand trembled. "Don't speak to me in that way," he murmured. "Come, Hilland, or I shall miss the train;" and in a moment he was gone.

Mrs. Mayburn never forgot the weeks he spent with her. Sometimes she would look at him wonderingly, and once she said: "Alford, it is hard for me to believe that you have passed through all that you have. Day after day passes, and you seem perfectly content with my quiet, monotonous life. You read to me my old favorite authors. You chaff me and Aunt Sheba about our little domestic economies. Beyond a hasty run through the morning paper you scarcely look at the daily journals. You are content with one vigorous walk each day. Indeed you seem to have settled down and adapted yourself to my old woman's life for the rest of time. I thought you would be restless, urging my earlier return to Washington, or seeking to abridge your leave, so that you might return to the excite-ment of the camp."

"No, aunty dear, I am not restless. I have outlived and outgrown that phase of my life. You will find that my pulse is as even as yours. Indeed I have a deep enjoyment of this profound quiet of our house. I have fully accepted my lot, and now expect only those changes that come from without and not from within. To be perfectly sincere with you, the feeling is growing that this profound quietude that has fallen upon me may be the prelude to final rest. It's right that I should accustom your mind to the possibilities of every day in our coming campaign, which I well foresee will be terribly severe. At first our generals did not know how to use cavalry, and beyond escort and picket duty little was asked of it. Now all this is changed. Cavalry has its part in every pitched battle, and in the intervals it has many severe conflicts of its own. Daring, ambitious

leaders are coming to the front, and the year will be one
of great and hazardous activity. My chief regret is that
Hilland's wound did not disable him wholly from further
service in the field. Still he will come out all right. He
always has and ever will. There are hidden laws that control and shape our lives. It seems to me that you were predestined to be just what you are. Your life is rounded
out and symmetrical according to its own law. The same
is true of Hilland and of myself thus far. The rudiments
of what we are to-day were clearly apparent when we were
boys. He is the same ardent, jolly, whole-souled fellow
that clapped me on the back after leaving the class-room.
Everybody liked him then, everything favored him. Often
when he had not looked at a lesson he would make a superb
recitation. I was moody and introspective; so I am to-day.
Even the unforeseen events of life league together to develop one's characteristics. The conditions of his life to-
day are in harmony with all that has been; the same is true
of mine, with the strange exception that I have found a
home and a dear staunch friend in one who I supposed would
ever be a stranger. See how true my theory is of Grace and
her father. Her blithesome girlhood has developed into
the happiest wifehood. Her brow is as smooth as ever, and
her eyes as bright. They have only gained in depth and
tenderness as the woman has taken the place of the girl.
Her form has only developed into lovelier proportions,
and her character into a more exquisite symmetry. She
has been one continuous growth according to the laws of
her being; and so it will be to the end. She will be just
as beautiful and lovable in old age as now; for nature, in
a genial mood, infused into her no discordant, disfiguring
elements. The major also is completing his life in conso-
nance with all that has gone before.''

"Alford, you are more of a fatalist than a materialist.
In my heart I feel, I know, you are wrong. What you say
seems so plausible as to be true; but my very soul revolts
at it all. There is a deep undertone of sadness in your

words, and they point to a possibility that would imbitter every moment of the remnant of my life. Suppose you should fall, what remedy would there be for me? Oh, in anguish I have learned what life would become then. I am a materialist like yourself, although all the clergymen in town would say I was orthodox. From earliest recollection mere things and certain people have been everything to me; and now you are everything, and yet at this hour the bullet may be molded which will strike you down. Grace, with her rich, beautiful life, is in equal danger. Hilland will go into the field and will expose himself as recklessly as yourself. I have no faith in your obscure laws. Thousands were killed in the last campaign, thousands are dying in hospitals this moment, and all this means thousands of broken hearts, unless they are sustained by something I have not. This world is all very well when all is well, but it can so easily become an accursed world!'' The old lady spoke with a strange bitterness, revealing the profound disquietude that existed under the serene amenities of her age and her methodical life.

Graham sought to give a lighter tone to their talk and said: ''Oh, well, aunty, perhaps we are darkening the sun with our own shadows. We must take life as we find it. There is no help for that. You have done so practically. With your strong good sense you could not do otherwise. The trouble is that you are haunted by old-time New England beliefs that, from your ancestry, have become infused into your very blood. You can't help them any more than other inherited infirmities which may have afflicted your grandfather. Let us speak of something else. Ah, here is a welcome diversion—the daily paper—and I'll read it through to you, and we'll gain another hint as to the drift of this great tide of events.''

The old lady shook her head sadly; and the fact that she watched the young man with hungry, wistful eyes, often blinded with tears, proved that neither state nor military policy was uppermost in her mind.

CHAPTER XXV

A PRESENTIMENT

ON Christmas morning Graham found his breakfast-plate pushed back, and in its place lay a superb sword and belt, fashioned much like the one he had lost in the rescue of his friend. With it was a genial letter from Hilland, and a little note from Grace, which only said:

"You will find my name engraved upon the sword with Warren's. We have added nothing else, for the good reason that our names mean everything—more than could be expressed, were the whole blade covered with symbols, each meaning a volume. You have taught us how you will use the weapon, my truest and best of friends.   GRACE HILLAND."

His eyes lingered on the name so long that his aunt asked: "Why don't you look at your gift?"

He slowly drew the long, keen, shining blade, and saw again the name "Grace Hilland," and for a time he saw nothing else. Suddenly he turned the sword and on the opposite side was "Warren Hilland," and he shook his head sadly.

"Alford, what *is* the matter?" his aunt asked impatiently.

"Why didn't they have their names engraved together?" he muttered slowly. "It's a bad omen. See, a sword is between their names. I wish they had been together. Oh, I wish Hilland could be kept out of the field!"

"There it is, Alford," began his aunt, irritably; "you men who don't believe anything are always the victims of superstition. Bad omen, indeed!"

"Well, I suppose I am a fool; but a strange chill at heart struck me for which I can't account;" and he sprang up and paced the floor uneasily. "Well," he continued, "I would bury it in my own heart rather than cause her one hour's sorrow, but I wish their names had been together." Then he took it up again and said: "Beautiful as it is, it may have to do some stern work, Grace—work far remote from your nature. All I ask is that it may come between Hilland and danger again. I wish I had not had that strange, cursed presentiment."

"Oh, Alford! I never saw you in such a mood, and on Christmas morning, too!"

"That is just what I don't like about it—it's not my habit to indulge such fancies, to say the least. Come what may, however, I dedicate the sword to her service without counting any cost;" and he kissed her name, and laid the weapon reverently aside.

"You are morbid this morning. Go to the door and see my present to you. You will find no bad omens on his shining coat."

Graham felt that it was weak to entertain such impressions as had mastered him, and hastened out. There, pawing the frozen ground, was a horse that satisfied even his fastidious eye. There was not a white hair in the coal-black coat. In his enthusiasm he forgot his hat, and led the beautiful creature up and down, observing with exultation his perfect action, clean-cut limbs, and deep, broad chest.

"Bring me a bridle," he said to the man in attendance, "and my hat."

A moment later he had mounted.

"Breakfast is getting cold," cried his aunt from the window, delighted, nevertheless, at the appreciation of her gift.

"This horse is breakfast and dinner both," he shouted, as he galloped down the path.

Then, to the old lady's horror, he dashed through the trees and shrubbery, took a picket-fence in a flying leap,

and circled round the house till Mrs. Mayburn's head was
dizzy.   Then she saw him coming toward the door as if he
would ride through the house; but the horse stopped almost
instantly, and Graham was on his feet, handing the bridle
to the gaping groom.

"Take good care of him," he said to the man, "for he is
a jewel."

"Alford," exclaimed his aunt, "could you make no better
return for my gift than to frighten me out of my wits?"

"Dear aunty, you are too well supplied ever to lose them
for so slight a cause.   I wanted to show the perfection of
your gift, and how well it may serve me.   You don't imagine that our cavalry evolutions are all performed on
straight turnpike roads, do you?   Now you know that
you have given me an animal that can carry me wherever
a horse can go, and so have added much to my chances of
safety.   I can skim out of a mêlée like a bird with Mayburn—for that shall be his name—where a blundering,
stupid horse would break my neck, if I wasn't shot.   I saw
at once from his action what he could do.   Where on earth
did you get such a creature?"

"Well," said the old lady, beaming with triumphant
happiness, "I have had agents on the lookout a long time.
The man of whom you had your first horse, then called
Firebrand, found him; and he knew well that he could not
impose any inferior animal upon you.   Are you really sincere in saying that such a horse as this adds to your chances
of safety?"

"Certainly.   That's what I was trying to show you.
Did you not see how he would wind in and out among the
trees and shrubbery—how he would take a fence lightly
without any floundering?   There is just as much difference
among horses as among men.   Some are simply awkward,
heavy, and stupid; others are vicious; more are good at
times and under ordinary circumstances, but fail you at a
pinch.   This horse is thoroughbred and well broken.   You
must have paid a small fortune for him."

"I never invested money that satisfied me better."

"It's like you to say so. Well, take the full comfort of thinking how much you have added to my comfort and prospective well-being. That gallop has already done me a world of good, and given me an appetite. I'll have another turn across the country after breakfast, and throw all evil presentiments to the winds."

"Why, now you talk sense. When you are in any more such moods as this morning I shall prescribe horse."

Before New Year's day Graham had installed his aunt comfortably in rooms adjoining the Hillands', and had thanked his friends for their gift in a way that proved it to be appreciated. Mrs. Mayburn had been cautioned never to speak of what he now regarded as a foolish and unaccountable presentiment, arising, perhaps, from a certain degree of morbidness of mind in all that related to Grace. Iss was on hand to act as groom, and Graham rode out with Hilland and Grace several times before his leave expired. Even at that day, when the city was full of gallant men and fair women, many turned to look as the three passed down the avenue.

Never had Grace looked so radiantly beautiful as when in the brilliant sunshine of a Washington winter and in the frosty air she galloped over the smooth, hard roads. Hilland was proud of the almost wondering looks of admiration that everywhere greeted her, and too much in love to note that the ladies they met looked at him in much the same way. The best that was said of Graham was that he looked a soldier, every inch of him, and that he rode the finest horse in the city as if he had been brought up in a saddle. He was regarded by society as reserved, unsocial, and proud; and at two or three receptions, to which he went because of the solicitation of his friends, he piqued the vanity of more than one handsome woman by his courteous indifference.

"What is the matter with your husband's friend?" a reigning belle asked Grace. "One might as well try to make an impression on a paving-stone."

"I think your illustration unhappy," was her quiet reply. "I cannot imagine Mr. Graham at any one's feet."

"Not even your own?" was the malicious retort.

"Not even my own," and a flash of anger from her dark eyes accompanied her answer.

Still, wherever he went he awakened interest in all natures not dull or sodden. He was felt to be a presence. There was a consciousness of power in his very attitudes; and one felt instinctively that he was far removed from the commonplace—that he had had a history which made him different from other men.

But before this slight curiosity was kindled to any extent, much less satisfied, his leave of absence expired; and with a sense of deep relief he prepared to say farewell. His friends expected to see him often in the city; he knew they would see him but seldom, if at all. He had made his visit with his aunt, and she understood him. His quiet poise was departing, and he longed for the stern, fierce excitement of active service.

Before he joined his regiment he spent the day with his friends, and took occasion once, when alone with Hilland, to make an appeal that was solemn and almost passionate in its earnestness, adjuring him to remain employed in duties like those which now occupied him. But he saw that his efforts were vain.

"No, Graham," was Hilland's emphatic reply; "just as soon as there is danger at the front I shall be with my regiment. Now I can do more here."

With Grace he took a short ride in the morning while Hilland was engaged in his duties, and he looked at the fair woman by his side with the thought that he might never see her again. It almost seemed as if Grace understood him, for although the rich color mantled in her cheeks and she abounded in smile and repartee, a look of deep sadness rarely left her eyes.

Once she said abruptly, "Alford, you will come and see

us often oefore the campaign opens? Oh, I dread this coming campaign. You will come often?''

"I fear not, Grace," he said, gravely and gently. "I will try to come, but not often." Then he added, with a short, abrupt laugh, "I wish I could break Hilland's leg." In answer to a look of surprise he continued, "Could not your father procure an order that would keep him in the city? He would have to obey orders."

"Ah, I understand you," and there was a quick rush of tears to her eyes. "It's of no use. I have thought of everything, but Warren's heart is set on joining his regiment in the spring."

"I know it. I have said all that I could say to a brother on the subject."

"From the first, Alford, you have tried to make the ordeal of this war less painful to me, and how well you have succeeded! You have been our good genius. Warren, in his impetuous, chivalrous feeling, would have gone into it unadvisedly, hastily; and before this might— Oh, I can't even think of it," she said with a shudder. "But years have passed since your influence guided him into a wiser and more useful course, and think how much of the time I have been able to be with him! And it has all been due to you, Alford. But the war seems no nearer its end. It rather assumes a larger and more threatening aspect. Why do not men think of us poor women before they go to war?''

"You think, then, that even your influence cannot keep him from the field?''

"No, it could not. Indeed, beyond a certain point I dare not exert it. I should be dumb before questions already asked, 'Why should I shrink when other husbands do not? What would be said of me here? what by my comrades in the regiment? What would your brave father think, though he might acquiesce? Nay, more, what would my wife think in her secret heart?' Alas! I find I am not made of such stern stuff as are some women. Pride and military fame could not sustain me if—if—''

"Do not look on the gloomy side, Grace. Hilland will come out of it all a major-general."

"Oh, I don't know, I don't know. I do know that he will often be in desperate danger; what a dread certainty that is for me! Oh, I wish you could be always near him; and yet 'tis a selfish wish, for you would not count the cost to yourself."

"No, Grace; I've sworn that on the sword you gave me."

"I might have known as much." Then she added earnestly, "Believe me, if you should fall it would also imbitter my life."

"Yes, you would grieve sincerely; but there would be an infinite difference, an infinite difference. One question, however, is settled beyond recall. If my life can serve you or Hilland, no power shall prevent my giving it. There is nothing more to be said: let us speak of something else."

"Yes, Alford, one thing more. Once I misjudged you. Forgive me;" and she caused her horse to spring into a gallop, resolving that no commonplace words should follow closely upon a conversation that had touched the most sacred feelings and impulses of each heart.

For some reason there was a shadow over their parting early in the evening, for Graham was to ride toward the front with the dawn. Even Hilland's genial spirits could not wholly dissipate it. Graham made heroic efforts, but he was oppressed with a despondency which was wellnigh overwhelming. He felt that he was becoming unmanned, and in bitter self-censure resolved to remain with his regiment until the end came, as he believed would be the case with him before the year closed.

"Alford, remember your promise. We all may need you yet," were his aunt's last words in the gray of the morning.

CHAPTER XXVI

AN IMPROVISED PICTURE GALLERY

MUCH to Graham's satisfaction, his regiment, soon after he joined it, was ordered into the Shenandoah Valley, and given some rough, dangerous picket duty that fully accorded with his mood. Even Hilland could not expect a visit from him now; and he explained to his friend that the other officers were taking their leaves of absence, and he, in turn, must perform their duties. And so the winter passed uneventfully away in a cheerful interchange of letters. Graham found that the front agreed with him better than Washington, and that his pulse resumed its former even beat. A dash at a Confederate picket post on a stormy night was far more tranquilizing than an evening in Hilland's luxurious rooms.

With the opening of the spring campaign Hilland joined his regiment, and was eager to remove by his courage and activity the slightest impression, if any existed, that he was disposed to shun dangerous service. There was no such impression, however; and he was most cordially welcomed, for he was a great favorite with both officers and men.

During the weeks that followed, the cavalry was called upon to do heavy work and severe fighting; and the two friends became more conspicuous than ever for their gallantry. They seemed, however, to bear charmed lives, for, while many fell or were wounded, they escaped unharmed.

At last the terrific and decisive campaign of Gettysburg opened; and from the war-wasted and guerilla-infested regions of Virginia the Northern troops found themselves

marching through the friendly and populous North. As
the cavalry brigade entered a thriving village in Pennsyl-
vania the people turned out almost *en masse* and gave them
more than an ovation. The troopers were tired, hungry,
and thirsty; and, since from every doorway was offered a
boundless hospitality, the column came to a halt. The
scene soon developed into a picturesque military picnic.
Young maids and venerable matrons, gray-bearded fathers,
shy, blushing girls, and eager-eyed children, all vied with
each other in pressing upon their defenders every delicacy
and substantial viand that their town could furnish at the
moment. A pretty miss of sixteen, with a peach-like bloom
in her cheeks, might be seen flitting here and there among
the bearded troopers with a tray bearing goblets of milk.
When they were emptied she would fly back and lift up
white arms to her mother for more, and the almost equally
blooming matron, smiling from the window, would fill the
glasses again to the brim. The magnates of the village
with their wives were foremost in the work, and were passing to and fro with great baskets of sandwiches, while stalwart men and boys were bringing from neighboring wells
and pumps cool, delicious water for the horses. How immensely the troopers enjoyed it all! No scowling faces
and cold looks here. All up and down the street, holding
bridle-reins over their arms or leaning against the flanks of
their horses, they feasted as they had not done since their
last Thanksgiving Day at home. Such generous cups of
coffee, enriched with cream almost too thick to flow from
the capacious pitchers, and sweetened not only with snow-
white sugar, but also with the smiles of some gracious
woman, perhaps motherly in appearance, perhaps so fair
and young that hearts beat faster under the weather-stained
cavalry jackets.

"How pretty it all is!" said a familiar voice to Graham,
as he was dividing a huge piece of cake with his pet Mayburn; and Hilland laid his hand on his friend's shoulder.

"Ah, Hilland, seeing you is the best part of this banquet *à la militaire.* Yes, it is a heavenly change after the dreary land we've been marching and fighting in. It makes me feel that I have a country, and that it's worth all it may cost."

"Look, Graham—look at that little fairy creature in white muslin, talking to that great bearded pard of a sergeant. Isn't that a picture? Oh, I wish Grace, with her eye for picturesque effects, could look upon this scene."

"Nonsense, Hilland! as if she would look at anybody or anything but you! See that white-haired old woman leading that exquisite little girl to yonder group of soldiers. See how they doff their hats to her. There's another picture for you."

Hilland's magnificent appearance soon attracted half a dozen village belles about him, each offering some dainty; and one—a black-eyed witch a little bolder than the others —offered to fasten a rose from her hair in his button-hole.

He entered into the spirit of the occasion with all the zest of his old student days, professed to be delighted with the favor as she stood on tiptoe to reach the lappet of his coat; and then he stooped down and pressed his lips to the fragrant petals, assuring the blushing little coquette, meanwhile, that it was the next best thing to her own red lips.

How vividly in after years Graham would recall him, as he stood there, his handsome head thrown back, looking the ideal of an old Norse viking, laughing and chatting with the merry, innocent girls around him, his deep-blue eyes emitting mirthful gleams on every side! According to his nature, Graham drew off to one side and watched the scene with a smile, as he had viewed similar ones far back in the years, and far away in Germany. He saw the ripples of laughter that his friend's words provoked, and recognized the old, easy grace, the light, French-like wit, that was wholly free from the French *double entendre,* and he thought: "Would that Grace could see him now, and she would fall in love with him anew, for her nature is too large for petty jealousy at a scene like that. Oh, Hilland, you and the

group around you make the finest picture of this long im-
provised gallery of pictures."

Suddenly there was a loud report of a cannon from a hill
above the village, and a shell shrieked over their heads.
Hilland's laughing aspect changed instantly. He seemed
almost to gather the young girls in his arms as he hurried
them into the nearest doorway, and then with a bound
reached Graham, who held his horse, vaulted into the saddle, and dashed up the street to his men who were standing
in line.

Graham sprang lightly on his horse, for in the scenes
resulting from the kaleidoscopic change that had taken
place he would be more at home.

"Mount!" he shouted; and the order, repeated up and
down the street, changed the jolly, feasting troopers of a
moment since into veterans who would sit like equestrian
statues, if so commanded, though a hundred guns thundered against them.

From the further end of the village came the wild yell
characteristic of the cavalry charges of the Confederates,
while shell after shell shrieked and exploded where had just
been unaffected gayety and hospitality.

The first shot had cleared the street of all except the
Union soldiers; and those who dared to peep from window
or door saw, with dismay, that the defenders whom they
had so honored and welcomed were retreating at a gallop
from the Rebel charge.

They were soon undeceived, however, for at a gallop the
national cavalry dashed into an open field near by, formed
with the precision of machinery, and by the time that the
Rebel charge had wellnigh spent itself in the sabring or
capture of a few tardy troopers, Hilland with platoon after
platoon was emerging upon the street again at a sharp trot,
which soon developed into a furious gallop as he dashed
against their assailants; and the pretty little coquette, bold
not only in love but in war, saw from a window her ideal
knight with her red rose upon his breast leading a charge

whose thunder caused the very earth to tremble; and she clapped her hands and cheered so loudly as he approached that he looked up, saw her, and for an instant a sunny smile passed over the visage that had become so stern. Then came the shock of battle.

Graham's company was held in reserve, but for some reason his horse seemed to grow unmanageable; and sabres had scarcely clashed before he, with the blade on which was engraved "Grace Hilland," was at her husband's side, striking blows which none could resist. The enemy could not stand the furious onset, and gave way slowly, sullenly, and at last precipitately. The tide of battle swept beyond and away from the village; and its street became quiet again, except for the groans of the wounded.

Mangled horses, mangled men, some dead, some dying, and others almost rejoicing in wounds that would secure for them such gentle nurses, strewed the streets that had been the scene of merry festivity.

The pretty little belle never saw her tawny, bearded knight again. She undoubtedly married and tormented some well-to-do dry-goods clerk; but a vision of a man of heroic mold, with a red rose upon his breast, smiling up to her just as he was about to face what might be death, will thrill her feminine soul until she is old and gray.

That night Graham and Hilland talked and laughed over the whole affair as they sat by a camp-fire.

"It has all turned out as usual," said Graham, ruefully. "You won a victory and no end of glory; I a reprimand from my colonel."

"If you have received nothing worse than a reprimand you are fortunate," was Hilland's response. "The idea of any horse becoming unmanageable in your hands! The colonel understands the case as well as I do, and knows that it was your own ravenous appetite for a fight that be- came unmanageable. But I told him of the good service you rendered, and gave him the wink to wink also. You were fearfully rash to-day, Graham. You were not content to fight at my side, but more than once were between me and the enemy. What the devil makes you so headlong in a fight—you that are usually so cool and self-controlled?"

Graham's hand rested on a fair woman's name engraved upon his sword, but he replied lightly: "When you teach me caution in a fight I'll learn."

"Well, excuse me, old fellow, I'm going to write to Grace. May not have a chance very soon again. I say, Graham, we'll have *the* battle of the war in a day or two."

"I know it," was the quiet response.

"And we must win, too," Hilland continued, "or the Johnnies will help themselves to Washington, Baltimore, Philadelphia, and perhaps New York. Every man should nerve himself to do the work of two. As I was saying, I shall write to Grace that your horse ran away with you and became uncontrollable until you were directly in front of me, when you seemed to manage him admirably, and struck blows worthy of the old French duellist who killed a man every morning before breakfast. I think she'll understand your sudden and amazingly poor horsemanship as well as I do."

She did, and far better.

Hilland's prediction proved true. The decisive battle of Gettysburg was fought, and its bloody field marked the highest point reached by the crimson tide of the Rebellion. From Cemetery Ridge it ebbed slowly and sullenly away to the south.

The brigade in which were the friends passed through another fearful baptism of fire in the main conflict and the pursuit which followed, and were in Virginia again, but with ranks almost decimated. Graham and Hilland still seemed to bear charmed lives, and in the brief pause in operations that followed, wrote cheerful letters to those so dear, now again at their seaside resort. Grace, who for days had been so pale, and in whose dark eyes lurked an ever-present dread of which she could not speak, smiled again. Her husband wrote in exuberant spirits over the victory, and signed himself "Lieutenant-Colonel." Graham in his letter said jestingly to his aunt that he had at last attained his "majority," and that she might therefore look for a little more discretion on his part.

"How the boys are coming on!" exulted the old major. "They will both wear the stars yet. But confound it all, why did Meade let Lee escape? He might have finished the whole thing up."

Alas! the immeasurable price of liberty was not yet paid.

One morning Hilland's and Graham's regiments were ordered out on what was deemed but a minor *reconnoissance;* and the friends, rested and strong, started in high spirits with their sadly shrunken forces. But they knew that the remaining handfuls were worth more than full ranks of untrained, unseasoned men. All grow callous, if not indifferent, to the vicissitudes of war; and while they missed regretfully many familiar faces, the thought that they had rendered the enemy's lines more meagre was consoling.

Graham and Hilland rode much of the long day together. They went over all the past, and dwelt upon the fact that their lives had been so different from what they had planned.

"By the way, Graham," said Hilland, abruptly, "it seems strange to me that you are so indifferent to women. Don't you expect ever to marry?"

Graham burst into a laugh as he replied: "I thought we had that subject out years ago, under the apple-tree—that night, you remember, when you talked like a schoolgirl till morning—"

"And you analyzed and philosophized till long after midnight—"

"Well, you knew then that Grace had spoiled me for every one else; and she's been improving ever since. When I find her equal I'll marry her, if I can."

"Poor, forlorn old bachelor that you are, and ever will

be!" cried Hilland. "You'll never find the equal of Grace Hilland."

"I think I shall survive, Hilland. My appetite is good. As I live, there are some Confederates in yonder clump of trees;" and he put spurs to his horse on a little private *reconnoissance*. The few horsemen vanished, in the thick woods beyond, the moment they saw that they were perceived; and they were regarded as prowling guerillas only.

That night they bivouacked in a grove where two roads intersected, threw out pickets and patrols, and kindled their fires, for they did not expect to strike the enemy in force till some time on the following day.

CHAPTER XXVII

A DREAM

GRAHAM and his friend had bidden each other an early and cordial good-night, for the entire force under the command of Hilland's colonel was to resume its march with the dawn. Although no immediate danger was apprehended, caution had been learned by long experience. The detachment was comparatively small, and it was far removed from any support; and while no hints of the presence of the enemy in formidable numbers had been obtained during the day, what was beyond them could not be known with any certainty. Therefore the horses had been carefully rubbed down, and the saddles replaced. In many instances the bridles also had been put on again, with the bit merely slipped from the mouth. In all cases they lay or hung within reach of the tired troopers, who, one after another, were dropping off into the cat-like slumber of a cavalry outpost.

As the fires died down, the shadows in the grove grew deeper and more obscure, and all was quiet, except when the hours came round for the relief of pickets and the men who were patrolling the roads. Graham remembered the evanescent group of Confederates toward whom he had spurred during the day. He knew that they were in a hostile region, and that their movements must be already well known to the enemy if strong in their vicinity. Therefore all his instincts as a soldier were on the alert. It so happened that he was second in command of his regiment on this occasion, and he felt the responsibility. He had been his own groom on their arrival at the grove, and his faithful charger, Mayburn, now stood saddled and bridled by his side, as he reclined, half dozing, again thinking deeply, by the low, flickering blaze of his fire. He had almost wholly lost the gloomy presentiments that had oppressed him at the beginning of the year. Both he and Hilland had passed through so many dangers that a sense of security was begotten. Still more potent had been the influence of his active out-of-door life. His nerves were braced, while his soldier's routine and the strong excitement of the campaign had become a preoccupying habit.

Only those who brood in idleness over the misfortunes and disappointments of life are destroyed by them.

He had not seen Grace for over half a year; and while she was and ever would be his fair ideal, he could now think of her with the quietude akin to that of the devout Catholic who worships a saint removed from him at a heavenly distance. The wisdom of this remoteness became more and more clear to him; for despite every power that he could put forth as a man, there was a deeper, stronger manhood within him which acknowledged this woman as sovereign. He foresaw that his lot would be one of comparative exile, and he accepted it with a calm and inflexible resolution.

Hearing a step he started up hastily, and saw Hilland appoaching from the opposite side of his fire.

"Ah, Graham, glad you are not asleep," said his friend, throwing himself down on the leaves, with his head resting on his hands. "Put a little wood on the fire, please; I'm chilly in the night air, and the dews are so confoundedly heavy."

"Why, Hilland, what's the matter?" Graham asked, as he complied. "You are an ideal cavalryman at a nap, and can sleep soundly with one eye open. It has seemed to me that you never lost a wink when there was a chance for it, even under fire."

"Why are you not sleeping?"

"Oh, I have been, after my fashion, dozing and thinking by turns. I always was an owl, you know. Moreover, I think it behooves us to be on the alert. We are a good way from support if hard pressed; and the enemy must be in force somewhere to the west of us."

"I've thought as much myself. My horse is ready, as yours is, and I left an orderly holding him. I suppose you will laugh at me, but I've had a cursed dream; and it has shaken me in spite of my reason. After all, how often our reason fails us at a pinch! I wish it was morning and we were on the road. I've half a mind to go out with the patrols and get my blood in circulation. I would were it not that I feel I should be with my men."

"Where's your colonel?"

"The old war-dog is sleeping like a top. Nothing ever disturbs him, much less a dream. I say, Graham, I made a good selection in him, didn't I?"

"Yes, but he'll be promoted soon, and you will be in command. What's more, I expect to see a star on *your* shoulder in less than six months."

"As I feel to-night, I don't care a picayune for stars or anything else relating to the cursed war. I'd give my fortune to be able to kiss Grace and tell her I'm well."

"You are morbid, Hilland. You will feel differently to-morrow, especially if there's a chance for a charge."

"No doubt, no doubt. The shadow of this confounded grove seems as black as death, and it oppresses me. Why should I, without apparent cause, have had such a dream?"

"Your supper and fatigue may have been the cause. If you don't mind, tell me this grisly vision."

"While you laugh at me as an old woman—you, in whom reason ever sits serene and dispassionate on her throne, except when you get into a fight."

"My reason's throne is often as rickety as a two-legged stool. No, I won't laugh at you. There's not a braver man in the service than you. If you feel as you say, there's some cause for it; and yet so complex is our organism that both cause and effect may not be worthy of very grave consideration, as I have hinted."

"Think what you please, this was my dream. I had made my dispositions for the night, and went to sleep as a matter of course. I had not slept an hour by my watch —I looked at it afterward—when I seemed to hear some one moaning and crying, and I thought I started up wide awake, and I saw the old library at home—the room you know so well. Every article of furniture was before me more distinctly than I can see any object now, and on the rug before the open fire Grace was crouching, while she moaned and wrung her hands and cried as if her heart was breaking. She was dressed in black—Oh, how white her hands and neck and face appeared against that mournful black!—and, strangest of all, her hair fell around her snowy white, like a silver veil. I started forward to clasp her in my arms, and then truly awoke, for there was nothing before me but my drooping horse, a few red coals of my expiring fire, and over all the black, black shadow of this accursed grove. Oh, for sunlight! Oh, for a gale of wind, that I might breathe freely again!" and the powerful man sprang to his feet and threw open his coat at his breast.

As he ceased speaking, the silence and darkness of the grove did seem ominous and oppressive, and Graham's old wretched presentiment of Christmas morning returned, but he strove with all the ingenuity in his power to reason his friend out of his morbid mood, as he termed it. He kindled his fire into a cheerful blaze, and Hilland cowered and shivered over it; then looking up abruptly, he said, "Graham, you and I accepted the belief long ago that man was only highly organized matter. I must admit to you that my mind has often revolted at this belief; and the thought that Grace was merely of the earth has always seemed to me sacrilegious. She never was what you would call a religious girl; but she once had a quiet, simple faith in a God and a hereafter, and she expected to see her mother again. I fear that our views have troubled her exceedingly; although

with that rare reserve in a woman, she never interfered with
one's strong personal convictions. The shallow woman tries
to set everybody right with the weighty reason, 'Oh, because
it *is* so; all good people say it is so.' I fear our views have
unsettled hers also. I wish they had not; indeed I wish
I could believe somewhat as she did.

"Once, only once, she spoke to me with a strange bitterness, but it revealed the workings of her mind. I, perhaps,
was showing a little too much eagerness in my spirit and
preparation for active service, and she broke out abruptly,
'Oh, yes, you and Alford can rush into scenes of carnage
very complacently. You believe that if the bullet is only
sure enough, your troubles are over forever, as Alford once
said. I suppose you are right, for you learned men have
studied into things as we poor women never can. If it's
true, those who love as we do should die together.' It has
often seemed that her very love—nay, that mine—was an
argument against our belief. That a feeling so pure, vivid,
and unselfish, so devoid of mere earthiness—a feeling that
apparently contains within itself the very essence of immortality—can be instantly blotted out as a flame is extin-
guished, has become a terrible thought. Grace Hilland is
worthy of an immortal life, and she has all the capacity for
it. It's not her lovely form and face that I love so much
as the lovely something—call it soul, spirit, or what you
choose—that will maintain her charm through all the
changes from youth to feeble and withered age. How
can I be sure that the same gentle, womanly spirit may not
exist after the final change we call death, and that to those
worthy of immortal life the boon is not given? Reason is
a grand thing, and I know we once thought we settled this
question; but reason fails me to-night, or else love and the
intense longings of the heart teach a truer and deeper
philosophy—

"You are silent, Graham. You think me morbid—that
wishes are fathers of my thoughts. Well, I'm not. I honestly don't know what the truth is. I only wish to-night

that I had the simple belief in a reunion with Grace which she had with regard to her mother. I fear we have unsettled her faith; not that we ever urged our views—indeed we have scarcely ever spoken of them—but there has been before her the ever-present and silent force of example. It was natural for her to believe that those were right in whom she most believed; and I'm not sure we are right—I'm not *sure*. I've not been sure for a long time."

"My dear Warren, you are not well. Exposure to all sorts of weather in this malarial country is telling on you; and I fear your feelings to-night are the prelude of a fever. You shall stay and sleep by my fire, and if I hear the slightest suspicious sound I will waken you. You need not hesitate, for I intend to watch till morning, whether you stay or not."

"Well, Graham, I will. I wish to get through this horrible night in the quickest way possible. But I'll first go and bring my horse here, so the poor orderly can have a nap."

He soon returned and lay down close to the genial fire, and Graham threw over him his own blankets.

"What a good, honest friend you are, Graham!—too honest even to say some hollow words favoring my doubts of my doubt and unbelief. If it hadn't been for you, I should have been dead long ago. In my blind confidence, I should have rushed into the war, and probably should have been knocked on the head at Bull Run. How many happy months I've passed with Grace since then!—how many since you virtually gave your life for me last autumn! You made sure that I took a man's, not a fool's, part in the war. Oh, Grace and I know it all and appreciate it; and —and—Alford, if I should fall, I commend Grace to your care."

"Hilland, stop, or you will unman me. This accursed grove *is* haunted, I half believe; and were I in command I would order 'Boots and Saddles' to be sounded at once. There, sleep, Warren, and in the morning you will be your own grand self. Why speak of anything I could do for you and Grace? How could I serve myself in any surer way? As schoolgirls say, 'I won't speak to you again.' I'm going to prowl around a little, and see that all is right;" and he disappeared among the shadowy boles of the trees.

When he returned from his rounds his friend was sleeping, but uneasily, with sudden fits and starts.

"He is surely going to have a fever," Graham muttered. "I'd give a year's pay if we were safe back in camp." He stood before the fire with folded arms, watching his boyhood's friend, his gigantic shadow stretching away into the obscurity as unwaveringly as those of the tree-trunks around him. His lips were compressed. He sought to make his will as inflexible as his form. He would not think of Grace, of danger to her and Hilland; and yet, by some horrible necromancy of the hour and place, the scene in Hilland's dream would rise before him with a vividness that was overawing. In the sighing of the wind through the foliage, he seemed to hear the poor wife's moans.

"Oh," he muttered, "would that I could die a thousand deaths to prevent a scene like that!"

When would the interminable night pass? At last he looked at his watch and saw that the dawn could not be far distant. How still everything had become! The men were in their deepest slumber. Even the wind had died out, and the silence was to his overwrought mind like the hush of expectancy.

This silence was at last broken by a shot on the road leading to the west. Other shots followed in quick succession.

Hilland was on his feet instantly. "We're attacked," he shouted, and was about to spring upon his horse when Graham grasped his hand in both of his as he said, "In the name of Grace Hilland, be prudent."

Then both the men were in the saddle, Hilland dashing toward his own command, and each shouting, "Awake! Mount!"

At the same instant the bugle from headquarters rang through the grove, giving the well-known order of "Boots and Saddles."

In place of the profound stillness of a moment before, there were a thousand discordant sounds—the trampling of feet, the jingling of sabres, the champing of bits by aroused, restless horses that understood the bugle call as well as the men, hoarse, rapid orders of officers, above all which in the distance could be heard Hilland's clarion voice.

Again and again from headquarters the brief, musical strains of the bugle echoed through the gloom, each one giving to the veterans a definite command. Within four minutes there was a line of battle on the western edge of the grove, and a charging column was in the road leading to the west, down which the patrols were galloping at a headlong pace. Pickets were rushing in, firing as they came. To the uninitiated it might have seemed a scene of dire confusion. In fact, it was one of perfect order and discipline. Even in the darkness each man knew just what to do and where to go, as he heard the bugle calls and the stern, brief, supplementary orders of the officers.

Graham found himself on the line of battle at the right of the road, and the sound that followed close upon the sharp gallop of the patrol was ominous indeed. It was the rushing, thunderous sound of a heavy body of cavalry —too heavy, his ear soon foretold him, to promise equal battle.

The experienced colonel recognized the fact at the same moment, and would not leave his men in the road to meet the furious onset. Again, sharp, quick, and decisive as the vocal order had been, the bugle rang out the command for a change of position. Its strains had not ceased when the officers were repeating the order all down the column that had been formed in the road for a charge, and scarcely a moment elapsed before the western pike was clear, and faced by a line of battle a little back among the trees. The Union force would now ask nothing better than that the enemy should charge down that road within pointblank range.

If the Nationals were veterans they were also dealing with veterans who were masters of the situation in their overwhelming force and their knowledge of the compara- tive insignificance of their opponents, whose numbers had been quite accurately estimated the day before.

The patrols were already within the Union lines and at their proper places when the Confederate column emerged into the narrow open space before the grove. Its advance had subsided into a sharp trot; but, instead of charging by column or platoon, the enemy deployed to right and left with incredible swiftness. Men dismounted and formed into line almost instantly, their gray forms looking phantom-like in the gray dawn that tinged the east.

The vigilant colonel was as prompt as they, and at the first evidence of their tactics the bugle resounded, and the line of battle facing the road which led westward wheeled at a gallop through the open trees and formed at right angles with the road behind the first line of battle. Again there was a bugle call. The men in both lines dismounted in- stantly, and as their horses were being led to the rear by those designated for the duty, a Union volley was poured into the Confederate line that had scarcely formed, causing many a gap. Then the first Union line retired behind the second, loading as they went, and, with the ready instinct of old fighters, putting trees between themselves and the swiftly advancing foe while forming a third line of battle. From the second Union line a deadly volley blazed in the dim obscurity of the woods. It had no perceptible effect in checking the impetuous onset of the enemy, who merely returned the fire as they advanced.

The veteran colonel, with cool alertness, saw that he was far outnumbered, and that his assailants' tactics were to drive him through the grove into the open fields, where his com- mand would be speedily dispersed and captured. His only chance was to run for it and get the start. Indeed the ob-

ject of his reconnoissance seemed already accomplished, for
the enemy was found to be in force in that direction. Therefore, as he galloped to the rear his bugler sounded "Retreat"
long and shrilly.

The dim Union lines under the trees melted away as by
magic, and a moment later there was a rush of horses through
the underbrush that fringed the eastern side of the grove.
But some men were shot, some sabred, and others captured
before they could mount and extricate themselves. The
majority, however, of the Union forces were galloping
swiftly away, scattering at first rather than keeping together, in order to distract the pursuit which for a time
was sharp and deadly. Not a few succumbed; others
would turn on their nearest pursuer in mortal combat,
which was soon decided in one way or the other. Graham
more than once wheeled and confronted an isolated foe, and
the sword bearing the name of the gentle Grace Hilland was
bloody indeed.

All the while his eye was ranging the field for Hilland,
and with his fleet steed, that could soon have carried him
beyond all danger, he diverged to right and left, as far as
their headlong retreat permitted, in his vain search for his
friend.

Suddenly the bugle from the Confederate side sounded a
recall. The enemy halted, fired parting shots, and retired
briskly over the field, gathering up the wounded and the
prisoners. The Union forces drew together on a distant
eminence, from which the bugler of the colonel in command was blowing a lively call to rendezvous.

"Where, Hilland?" cried Graham, dashing up.

The colonel removed a cigar from his mouth and said,
"Haven't seen him since I ordered the retreat. Don't
worry. He'll be here soon. Hilland is sure to come out
all right. It's a way he has. 'Twas a rather rapid change
of base, Major Graham. That the enemy should have ceased
their pursuit so abruptly puzzles me. Ah, here comes your
colonel, and when Hilland puts in an appearance we must

hold a brief council, although I suppose there is nothing left for us but to make our way back to camp and report as speedily as possible. I'd like to come back with a division, and turn the tables on those fellows. I believe we fought a divis—"

"Hilland!" shouted Graham, in a voice that drowned the colonel's words, and echoed far and wide.

There was no answer, and the fugitives were nearly all in.

Graham galloped out beyond the last lagging trooper, and with a cry that smote the hearts of those that heard it he shouted, "Hilland!" and strained his eyes in every direction. There was no response—no form in view that resembled his friend.

At wild speed he returned and rode among Hilland's command. His manner was so desperate that he drew all eyes upon him, and none seemed able or willing to answer. At last a man said, "I heard his voice just as we were breaking from that cursed grove, and I've seen or heard nothing of him since. I supposed he was on ahead with the colonel;" and that was all the information that could be obtained.

The men looked very downcast, for Hilland was almost idolized by them. Graham saw that there was an eager quest of information among themselves, and he waited with feverish impatience for further light; but nothing could be elicited from officers or privates beyond the fact that Hilland had been bravely doing his duty up to the moment when, as one of the captains said, "It was a scramble, 'each man for himself, and the devil take the hindmost.'"

As long as there had been a gleam of hope that Hilland had escaped with the rest, Graham had been almost beside himself in his feverish impatience.

He now rode to where the two colonels were standing, and the senior began rapidly, "Major Graham, we sympathize with you deeply. We all, and indeed the army, have sustained a severe loss in even the temporary absence of

Lieutenant-Colonel Hilland; for I will not believe that worse has happened than a wound and brief captivity. The enemy has acted peculiarily. I have fears that they may be flanking us and trying to intercept us on some parallel road. Therefore I shall order that we return to camp in the quickest possible time. Good God, Graham! don't take it so to heart. You've no proof that Hilland is dead. You look desperate, man. Come, remember that you are a soldier and that Hilland was one too. We've had to discount such experiences from the start."

"Gentlemen," said Graham, in a low, concentrated voice, and touching his hat to the two colonels, "I am under the command of you both—one as my superior officer, the other as leader of the expedition. I ask permission to return in search of my friend."

"I forbid it," they both cried simultaneously, while the senior officer continued, "Graham, you are beside yourself. It would be almost suicide to go back. It would certainly result in your capture, while there is not one chance in a thousand that you could do Hilland any good."

Graham made no immediate reply, but was studying the ill-omened grove with his glass. After a moment he said, "I do not think there will be any further pursuit. The enemy are retiring from the grove. My explanation of their conduct is this: There is some large decisive movement in progress, and we were merely brushed out of the way that we might learn nothing of it. My advice is that we retain this commanding position, throw out scouts on every side, and I doubt whether we find anything beyond a small rearguard in ten miles of us within a few hours."

"Your anxiety for your friend warps your judgment, and it is contrary to my instructions, which were simply to learn if there was any considerable force of the enemy in this region. Your explanation of the enemy's conduct is plausible, and has already occurred to me as a possibility. If it be the true explanation, all the more reason that we should return promptly and report what we know and what we surmise. I shall therefore order 'Retreat' to be sounded at once.''

"And I, Major Graham," said his own colonel, "must add, that while you have my sympathy, I nevertheless order you to your place in the march. Rather than permit you to carry out your mad project, I would place you under arrest."

"Gentlemen, I cannot complain of your course, or criticise your military action. You are in a better condition of mind to judge what is wise than I; and under ordinary circumstances I would submit without a word. But the circumstances are extraordinary. Hilland has been my friend since boyhood. I will not remain in suspense as to his fate; much less will I leave his wife and friends in suspense. I know that disobedience of orders in the face of the enemy is one of the gravest offences, but I must disobey them, be the consequences what they may."

As he wheeled his horse, his colonel cried, "Stop him. He's under arrest!" But Mayburn, feeling the touch of the spur, sprang into his fleet gallop, and they might as well have pursued a bird.

They saw this at once, and the colonel in command only growled, "—— this reconnoissance. Here we've lost two of the finest officers in the brigade, as well as some of our best men. Sound 'Retreat.' ''

There was a hesitancy, and a wild impulse among Hilland's men to follow Graham to the rescue, but it was sternly repressed by their officers, and the whole command was within a few moments on a sharp trot toward camp.

CHAPTER XXVIII

ITS FULFILMENT

GRAHAM soon slackened his pace when he found that he was not pursued, and as his friends disappeared he returned warily to the brow of the eminence and watched their rapid march away from the ill-fated locality. He rode over the brow of the hill as if he was following, for he had little doubt that the movements of the Union force were watched. Having tied his horse where he could not be seen from the grove, he crept back behind a sheltering bush, and with his glass scanned the scene of conflict. In the road leading through the grove there were ambulances removing the wounded. At last these disappeared, and there was not a living object in sight. He watched a little longer, and buzzards began to wheel over and settle upon the battleground—sure evidence that for the time it was deserted.

He hesitated no longer. Mounting his horse he continued down the hill so as to be screened from any possible observers, then struck off to his left to a belt of woods that extended well up to the vicinity of the grove. Making his way through this bit of forest, he soon came to an old wood-road partially grown up with bushes, and pushed his way rapidly back toward the point he wished to attain. Having approached the limits of the belt of woods, he tied his horse in a thicket, listened, then stole to the edge nearest the grove. It appeared deserted. Crouching along a rail fence with revolver in hand, he at last reached its fatal shade, and pushing through its fringe of lower growth, peered cautiously around. Here and there he saw a lifeless body or a struggling, wounded horse, over which the buzzards hovered, or on which they had already settled. Disgusting as was their presence, they reassured him, and he boldly and yet with an awful dread at heart began his search, scanning with rapid eye each prostrate form along the entire back edge of the grove through which the Union forces had burst in their swift retreat.

He soon passed beyond all traces of conflict, and then retraced his steps, uttering half-unconsciously and in a tone of anguish his friend's name. As he approached what had been the extreme right of the Union line in their retreat, and their left in the advance, he beheld a dead horse that looked familiar. He sprang forward and saw that it was Hilland's.

"Hilland! Warren!" he shouted, wild with awful foreboding.

From a dense thicket near he head a feeble groan. Rushing into it, he stumbled against the immense mossy trunk of a prostrate, decaying tree. Concealed beyond it lay his friend, apparently dying.

"Oh, Warren!" he cried, "my friend, my brother, don't you know me? Oh, live, live! I can rescue you."

There was no response from the slowly gasping man.

Graham snatched a flask from his pocket and wet the pallid lips with brandy, and then caused Hilland to swallow a little. The stimulant kindled for a few moments the flame of life, and the dying man slowly became conscious.

"Graham," he murmured feebly—"Graham, is that you?"

"Yes, yes, and I'll save you yet. Oh, in the name of Grace, I adjure you to live."

"Alas for Grace! My dream—will come true."

"Oh, Hilland, no, no! Oh, that I could die in your place! What is my life to yours! Rally, Warren, rally. My fleet horse is tied near, or if you are too badly wounded I will stay and nurse you. I'll fire a pistol shot through my arm, and then we can be sent to the hospital together.

Here, take more brandy. That's right. With **your** physique you should not think of death. Let me lift you up and stanch your wound."

"Don't move me, Graham, or I'll bleed to death instantly, and—and—I want to look in your face—once more, and send my—true love to Grace. More brandy, please. It's getting light again. Before it was dark—oh, so dark! How is it you are here?"

"I came back for you. Could I ride away and you not with me? Oh, Warren! I must save your life. I must, I must!"

"Leave me, Graham; leave me at once. You will be captured, if not killed," and Hilland spoke with energy.

"I will never leave you. There, your voice proves that your strength is coming back. Warren, Warren, can't you live for Grace's sake?"

"Graham," said Hilland, solemnly, "even my moments are numbered. One more gush of blood from my side and I'm gone. Oh, shall I become nothing? Shall I be no more than the decaying tree behind which I crawled when struck down? Shall I never see my peerless bride again? She would always have been a bride to me. I can't believe it. There must be amends somewhere for the agony of mind, not body, that I've endured as I lay here, and for the anguish that Grace will suffer. Oh, Graham, my philosophy fails me in this strait, my whole nature revolts at it. Mere corruption, chemical change, ought not to be the end of a *man*."

"Do not waste your strength in words. Live, and in a few short weeks Grace may be your nurse. Take more brandy, and then I'll go for assistance."

"No, Graham, no. Don't leave me. Life is ebbing again. Ah, ah! farewell—true friend. Un—bounded love —Grace. Commit—her—your care!"

There was a convulsive shudder and the noble form was still.

Graham knelt over him for a few moments in silent

horror. Then he tore open Hilland's vest and placed his hand over his heart. It was motionless. His hand, as he withdrew it, was bathed in blood. He poured brandy into the open lips, but the powerful stimulant was without effect. The awful truth overwhelmed him.

Hilland was dead.

He sat down, lifted his friend up against his breast, and hung over him with short, dry sobs—with a grief far beyond tears, careless, reckless of his own safety.

The bushes near him were parted, and a sweet girlish face, full of fear, wonder, and pity, looked upon him. The interpretation of the scene was but too evident, and tears gushed from the young girl's eyes.

"Oh, sir," she began in a low, faltering voice.

The mourner paid no heed.

"Please, sir," she cried, "do not grieve so. I never saw a man grieve like that. Oh, papa, papa, come, come here."

The quick pride of manhood was touched, and Graham laid his friend reverently down, and stood erect, quiet, but with heaving breast. Hasty steps approached, and a gray-haired man stood beside the young girl.

"I am your prisoner, sir," said Graham, "but in the name of humanity I ask you to let me bury my dead."

"My dear young sir, in the name of humanity and a more sacred Name, I will do all for you in my power. I am a clergyman, and am here with a party from a neighboring village, charged with the office of burying the dead with appropriate rites. I have no desire to take you prisoner, but will be glad to entertain you as my guest if the authorities will permit. Will you not give me some brief explanation of this scene while they are gathering up the dead?"

Graham did so in a few sad words. The daughter sat crying on the mossy log meanwhile, and the old man wiped his eyes again and again.

"Was there ever a nobler-looking man?" sobbed the girl; "and to think of his poor wife! Papa, he must not be buried here. He must be taken to our little cemetery by the church, and I will often put flowers on his grave."

"If you will carry out this plan, sweet child," said Graham, "one broken-hearted woman will bless you while she lives."

"Think, papa," resumed the girl—"think if it was our Henry what we would wish."

"I'm glad you feel as you do, my child. It proves that this horrible war is not hardening your heart or making you less gentle or compassionate. I will carry out your wishes and yours, sir, and will use my whole influence to prevent your noble fidelity to your friend from becoming the cause of your captivity. I will now summon assistance to carry your friend to the road, where a wagon can take him to the village."

In a few moments two negro slaves, part of the force sent to bury the dead, with their tattered hats doffed out of respect, slowly bore the body of Hilland to the roadside. Graham, with his bare head bowed under a weight of grief that seemed wellnigh crushing, followed closely, and then the old clergyman and his daughter. They laid the princely form down on the grass beside a dark-haired young Confederate officer, who was also to be taken to the cemetery.

The sad rites of burial which the good old man now performed over both friend and foe of subordinate rank need not be dwelt upon. While they were taking place Graham stood beside his friend as motionless as if he had become a statue, heedless of the crowd of villagers and country people that had gathered to the scene.

At last a sweet voice said: "Please, sir, it's time to go. You ride with papa. I am young and strong and can walk."

His only response was to take her hand and kiss it fervently. Then he turned to her father and told him of his horse that was hidden in the nearest edge of the belt of woods, and asked that it might be sent for by some one who was trustworthy.

"Here is Sampson, one of my own people; I'd trust him

with all I have;" and one of the negroes who had borne the body of Hilland hastened away as directed, and soon returned with the beautiful horse that awakened the admiration of all and the cupidity of a few of the nondescript characters that had been drawn to the place.

A rude wagon was drawn to the roadside, its rough boards covered with leafy boughs, and the Union and the Confederate officer were placed in it side by side. Then the minister climbed into his old-fashioned gig, his daughter sprang lightly in by his side, took the reins and slowly led the way, followed by the extemporized hearse, while Graham on his horse rode at the feet of his friend, chief mourner in bitter truth. The negroes who had buried the dead walked on either side of the wagon bareheaded and oblivious of the summer sun, and the country people and villagers streamed along the road after the simple procession.

The bodies were first taken to the parsonage, and the stains of battle removed by an old colored aunty, a slave of the clergyman. Graham gave into the care of the clergyman's daughter Hilland's sword and some other articles that he did not wish to carry on his return to the Union lines. Among these was an exquisite likeness of Grace smiling in her happy loveliness.

Tears again rushed into the young girl's eyes as she asked in accents of deepest commiseration: "And will you have to break the news to her?"

"No," said Graham hoarsely; "I could not do that. I'd rather face a thousand guns than that poor wife."

"Why do you not keep the likeness?"

"I could not look upon it and think of the change which this fatal day will bring to those features. I shall leave it with you until she comes for his sword and to visit his grave. No one has a better right to it than you, and in this lovely face you see the promise of your own womanhood reflected. You have not told me your name. I wish to know it, for I shall love and cherish it as one of my most sacred memories."

"Margarita Anderson," was the blushing reply. "Papa and my friends call me Rita."

"Let me call you what your name signifies, and what you have proved yourself to be—Pearl. Who is Henry?"

"My only brother. He is a captain in our army."

"You are a true Southern girl?"

"Yes, in body and soul I'm a Southern girl;" and her dark eyes flashed through her tears.

"So was the original of this likeness. She is kin to you in blood and feeling as well as in her noble qualities; but she loved her Northern husband more than the whole world, and all in it was nothing compared with him. She will come and see you some day, and words will fail her in thanks."

"And will you come with her?"

"I don't know. I may be dead long before that time."

The young girl turned away, and for some reason her tears flowed faster than ever before.

"Pearl, my tender-hearted child, don't grieve over what would be so small a grief to me. This evil day has clouded your young life with the sadness of others. But at your age it will soon pass;" and he returned to his friend and took from him the little mementoes that he knew would be so dear to Grace.

Soon after, the two bodies were borne to the quaint old church and placed before the altar. Both were dressed in their full uniforms, and there was a noble calmness on the face of each as they slumbered side by side in the place sacred to the God of peace, and at peace with each other for evermore.

For an hour the bell tolled slowly, and the people passed in at one door, looked upon the manly forms, and with awed faces crept out at the other.

It was indeed a memorable day for the villagers. They had been awakened in the dawn by sounds of distant conflict. They had exulted over a brilliant victory as the Confederate forces came marching rapidly through their streets.

They had been put on the *qui vive* to know what the rapid movement of their troops meant. Some of the most severely wounded had been left in their care. The battlefield with its horrors had been visited, and there was to be a funeral service over two actors in the bloody drama, whose untimely fate excited not only sympathy, but the deep interest and curiosity which ever attend upon those around whom rumor has woven a romantic history. The story of Graham's return in search of his friend, of the circumstances of their discovery by Rita, of the likeness of the lovely wife who would soon be heart-broken from the knowledge of what was known to them, had got abroad among the people, and their warm Southern hearts were more touched by the fate of their Northern foe than by that of the officer wearing the livery of their own service, but of whom little was known.

Graham's profound grief also impressed them deeply; and the presence of a Union officer, sitting among them, forgetful of his danger, of all except that his friend was dead, formed a theme which would be dwelt upon for months to come.

Near the close of the day, after some appropriate words in the church, the venerable clergyman, with his white locks uncovered, led the way through the cemetery to its further side, where, under the shade of an immense juniper-tree, were two open graves. As before, Graham followed his friend, and after him came Rita with a number of her young companions, dressed in white and carrying baskets of flowers. After an impressive burial service had been read, the young girls passed to and fro between the graves, throwing flowers in each and singing as they went a hymn breathing the certainty of the immortality that had been the object of poor Hilland's longing aspiration. Graham's heart thrilled as he heard the words, for they seemed the answer to his friend's questions. But, though his feelings might be touched deeply, he was the last man to be moved by sentiment or emotion from a position to which his inexorable reason had conducted him.

The sun threw its level rays over a scene that he never forgot—the white-haired clergyman standing between the open graves; the young maidens, led by the dark-eyed Rita, weaving in and out, their white hands and arms glowing like ivory as they strewed the flowers, meanwhile singing with an unconscious grace and pathos that touched the rudest hearts; the concourse of people, chiefly women, old men, and children, for the young and strong were either mouldering on battlefields or marching to others; the awed sable faces of the negroes in the further background; the exquisite evening. sky; the songs of unheeding birds, so near to man in their choice of habitation, so remote from his sorrows and anxieties—all combined to form a picture and a memory which would be vivid and real to his latest day.

The graves were at last filled and piled up with flowers. Then Graham, standing uncovered before them all, spoke slowly and earnestly:

"People of the South, you see before you a Northern man, an officer in the Union army; but as I live I cherish no thought of enmity toward one of you. On the contrary, my heart is overwhelmed with gratitude. You have placed here side by side two brave men. You have rendered to their dust equal reverence and honor. I am in accord with you. I believe that the patriotism of one was as sincere as that of the other, the courage of one as high as that of the other, that the impulses which led them to offer up their lives were equally noble. In your generous sympathy for a fallen foe you have proved yourselves Americans in the best sense of the word. May the day come when that name shall suffice for us all. Believe me, I would defend your homes and my own with equal zeal;" and with a bow of profound respect he turned to the grave of his friend.

With a delicate appreciation of his wish, the people, casting backward lingering, sympathetic glances, ebbed away and he was soon left alone.

CHAPTER XXIX

A SOUTHERN GIRL

WHEN Graham was left alone he knelt and bowed his head in the flowers that Rita had placed on Hilland's grave, and the whole horrible truth seemed to grow, to broaden and deepen, like a gulf that had opened at his feet. Hilland, who had become a part of his own life and seemed inseparable from all its interests, had disappeared forever. But yesterday he was the centre of vast interests and boundless love; now he had ceased to be. The love would remain, but oh, the torture of a boundless love when its object has passed beyond its reach!

The thought of Grace brought to the mourner an indescribable anguish. Once his profound love for her had asserted itself in a way that had stung him to madness, and the evil thought had never returned. Now she seemed to belong to the dead husband even more than when he was living. The thought that tortured him most was that Grace would not long survive Hilland. The union between the two had been so close and vital that the separation might mean death. The possibility overwhelmed him, and he grew faint and sick. Indeed it would seem that he partially lost consciousness, for at last he became aware that some one was standing near and pleading with him. Then he saw it was Rita.

"Oh, sir," she entreated, "do not grieve so. It breaks my heart to see a man so overcome. It seems terrible. It makes me feel that there are depths of sorrow that frighten me. Oh, come with me—do, please. I fear you've eaten nothing to-day, and we have supper all ready for you."

Graham tottered to his feet and passed his hand across his brow, as if to brush away an evil dream.

"Indeed, sir, you look sick and faint. Take my arm and lean on me. I assure you I am very strong."

"Yes, Pearl, you are strong. Many live to old age and never become as true a woman as you are to-day. This awful event has wellnigh crushed me, and, now I think of it, I have scarcely tasted food since last evening. Thank you, my child, I will take your arm. In an hour or two I shall gain self-control."

"My heart aches for you, sir," she said, as they passed slowly through the twilight.

"May it be long before it aches from any sorrow of your own, Pearl."

The parsonage adjoined the church. The old clergyman abounded in almost paternal kindness, and pressed upon Graham a glass of home-made wine. After he had taken this and eaten a little, his strength and poise returned, and he gave his entertainers a fuller account of Hilland and his relations, and in that Southern home there was as genuine sympathy for the inmates of the Northern home as if they all had been devoted to the same cause.

"There are many subjects on which we differ," said his host. "You perceive that I have slaves, but they are so attached to me that I do not think they would leave me if I offered them their freedom. I have been brought up to think slavery right. My father and grandfather before me held slaves and always treated them well. I truly think they did better by them than the bondmen could have done for themselves. To give them liberty and send them adrift would be almost like throwing little children out into the world. I know that there are evils and abuses connected with our system, but I feel sure that liberty given to a people unfitted for it would be followed by far greater evils."

"It's a subject to which I have given very little attention," Graham replied. "I have spent much of my life abroad, and certainly your servants are better off than the peasantry and very poor in many lands that I have visited."

With a kind of wonder, he thought of the truth that Hilland, who so hated slavery, had been lifted from the battle-field by slaves, and that his remains had been treated with reverent honor by a slave-holder.

The old clergyman's words also proved that, while he deprecated the war unspeakably, his whole sympathy was with the South. His only son, of whom neither he nor Rita could speak without looks of pride and affection kindling in their faces, was in the Confederate service, and the old man prayed as fervently for success to the cause to which he had devoted the treasure of his life as any Northern father could petition the God of nations for his boy and the restoration of the Union. At the same time his nature was too large, too highly ennobled by Christianity, for a narrow, vindictive bitterness. He could love the enemy that he was willing his son should oppose in deadly battle.

"We hope to secure our independence," he added, "and to work out our national development according to the genius of our own people. I pray and hope for the time when the North and South may exist side by side as two friendly nations. Your noble words this afternoon found their echo in my heart. Even though my son should be slain by a Northern hand, as your friend has been by a Southern, I wish to cherish no vindictive bitterness and enmity. The question must now be settled by the stern arbitrament of battle; but when the war is over let it not be followed by an era of hate."

He then told Graham how he had lost his beloved wife years before, and how lonely and desolate he had been until Rita had learned to care for him and provide for his comfort with almost hourly vigilance.

"Yes," said Graham, "I have seen it; she is to you what my friend's wife is to her invalid father, the immeasurable blessing of his life. How it will be now I hardly know, for

I fear that her grief will destroy her, and the old major, her father, could not long survive.''

A note was now handed to the old gentleman, who, having read it, appeared greatly distressed. After a moment's hesitancy he gave it to Graham, who read as follows:

"I heard the North'ner speak this arternoon, an' I can't be one to take and rob him of his horse and send him to prison. But it'll be done to-night if you can't manage his escape. Every rode is watched, an' your house will be searched to-night.   ONE OF THE BAND.

"You'll burn this an' keep mum or my neck will be stretched.''

"Who brought the note?'' Mr. Anderson asked, going to the door and questioning a colored woman.

"Dunno, mas'r. De do' open a little, and de ting flew in on de flo'.''

"Well,''' said Graham, "I must mount and go at once;'' and he was about to resume his arms.

"Wait, wait; I must think!'' cried his host. "For you to go alone would be to rush into the very evils we are warned against. I am pained and humiliated beyond measure by this communication. Mr. Graham, do not judge us harshly. There is, I suppose, a vile sediment in every community, and there is here a class that won't enlist in open, honorable warfare, but prowl around, chiefly at night, intent on deeds like this.''

"Papa,'' said Rita, who had read the warning, "I know what to do;'' and her brave spirit flashed in her eyes.

"You, my child?''

"Yes. I'll prove to Mr. Graham what a Southern girl will do for a guest—for one who has trusted her. The deep, deep disgrace of his capture and robbery shall not come on our heads. I will guide him at once through the woods to old Uncle Jehu's cabin. No one will think of looking for him there; for there is little more than a bridle-path leading to it; but I know the way, every inch of it.''

"But, Rita, I could send one of the servants with Mr. Graham.''

"No, papa; he would be missed and afterward questioned, and some awful revenge taken on him. You must say that I have retired when the villains come. You must keep all our servants in. Mr. Graham and I will slip out. He can saddle his horse, and I, you know well, can saddle mine. Now we must apparently go to our rooms and within half an hour slip out unperceived and start. No one will ever dare touch me, even if it is found out."

"Pearl, priceless Pearl, I'll fight my way through all the guerillas in the land, rather than subject you to peril."

"You could not fight your way through them, the cowardly skulkers. What chance would you have in darkness? My plan brings me no peril, for if they met us they would not dare to touch me. But if it costs me my life I *will* go," she concluded passionately. "This disgrace must not fall on our people."

"Rita is right," said the old clergyman, solemnly. "I could scarcely survive the disgrace of having a guest taken from my home, and they would have to walk over my prostrate form before it could be done; and to send you out alone would be even more shameful. The plan does not involve much peril to Rita. Although, in a sense, you are my enemy, I will trust this pearl beyond price to your protection, and old Jehu will return with her until within a short distance of the house. As she says, I think no one in this region would harm her. I will co-operate with you, Rita, and entreat the Heavenly Father until I clasp you in my arms again. Act, act at once."

Graham was about to protest again, but she silenced him by a gesture that was almost imperious. "Don't you see that for papa's sake, for my own, as well as yours, I must go? Now let us say good-night as if we were parting unsuspicious of trouble. When I tap at your door, Mr. Graham, you will follow me; and you, papa, try to keep our people in ignorance."

Graham wrung the clergyman's hand in parting, and said, "You will always be to me a type of the noblest development of humanity."

"God bless you, sir," was the reply, "and sustain you through the dangers and trying scenes before you. I am but a simple old man, trying to do right with God's help. And, believe me, sir, the South is full of men as sincere as I am."

Within half an hour Graham followed his fair guide down a back stairway and out into the darkness. Rita's pony was at pasture in a field adjoining the stable, but he came instantly at her soft call.

"I shall not put on my saddle," she whispered. "If I leave it hanging in the stable it will be good evidence that I am in my room. There will be no need of our riding fast, and, indeed, I have often ridden without a saddle for fun. I will guide you to your horse and saddle in the dark stable, for we must take him out of a back door, so that there will be no sound of his feet on the boards."

Within a few moments they were passing like shadows down a shaded lane that led from the house to the forest, and then entered what was a mere bridle-path, the starlight barely enabling the keen-eyed Rita to make it out at times. The thick woods on either side prevented all danger of flank attacks. After riding some little time they stopped and listened. The absolute silence, broken only by the cries of the wild creatures of the night, convinced them that they were not followed. Then Rita said, "Old Jehu has a bright boy of sixteen or thereabout, and he'll guide you north through the woods as far as he can, and then God will protect and guide you until you are safe. I know He will help you to escape, that you may say words of comfort to the poor, broken-hearted wife."

"Yes, Pearl, I think I shall escape. I take your guidance as a good omen. If I could only be sure that no harm came to you and your noble father!"

"The worst of harm would have come to us had we permitted the evil that was threatened."

"You seem very young, Pearl, and yet you are in many ways very mature and womanly."

"I am young—only sixteen—but mamma's death and the responsibility it brought me made my childhood brief. Then Henry is five years older than I, and I always played with him, and, of course, you know I tried to reach up to those things that he thought about and did. I've never been to school. Papa is educating me, and oh, he knows so much, and he makes knowledge so interesting, that I can't help learning a little. And then Henry's going into the war, and all that is happening, makes me feel so very, very old and sad at times;" and so she continued in low tones to tell about herself and Henry and her father, of their hopes of final victory, and all that made up her life. This she did with a guileless frankness, and yet with a refined reserve that was indescribable in its simple pathos and beauty. In spite of himself Graham was charmed and soothed, while he wondered at the exquisite blending of girlhood and womanhood in his guide. She also questioned him about the North and the lands he had visited, about his aunt and Grace and her father; and Graham's tremulous tones as he spoke of Grace led her to say sorrowfully, "Ah, she is very, very dear to you also."

"Yes," he said, imitating her frankness, "she is dearer to me than my life. I would gladly have died in Hilland's place to have saved her this sorrow. Were it not for the hope of serving her in some way, death would have few terrors to me. There, my child, I have spoken to you as I have to only one other, my dear old aunty, who is like a mother. Your noble trust begets trust."

Then he became aware that she was crying bitterly.

"Pearl, Pearl," he said, "don't cry. I have become accustomed to a sad heart, and it's an old, old story."

"Oh, Mr. Graham, I remember hearing mamma say once that women learn more through their hearts than their heads. I have often thought of her words, and I think they must be true. Almost from the first my heart told me that there was something about you which made you different from other people. Why is the world so full of trouble of every kind?

Ah, well, papa has taught me that heaven will make amends for everything."

They had now reached a little clearing, and Rita said that they were near Jehu's cabin, and that their final words had better be said before awakening the old man. "I must bathe my face, too," she added, "for he would not understand my tears," and went to a clear little spring but a few paces away.

Graham also dismounted. When she returned he took her hand and raised it reverently to his lips as he said, "Pearl, this is not a case for ordinary thanks. I no doubt owe my life, certainly my liberty, to you. On that I will not dwell. I owe to you and your father far more, and so does poor Grace Hilland. You insured a burial for my friend that will bring a world of comfort to those who loved him. The thought of your going to his grave and placing upon it fresh flowers from time to time will contain more balm than a thousand words of well-meant condolence. Pearl, my sweet, pure, noble child, is there nothing I can do for you?"

"Yes," she faltered; "it may be that you can return all that we have done a hundred-fold. It may be that you will meet Henry in battle. In the memory of his little sister you will spare him, will you not? If he should be captured I will tell him to write to you, and I feel sure that you will remember our lonely ride and the gray old father who is praying for you now, and will not leave him to suffer."

Graham drew a seal ring from his finger and said: "Dear Pearl, take this as a pledge that I will serve him in any way in my power and at any cost to myself. I hope the day will come when he will honor me with his friendship, and I would as soon strike the friend I have lost as your brother."

"Now I am content," she said. "I believe every word you say."

"And Grace Hilland will come some day and claim you as a sister dearly beloved. And I, sweet Pearl, will honor your memory in my heart of hearts. The man who wins you as his bride may well be prouder than an emperor."

"Oh, no, Mr. Graham, I'm just a simple Southern girl."

"There are few like you, I fear, South or North. You are a girl to kindle every manly instinct and power, and I shall be better for having known you. The hope of serving you and yours in some way and at some time will give a new zest and value to my life."

"Do not speak so kindly or I shall cry again. I've been afraid you would think me silly, I cry so easily. I do not think we Southern girls are like those at the North. They are colder, I imagine, or at least more able to control their feelings. Papa says I am a child of the South. I can't decide just how much or how little I ought to feel on all occasions, and ever since I saw you mourning over your friend with just such passionate grief as I should feel, my whole heart has ached for you. You will come and see us again if you have a chance?"

"I will make chances, Pearl, even though they involve no little risk."

"No, no; don't do that. You ought to care too much for us to do that. Nothing would give me pleasure that brought danger to you. If I could only know that you reached your friends in safety!"

"I'll find a way of letting you know if I can."

"Well, then, good-by. It's strange, but you seem like an old, old friend. Oh, I know Henry will like you, and that you will like him. Next to mamma's, your ring shall be my dearest treasure. I shall look at it every night and think I have added one more chance of Henry's safety. Oh, I could worship the man who saved his life."

"And any man might worship you. Good-by, Pearl;" and he kissed her hand again and again, then lifted her on her pony with a tenderness that was almost an embrace, and she rode slowly to the door of a little log cabin, while Graham remained concealed in the shadow of the woods until it was made certain that no one was in the vicinity except Jehu and his family.

The old man was soon aroused, and his ejaculations and exclamations were innumerable.

"No, missy, dars no un been roun' heah for right smart days. It's all safe, an' Jehu an' his ole ooman knows how ter keep mum when Mas'r Anderson says mum; an' so does my peart boy Huey"—who, named for his father, was thus distinguished from him. "An' de hossifer is a Linkum man? Sho, sho! who'd a tink it, and his own son a 'Federate! Well, well, Mas'r Anderson isn't low-down white trash. If he thought a ting was right I reckon de hull worl' couldn't make him cut up any white-trash didoes."

When Rita explained further the old negro replied with alacrity: "Ob cose Jehu will took you home safe, an' proud he'll be ter go wid you, honey. You'se a mighty peart little gal, an' does youse blood an' broughten up jestice. Mighty few would dar' ride fi e mile troo de lonesome woods wid a strange hossifer, if he be a Linkum man. He mus' be sumpen like Linkum hisself. Yes, if you bain't afeared ter show him de way, Huey needn't be;" and the boy, who was now wide awake, said he'd "like notten better dan showin' a Linkum man troo de woods."

Graham was summoned, and in a few moments all was arranged.

He then drew the old man aside and said, "You good, faithful old soul, take care of that girl as the apple of your eye, for she has only one equal in the world. Here is one hundred dollars. That will pay for a good many chickens and vegetables, won't it?"

"Lor' bless you, mas'r, dey ain't chickens nuff in Ole Virginny to brought hundred dollars."

"Well, I'll tell you what I'm afraid of. This region may be wasted by war, like so many others. You may not be troubled in this out-of-the-way place. If Mr. Anderson's family is ever in need, you are now paid to supply them with all that you can furnish."

" 'Deed I is, mas'r, double paid."

"Be faithful to them and you shall have more 'Linkum money,' as you call it. Keep it, for your money down here won't be worth much soon."

"Dat's shoah. De cullud people bain't all prayin' for Linkum for notten."

"Good-by. Do as I say and you shall be taken care of some day. Say nothing about this."

"Mum's de word all roun' ter-night, mas'r."

"Huey, are you ready?"

"I is, mas'r."

"Lead the way, then;" and again approaching Rita, Graham took off his hat and bowed low as he said, "Give my grateful greeting to your honored father, and may every hope of his heart be fulfilled in return for his good deeds to-day. As for you, Miss Anderson, no words can express my profound respect and unbounded gratitude. We shall meet again in happier times;" and backing his horse, while he still remained uncovered, he soon turned and followed Huey.

"Well, now," ejaculated Jehu. " 'Clar ter you ef dat ar Linkum hossifer bain't nigh onter bein' as fine a gemman as Mas'r Henry hisself. Won't you take some 'freshment, missy? No? Den I'se go right 'long wid you."

Rita enjoined silence, ostensibly for the reason that it was prudent, but chiefly that she might have a respite from the old man's garrulousness. Her thoughts were very busy. The first romance of her young life had come, and she still felt on her hands the kisses that had been so warm and sincere, although she knew they were given by one who cherished a hopeless love. After all, it was but her vivid Southern imagination that had been kindled by the swift, strange events of the past twenty-four hours. With the fine sense of the best type of dawning womanhood, she had been deeply moved by Graham's strong nature. She had seen in him a love for another man that was as tender and passionate as that of a woman, and yet it was bestowed upon the husband of the woman whom he had loved for years. That he had not hesitated to risk captivity and death in returning for his friend proved his bravery to be unlimited, and a Southern girl adores courage. For a time Graham would be the ideal of her girlish heart. His words of admiration and respect were dwelt upon, and her cheeks flushed up seen in the deep shadow of the forest. Again her tears would fall fast as she thought of his peril and of all the sad scenes of the day and the sadder ones still to come. Grace Hilland, a Southern girl like herself, became a glorified image to her fancy, and it would now be her chief ambition to be like her. She would keep her lovely portrait on her bureau beside her Bible, and it should be almost equally sacred.

In the edge of the forest she parted from Jehu with many and warm thanks, for she thought it wise that there should not be the slightest chance of his being seen. She also handed him a Confederate bill out of her slender allowance, patted him on the shoulder as she would some faithful animal, and rode away. He crept along after her till he saw her let down some bars and turn her pony into the fields. He then crept on till he saw her enter a door, and then stole back to the forest and shambled homeward as dusky as the shadows in which he walked, chuckling, "Missy Rita, sweet honey, guv me one of dem 'Federate rags. Oh, golly! I'se got more money—live Linkum money —dan Mas'r Anderson hisself, and I'se got notten ter do but raise chickens an' garden sass all my born days. Missy Rita's red cheeks never grow pale long as Jehu or Huey can tote chickens and sass."

CHAPTER XXX

GUERILLAS

G RAHAM, beyond a few low, encouraging words, held his peace and also enjoined silence on his youthful guide. His plan was to make a wide circuit around the battlefield of the previous day, and then strike the trail of the Union forces, which he believed he could follow at night. Huey thought that this could be done and that they could keep in the shelter of the woods most of the distance, and this they accomplished, reconnoitring the roads most carefully before crossing them. Huey was an inveterate trapper; and as his pursuit was quite as profitable as raising "sass," old Jehu gave the boy his own way. Therefore he knew every path through the woods for miles around.

The dawn was in the east before Graham reached the Union trail, and he decided to spend the day in a dense piece of woods not very far distant. Huey soon settled the question of Mayburn's provender by purloining a few sheaves of late oats from a field that they passed; but when they reached their hiding-place Graham was conscious that he was in need of food himself, and he also remembered that a boy is always ravenous.

"Well, Huey," he said, "in providing for the horse you have attended to the main business, but what are we going to do?"

"We'se gwine ter do better'n de hoss. If mas'r 'll 'zamine his saddle-bags, reckon he'll fine dat Missy Rita hain't de leddy to sen' us off on a hunt widout a bite of suthin' good. She sez, sez she to me, in kind o' whisper like, 'Mas'r Graham 'll fine suthin' you'll like, Huey;'" and the boy eyed the saddle-bags like a young wolf.

"Was there ever such a blessed girl!" cried Graham, as he pulled out a flask of wine, a fowl cut into nice portions, bread, butter, and relishes—indeed, the best that her simple housekeeping afforded in the emergency. In the other bag there was also a piece of cake of such portentous size that Huey clasped his hands and rolled up his eyes as he had seen his parents do when the glories of heaven were expatiated upon in the negro prayer-meetings.

"That's all for you, Huey, and here's some bread and cold ham to go with it. When could she have provided these things so thoughtfully? It must have been before she called me last night. Now, Huey, if you ever catch anything extra nice in the woods you take it to Miss Rita. There is ten dollars to pay you; and when the Lincoln men get possession here I'll look after you and give you a fine chance, if you have been faithful. You must not tell Miss Rita what I say, but seem to do all of your own accord. I wish I had more money with me, but you will see me again, and I will make it all right with you."

"It's all right now, mas'r. What wouldn't I do for Missy Rita? When my ole mammy was sick she bro't med'cin, and a right smart lot ob tings, and brung her troo de weariness. Golly! Wonder Missy Rita don't go straight up ter heben like dem rackets dey shoots when de 'Federates say dey hab a vict'ry;" and then the boy's mouth became so full that he was speechless for a long time.

The sense of danger, and the necessity for the utmost vigilance, had diverted Graham's thoughts during his long night ride; and with a soldier's habit he had concentrated his faculties on the immediate problem of finding the trail, verifying Huey's local knowledge by observation of the stars. Now, in the cool summer morning, with Rita's delicious repast before him, life did not seem so desperate a thing as on the day before. Although exceedingly wea-

ried, the strength of mind which would enable him to face
his sad tasks was returning. He thought little about the
consequences of his disobedience to orders, and cared less.
If he lost his rank he would enlist as a private soldier after
he had done all in his power for Grace, who had been committed to his care by Hilland's last words. He felt that she
had the most sacred claims upon him, and yet he queried,
"What can I do for her beyond communicating every detail
of her husband's last hours and his burial? What remedy
is there for a sorrow like hers?"

At the same time he felt that a lifelong and devoted
friendship might bring solace and help at times, and this
hope gave a new value to his life. He also thought it very
possible that the strange vicissitudes of war might put it in
his power to serve the Andersons, in whom he felt a grateful interest that only such scenes as had just occurred could
have awakened. It would ever be to him a source of unalloyed joy to add anything to Rita Anderson's happiness.

His kind old aunt, too, had her full share of his thoughts
as he reclined on the dun-colored leaves of the previous
year and reviewed the past and planned for the future.
He recalled her words, "that good would come of it," when
he had promised to "live and do his best." Although in
his own life he had missed happiness, there was still a prospect of his adding much to the well-being of others.

But how could he meet Grace again? He trembled at
the very thought. Her grief would unman him. It was
agony even to imagine it; and she might, in her ignorance
of an officer's duties in battle, think that if he had kept
near Hilland the awful event might have been averted.

After all, he could reach but one conclusion—to keep his
old promise "to do his best," as circumstances indicated.

Asking Huey, who had the trained ear of a hunter, to
watch and listen, he took some sleep in preparation for the
coming night, and then gave the boy a chance to rest.

The day passed quietly, and in the evening he dismissed
Huey, with assurances to Rita and her father that a night's

ride would bring him within the Union lines, and that he now knew the way well. The boy departed in high spirits, feeling that he would like "showin' Linkum men troo de woods" even better than trapping.

Then looking well to his arms, and seeing that they were ready for instant use, Graham started on his perilous ride, walking his horse and stopping to listen from time to time. Once in the earlier part of the night he heard the sound of horses' feet, and drawing back into the deep shadow of the woods he saw three or four men gallop by. They were undoubtedly guerillas looking for him, or on some prowl with other objects in view. At last he knew he must be near his friends, and he determined to push on, even though the dawn was growing bright; but he had hardly reached this conclusion when but a short distance in advance a dozen horsemen dashed out of a grove and started toward him.

They were part of "The Band," who, with the instincts of their class, conjectured too truly that, since he had eluded them thus far, their best chance to intercept him would be at his natural approach to the Union lines; and now, with the kind of joy peculiar to themselves, they felt that their prey was in their power, beyond all hope of escape, for Graham was in plain sight upon a road inclosed on either side by a high rail fence. There were so many guerillas that there was not a ghost of a chance in fighting or riding through them, and for a moment his position seemed desperate.

"It's Mayburn to the rescue now," he muttered, and he turned and sped away, and every leap of his noble horse increased the distance between him and his pursuers. His confidence soon returned, for he felt that unless something unforeseen occurred he could ride all around them. His pursuers fired two shots, which were harmless enough, but to his dismay Graham soon learned that they were signals, for from a farmhouse near other horsemen entered the road, and he was between two parties.

There was not a moment to lose. Glancing ahead, he

saw a place where the fence had lost a rail or two. He spurred toward it, and the gallant horse flew over like a bird into a wide field fringed on the further side by a thick growth of timber. Bullets from the intercepting party whizzed around him; but he sped on unharmed, while his pursuers only stopped long enough to throw off a few rails, and then both of the guerilla squads rode straight for the woods, with the plan of keeping the fugitive between them, knowing that in its tangle he must be caught.

Graham resolved to risk another volley in order to ride around the pursuers nearest the Union lines, thus throwing them in the rear, with no better chance than a stern chase would give them. In order to accomplish this, however, he had to circle very near the woods, and in doing so saw a promising wood-road leading into them. The yelling guerillas were so close as to make his first plan of escape extremely hazardous; therefore, following some happy instinct he plunged into the shade of the forest. The road proved narrow, but it was open and unimpeded by overhanging boughs. Indeed, the trees were the straight, slender pines in which the region abounded, and he gained on all of his pursuers except two, who, like himself, were superbly mounted. The thud of their horses' hoofs kept near, and he feared that he might soon come to some obstruction which would bring them to close quarters. Mayburn was giving signs of weariness, for his mettle had been sorely tried of late, and Graham resolved to ambush his pursuers if possible. An opportunity occurred speedily, for the road made a sharp turn, and there was a small clearing where the timber had been cut. The dawn had as yet created but a twilight in the woods, and the obscurity aided his purpose. He drew up by the roadside at the beginning of the clearing, and in a position where he could not readily be seen until the guerillas were nearly abreast, and waited, with his heavy revolver in hand and his drawn sword lying across the pommel of his saddle.

On they came at a headlong pace, and passed into the

clearing but a few feet away. There were two sharp reports, with the slightest possible interval. The first man dropped instantly; the other rode wildly for a few moments and then fell headlong, while the riderless horses galloped on for a time.

Graham, however, soon overtook them, and with far more compunction than he had felt in shooting their riders, he struck them such a blow with his sword on their necks, a little back of their ears, that they reeled and fell by the roadside. He feared those horses more than all "The Band"; for if mounted again they might tire Mayburn out in a prolonged chase.

To his great joy the wood lane soon emerged into another large open field, and he now felt comparatively safe.

The guerillas, on hearing the shots, spurred on exultantly, feeling sure of their prey, but only to stumble over their fallen comrades. One was still able to explain the mode of their discomfiture; and the dusky road beyond at once acquired wholesome terrors for the survivors, who rode on more slowly and warily, hoping now for little more than the recapture of the horses, which were the envy of all their lawless hearts. Your genuine guerilla will always incur a heavy risk for a fine horse. They soon discovered the poor brutes, and saw at a glance that they would be of no more service in irregular prowlings. Infuriated more at the loss of the beasts than at that of the men, they again rushed forward only to see Graham galloping easily away in the distance.

Even in their fury they recognized that further pursuit was useless, and with bitter curses on their luck, they took the saddles from the fallen horses, and carried their associates, one dead and the other dying, to the farmhouse in which dwelt a sympathizer, who had given them refreshment during the night.

A few hours later—for he travelled the rest of the way very warily—Graham reported to his colonel, and found the brigade under orders to move on the following morning, provided with ten days' rations.

The officer was both delighted and perplexed. "It's a hard case," he said. "You acted from the noblest impulses; but it was flat disobedience to orders."

"I know it. I shall probably be dismissed from the service. If so, colonel, I will enlist as a private in your regiment. Then you can shoot me if I disobey again."

"Well, you are the coolest fellow that ever wore the blue. Come with me to headquarters."

The fact of his arrival, and an imperfect story of what had occurred, soon got abroad among the men; and they were wild in their approval, cheering him with the utmost enthusiasm as he passed to the brigadier's tent. The general was a genuine cavalryman; and was too wise in his day and generation to alienate his whole brigade by any martinetism. He knew Graham's reputation well, and he was about starting on a dangerous service. The cheers of the men crowding to his tent spoke volumes. Hilland's regiment seemed half beside themselves when they learned that Graham had found their lieutenant-colonel dying on the field, and that he had been given an honorable burial. The general, therefore, gave Graham a most cordial welcome; and said that the question was not within his jurisdiction, and that he would forward full particulars at once through the proper channels to the Secretary of War, adding, "We'll be on the march before orders can reach you. Meanwhile take your old command."

Then the story had to be repeated in detail to the chief officers of the brigade. Graham told it in as few words as possible, and they all saw that his grief was so profound that the question of his future position in the army was scarcely thought of. "I am not a sentimental recruit," he said in conclusion. "I know the nature of my offence, and will make no plea beyond that I believed that all danger to our command had passed, and that it would ride quietly into camp, as it did. I also thought that my superiors in giving the order were more concerned for my safety than for anything else. What the consequences are to myself personally, I don't care a straw. There are some misfortunes which dwarf all others." The conference broke up with the most hearty expressions of sympathy, and the regret for Hilland's death was both deep and genuine.

"I have a favor to ask my colonel, with your approval, General," said Graham. "I would like to take a small detachment and capture the owner of the farmhouse at which was harbored part of the guerilla band from which I escaped. I would like to make him confess the names of his associates, and send word to them that if harm comes to any who showed kindness or respect to officers of our brigade, severe punishment will be meted out on every one whenever the region is occupied by Union forces."

"I order the thing to be done at once," cried the general. "Colonel, give Major Graham as many men as he needs; and, Graham, send word we'll hang every mother's son of 'em and burn their ranches if they indulge in any more of their devilish outrages. Bring the farmer into camp, and I will send him to Washington as a hostage."

On this occasion Graham obeyed orders literally. The farmer and two of the guerillas were captured; and when threatened with a noosed rope confessed the names of the others. A nearly grown son of the farmer was intrusted with the general's message to their associates; and Graham added emphatically that he intended to come himself some day and see that it was obeyed. "Tell them to go into the army and become straightforward soldiers if they wish, but if I ever hear of another outrage I'll never rest till the general's threat is carried out."

Graham's deadly pistol shots and the reputation he had gained in the vicinity gave weight to his words; and "The Band" subsided into the most humdrum farmers of the region. Rita had ample information of his safety, for it soon became known that he had killed two of the most active and daring of the guerillas and captured three others; and she worshipped the hero of her girlish fancy all the more devoutly.

CHAPTER XXXI

JUST IN TIME

GRAHAM returned to camp early in the afternoon, and was again greeted with acclamations, for the events that had occurred had become better known. The men soon saw, however, from his sad, stern visage that he was in no mood for ovations, and that noisy approval of his course was very distasteful. After reporting, he went directly to his tent; its flaps were closed, and Iss was instructed to permit no one to approach unless bearing orders. The faithful negro, overjoyed at his master's safe return, marched to and fro like a belligerent watch-dog.

Graham wrote the whole story to his aunt, and besought her to make known to Grace with all the gentleness and tact that she possessed the awful certainty of her husband's death. A telegram announcing him among the missing had already been sent. "Say to her," he said, in conclusion, "that during every waking moment I am grieving for her and with her. Oh, I tremble at the effect of her grief: I dread its consequences beyond all words. You know that every power I possess is wholly at her service. Write me daily and direct me what to do—if, alas! it is within my power to do anything in regard to a grief that is without remedy."

He then explained that the command was under orders to move the following day, and that he would write again when he could.

During the next two weeks he saw some active service, taking part in several skirmishes and one severe engagement. In the last it was his fortune to receive on the shoulder a sabre-cut which promised to be a painful though not a dangerous wound, his epaulet having broken the force of the blow.

On the evening of the battle a telegram was forwarded to him containing the words:

"Have written fully. Come home if you can for a short time. All need you.   CHARLOTTE MAYBURN."

In the rapid movements of his brigade his aunt's letters had failed to reach him, and now he esteemed his wound most fortunate since it secured him a leave of absence.

His journey home was painful in every sense of the word. He was oppressed by the saddest of memories. He both longed and dreaded unspeakably to see Grace, and the lack of definite tidings from her left his mind a prey to the dreariest forebodings, which were enhanced by his aunt's telegram. The physical pain from which he was never free was almost welcomed as a diversion from his distress of mind. He stopped in Washington only long enough to have his wound re-dressed, and pushed northward. A fatality of delays irritated him beyond measure; and it was late at night when he left the cars and was driven to his aunt's residence.

A yearning and uncontrollable interest impelled him to approach first the cottage which contained the woman, dearer to him than all the world, who had been so strangely committed to his care. To his surprise there was a faint light in the library; and Hilland's ill-omened dream flashed across his mind. With a prophetic dread at heart, he stepped lightly up the piazza to a window. As he turned the blinds he witnessed a scene that so smote his heart that he had to lean against the house for support. Before him was the reality of poor Hilland's vision.

On the rug before the flickering fire the stricken wife crouched, wringing her hands, which looked ghostly in their whiteness. A candle burning dimly on a table in-

creased the light of the fire; and by their united rays he
saw, with a thrill of horror, that her loosened hair, which
covered her bowed face and shoulders, was, in truth, silver
white; and its contrast with her black wrapper made the
whole scene, linked as it was with a dead man's dream, so
ghostly that he shuddered, and was inclined to believe it to
be the creation of his overwrought senses. In self-distrust
he looked around. Other objects were clear in the faint
moonlight. He was perfectly conscious of the dull ache
of his wound. Had the phantom crouched before the fire
vanished? No; but now the silver hair was thrown back,
and Grace Hilland's white, agonized face was lifted heaven-
ward. Oh, how white it was!

She slowly took a dark-colored vial from her bosom.

Thrilled with unspeakable horror, "Grace!" he shouted,
and by a desperate effort threw the blind upward and off
from its hinges, and it fell with a crash on the veranda.
Springing into the apartment, he had not reached her side
before the door opened, and his aunt's frightened face
appeared.

"Great God! what does this mean, Alford?"

"What *does* it mean, indeed!" he echoed in agonized
tones, as he knelt beside Grace, who had fallen on the floor
utterly unconscious. "Bring the candle here," he added
hoarsely.

She mechanically obeyed and seemed almost paralyzed.
After a moment's search he snatched up something and
cried: "She's safe, she's safe! The cork is not removed."
Then he thrust the vial into his pocket, and lifted Grace
gently on the lounge, saying meanwhile: "She has only
fainted; surely 'tis no more. Oh, as you value my life and
hers, act. You should know what to do. I will send the
coachman for a physician instantly, and will come when
you need me."

Rushing to the man's room, he dragged him from his
bed, shook him awake, and gave him instructions and offers
of reward that stirred the fellow's blood as it had never

been stirred before; and yet when he reached the stable he found that Graham had broken the lock and had a horse saddled and ready.

"Now ride," he was commanded, "as if the devil you believe in was after you."

Then Graham rushed back into the house, for he was almost beside himself. But when he heard the poor old major calling piteously, and asking what was the matter, he was taught his need of self-control. Going up to the veteran's room, he soothed him by saying that he had returned late in the night in response to his aunt's telegram, and that he had found Grace fainting on the floor, that Mrs. Mayburn and the servants were with her, and that a physician had been sent for.

"Oh, Graham, Graham," moaned the old man, "I fear my peerless girl is losing her mind, she has acted so strangely of late. It's time you came. It's time something was done, or the worst may happen."

With an almost overwhelming sense of horror, Graham remembered how nearly the worst had happened, but he only said: "Let us hope the worst has passed. I will bring you word from Mrs. Mayburn from time to time."

His terrible anxiety was only partially relieved, for his aunt said that Grace's swoon was obstinate, and would not yield to the remedies she was using. "Come in," she cried. "This is no time for ceremony. Take brandy and chafe her wrists."

What a mortal chill her cold hands gave him! It was worse than when Hilland's hands were cold in his.

"Oh, aunt, she will live?"

"Certainly," was the brusque reply. "A fainting turn is nothing. Come, you are cool in a battle: be cool now. It won't do for us all to lose our wits, although Heaven knows there's cause enough."

"How white her face and neck are!"—for Mrs. Mayburn had opened her wrapper at the throat, that she might breathe more easily—"just as Hilland saw her in his dream."

"Have done with your dreams, and omens, and all your weird nonsense. It's time for a little more *common*-sense. Rub her wrists gently but strongly; and if she shows signs of consciousness, disappear."

At last she said hastily, "Go."

Listening at the door, he heard Grace ask, a few moments later, in a faint voice, "What has happened?"

"You only fainted, deary."

"Why—why—I'm in the library."

"Yes, you got up in your sleep, and I followed you; and the doctor will soon be here, although little need we have of him."

"Oh, I've had a fearful dream. I thought I saw Warren or Alford. I surely heard Alford's voice."

"Yes, dear, I've no doubt you had a bad dream; and it may be that Alford's voice caused it, for he arrived late last night and has been talking with your father."

"That must be it," she sighed; "but my head is so confused. Oh, I am so glad he's come! When can I see him?"

"Not till after the doctor comes and you are much stronger."

"I wish to thank him; I can't wait to thank him."

"He doesn't want thanks, deary; he wants you to get well. You owe it to him and your father to get well—as well as your great and lifelong sorrow permits. Now, deary, take a little more stimulant, and then don't talk. I've explained everything, and shown you your duty; and I know that my brave Grace will do it."

"I'll try," she said, with a pathetic weariness in her voice that brought a rush of tears to Graham's eyes.

Returning to Major St. John, he assured him that Grace had revived, and that he believed she would be herself hereafter.

"Oh, this cursed war!" groaned the old man; "and how I have exulted in it and Warren's career! I had a blind confidence that he would come out of it a veteran general while yet little more than a boy. My ambition has been punished, punished; and I may lose both the children of whom I was so proud. Oh, Graham, the whole world is turning as black as Grace's mourning robes."

"I have felt that way myself. But, Major, as soldiers we must face this thing like men. The doctor has come; and I will bring him here before he goes, to give his report."

"Well, Graham, a father's blessing on you for going back for Warren. If Grace had been left in suspense as to his fate she would have gone mad in very truth. God only knows how it will be now; but she has a better chance in meeting and overcoming the sharp agony of certainty."

Under the physician's remedies Grace rallied more rapidly; and he said that if carried to her room she would soon sleep quietly.

"I wish to see Mr. Graham first," she said, decisively.

To Mrs. Mayburn's questioning glance, he added, "Gratify her. I have quieting remedies at hand."

"He will prove more quieting than all remedies. He saved my husband's life once, and tried to do so again; and I wish to tell him I never forget it night or day. He is brave, and strong, and tranquil; and I feel that to take his hand will allay the fever in my brain."

"Grace, I am here," he said, pushing open the door and bending his knee at her side while taking her hand. "Waste no strength in thanks. School your broken heart into patience; and remember how dear, beyond all words, your life is to others. Your father's life depends on yours."

"I'll try," she again said; "I think I feel better, differently. An oppression that seemed stifling, crushing me, is passing away. Alford, was there no chance—no chance at all of saving him?"

"Alas! no; and yet it is all so much better than it might have been! His grave is in a quiet, beautiful spot, which you can visit; and fresh flowers are placed upon it every day. Dear Grace, compare your lot with that of so many others whose loved ones are left on the field."

"As he would have been were it not for you, my true,

true friend," and she carried his hand to her lips in passionate gratitude. Then tears gushed from her eyes, and she sobbed like a child.

"Thank the good God!" ejaculated Mrs. Mayburn. "These are the first tears she has shed. She will be better now. Come, deary, you have seen Alford. He is to stop with us a long time, and will tell you everything over and over. You must sleep now."

Graham kissed her hand and left the room, and the servants carried her to her apartment. Mrs. Mayburn and the physician soon joined him in the library, which was haunted by a memory that would shake his soul to his dying day.

The physician in a cheerful mood said, "I now predict a decided change for the better. It would almost seem that she had had some shock which has broken the evil spell; and this natural flow of tears is better than all the medicine in the world;" and then he and Mrs. Mayburn explained how Grace's manner had been growing so strange and unnatural that they feared her mind was giving way.

"I fear you were right," Graham replied sadly; and he told them of the scene he had witnessed, and produced the vial of laudanum.

The physician was much shocked, but Mrs. Mayburn had already guessed the truth from her nephew's words and manner when she first discovered him.

"Neither Grace nor her father must ever know of this," she said, with a shudder.

"Certainly not; but Dr. Markham should know. As her physician, he should know the whole truth."

"I think that phase of her trouble has passed," said the doctor, thoughtfully; "but, as you say, I must be on my guard. Pardon me, you do not look well yourself. Indeed, you look faint;" for Graham had sunk into a chair.

"I fear I have been losing considerable blood," said Graham, carelessly; "and now that this strong excitement is passing, it begins to tell. I owe my leave of absence to a wound."

"A wound!" cried his aunt, coming to his side. "Why did you not speak of it?"

"Indeed, there has been enough to speak of beyond this trifle. Take a look at my shoulder, doctor, and do what you think best."

"And here is enough to do," was his reply as soon as Graham's shoulder was bared: "an ugly cut, and all broken loose by your exertions this evening. You must keep very quiet and have good care, or this reopened wound will make you serious trouble."

"Well, doctor, we have so much serious trouble on hand that a little more won't matter much."

His aunt inspected the wound with grim satisfaction, and then said, sententiously: "I'm glad you have got it, Alford, for it will keep you home and divert Grace's thoughts. In these times a wound that leaves the heart untouched may be useful; and nothing cures a woman's trouble better than having to take up the troubles of others. I predict a deal of healing for Grace in your wound."

"All which goes to prove," added the busy physician, "that woman's nature is different from man's."

When he was gone, having first assured the major over and over again that all danger was past, Graham said, "Aunt, Grace's hair is as white as yours."

"Yes; it turned white within a week after she learned the certainty of her husband's death."

"Would that I could have died in Hilland's place!"

"Yes," said the old lady, bitterly; "you were always too ready to die."

He drew her down to him as he lay on the lounge, and kissed her tenderly, as he said, "But I have kept my promise 'to live and do my best.'"

"You have kept your promise *to live* after a fashion. My words have also proved true, 'Good has come of it, and more good will come of it.'"

CHAPTER XXXII

A WOUNDED SPIRIT

GRACE'S chief symptom when she awoke on the following morning was an extreme lassitude. She was almost as weak as a violent fever would have left her, but her former unnatural and fitful manner was gone. Mrs. Mayburn told Graham that she had had long moods of deep abstraction, during which her eyes would be fixed on vacancy, with a stare terrible to witness, and then would follow uncontrollable paroxysms of grief.

"This morning," said her anxious nurse, "she is more like a broken lily that has not strength to raise its head. But the weakness will pass; she'll rally. Not many die of grief, especially when young."

"Save her life, aunty, and I can still do a man's part in the world."

"Well, Alford, you must help me. She has been committed to your care; and it's a sacred trust."

Graham was now installed in his old quarters, and placed under Aunt Sheba's care. His energetic aunt, however, promised to look in upon him often, and kept her word. The doctor predicted a tedious time with his wound, and insisted on absolute quiet for a few days. He was mistaken, however. Time would not be tedious, with frequent tidings of Grace's convalescence and her many proofs of deep solicitude about his wound.

Grace did rally faster than had been expected. Her system had received a terrible shock, but it had not been enfeebled by disease. With returning strength came an insatiate craving for action—an almost desperate effort to occupy her hands and mind. Before it was prudent for Graham to go out or exert himself—for his wound had developed some bad symptoms—she came to see him, bringing delicacies made with her own hands.

Never had her appearance so appealed to his heart. Her face had grown thin, but its lovely outlines remained; and her dark eyes seemed tenfold more lustrous in contrast with her white hair. She had now a presence that the most stolid would turn and look after with a wondering pity and admiration, while those gifted with a fine perception could scarcely see her without tears. Graham often thought that if she could be turned into marble she would make the ideal statue representing the women of both the contending sections whose hearts the war had broken.

As she came and went, and as he eventually spent long hours with her and her father, she became to him a study of absorbing interest, in which his old analytical bent was not wholly wanting. "What," he asked himself every hour in the day, "will be the effect of an experience like this on such a woman? what the final outcome?" There was in this interest no curiosity, in the vulgar sense of the word. It was rather the almost sleepless suspense of a man who has everything at stake, and who, in watching the struggle of another mind to cope with misfortune, must learn at the same time his own fate. It was far more than this—it was the vigilance of one who would offer help at all times and at any cost. Still, so strong are natural or acquired characteristics that he could not do this without manifesting some of the traits of the Alford Graham who years before had studied the mirthful Grace St. John with the hope of analyzing her power and influence. And had he been wholly indifferent to her, and as philosophical and cynical as once it was his pride to think he was, she would still have remained an absorbing study. Her sudden and awful bereavement had struck her strong and exceptional spiritual nature with the shattering force of the ball that crashes through muscle, bone, and nerves. In the latter case the wound may be mortal, or it may cause weakness and deformity. The wounded spirit must survive, although the effects of the wound may be even more serious and far-reaching—changing, developing, or warping character to a degree that even the most experienced cannot predict. Next to God, time is the great healer; and human love, guided by tact, can often achieve signal success.

But for Graham there was no God; and it must be said that this was becoming true of Grace also. As Hilland had feared, the influence of those she loved and trusted most had gradually sapped her faith, which in her case had been more a cherished tradition, received from her mother, than a vital experience.

Hilland's longings for a life hereafter, and his words of regret that she had lost the faith of her girlhood, were neutralized by the bitter revolt of her spirit against her immeasurable misfortune. Her own experience was to her a type of all the desolating evil and sorrow of the world; and in her agony she could not turn to a God who permitted such evil and suffering. It seemed to her that there could be no merciful, overruling Providence—that her husband's view, when his mind was in its most vigorous and normal state, was more rational than a religion which taught that a God who loved good left evil to make such general havoc.

"It's the same blind contention of forces in men as in nature," she said to herself; "and only the strong or the fortunate survive."

One day she asked Graham abruptly, "Do you believe that the human spirit lives on after death?"

He was sorely troubled to know how to answer her, but after a little hesitation said, "I feel, as your husband did, that I should be glad if you had the faith of your girlhood. I think it would be a comfort to you."

"That's truly the continental view, that superstition is useful to women. Will you not honestly treat me as your equal, and tell me what you, as an educated man, believe?"

"No," he replied, gravely and sadly, "I will only recall with emphasis your husband's last words."

"You are loyal to him, at least; and I respect you for it. But I know what you believe, and what Warren believed when his faculties were normal and unbiased by the intense longing of his heart. I am only a woman, Alford, but I must use such little reason as I have; and no being except one created by man's ruthless imagination could permit the suffering which this war daily entails. It's all of the earth, earthy. Alford," she added, in low, passionate utterance, "I could believe in a devil more easily than in a God; and yet my unbelief sinks me into the very depths of a hopeless desolation. What am I? A mere little atom among these mighty forces and passions which rock the world with their violence. Oh, I was so happy! and now I am crushed by some haphazard bullet shot in the darkness."

He looked at her wonderingly, and was silent.

"Alford," she continued, her eyes glowing in the excitement of her strong, passionate spirit, "I will not succumb to all this monstrous evil. If I am but a transient emanation of the earth, and must soon return to my kindred dust, still I can do a little to diminish the awful aggregate of suffering. My nature, earth-born as it is, revolts at a selfish indifference to it all. Oh, if there is a God, why does He not rend the heavens in His haste to stay the black torrents of evil? Why does He not send the angels of whom my mother told me when a child, and bid them stand between the armies that are desolating thousands of hearts like mine? Or if He chooses to work by silent, gentle influences like those of spring, why does He not bring human hearts together that are akin, and enhance the content and happiness which our brief life permits? But no. Unhappy mistakes are made. Alas, my friend, we both know it to our sorrow! Why should I feign ignorance of that which your unbounded and unselfish devotion has proved so often? Why should you not know that before this deadly

stroke fell my one grief was that you suffered; and that as
long as I could pray I prayed for your happiness? Now I
can see only merciless force or blind chance, that in nature
smites with the tornado the lonely forest or the thriving
village, the desolate waves or some ship upon them. Men,
with all their boasted reason, are even worse. What could
be more mad and useless than this war? Alford, I alone
have suffered enough to make the thing accursed; and I
must suffer to the end: and I am only one of countless
women. What is there for me, what for them, but to grow
lonelier and sadder every day? But I won't submit to the
evil. I won't be a mere bit of helpless drift. While I live
there shall be a little less suffering in the world. Ah, Alford! you see how far removed I am from the sportive girl
you saw on that May evening years ago. I am an old, white-
haired, broken-hearted woman; and yet," with a grand
look in her eyes, she concluded, "I have spirit enough left
to take up arms against all the evil and suffering within my
reach. I know how puny my efforts will be; but I would
rather try to push back an avalanche than cower before it."

Thus she revealed to him the workings of her mind;
and he worshipped her anew as one of the gentlest and most
loving of women, and yet possessed of a nature so strong
that under the guidance of reason it could throw off the
shackles of superstition and defy even fate. Under the spell
of her words the evil of the world did seem an avalanche,
not of snow, but of black molten lava; while she, too brave
and noble to cower and cringe, stood before it, her little
hand outstretchd to stay its deadly onset.

CHAPTER XXXIII

THE WHITE-HAIRED NURSE

LIFE at the two cottages was extremely secluded. All who felt entitled to do so made calls, partly of condolence and partly from curiosity. The occupants of the two unpretending dwellings had the respect of the community; but from their rather unsocial ways could not be popular. The old major had ever detested society in one of its phases—that is, the claims of mere vicinage, the duty to call and be called upon by people who live near, when there is scarcely a thought or taste in common. With his Southern and army associations he had drifted to a New England city; but he ignored the city except as it furnished friends and things that pleased him. His attitude was not contemptuous or unneighborly, but simply indifferent.

"I don't thrust my life on any one," he once said to Mrs. Mayburn, "except you and Grace. Why should other people thrust their lives on me?"

His limited income had required economy, and his infirmities a life free from annoyance. As has been shown, Grace had practiced the one with heart as light as her purse; and had interposed her own sweet self between the irritable veteran and everything that could vex him. The calling world had had its revenge. The major was profane, they had said; Grace was proud, or led a slavish life. The most heinous sin of all was, they were poor. There were several families, however, whom Grace and the major had found congenial, with various shades of difference; and the young girl had never lacked all the society she cared for. Books had been her chief pleasure; the acquaintance of good whist-players had been cultivated; army and Southern friends had appeared occasionally; and when Mrs. Mayburn had become a neighbor, she had been speedily adopted into the closest intimacy. When Hilland had risen above their horizon he soon glorified the world to Grace. To the astonishment of society, she had married a millionaire, and they had all continued to live as quietly and unostentatiously as before. There had been another slight effort to "know the people at the St. John cottage," but it had speedily died out. The war had brought chiefly military associations and absence. Now again there was an influx of callers largely from the church that Grace had once attended. Mrs. Mayburn received the majority with a grim politeness, but discriminated very favorably in case of those who came solely from honest sympathy. All were made to feel, however, that, like a mourning veil, sorrow should shield its victims from uninvited observation.

Hilland's mother had long been dead, and his father died at the time when he was summoned from his studies in Germany. While on good terms with his surviving relatives, there had been no very close relationship or intimacy remaining. Grace had declared that she wished no other funeral service than the one conducted by the good old Confederate pastor; and the relatives, learning that they had no interest in the will, speedily discovered that they had no further interest whatever. Thus the inmates of the two cottages were left to pursue their own shadowed paths, with little interference from the outside world. The major treasured a few cordial eulogies of Hilland cut from the journals at the time; and except in the hearts wherein he was enshrined a living image, the brave, genial, high-souled man passed from men's thoughts and memories, like thousands of others in that long harvest of death.

Graham's wound at last was wellnigh healed, and the time was drawing near for his return to the army. His general had given such a very favorable account of the

circumstances attending his offence, and of his career as a
soldier both before and after the affair, that the matter was
quietly ignored.   Moreover, Hilland, as a soldier and by
reason of the loyal use of his wealth, stood very high in
the estimation of the war authorities; and the veteran
major was not without his surviving circle of influential
friends.   Graham, therefore, not only retained his rank,
but was marked for promotion.

Of all this, however, he thought and cared little. If he
had loved Grace before, he idolized her now. And yet with
all her deep affection for him and her absolute trust, she
seemed more remote than ever. In the new phase of her
grief she was ever seeking to do little things which she
thought would please him. But this was also true of her
course toward Mrs. Mayburn, especially so toward her
father, and also, to a certain extent, toward the poor and
sick in the vicinity. Her one effort seemed to be to escape
from her thoughts, herself, in a ceaseless ministry to others.
And the effort sometimes degenerated into restlessness.
There was such a lack of repose in her manner that even
those who loved her most were pained and troubled. There
was not enough to keep her busy all the time, and yet she
was ever impelled to do something.

One day she said to Graham, "I wish I could go back
with you to the war; not that I wish to shed another drop
of blood, but I would like to march, march forever."

Shrewd Mrs. Mayburn, who had been watching Grace
closely for the last week or two, said quietly: "Take her
back with you, Alford. Let her become a nurse in some
hospital. It will do both her and a lot of poor fellows a
world of good."

"Mrs. Mayburn, you have thought of just the thing,"
cried Grace. "In a hospital full of sick and wounded men
I could make my life amount to something; I should never
need to be idle then."

"Yes, you would. You would be under orders like
Alford, and would have to rest when off duty. But, as

you say, you could be of great service, instead of wasting your energy in coddling two old people. You might save many a poor fellow's life."

"Oh," she exclaimed, clasping her hands, "the bare thought of saving one poor woman from such suffering as mine is almost overwhelming. But how can I leave papa?"

"I'll take care of the major and insure his consent. If men are so possessed to make wounds, it's time women did more to cure them. It's all settled: you are to go. I'll see the major about it now, if he *has* just begun his newspaper;" and the old lady took her knitting and departed with her wonted prompt energy.

At first Graham was almost speechless from surprise, mingled doubt and pleasure; but the more he thought of it, the more he was convinced that the plan was an inspiration.

"Alford, you will take me?" she said, appealingly.

"Yes," he replied, smilingly, "if you will promise to obey my orders in part, as well as those of your superiors."

"I'll promise anything if you will only take me. Am I not under your care?"

"Oh, Grace, Grace, I can do so little for you!"

"No one living can do more. In providing this chance of relieving a little pain, of preventing a little suffering, you help me, you serve me, you comfort me, as no one else could. And, Alford, if you are wounded, come to the hospital where I am; I will never leave you till you are well. Take me to some exposed place in the field, where there is danger, where men are brought in desperately wounded, where you would be apt to be."

"I don't know where I shall be, but I would covet any wound that would bring you to my side as nurse."

She thought a few moments, and then said, resolutely: "I will keep as near to you as I can. I ask no pay for my services. On the contrary, I will employ my useless wealth in providing for exposed hospitals. When I attempt to take care of the sick or wounded, I will act scrupulously under the orders of the surgeon in charge; but I do not see why,

M—ROE—XIII

if I pay my own way, I cannot come and go as I think I can be the most useful."

"Perhaps you could, to a certain extent, if you had a permit," said Graham, thoughtfully; "but I think you would accomplish more by remaining in one hospital and acquiring skill by regular work. It would be a source of indescribable anxiety to me to think of your going about alone. If I know just where you are, I can find you and write to you."

"I will do just what you wish," she said, gently.

"I wish for only what is best for you."

"I know that. It would be strange if I did not."

Mrs. Mayburn was not long in convincing the major that her plan might be the means of incalculable benefit to Grace as well as to others. He, as well as herself and Graham, had seen with deep anxiety that Grace was giving way to a fever of unrest; and he acquiesced in the view that it might better run its course in wholesome and useful activity, amid scenes of suffering that might tend to reconcile her to her own sorrow.

Graham, however, took the precaution of calling on Dr. Markham, who, to his relief, heartily approved of the measure. On one point Graham was firm. He would not permit her to go to a hospital in the field, liable to vicissitudes from sudden movements of the contending armies. He found one for her, however, in which she would have ample scope for all her efforts; and before he left he interested those in charge so deeply in the white-haired nurse that he felt she would always be under watchful, friendly eyes.

"Grace," he said, as he was taking leave, "I have tried to be a true friend to you."

"Oh, Alford!" she exclaimed, and she seized his hand and held it in both of hers.

His face grew stern rather than tender as he added: "You will not be a true friend to me—you will wrong me deeply—if you are reckless of your health and strength.

Remember that, like myself, you have entered the service, and that you are pledged to do your duty, and not to work with feverish zeal until your strength fails. You are just as much under obligation to take essential rest as to care for the most sorely wounded in your ward. I shall take the advice I give. Believing that I am somewhat essential to your welfare and the happiness of those whom we have left at home, I shall incur no risks beyond those which properly fall to my lot. I ask you to be equally conscientious and considerate of those whose lives are bound up in you."

"I'll try," she said, with that same pathetic look and utterance which had so moved him on the fearful night of his return from the army. "But, Alford, do not speak to me so gravely, I had almost said sternly, just as we are saying good-by."

He raised her hand to his lips, and smiled into her pleading face as he replied, "I only meant to impress you with the truth that you have a patient who is not in your ward— one who will often be sleeping under the open sky, I know not where. Care a little for him, as well as for the unknown men in your charge. This you can do only by taking care of yourself. You, of all others, should know that there are wounds besides those which will bring men to this hospital."

Tears rushed into her eyes as she faltered, "You could not have made a stronger appeal."

"You will write to me often?"

"Yes, and you cannot write too often. Oh, Alford, I cannot wish you had never seen me; but it would have been far, far better for you if you had not."

"No, no," he said, in low, strong emphasis. "Grace Hilland, I would rather be your friend than have the love of any woman that ever lived."

"You do yourself great wrong (pardon me for saying it, but your happiness is so dear to me), you do yourself great wrong. A girl like Pearl Anderson could make you truly happy; and you could make her happy."

"Sweet little Pearl will be happy some day; and I may

be one of the causes, but not in the way you suggest. It is hard to say good-by and leave you here alone, and every moment I stay only makes it harder ''

He raised her hand once more to his lips, then almost rushed away.

Days lapsed into weeks, and weeks into months. The tireless nurse alleviated suffering of every kind; and her silvery hair was like a halo around a saintly head to many a poor fellow. She had the deep solace of knowing that not a few wives and mothers would have mourned had it not been for her faithfulness.

But her own wound would not heal. She sometimes felt that she was slowly bleeding to death. The deep, dark tide of suffering, in spite of all she could do, grew deeper and darker; and she was growing weary and discouraged.

Graham saw her at rare intervals; and although she brightened greatly at his presence, and made heroic efforts to satisfy him that she was doing well, he grew anxious and depressed. But there was nothing tangible, nothing definite. She was only a little paler, a little thinner; and when he spoke of it she smilingly told him that he was growing gaunt himself with his hard campaigning.

"But you, Grace," he complained, "are beginning to look like a wraith that may vanish some moonlight night."

Her letters were frequent, sometimes even cheerful, but brief. He wrote at great length, filling his pages with descriptions of nature, with scenes that were often humorous but not trivial, with genuine life, but none of its froth. Life for both had become too deep a tragedy for any nonsense. He passed through many dangers, but these, as far as possible, he kept in the background; and fate, pitying his one deep wound, spared him any others.

At last there came the terrible battle of the Wilderness, and the wards were filled with desperately wounded men. The poor nurse gathered up her failing powers for one more effort; and Confederate and Union men looked after her wonderingly and reverently, even in their mortal weakness. To many she seemed like a ministering spirit rather than a woman of flesh and blood; and lips of dying men blessed her again and again. But they brought no blessing. She only shuddered and grew more faint of heart as the scenes of agony and death increased. Each wound was a type of Hilland's wound, and in every expiring man she saw her husband die. Her poor little hands trembled now as she sought to stem the black, black tide that deepened and broadened and foamed around her.

Late one night, after a new influx of the wounded, she was greatly startled while passing down her ward by hearing a voice exclaim, "Grace—Grace Brentford!"

It was her mother's name.

The call was repeated; and she tremblingly approached a cot on which was lying a gray-haired man.

"Great God!" he exclaimed, "am I dreaming? am I delirious? How is it that I see before me the woman I loved forty-odd years ago? You cannot be Grace Brentford, for she died long years since."

"No, but I am her daughter."

"Her daughter!" said the man, struggling to rise upon his elbow—"her daughter! She should not look older than you."

"Alas, sir, my age is not the work of time, but of grief. I grew old in a day. But if you knew and loved my mother, you have sacred claims upon me. I am a nurse in this ward, and will devote myself to you."

The man sank back exhausted. "This is strange, strange indeed," he said. "It is God's own providence. Yes, my child, I loved your mother, and I love her still. Harry St. John won her fairly; but he could not have loved her better than I. I am now a lonely old man, dying, I believe, in my enemy's hands, but I thank God that I've seen Grace Brentford's child, and that she can soothe my last hours."

"Do not feel so discouraged about yourself," said Grace, her tears falling fast. "Think rather that you have been brought here that I might nurse you back to life. Believe me, I will do so with tender, loving care."

"How strange it all is!" the man said again. "You have her very voice, her manner. But it was by your eyes that I recognized you. Your eyes are young and beautiful like hers, and full of tears, as hers were when she sent me away with an ache in my heart that has never ceased. It will soon be cured now. Your father will remember a wild young planter down in Georgia by the name of Phil Harkness."

"Indeed, sir, I've heard both of my parents speak of you, and it was ever with respect and esteem."

"Give my greeting to your father, and say I never bore him any ill-will. In the saddest life there is always some compensation. I have had wealth and honors; I am a colonel in our army, and have been able to serve the cause I loved; but, chief of all, the child of Grace Brentford is by my side at the end. Is your name Grace also?"

"Yes. Oh, why is the world so full of hopeless trouble?"

"Not hopeless trouble, my child. I am not hopeless. For long years I have had peace, if not happiness—a deep inward calm which the confusion and roar of the bloodiest battles could not disturb. I can close my eyes now in my final sleep as quietly as a child. In a few hours, my dear, I may see your mother; and I shall tell her that I left her child assuaging her own sorrow by ministering to others."

"Oh, oh!" sobbed Grace, "pray cease, or I shall not be fit for my duties; your words pierce my very soul. Let me nurse you back to health. Let me take you to my home until you are exchanged, for I must return. I must, must. My strength is going fast; and you bring before me my dear old father whom I have left too long."

"My poor child! God comfort and sustain you. Do not let me keep you longer from your duties, and from those who need you more than I. Come and say a word to me when you can. That's all I ask. My wound was dressed before your watch began, and I am doing as well as I could expect. When you feel like it, you can tell me more about yourself."

Their conversation had been in a low tone as she sat beside him, the patients near either sleeping or too preoccupied by their own sufferings to give much heed.

Weary and oppressed by bitter despondency, she went from cot to cot, attending to the wants of those in her charge. To her the old colonel's sad history seemed a mockery of his faith, and but another proof of a godless or God-forgotten world. She envied his belief, with its hope and peace; but he had only increased her unbelief. But all through the long night she watched over him, coming often to his side with delicacies and wine, and with gentle words that were far more grateful.

Once, as she was smoothing back his gray locks from his damp forehead, he smiled, and murmured, "God bless you, my child. This is a foretaste of heaven."

In the gray dawn she came to him and said, "My watch is over, and I must leave you for a little while; but as soon as I have rested I will come again."

"Grace," he faltered, hesitatingly, "would you mind kissing an old, old man? I never had a child of my own to kiss me."

She stooped down and kissed him again and again, and he felt her hot tears upon his face.

"You have a tender heart, my dear," he said, gently. "Good-by, Grace—Grace Brentford's child. Dear Grace, when we meet again perhaps all tears will be wiped from your eyes forever."

She stole away exhausted and almost despairing. On reaching her little room she sank on her couch, moaning; "Oh, Warren, Warren, would that I were sleeping your dreamless sleep beside you!"

Long before it was time for her to go on duty again she returned to the ward to visit her aged friend. His cot was empty. In reply to her eager question she was told that he had died suddenly from internal hemorrhage soon after she had left him.

She looked dazed for a moment, as if she had received a blow, then fell fainting on the cot from which her mother's friend had been taken. The limit of her endurance was passed.

Before the day closed, the surgeon in charge of the hospital told her gently and firmly that she must take an indefinite leave of absence. She departed at once in the care of an attendant; but stories of the white-haired nurse lingered so long in the ward and hospital that at last they began to grow vague and marvellous, like the legends of a saint.

CHAPTER XXXIV

RITA'S BROTHER

ALL through the campaign of '64 the crimson tide of war deepened and broadened. Even Graham's cool and veteran spirit was appalled at the awful slaughter on either side. The Army of the Potomac—the grandest army ever organized, and always made more sublime and heroic by defeat—was led by a man as remorseless as fate. He was fate to thousands of loyal men, whom he placed at will as coolly as if they had been the pieces on a chessboard. He was fate to the Confederacy, upon whose throat he placed his iron grasp, never relaxed until life was extinct. In May, 1864, he quietly crossed the Rapidan for the death-grapple. He took the most direct route for Richmond, ignoring all obstacles and the fate of his predecessors. To think that General Grant wished to fight the battle of the Wilderness is pure idiocy. One would almost as soon choose the Dismal Swamp for a battleground. It was undoubtedly his hope to pass beyond that gloomy tangle, over which the shadow of death had brooded ever since fatal Chancellorsville. But Lee, his brilliant and vigilant opponent, rarely lost an advantage; and Graham's experienced eye, as with the cavalry he was in the extreme advance, clearly saw that their position would give their foes enormous advantages. Lee's movements would be completely masked by the almost impervious growth. He and his lieutenants could approach within striking distance, whenever they chose, without being seen, and had little to fear from the Union artillery, which the past had given them much cause to dread. It was a region also to disgust the very soul of a cavalryman; for the low, scrubby growth lined the narrow roads almost as effectually as the most scientifically prepared *abatis.*

Graham's surmise was correct. Lee would not wait till his antagonist had reached open and favorable ground, but he made an attack at once, where, owing to peculiarities of position, one of his thin regiments had often the strength of a brigade.

On the morning of the 5th of May began one of the most awful and bloody battles in the annals of warfare. Indeed it was the beginning of one long and almost continuous struggle which ended only at Appomattox.

With a hundred thousand more, Graham was swept into the bloody vortex, and through summer heat, autumn rains, and winter cold, he marched and fought with little rest. He was eventually given the colonelcy of his regiment, and at times commanded a brigade. He passed through unnumbered dangers unscathed; and his invulnerability became a proverb among his associates. Indeed he was a mystery to them, for his face grew sadder and sterner every day, and his reticence about himself and all his affairs was often remarked upon. His men and officers had unbounded respect for him, that was not wholly unmixed with fear; for while he was considerate, and asked for no exposure to danger in which he did not share, his steady discipline was never relaxed, and he kept himself almost wholly aloof, except as their military relations required contact. He could not, therefore, be popular among the hard-swearing, rollicking, and convivial cavalrymen. In a long period of inaction he might have become very unpopular, but the admirable manner in which he led them in action, and his sagacious care of them and their horses on the march and in camp, led them to trust him implicitly. Chief of all, he had acquired that which with the stern veterans of that day went further than anything else—a reputation for dauntless courage. What they objected to were his "glum looks and unsocial ways," as they termed them.

They little knew that his cold, stern face hid suffering that was growing almost desperate in its intensity. They little knew that he was chained to his military duty as to a rock, while a vulture of anxiety was eating out his very heart. What was a pale, thin, white-haired woman to them? But what to him? How true it is that often the heaviest burdens of life are those at which the world would laugh, and of which the overweighted heart cannot and will not speak!

For a long time after his plunge into the dreary depths of the Wilderness he had received no letters. Then he had learned of Grace's return home; and at first he was glad indeed. His aunt had written nothing more alarming than that Grace had overtaxed her strength in caring for the throngs of wounded men sent from the Wilderness, that she needed rest and good tonic treatment. Then came word that she was "better"; then they "hoped she was gaining"; then they were about to go to "the seashore, and Grace had always improved in salt air." It was then intimated that she had found "the summer heat very enervating, and now that fall winds were blowing she would grow stronger." At last, at the beginning of winter, it was admitted that she had not improved as they had hoped; but they thought she was holding her own very well—that the continued and terrific character of the war oppressed her —and that every day she dreaded to hear that he had been stricken among other thousands.

Thus, little by little, ever softened by some excuse or some hope, the bitter truth grew plain: Grace was failing, fading, threatening to vanish. He wrote as often as he could, and sought with all his skill to cheer, sustain, and reconcile her to life. At first she wrote to him not infrequently, but her letters grew further and further apart, and at last she wrote, in the early spring of '65.

"I wish I could see you, Alford; but I know it is impossible. You are strong, you are doing much to end this awful war, and it's your duty to remain at your post. You must not sully your perfect image in my mind, or add to my unhappiness by leaving the service now for my sake. I have learned the one bitter lesson of the times. No matter how much *personal* agony, physical or mental, is involved, the war must go on; and each one must keep his place in the ranks till he falls or is disabled. I have fallen. I am disabled. My wound will not close, and drop by drop life and strength are ebbing. I know I disappoint you, my true, true friend; but I cannot help it. Do not reproach me. Do not blame me too harshly. Think me weak, as I truly am. Indeed, when I am gone your chances will be far better. It costs me a great effort to write this. There is a weight on my hand and brain as well as on my heart. Hereafter I will send my messages through dear, kind Mrs. Mayburn, who has been a mother to me in all my sorrow. Do not fear: I will wait till you can come with honor; for I must see you once more."

For a long time after receiving this letter a despair fell on Graham. He was so mechanical in the performance of his duties that his associates wondered at him, and he grew more gaunt and haggard than ever. Then in sharp reaction came a feverish eagerness to see the war ended.

Indeed all saw that the end was near, and none, probably, more clearly than the gallant and indomitable Lee himself. At last the Confederate army was outflanked, the lines around Petersburg were broken through, and the final pursuit began. It was noted that Graham fought and charged with an almost tiger-like fierceness; and for once his men said with reason that he had no mercy on them. He was almost counting the hours until the time when he could sheathe his sword and say with honor, "I resign."

One morning they struck a large force of the enemy, and he led a headlong charge. For a time the fortunes of the battle wavered, for the Confederates fought with the courage of desperation. Graham on his powerful horse soon became a conspicuous object, and all gave way before him as if he were a messenger of death, at the same time wondering at his invulnerability.

The battle surged on and forward until the enemy were driven into a thick piece of woods. Graham on the right of his line directed his bugler to give the order to dismount, and a moment later his line of battle plunged into the forest. In the desperate *mêlée* that followed in the underbrush, he was lost to sight except to a few of his men. It was here that he found himself confronted by a Confederate officer, from whose eyes flashed the determination either to slay or to be slain. Graham had crossed swords with him but a moment when he recognized that he had no ordinary antagonist; and with his instinct of fight aroused to its highest pitch he gave himself up wholly to a personal and mortal combat, shouting meantime to those near, "Leave this man to me."

Looking his opponent steadily in the eye, like a true swordsman, he remained first on the defensive; and such was his skill that his long, straight blade was a shield as well as a weapon. Suddenly the dark eyes and features of his opponent raised before him the image of Rita Anderson; and he was so overcome for a second that the Confederate touched his breast with his sabre and drew blood. That sharp prick and the thought that Rita's brother might be before him aroused every faculty and power of his mind and body. His sword was a shield again, and he shouted, "Is not your name Henry Anderson?"

"My name is our cause," was the defiant answer; "with it I will live or die."

Then came upon Graham one of those rare moments in his life when no mortal man could stand before him. Ceasing his wary, rapid fence, his sword played like lightning; and in less than a moment the Confederate's sabre flew from his hand, and he stood helpless.

"Strike," he said, sullenly; "I won't surrender."

"I'd sooner cut off my right hand," replied Graham, smiling upon him, "than strike the brother of Rita Anderson."

"Is your name Graham?" asked his opponent, his aspect changing instantly.

"Yes; and you are Henry. I saw your sister's eyes in yours. Take up your sword, and go quietly to the rear as my friend, not prisoner. I adjure you, by the name of your old and honored father and your noble-hearted sister, to let me keep my promise to them to save your life, were it ever in my power."

"I yield," said the young man, in deep despondency. "Our cause *is* lost, and you are the only man in the North to whom I should be willing to surrender. Colonel, I will obey your orders."

Summoning his orderly and another soldier, he said to them, "Escort this gentleman to the rear. Let him keep his arms. I have too much confidence in you, Colonel Anderson, even to ask that you promise not to escape. Treat him with respect. He will share my quarters to-night." And then he turned and rushed onward to overtake the extreme advance of his line, wondering at the strange scene which had passed with almost the rapidity of thought.

That night by Graham's camp-fire began a friendship between himself and Henry Anderson which would be life-long. The latter asked, "Have you heard from my father and sister since you parted with them?"

"No. My duties have carried me far away from that region. But it is a source of unspeakable gratification that we have met, and that you can tell me of their welfare."

"It does seem as if destiny, or, as father would say, Providence, had linked my fortunes and those of my family with you. He and Rita would actually have suffered with hunger but for you. Since you were there the region has been tramped and fought over by the forces of both sides, and swept bare. My father mentioned your name and that of Colonel Hilland; and a guard was placed over his house, and he and Rita were saved from any personal annoyance. But all of his slaves, except the old woman you remember, were either run off or enticed away, and his means of livelihood practically destroyed. Old Uncle Jehu and his son Huey have almost supported them. They, simple souls, could not keep your secret, though they tried to after their clumsy fashion. My pay, you know, was almost worthless; and indeed there was little left for them to buy. Colonel Graham, I am indebted to you for far more than life, which has become wellnigh a burden to me.''

"Life has brought far heavier burdens to others than to you, Colonel Anderson. Those you love are living; and to provide for and protect such a father and sister as you possess might well give zest to any life. Your cause *is* lost; and the time may come sooner than you expect when you will be right glad of it. I know you cannot think so now, and we will not dwell on this topic. I can testify from four years' experience that no cause was ever defended with higher courage or more heroic self-sacrifice. But your South is not lost; and it will be the fault of its own people if it does not work out a grander destiny within the Union than it could ever achieve alone. But don't let us discuss politics. You have the same right to your views that I have to mine. I will tell you how much I owe to your father and sister, and then you will see that the burden of obligation rests upon me;" and he gave his own version of that memorable day whose consequences threatened to culminate in Grace Hilland's death.

Under the dominion of this thought he could not hide the anguish of his mind; and Rita had hinted enough in her letters to enable Anderson to comprehend his newfound friend. He took Graham's hand, and as he wrung it he said, "Yes, life has brought to others heavier burdens than to me.''

"You may have thought," resumed Graham, "that I fought savagely to-day; but I felt that it is best for all to end this useless, bloody struggle as soon as possible. As for myself, I'm just crazed with anxiety to get away and return home. Of course we cannot be together after tonight, for with the dawn I must be in the saddle. Tonight you shall share my blankets. You must let me treat you as your father and Rita treated me. I will divide my

money with you: don't grieve me by objecting.   Call it a
loan if you will.   Your currency is now worthless.   You
must go with the other prisoners; but I can soon obtain
your release on parole, and then, in the name of all that is
sacred, return home to those who idolize you.   Do this,
Colonel Anderson, and you will lift a heavy burden from
one already overweighted."

"As you put the case I cannot do otherwise," was the
sad reply.   "Indeed I have no heart for any more useless
fighting.   My duty now is clearly to my father and sister."

That night the two men slumbered side by side, and in
the dawn parted more like brothers than like foes.

As Graham had predicted, but a brief time elapsed before Lee surrendered, and Colonel Anderson's liberty on
parole was soon secured.   They parted with the assurance
that they would meet again as soon as circumstances would
permit.

At the earliest hour in which he could depart with honor,
Graham's urgent entreaty secured him a leave of absence;
and he lost not a moment in his return, sending to his aunt
in advance a telegram to announce his coming.

CHAPTER XXXV

HIS SOMBRE RIVALS

NEVER had his noble horse Mayburn seemed to fail him until the hour that severed the military chain which had so long bound him to inexorable duty, and yet the faithful beast was carrying him like the wind. Iss, his servant, soon fell so far behind that Graham paused and told him to come on more leisurely, that Mayburn would be at the terminus of the military railroad. And there Iss found him, with drooping head and white with foam. The steam-engine was driven to City Point with the reckless speed characteristic of military railroads; but to Graham the train seemed to crawl. He caught a steamer bound for Washington, and paced the deck, while in the moonlight the dark shores of the James looked stationary. From Washington the lightning express was in his view more dilatory than the most lumbering stage of the old régime.

When at last he reached the gate to his aunt's cottage and walked swiftly up the path, the hour and the scene were almost the same as when he had first come, an indifferent stranger, long years before. The fruit-trees were as snowy white with blossoms, the air as fragrant, the birds singing as jubilantly, as when he had stood at the window and gazed with critical admiration on a sportive girl, a child-woman, playing with her little Spitz dog. As he passed the spot where she had stood, beneath his ambush behind the curtains, his excited mind brought back her image with life-like realism—the breeze in her light hair, her dark eyes brimming with mirth, her bosom panting from her swift advance, and the color of the red rose in her cheeks.

He groaned as he thought of her now.

His aunt saw him from the window, and a moment later was sobbing on his breast.

"Aunt," he gasped, "I'm not too late?"

"Oh, no," she said, wearily; "Grace is alive; but one can scarcely say much more. Alford, you must be prepared for a sad change."

He placed her in her chair, and stood before her with heaving breast. "Now tell me all," he said, hoarsely.

"Oh, Alford, you frighten me. You must be more composed. You cannot see Grace, looking and feeling as you do. She is weakness itself;" and she told him how the idol of his heart was slowly, gradually, but inevitably sinking into the grave.

"Alford, Alford," she cried, entreatingly, "why do you look so stern? You could not look more terrible in the most desperate battle."

In low, deep utterance, he said, "This is my most desperate battle; and in it are the issues of life and death."

"You terrify *me*, and can you think that a weak, dying woman can look upon you as you now appear?"

"She shall not die," he continued, in the same low, stern utterance, "and she must look upon me, and listen, too. Aunt, you have been faithful to me all these years. You have been my mother. I must entreat one more service. You must second me, sustain me, co-work with me. You must ally all your experienced womanhood with my manhood, and with my will, which may be broken, but which shall not yield to my cruel fate."

"What do you propose to do?"

"That will soon be manifest. Go and prepare Grace for my visit. I wish to see her alone. You will please be near, however;" and he abruptly turned and went to his room to remove his military suit and the dust of travel.

He had given his directions as if in the field, and she wonderingly and tremblingly obeyed, feeling that some crisis was near.

Grace was greatly agitated when she heard of Graham's arrival; and two or three hours elapsed before she was able to be carried down and placed on the sofa in the library. He, out in the darkness on the piazza, watched with eyes that glowed like coals—watched as he had done in the most desperate emergency of all the bloody years of battle. He saw her again, and in her wasted, helpless form, her hollow cheeks, her bloodless face, with its weary, hopeless look, her mortal weakness, he clearly recognized his *sombre rivals*, *Grief and Death;* and with a look of indomitable resolution he raised his hand and vowed that he would enter the lists against them. If it were within the scope of human will he would drive them from their prey.

His aunt met him in the hall and whispered, "Be gentle."

"Remain here," was his low reply. "I have also sent for Dr. Markham;" and he entered.

Grace reached out to him both her hands as she said, "Oh, Alford, you are barely in time. It is a comfort beyond all words to see you before—before—" She could not finish the sinister sentence.

He gravely and silently took her hands, and sat down beside her.

"I know I disappoint you," she continued. "I've been your evil genius, I've saddened your whole life; and you have been so true and faithful! Promise me, Alford, that after I'm gone you will not let my blighted life cast its shadow over your future years. How strangely stern you look!"

"So you intend to die, Grace?" were his first, low words.

"Intend to die?"

"Yes. Do you think you are doing right by your father in dying?"

"Dear, dear papa! I have long ceased to be a comfort to him. He, too, will be better when I am gone. I am now a hopeless grief to him. Alford, dear Alford, do not look at me in that way."

"How else can I look? Do you not comprehend what your death means to *me*, if not to others?"

"Alford, can I help it?"

"Certainly you can. It will be sheer, downright selfishness for you to die. It will be your one unworthy act. You have no disease: you have only to comply with the conditions of life in order to live."

"You are mistaken," she said, the faintest possible color coming into her face. "The bullet that caused Warren's death has been equally fatal to me. Have I not tried to live?"

"I do not ask you to *try* to live, but to *live*. Nay, more, I demand it; and I have the right. I ask for nothing more. Although I have loved you, idolized you, all these years, I ask only that you comply with the conditions of life and live."

The color deepened perceptibly under his emphatic words, and she said, "Can a woman live whose heart, and hope, and soul, if she has one, are dead and buried?"

"Yes, as surely as a man whose heart and hope were buried long years before. There was a time when I weakly purposed to throw off the burden of life; but I promised to live and do my best, and I am here to-day. You must make me the same promise. In the name of all the past, I demand it. Do you imaigne that I am going to sit down tamely and shed a few helpless tears if you do me this immeasurable wrong?"

"Oh, Alford!" she gasped, "what do you mean?"

"I am not here, Grace, to make threats," he said gravely; "but I fear you have made a merely superficial estimate of my nature. Hilland is not. You know that I would have died a hundred times in his place. He committed you to my care with his last breath, and that trust gave value to my life. What right have you to die and bring to me the blackness of despair? I am willing to bear my burden patiently to the end. You should be willing to bear yours."

"I admit your claim," she cried, wringing her hands. "You have made death, that I welcome, a terror. How can I live? What is there left of me but a shadow? What am

I but a mere semblance of a woman? The snow is not whiter than my hair, or colder than my heart. Oh, Alford, you have grown morbid in all these years. You cannot know what is best. Your true chance is to let me go. I am virtually dead now, and when my flickering breath ceases, the change will be slight indeed."

"It will be a fatal change for me," he replied, with such calm emphasis that she shuddered. "You ask how you can live. Again I repeat, by complying with the conditions of life. You have been complying with the conditions of death; and I will not yield you to him. Grief has been a far closer and more cherished friend than I; and you have permitted it, like a shadow, to stand between us. The time has now come when you must choose between this fatal shadow, this useless, selfish grief, and a loyal friend, who only asks that he may see you at times, that he may know where to find the one life that is essential to his life. Can you not understand from your own experience that a word from you is sweeter to me than all the music of the world?—that smiles from you will give me courage to fight the battle of life to the last? Had Hilland come back wounded, would you have listened if he had reasoned, 'I am weak and maimed—not like my old self: you will be better off without me'?"

"Say no more," she faltered. "If a shadow can live, I will. If a poor, heartless, hopeless creature can continue to breathe, I will. If I die, as I believe I must, I will die doing just what you ask. If it is possible for me to live, I shall disappoint you more bitterly than ever. Alford, believe me, the woman is dead within me. If I live I shall become I know not what—a sort of unnatural creature, having little more than physical life."

"Grace, our mutual belief forbids such a thought. If a plant is deeply shadowed, and moisture is withdrawn, it begins to die. Bring to it again light and moisture, the conditions of its life, and it gradually revives and resumes its normal state. This principle applies equally to you in your higher order of existence. Will you promise me that, at the utmost exertion of your will and intelligence, you will try to live?"

"Yes, Alford; but again I warn you. You will be disappointed."

He kissed both her hands with a manner that evinced profound gratitude and respect, but nothing more; and then summoned his aunt and Dr. Markham.

Grace lay back on the sofa, white and faint, with closed eyes.

"Oh, Alford, what have you done?" exclaimed Mrs. Mayburn.

"What is right and rational. Dr. Markham, Mrs. Hilland has promised to use the utmost exertion of her will and intelligence to live. I ask that you and my aunt employ your utmost skill and intelligence in co-operation with her effort. We here—all four of us—enter upon a battle; and, like all battles, it should be fought with skill and indomitable courage, not sentimental impulse. I know that Mrs. Hilland will honestly make the effort, for she is one to keep her word. Am I not right, Grace?"

"Yes," was the faint reply.

"Why, now I can go to work with hope," said the physician briskly, as he gave his patient a little stimulant.

"And I also," cried the old lady, tears streaming down her face. "Oh, darling Grace, you will live and keep all our hearts from breaking."

"I'll try," she said, in almost mortal weariness.

When she had been revived somewhat by his restoratives, Dr. Markham said, "I now advise that she be carried back to her room, and I promise to be unwearied in my care."

"No," said Graham to his aunt. "Do not call the servants; I shall carry her to her room myself;" and he lifted her as gently as he would take up a child, and bore her strongly and easily to her room.

"Poor, poor Alford!" she whispered—"wasting your rich, full heart on a shadow."

CHAPTER XXXVI

ALL MATERIALISTS

WHEN Graham returned to the library he found that the major had tottered in, and was awaiting him with a look of intense anxiety.

"Graham, Graham!" he cried, "do you think there is any hope?"

"I do, sir. I think there is almost a certainty that your daughter will live."

"Now God be praised! although I have little right to say it, for I've put His name to a bad use all my life."

"I don't think any harm has been done," said Graham, smiling.

"Oh, I know, I know how wise you German students are. You can't find God with a microscope or a telescope, and therefore there is none. But I'm the last man to criticise. Grace has been my divinity since her mother died; and if you can give a reasonable hope that she'll live to close my eyes, I'll thank the God that my wife worshipped, in spite of all your new-fangled philosophies."

"And I hope I shall never be so wanting in courtesy, to say the least, as to show anything but respect for your convictions. You shall know the whole truth about Grace; and I shall look to you also for aid in a combined effort to rally and strengthen her forces of life. You know, Major, that I have seen some service."

"Yes, yes; boy that you are, you are a hundred-fold more of a veteran than I am. At the beginning of the war I felt very superior and experienced. But the war that I saw was mere child's-play."

"Well, sir, the war that I've been through was child's play to me compared with the battle begun to-night. I never feared death, except as it might bring trouble to others, and for long years I coveted it; but I fear the death of Grace Hilland beyond anything in this world or any other. As her father, you now shall learn the whole truth;" and he told his story from the evening of their first game of whist together.

"Strange, strange!" muttered the old man. "It's the story of Philip Harkness over again. But, by the God who made me, she shall reward you if she lives."

"No, Major St. John, no. She shall devote herself to you, and live the life that her own feelings dictate. She understands this, and I *will* it. I assure you that whatever else I lack it's not a will."

"You've proved that, Graham, if ever a man did. Well, well, well, your coming has brought a strange and most welcome state of affairs. Somehow you've given me a new lease of life and courage. Of late we've all felt like hauling down the flag, and letting grim death do his worst. I couldn't have survived Grace, and didn't want to. Only plucky Mrs. Mayburn held on to your coming as a forlorn hope. You now make me feel like nailing the flag to the staff, and opening again with every gun. Grace is like her mother, if I do say it. Grace Brentford never lacked for suitors, and she had the faculty of waking up *men*. Forgive an old man's vanity. Phil Harkness was a little wild as a young fellow, but he had grand mettle in him. He made more of a figure in the world than I—was sent to Congress, owned a big plantation, and all that—but sweet Grace Brentford always looked at me reproachfully when I rallied her on the mistake she had made, and was contentment itself in my rough soldier's quarters," and the old man took off his spectacles to wipe his tear-dimmed eyes. "Grace is just like her. She, too, has waked up men. Hilland was a grand fellow; and, Graham, you are a soldier every inch of you, and that's the highest praise I can bestow. You are in command in this battle, and God be with you. Your unbelief doesn't affect *Him* any more than a mole's."

Graham laughed—he could laugh in his present hopefulness—as he replied, "I agree with you fully. If there is a personal Creator of the universe, I certainly am a small object in it."

"That's not what I've been taught to believe either; nor is it according to my reason. An infinite God could give as much attention to you as to the solar system."

"From the present aspect of the world, a great deal would appear neglected," Graham replied, with a shrug.

"Come, Colonel Graham," said the major, a little sharply, "you and I have both heard the rank and file grumble over the tactics of their general. It often turned out that the general knew more than the men. But it's nice business for me to be talking religion to you or any one else;" and the idea struck him as so comical that he laughed outright.

Mrs. Mayburn, who entered at that moment, said: "That's a welcome sound. I can't remember, Major, when I've heard you laugh. Alford, you are a magician. Grace is sleeping quietly."

"Little wonder! What have I had to laugh about?" said the major. "But melancholy itself would laugh at my joke to-night. Would you believe it, I've been talking religion to the colonel, —— if I haven't!"

"I think it's time religion was talked to all of us."

"Oh, now, Mrs. Mayburn, don't you begin. You haven't any God any more than Graham has. You have a jumble of old-fashioned theological attributes, that are of no more practical use to you than the doctrines of Aristotle. Please ring for Jinny, and tell her to bring us a bottle of wine and some cake. I want to drink to Grace's health. If I could see her smile again I'd fire a *feu de joie* if I could find any ordnance larger than a popgun. Don't laugh at me, friends," he added, wiping the tears from his dim old eyes; "but the bare thought that Grace will live to bless my last few days almost turns my head. Where is Dr. Markham?"

"He had other patients to see, and said he would return by and by," Mrs. Mayburn replied.

"It's time we had a little relief," she continued, "whatever the future may be. The slow, steady pressure of anxiety and fear was becoming unendurable. I could scarcely have suffered more if Grace had been my own child; and I feared for you, Alford, quite as much."

"And with good reason," he said, quietly.

She gave him a keen look, and then did as the major had requested.

"Come, friends," cried he, "let us give up this evening to hope and cheer. Let what will come on the morrow, we'll have at least one more gleam of wintry sunshine to-day."

Filling the glasses of all with his trembling hand, he added, when they were alone: "Here's to my darling's health. May the good God spare her, and spare us all, to see brighter days. Because I'm not good, is no reason why He isn't."

"Amen!" cried the old lady, with Methodistic fervor.

"What are you saying amen to?—that I'm not good?"

"Oh, I imagine we all average about alike," was her grim reply—"the more shame to us all!"

"Dear, conscience-stricken old aunty!" said Graham, smiling at her. "Will nothing ever lay your theological ghosts?"

"No, Alford," she said, gravely. "Let us change the subject."

"I've told Major St. John everything from the day I first came here," Graham explained; "and now before we separate let it be understood that he joins us as a powerful ally. His influence over Grace, after all, is more potent than that of all the rest of us united. My words to-night have acted more like a shock than anything else. I have placed before her clearly and sharply the consequences of yielding passively, and of drifting further toward darkness. We must possess ourselves with an almost infinite patience and vigilance. She, after all, must bear the brunt of this fight with death; but we must be ever on hand to give her support, and it must be given also unobtrusively, with all the tact we possess. We can let her see that we are more cheerful in our renewed hope, but we must be profoundly sympathetic and considerate."

"Well, Graham, as I said before, you are captain. I learned to obey orders long ago as well as to give them;" and the major summoned his valet and bade them good-night.

Graham, weary in the reaction from his intense feeling and excitement, threw himself on the sofa, and his aunt came and sat beside him.

"Alford," she said, "what an immense change your coming has made!"

"The beginning of a change, I hope."

"It was time—it was time. A drearier household could scarcely be imagined. Oh, how dreary life can become! Grace was dying. Every day I expected tidings of your death. It's a miracle that you are alive after all these bloody years. All zest in living had departed from the major. We are all materialists, after our own fashion, wholly dependent on earthly things, and earthly things were failing us. In losing Grace, you and the major would have lost everything; so would I in losing you. Alford, you have become a son to me. Would you break a mother's heart? Can you not still promise to live and do your best?"

"Dear aunt, we shall all live and do our best."

"Is that the best you can say, Alford?"

"Aunty, there are limitations to the strength of every man. I have reached the boundary of mine. From the time I began the struggle in the Vermont woods, and all through my exile, I fought this passion. I hesitated at no danger, and the wilder and more desolate the region, the greater were its attractions to me. I sought to occupy my mind with all that was new and strange; but such was my nature that this love became an inseparable part of my being. I might just as well have said I would forget my sad childhood, the studies that have interested me, your kindness. I might as well have decreed that I should not look the same and be the same—that all my habits of thought and traits of character should not be my own. Imagine that a tree in your garden had will and intelligence. Could it ignore the law of its being, all the long years which had made it what it is, and decide to be some other kind of tree, totally different? A man who from childhood has had many interests, many affections, loses, no doubt, a sort of concentration when the one supreme love of his life takes possession of him. If Grace lives, and I can see that she has at last tranquilly and patiently accepted her lot, you will find that I can be tranquil and patient. If she dies, I feel that I shall break utterly. I can't look into the abyss that her grave would open. Do not think that I would consciously and deliberately become a vulgar suicide—I hope I long since passed that point, and love and respect for you forbid the thought—but the long strain that I have been under, and the dominating influence of my life, would culminate. I should give way like a man before a cold, deadly avalanche. I have been frank with you, for in my profound gratitude for your love and kindness I would not have you misunderstand me, or think for a moment that I proposed deliberately to forget you in my own trouble. The truth is just this, aunt: I have not strength enough to endure Grace Hilland's death. It would be such a lame, dreary, impotent conclusion that I should sink under it, as truly as a man who found himself in the sea weighted by a ton of lead. But don't let us dwell on this thought. I truly believe that Grace will live, if we give her all the aid she requires. If she honestly makes the effort to live—as she will, I feel sure—she can scarcely help living when the conditions of life are supplied."

"I think I understand you, Alford," said the old lady, musingly; "and yet your attitude seems a strange one."

"It's not an unnatural one. I am what I have been

growing to be all these years. I can trace the sequence of cause and effect until this moment.''

"Well, then," said the old lady, grimly, "Grace must live, if it be in the power of human will and effort to save her. Would that I had the faith in God that I ought to have! But He is afar off, and He acts in accordance with an infinite wisdom that I can't understand. The happiness of His creatures seems a very secondary affair.''

"Now, aunty, we are on ground where we differ theoretically, to say the least; but I accord to you full right to think what you please, because I know you will employ all the natural and rational expedients of a skilful nurse.''

"Yes, Alford; you and Grace only make me unhappy when you talk in that way. I know you are wrong, just as certainly as the people who believed the sun moved round the earth. The trouble is that I know it only with the same cold mental conviction, and therefore can be of no help to either of you. Pardon me for my bluntness: do you expect to marry Grace, should she become strong and well?''

"No, I can scarcely say I have any such hope. It is a thought I do not even entertain at present, nor does she. I am content to be her friend through life, and am convinced that she could not think of marriage again for years, if ever. That is a matter of secondary importance. All that I ask is that she shall live.''

"Well, compared with most men, a very little contents you," said his aunt dryly. "We shall see, we shall see. But you have given me such an incentive that, were it possible, I'd open my withered veins and give her half of my poor blood.''

"Dear aunty, how true and stanch your love is! I cannot believe it will be disappointed.''

"I must go back to my post now, nor shall I leave it very often.''

"Here is Dr. Markham. He will see that you have it often enough to maintain your own health, and I will too. I've been a soldier too long to permit my chief of staff to be disabled. Pardon me, doctor, but it seems to me that this is more of a case for nursing and nourishment than for drugs.''

''You are right, and yet a drug can also become a useful ally. In my opinion, it is more a case for change than anything else. When Mrs. Hilland is strong enough, you must take her from this atmosphere and these associations. In a certain sense she must begin life over again, and take root elsewhere.''

''There may be truth in what you say;'' and Graham was merged in deep thought when he was left alone. The doctor, in passing out a few moments later, assured him that all promised well.

CHAPTER XXXVII

THE EFFORT TO LIVE

AS Graham had said, it did seem that infinite patience and courage would be required to defeat the dark adversaries now threatening the life upon which he felt that his own depended. He had full assurance that Grace made her promised effort, but it was little more than an effort of will, dictated by a sense of duty. She had lost her hold on life, which to her enfeebled mind and body promised little beyond renewed weariness and disappointment. How she could live again in any proper sense of the word was beyond her comprehension; and what was bare existence? It would be burdensome to herself and become wearisome to others. The mind acts through its own natural medium, and all the light that came to her was colored by almost despairing memories.

Too little allowance is often made for those in her condition. The strong man smiles half contemptuously at the efforts of one who is feeble to lift a trifling weight. Still, he is charitable. He knows that if the man has not the muscle, all is explained. So material are the conceptions of many that they have no patience with those who have been enfeebled in mind, will, and courage. Such persons would say, "Of course Mrs. Hilland cannot attend to her household as before; but she ought to have faith, resignation; she ought to make up her mind cheerfully to submit, and she would soon be well. Great heavens! haven't other women lost their husbands? Yes, indeed, and they worried along quite comfortably."

Graham took no such superficial view. "Other women" were not Grace. He was philosophical, and tried to estimate the effect of her own peculiar experience on her own nature, and was not guilty of the absurdity of generalizing. It was his problem to save Grace as she was, and not as some good people said she ought to be. Still, his firm belief remained, that she could live if she would comply with what he believed to be the conditions of life; indeed, that she could scarcely help living. If the time could come when her brain would be nourished by an abundance of healthful blood, he might hope for almost anything. She would then be able to view the past dispassionately, to recognize that what *was past* was gone forever, and to see the folly of a grief which wasted the present and the future. If she never became strong enough for that—and the prospect was only a faint, half-acknowledged hope—then he would reverently worship a patient, gentle, white-haired woman, who should choose her own secluded path, he being content to make it as smooth and thornless as possible.

Beyond a brief absence at the time his regiment was mustered out of the service, he was always at home, and the allies against death—with their several hopes, wishes, and interests—worked faithfully. At last there was a more decided response in the patient. Her sleep became prolonged, as if she were making amends for the weariness of years. Skilful tonic treatment told on the wasted form. New blood was made, and that, in Graham's creed, was new life.

His materialistic theory, however, was far removed from any gross conception of the problem. He did not propose to feed a woman into a new and healthful existence, except as he fed what he deemed to be her whole nature. In his idea, flowers, beauty in as many forms as he could command and she enjoy at the time, were essential. He ransacked nature in his walks for things to interest her. He brought her out into the sunshine, and taught her to distinguish the different birds by their notes. He had Mrs. Mayburn talk to her and consult with her over the homely and wholesome details of housekeeping. Much of the news of the day was brought to her attention as that which should naturally interest her, especially the reconstruction of the South, as represented and made definite by the experience of Henry Anderson and his sister. He told her that he had bought at a nominal sum a large plantation in the vicinity of the parsonage, and that Colonel Anderson should be his agent, with the privilege of buying at no more of an advance than would satisfy the proud young Southerner's self respect.

Thus from every side he sought to bring natural and healthful influences to bear upon her mind, to interest her in life at every point where it touched her, and to reconnect the broken threads which had bound her to the world.

He was aided earnestly and skilfully on all sides. Their success, however, was discouragingly slow. In her weakness Grace made pathetic attempts to respond, but not from much genuine interest. As she grew stronger her manner toward her father was more like that of her former self than was the rest of her conduct. Almost as if from the force of habit, she resumed her thoughtful care for his comfort; but beyond that there seemed to be an apathy, an indifference, a dreary preoccupation hard to combat.

In Graham's presence she would make visible effort to do all he wished, but it was painfully visible, and sometimes she would recognize his unobtrusive attentions with a smile that was sadder than any words could be. One day she seemed almost wholly free from the deep apathy that was becoming characteristic, and she said to him, "Alas, my friend! as I said to you at first, the woman *is* dead within me. My body grows stronger, as the result of the skill and help you all are bringing to bear on my sad problem, but my heart is dead, and my hope takes no hold on life. I cannot overcome the feeling that I am a mere shadow, and have no right to be here among the living. You are so brave, patient, and faithful that I am ever conscious of a sort of dull remorse; but there is a weight on

my brain and a despairing numbness at my heart, making
everything seem vain and unreal. Please do not blame
me. Asking me to feel is like requiring sight of the blind.
I've lost the faculty. I have suffered so much that I have
become numb, if not dead. The shadows of the past mingle
with the shadows of to-day. Only you seem real in your
strong, vain effort, and as far as I can suffer any more it
pains me to see you thus waste yourself on a hopeless
shadow of a woman. I told you I should disappoint you."

"I am not wasting myself, Grace. Remain a shadow
till you can be more. I will bear my part of the burden,
if you will be patient with yours. Won't you believe that
I am infinitely happier in caring for you as you are than I
should be if I could not thus take your hand and express
to you my thought, my sympathy? Dear Grace, the causes
which led to your depression were strong and terrible.
Should we expect them to be counteracted in a few short
weeks?"

"Alas, Alford! is there any adequate remedy? Forgive me for saying this to you, and yet you, of all people,
can understand me best. You cling to me who should be
nothing to a man of your power and force. You say you
cannot go on in life without me, even as a weak, dependent
friend—that you would lose all zest, incentive, and interest;
for I cannot think you mean more. If you feel in this way
toward me, who in the eyes of other men would be a dismal
burden, think how Warren dwells in my memory, what he
was to me, how his strong sunny nature was the sun of my
life. Do you not see you are asking of me what you say
you could not do yourself, although you would, after your
own brave, manly fashion? But your own belief should
teach you the nature of my task when you ask me to go on
and take up life again, from which I was torn more completely than the vine which falls with the tree to which it
clung."

"Dear Grace, do not think for a moment that I am not
always gratefully conscious of the immense self-sacrifice

you are making for me and others. You long for rest and
forgetfulness, and yet you know well that your absence
would leave an abyss of despair. You now add so much
to the comfort of your father! Mrs. Mayburn clings to
you with all the love of a mother. And I, Grace—what
else can I do? Even your frail, sad presence is more to
me than the sun in the sky. Is it pure selfishness on my
part to wish to keep you? Time, the healer, will gradually bring to you rest from pain, and serenity to us all.
When you are stronger I will take you to Hilland's grave—"

"No, no, no!" she cried, almost passionately. "Why
should I go there? Oh, this is the awful part of it! What
I so loved has become nothing, worse than nothing—that
from which I shrink as something horrible. Oh, Alford!
why are we endowed with such natures if corruption is to
be the end? It is this thought that paralyzes me. It seems
as if pure, unselfish love is singled out for the most diabol-
ical punishment. To think that a form which has become
sacred to you may be put away at any moment as a horrible
and unsightly thing! and that such should be the end of the
noblest devotion of which man is capable! My whole being
revolts at it; and yet how can I escape from its truth? I
am beset by despairing thoughts on every side when able to
think at all, and my best remedy seems a sort of dreary
apathy, in which I do little more than breathe. I have
read that there comes a time when the tortured cease to
feel much pain. There was a time, especially at the hospital, when I suffered constantly—when almost everything
but you suggested torturing thoughts. I suffered with you
and for you, but there was always something sustaining in
your presence. There is still. I should not live a month
in your absence, but it seems as if it were your strong will
that holds me, not my own. You have given me the power,
the incentive, to make such poor effort as I am putting forth.
Moreover, in intent, you gave your life for Warren again and
again, and as long as I have any volition left I will try and
do all you wish, since you so wish it. But my hope is dead.

I do not see how any more good can come to me or through me."

"You are still willing, however, to permit me to think for you, to guide you? You will still use your utmost effort to live?"

"Yes. I can refuse to the man who went back to my dying husband nothing within my power to grant. It is indeed little. Besides, I am in your care, but I fear I shall prove a sad, if not a fatal legacy."

"Of that, dear Grace, you must permit me to be the judge. All that you have said only adds strength to my purpose. Does not the thought that you are doing so very much for me and for all who love you bring some solace?"

"It should. But what have I brought you but pain and deep anxiety? Oh, Alford, Alford! you will waken some bitter day to the truth that you love but the wraith of the girl who unconsciously won your heart. You have idealized her, and the being you now love does not exist. How can I let you go on thus wronging yourself?"

"Grace," replied he, gravely and almost sternly, "I learned in the northern woods, among the fiords of Norway, under the shadow of the Himalayas, and in my long, lonely hours in the war, whom I loved, and why I loved her. I made every effort at forgetfulness that I, at least, was capable of exerting, and never forgot for an hour. Am I a sentimental boy, that you should talk to me in this way? Let us leave that question as settled for all time. Moreover, never entertain the thought that I am planning and hoping for the future. I see in your affection for me only a pale reflection of your love for Hilland."

"No, Alford, I love you for your own sake. How tenderly you have ever spoken of little Rita Anderson, and yet—"

"And yet, as I have told you more than once, the thought of loving her never entered my mind. I could plan for her happiness as I would for a sister, had I one."

"Therefore you can interpret me."

"Therefore I have interpreted you, and, from the first, have asked for nothing more than that you still make one of our little circle, each member of which would be sadly missed, you most of all."

"I ought to be able to do so little as that for you. Indeed, I am trying."

"I know you are, and, as you succeed, you will see that I am content. Do not feel that when I am present you must struggle and make unwonted effort. The tide is setting toward life; float gently on with it. Do not try to force nature. Let time and rest daily bring their imperceptible healing. The war is over. I now have but one object in life, and if you improve I shall come and go and do some man's work in the world. My plantation in Virginia will soon give me plenty of wholesome out-of-door thoughts."

She gave him one of her sad smiles as she replied wearily, "You set me a good example."

This frank interchange of thought appeared at first to have a good effect on Grace, and brought something of the rest which comes from submission to the inevitable. She found that Graham's purpose was as immovable as the hills, and at the same time was more absolutely convinced that he was not looking forward to what seemed an impossible future. Nor did he ask that her effort should be one of feeble struggles to manifest an interest before him which she did not feel. She yielded to her listlessness and apathy to a degree that alarmed her father and Mrs. Mayburn, but Graham said: "It's the course of nature. After such prolonged suffering, both body and mind need this lethargy. Reaction from one extreme to another might be expected."

Dr. Markham agreed in the main with this view, and yet there was a slight contraction of perplexity on his brows as he added: "I should not like to see this tendency increase beyond a certain point, or continue too long. From the first shock of her bereavement Mrs. Hilland's mind has not been exactly in a normal condition. There are phases of her trouble difficult to account for and difficult to treat. The very fineness of her organization made the terrible shock more serious in its injury. I do not say this to discourage you—far from it—but in sincerity I must call your attention to the fact that every new phase of her grief has tended to some extreme manifestation, showing a disposition toward, not exactly mental weakness, but certainly an abnormal mental condition. I speak of this that you may intelligently guard against it. If due precaution is used, the happy mean between these reactions may be reached, and both mind and body recover a healthful tone. I advise that you all seek some resort by the sea, a new one, without any associations with the past."

Within a few days they were at a seaside inn, a large one whose very size offered seclusion. From their wide and lofty balconies they could watch the world come and go on the sea and on the land; and the world was too large and too distant for close scrutiny or petty gossip. They could have their meals in their rooms, or in the immense dining-hall, as they chose; and in the latter place the quiet party would scarcely attract a second glance from the young, gay, and sensation-loving. Their transient gaze would see two old ladies, one an invalid, an old and crippled man, and one much younger, who evidently would never take part in a german.

It was thought and hoped that this nearness to the complex world, with the consciousness that it could not approach her to annoy and pry, might tend to awaken in Grace a passing interest in its many phases. She could see without feeling that she was scanned and surmised about, as is too often the case in smaller houses wherein the guests are not content until they have investigated all newcomers.

But Grace disappointed her friends. She was as indifferent to the world about her as the world was to her. At first she was regarded as a quiet invalid, and scarcely noticed. The sea seemed to interest her more than all things else, and, if uninterrupted, she would sit and gaze at its vary-ing aspects for hours.

According to Graham's plan, she was permitted, with little interference, to follow her mood. Mrs. Mayburn was like a watchful mother, the major much his former self, for his habits were too fixed for radical changes. Grace would quietly do anything he asked, but she grew more forgetful and inattentive, coming out of her deep abstraction—if such it could be termed—with increasing effort. With Graham she seemed more content than with any one else. With him she took lengthening walks on the beach. He sat quietly beside her while she watched the billows chasing one another to the shore. Their swift onset, their defeat, over which they appeared to foam in wrath, their backward and disheartened retreat, ever seemed to tell her in some dim way a story of which she never wearied. Often she would turn and look at him with a vague trouble in her face, as if faintly remembering something that was a sorrow to them both; but his reassuring smile quieted her, and she would take his hand as a little child might have done, and sit for an hour without removing her eyes from the waves. He waited patiently day after day, week after week, reiter-ating to himself, "She will waken, she will remember all, and then will have strength and calmness to meet it. This is nature's long repose."

It was growing strangely long and deep.

Meanwhile Grace, in her outward appearance, was under-going a subtle change. Graham was the first to observe it, and at last it was apparent to all. As her mind became inert, sleeping on a downy couch of forgetfulness, closely curtained, the silent forces of physical life, in her deep tranquillity, were doing an artist's work. The hollow cheeks were gradually rounded and given the faintest pos-sible bloom. Her form was gaining a contour that might satisfy a sculptor's dream.

The major had met old friends, and it was whispered about who they were—the widow of a millionaire; Colonel

Graham, one of the most dashing cavalry officers in the war which was still in all minds; Major St. John, a veteran soldier of the regular service, who had been wounded in the Mexican War and who was well and honorably known to the chief dignitaries of the former generation. Knowing all this, the quidnuncs complacently felt at first that they knew all. The next thing was to know the people. This proved to be difficult indeed. The major soon found a few veteran cronies at whist, but to others was more unapproachable than a major-general of the old school. Graham was far worse, and belles tossed their heads at the idea that he had ever been a "dashing cavalry officer" or dashing anything else. Before the summer was over the men began to discover that Mrs. Hilland was the most beautiful woman in the house—strangely, marvellously, supernaturally beautiful.

An artist, who had found opportunity to watch the poor unconscious woman furtively—not so furtively either but that any belle in the hostelry would know all about it in half a minute—raved about the combination of charms he had discovered.

"Just imagine," he said, "what a picture she made as she sat alone on the beach! She was so remarkable in her appearance that one might think she had arisen from the sea, and was not a creature of the earth. Her black, close-fitting dress suggested the form of Aphrodite as she rose from the waves. Her profile was almost faultless in its exquisite lines. Her complexion, with just a slight warm tinge imparted by the breeze, had not the cold, dead white of snow, but the clear transparency which good aristocratic blood imparts. But her eyes and hair were her crowning features. How shall I describe the deep, dreamy languor of her large, dark eyes, made a hundred-fold more effective by the silvery whiteness of her hair, which had partly escaped from her comb, and fell upon her neck! And then her sublime, tranquil indifference! That I was near, spellbound with admiration, did not interest her so much as a sail, no larger than a gull's wing, far out at sea. '

"Strange, strange!" said one of his friends, laughing; "her unconsciousness of your presence was the strangest part of it all. Why did you not make a sketch?"

"I did, but that infernal Colonel Graham, who is said to be her shadow—after her million, you know—suddenly appeared and asked sternly: 'Have you the lady's permission for this sketch?' I stammered about being 'so impressed, that in the interests of art,' etc. He then snatched my sketch and threw it into the waves. Of course I was angry, and I suppose my words and manner· became threatening. He took a step toward me, looking as I never saw a man look. 'Hush,' he said, in a low voice. 'Say or do a thing to annoy that lady, and I'll wring your neck and toss you after your sketch. Do you think I've been through a hundred battles to fear your insignificance?' By Jove! he looked as if he could do it as easily as say it. Of course I was not going to brawl before a lady."

"No; it wouldn't have been prudent—I mean gentlemanly," remarked his bantering friend.

"Well, laugh at me," replied the young fellow, who was as honest as light-hearted and vain. "I'd risk the chance of having my neck wrung for another glimpse at such marvellous beauty. Would you believe it? the superb creature never so much as once turned to glance at us. She left me to her attendant as completely as if he were removing an annoying insect. Heavens! but it was the perfection of high breeding. But I shall have my revenge: I'll paint her yet."

"Right, my friend, right you are; and your revenge will be terrible. Her supernatural and high-bred nonchalance will be lost forever should she see her portrait;" and with mutual chaffing, spiced with good-natured satire, as good-naturedly received, the little party in a smoking-room separated.

But furtive eyes soon relieved the artist from the charge of exaggeration. Thus far Grace's manner had been ascribed to high-bred reserve and the natural desire for seclusion in her widowhood.   Now, however, that attention was concentrated upon her, Graham feared that more than her beauty would be discovered.

He himself also longed inexpressibly to hide his new phase of trouble from the chattering throng of people who were curious to know about them.   To know?   As if they could know!   They might better sit down to gossip over the secrets of the differential and the integral calculus.

But he saw increasing evidences that they were becoming objects of "interest," and the beautiful millionaire widow "very interesting," as it was phrased; and he knew that there is no curiosity so penetrating as that of the fashionable world when once it is aroused, and the game deemed worthy of pursuit.

People appeared from Washington who had known Lieutenant-Colonel Hilland and heard something of Graham, and the past was being ferreted out.   "Her hair had turned white from grief in a night," it was confidently affirmed.

Poor Jones shrugged his shoulders as he thought: "I shall never be the cause of my wife's hair turning white, unless I may, in the future, prevent her from dyeing it."

After all, sympathy was not very deep.   It was generally concluded that Colonel Graham would console her, and one lady of elegant leisure, proud of her superior research, declared that she had seen the colonel "holding Mrs. Hilland's hand," as they sat in a secluded angle of the rocks.

Up to a certain time it was comparatively easy to shield Grace; but now, except as she would turn her large, dreamy eyes and unresponsive lips upon those who sought her acquaintance, she was as helpless as a child.   The major and Mrs. Mayburn at once acquiesced in Graham's wish to depart.   Within a day or two the gossips found that their prey had escaped, and Grace was once more in her cottage home.

At first she recognized familiar surroundings with a sigh of content.   Then a deeply troubled look flitted across her face and she looked at Graham inquiringly.

"What is it, Grace?" he asked, gently.

She pressed her hand to her brow, glanced around once more, shook her head sadly, and went to her room to throw off her wraps

They all looked at one another with consternation. Hitherto they had tried to be dumb and blind, each hiding the growing and awful conviction that Grace was drifting away from them almost as surely as if she had died.

"Something must be done at once," said practical Mrs. Mayburn.

"I have telegraphed for Dr. Markham," replied Graham, gloomily. "Nothing can be done till he returns. He is away on a distant trip."

"Oh!" groaned the old major, "there will be an end of me before there is to all this trouble."

CHAPTER XXXVIII

GRAHAM'S LAST SACRIFICE

A TERRIBLE foreboding oppressed Graham. Would
Grace fulfil her prediction and disappoint him, after
all? Would she elude him, escape, *die*, and yet remain at his side, beautiful as a dream? Oh, the agony of
possessing this perfect casket, remembering the jewel that
had vanished! He had vowed to defeat his gloomy rivals,
Grief and Death, and they were mocking him, giving the
semblance of what he craved beyond even imagined perfection, but carrying away into their own inscrutable darkness
the woman herself.

What was Grace?—what becoming? As he looked he
thought of her as a sculptor's ideal embodied, a dream of
beauty only, not a woman—as the legend of Eve, who
might, before becoming a living soul, have harmonized
with the loveliness of her garden without seeing or feeling it.

He could not think of her mind as blotted out or perverted; he could not conceive of it otherwise than as corresponding with her outward symmetry. To his thought
it slumbered, as her form might repose upon her couch, in
a death-like trance. She went and came among them like
a somnambulist, guided by unconscious instincts, memories,
and habits.

She knew their voices, did, within limitations, as they
requested; but when she waited on her father there was a
sad, mechanical repetition of what she had done since

childhood. Mrs. Mayburn found her docile and easily controlled, and the heart-stricken old lady was vigilance itself.

Toward Graham, however, her manner had a marked characteristic. He was her master, and she a dumb, lovely, unreasoning creature, that looked into his eyes for guidance, and gathered more from his tones than from his words. Some faint consciousness of the past had grown into an instinct that to him she must look for care and direction; and she never thought of resisting his will. If he read to her, she turned to him her lovely face, across which not a gleam of interest or intelligence would pass. If he brought her flowers, she would hold them until they were taken from her. She would pace the garden walks by his side, with her hand upon his arm, by the hour if he wished it, sometimes smiling faintly at his gentle tones, but giving no proof that she understood the import of his words. At Hilland's name only she would start and tremble as if some deep chord were struck, which could merely vibrate until its sounds were faint and meaningless.

It was deeply touching also to observe in her sad eclipse how her ingrained refinement asserted itself. In all her half-conscious action there was never a coarse look or word. She was a rose without its perfume. She was a woman without a woman's mind and heart. These had been subtracted, with all the differences they made; otherwise she was Grace Hilland.

Graham was profoundly perplexed and distressed. The problem had become too deep for him. The brain, nourished by good blood, had not brought life. All his skill and that of those allied with him had failed. The materialist had matter in the perfection of breathing outline, but where was the woman he loved? How could he reach her, how make himself understood by her, except as some timid, docile creature responds to a caress or a tone? His very power over her was terrifying. It was built upon the instinct, the allegiance that cannot reason but is unquestioning. Nothing could so have daunted his hope, courage, and will as the exquisite being Grace had become, as she looked up to him with her large, mild, trusting eyes, from which thought, intelligence, and volition had departed.

At last Dr. Markham came, and for several days watched his patient closely, she giving little heed to his presence. They all hung on his perturbed looks with a painful anxiety. For a time he was very reticent, but one day he followed Graham to his quarters in Mrs. Mayburn's cottage, where he was now much alone. Grace seemed to miss him but slightly, although she always gave some sign of welcome on his return. The mocking semblance of all that he could desire often so tantalized him that her presence became unendurable. The doctor found him pacing his room in a manner betokening his half-despairing perplexity.

"Colonel Graham," he said, "shall I surprise you when I say physicians are very fallible? I know that it is not the habit of the profession to admit this, but I have not come here to talk nonsense to you. You have trusted me in this matter, and admitted me largely into your confidence, and I shall speak to you in honest, plain English. Mrs. Hilland's symptoms are very serious. What I feared has taken place. From her acute and prolonged mental distress and depression, of which she would have died had you not come, she reacted first into mental lethargy, and now into almost complete mental inactivity. I cannot discover that any disturbed physical functions have been an element in her mental aberration, for more perfect physical life and loveliness I have never seen. Her white hair, which might have made her look old, is a foil to a beauty which seems to defy age.

"Pardon me for saying it, but I fear our treatment has been superficial. We men of the world may believe what we please, but to many natures, especially to an organization like Mrs. Hilland's, hope and faith are essential. She has practically been without these from the first, and, as you know, she was sinking under the struggle maintained by her own brave, womanly spirit. She was contending with more than actual bereavement. It was the hopelessness of the struggle that crushed her, for she is not one of that large class of women who can find consolation in crape and becoming mourning.

"In response to your appeal, she did make the effort you required, but it was the effort of a mind still without hope or faith—one that saw no remedy for the evils that had already overwhelmed her—and I must bear witness that her efforts were as sincere as they were pathetic. We all watched to give every assistance in our power. I've lain awake nights, Colonel Graham, to think of remedies that would meet her needs; and good Mrs. Mayburn and your old black cook, Aunt Sheba, prepared food fit for the gods. You were more untiring and effective than any of us, and the major's very infirmities were among her strongest allies. Well, we have the result—a woman who might be a model for a goddess, even to her tranquil face, in which there is no trace of varying human feeling. Explanation of the evil that crushed her, hope, and faith were not given—who can give them?—but they were essential to her from the first. Unbelief, which is a refuge to some, was an abyss to her. In it she struggled and groped until her mind, appalled and discouraged and overwhelmed, refused to act at all. In one sense it is a merciful oblivion, in another a fatal one, from which she must be aroused if possible. But it's a hard, hard case."

"You make it hard indeed," said Graham, desperately. "What faith can I instil except the one I have? I can't lie, even for Grace Hilland. She knew well once that I could easily die for her."

"Well, then," said the physician, "permit a plain, direct question. Will you marry her?"

"Marry her—as she now is?" cried Graham, in unfeigned astonishment.

"You said you could die for her. This may be going much further. Indeed I should call it the triumph of human affection, for in honesty I must tell you that she may

never be better, she may become worse. But I regard it as
her only chance. At any rate, she needs a vigilant care-
taker. Old Mrs. Mayburn will not be equal to the task
much longer, and her place will have to be filled by hired
service. I know it is like suggesting an almost impossible
sacrifice to broach even the thought, remembering her condition, but—"

"Dr. Markham," said Graham, pacing the floor in great
agitation, "you wholly misunderstand me. I was thinking
of her, not of myself. What right have I to marry Grace
Hilland without her consent? She could give no intelligent
assent at present."

"The right of your love; the right her husband gave
when he committed her to your care; the right of your desire to prevent her from drifting into hopeless, lifelong im-
becility, wherein she would be almost at the mercy of hired
attendants, helpless to shield herself from any and every
wrong; the right of a man to sacrifice himself absolutely
for another if he chooses."

"But she might waken from this mental trance and feel
that I had taken a most dishonorable advantage of her helplessness."

"Yes, you run that risk; but here is one man who will
assure her to the contrary, and you would be sustained by
the consciousnes of the purest motives. It is that she may
waken that I suggest the step; mark, I do not advise it.
As I said at first, I am simply treating you with absolute
confidence and sincerity. If matters go on as they are, I
have little or no hope. Mrs. Mayburn is giving way under
the strain, and symptoms of her old disorder are returning.
She cannot watch Mrs. Hilland much longer as she has been
doing. Whom will you put in her place? Will you send
Mrs. Hilland to an asylum, with its rules and systems and
its unknown attendants? Moreover, her present tranquil
condition may not last. She may become as violent as she
now is gentle. She may gradually regain her intelligence,
or it may be restored to her by some sudden shock. If the

mysteries of the physical nature so baffle us, who can predict the future of a disordered intellect? I have presented the darkest side of the picture; I still think it has its bright side. She has no hereditary mental weakness to contend with. As it developed somewhat gradually, it may pass in the same manner. If you should marry her and take her at once to Europe, change of scene, of life, with your vigilant presence ever near, might become important factors in the problem. The memory that she was committed to your care has degenerated into a controlling instinct; but that is far better than nothing. The only real question in my mind is, Are you willing to make the sacrifice and take the risks? You know the world will say you married her for her money, and that will be hard on a man like you."

Graham made a gesture of contempt: "That for the world," he said. "Have you broached this subject to her father and my aunt?"

"Certainly not before speaking to you."

"You then give me your assurance, as a man, that you believe this right, and that it is Grace Hilland's best chance —indeed, almost her only chance—for recovery?"

"I do most unhesitatingly, and I shall do more. I shall bring from New York an eminent physician who has made mental disease a study all his life, and he shall either confirm my opinion or advise you better."

"Do so, Dr. Markham," said Graham, very gravely. "I have incurred risks before in my life, but none like this. If from any cause Mrs. Hilland should recover memory and full intelligence, and reproach me for having taken advantage of a condition which, even among savage tribes, renders the afflicted one sacred, all the fiendish tortures of the Inquisition would be nothing to what I should suffer. Still, prove to me, prove to her father, that it is her best chance, and for Grace Hilland I will take even this risk. Please remember there must be no professional generalities. I must have your solemn written statement that it is for Mrs. Hilland's sake I adopt the measure."

"So be it," was the reply. "I shall telegraph to Dr. Armand immediately to expect me, and shall say that I wish him to be prepared to come at once."

"Do so, and consider no question of expense. I am no longer poor, and if I were, I would mortgage my blood at this juncture."

On the following evening Dr. Armand was almost startled by the vision on the veranda of the St. John cottage. A silvery-haired woman sat looking placidly at the glowing sunset, with its light and its rose-hues reflected in her face.

"If ever there was a picture of a glorified saint, there is one," he muttered, as he advanced and bowed.

She gave him no attention, but with dark eyes, made brilliant by the level rays, she gazed steadily on the closing day. The physician stole a step or two nearer, and looked as steadily at her, while his experienced eye detected in all her illuminated beauty the absence of the higher, more subtle light of reason. Dr. Markham had told him next to nothing about the case, and had asked him to go and see for himself, impressing him only with the fact that it was a question of vital importance that he was to aid in deciding; that he must give it his whole professional skill, and all the necessary time, regardless of expense. The moment he saw Grace, however, the business aspect of the affair passed from his mind. His ruling passion was aroused, and he was more than physician—a student—as the great in any calling ever are.

Graham came to the door and recognized instinctively the intent, eagle-eyed man, who merely nodded and motioned him to approach his patient. Graham did so, and Grace turned her eyes to him with a timid, questioning glance. He offered her his arm; she rose instantly and took it, and began walking with him.

"Were you looking at the sunset, Grace?"

She turned upon him the same inquiring eyes, but did not answer.

"Do you not think it very beautiful? Does it not remind you of the sunset you saw on the evening when I returned from my first battle?"

She shook her head, and only looked perplexed.

"Why, Grace," he continued, as if provoked, "you *must* remember. I was carried, you know, and you and Mrs. Mayburn acted as if my scratches were mortal wounds."

She looked frightened at his angry tones, clasped her hands, and with tears in her eyes looked pleadingly up to him.

"Dear Grace, don't be worried." He now spoke in the gentlest tones, and lifted her hand to his lips. A quick, evanescent smile illumined her face. She fawned against his shoulder a moment, placed his hand against her cheek, and then leaned upon his arm as they resumed their walk, Dr. Armand keeping near them without in the least attracting her attention.

"Grace," resumed Graham, "you must remember. Hilland, Warren, you know."

She dropped his arm, looked wildly around, covered her face with her hands, and shuddered convulsively.

After a moment he said, kindly but firmly, "Grace, dear Grace."

She sprang to him, seized his hand, and casting a look of suspicion at Dr. Armand, drew him away.

A few moments later she was again looking tranquilly at the west, but the light had departed from the sky and from her face. It had the look of one who saw not, thought and felt not. It was breathing, living death.

Graham looked at her mournfully for a few moments, and then, with a gesture that was almost despairing, turned to the physician, who had not lost a single expression.

"Thank you," was that gentleman's first laconic remark; and he dropped into a chair, still with his eyes on the motionless figure of Grace.

At last he asked, "How long would she maintain that position?"

"I scarcely know," was the sad response; "many hours certainly."

"Please let her retain it till I request you to interfere. The moon is rising almost full, the evening is warm, and she can take no harm."

The major tottered out on his crutches, and was given his chair, the physician meanwhile being introduced. Brief and courteous was Dr. Armand's acknowledgment, but he never took his eyes from his patient. The same was true of his greeting to Mrs. Mayburn; but that good lady's hospitable instincts soon asserted themselves, and she announced that dinner was ready.

"Take Mrs. Hilland to dinner," said the physician to Graham; "but first introduce me."

The young man approached and said, "Grace." She rose instantly and took his arm. "This is Dr. Armand, Grace. He has called to see you." She made him a courteous inclination, and then turned to Graham to see what next was expected of her, but he only led her to the dining-room.

"Gracie, darling, bring me my cushion," said her father, speaking as he had been used to do when she was a little girl.

She brought it mechanically and arranged it, then stood in expectancy. "That will do, dear;" and she returned to her seat in silence. Throughout the meal she maintained this silence, although Dr. Armand broached many topics, avoiding only the name of her husband. Her manner was that of a little, quiet, well-bred child, who did not understand what was said, and had no interest in it. The physician's scrutiny did not embarrass her; she had never remembered, much less forgotten him.

When the meal was over they all returned to the piazza. At the physician's request she was placed in her old seat, and they all sat down to watch. The moon rose higher and higher, made her hair more silvery, touched her still face with a strange, ethereal beauty, and threw the swaying shadow of a spray of woodbine across her motionless figure —so motionless that she seemed a sculptured rather than a breathing woman.

After a while the old major rose and groaned as he tottered away. Mrs. Mayburn, in uncontrollable nervous restlessness, soon followed, that she might find relief in household cares. The two men watched on till hours had passed, and still the lovely image had not stirred. At last Dr. Armand approached her and said, "Mrs. Hilland."

She rose, and stood coldly aloof. The name, with her prefix, did not trouble her. She had long been accustomed to that. "Hilland," as Graham uttered the word, alone affected her, touching some last deep chord of memory.

"Mrs. Hilland," the doctor continued, "it is getting late. Do you not think you had better retire?"

She looked at him blankly, and glanced around as if in search of some one.

"I am here, Grace," said Graham, emerging from the doorway.

She came to him at once, and he led her to Mrs. Mayburn, kissing her hand, and receiving, in return, her strange, brief, fawning caress.

"I would like to know the history of Mrs. Hilland's malady from the beginning," said Dr. Armand, when Graham returned.

"I cannot go over it again," replied Graham, hoarsely. "Dr. Markham can tell you about all, and I will answer any questions. Your room is ready for you here, where Dr. Markham will join you presently. I must bid you good-night;" and he strode away.

But as he passed under the apple-tree and recalled all that had occurred there, he was so overcome that once more he leaned against it for support.

CHAPTER XXXIX

MARRIED UNCONSCIOUSLY

THERE was no sleep for Graham that night, for he knew that two skilful men were consulting on a question beyond any that had agitated his heart before. As he paced the little parlor with restless steps, Aunt Sheba's ample form filled the doorway, and in her hands was a tray bearing such coffee as only she knew how to brew.

"Thanks, Aunt Sheba," he said, motioning to a table, without pausing in his distracted walk.

She put down the tray, retreated hesitatingly, and then began: "Dear Mas'r Graham, my ole heart jes aches for yer. But don't yer be so cast down, mas'r; de good Lord knows it all, and I'se a-prayin' for yer and de lubly Miss Grace night and day."

He was so utterly miserable that he was grateful for even this homely sympathy, and he took the old woman's hand in his as he said kindly, "Pray on, then, good old aunty, if it's any comfort to you. It certainly can do no harm."

"Oh, Mas'r Graham, you dunno, you dunno. Wid all yer wise knowin', yer dunno. You'se all—good Mis' Mayburn, de ole major, an' all—are in de dark land ob unbelievin', like poor Missy Grace. She doesn't know how you'se all tink about her an' lub her; needer does you know how de good Lord tinks about you and lubs you. You guv me my liberty; you guv what I tinks a sight more on; you'se been kind to de poor old slave dat los' all her chillen in de weary days dat's gone. I'se a 'memberin' yer all de time. You hab no faith, Mas'r Graham, and poor ole Aunt Sheba mus' hab faith for yer. An' so I will. I'se a wrastlin' wid de Lord for yer all de time, an' I'se a-gwine to wrastle on till I sees yer an' Missy Grace an' all comin' inter de light;'' and she threw her apron over her head, and went sobbing away.

He paused for a moment when she left him, touched deeply by the strong, homely, human sympathy and gratitude of the kind old soul who fed him—as he never forgot —when he was a fugitive in a hostile land. That she had manifested her feeling after what he deemed her own ignorant, superstitious fashion was nothing. It was the genuine manifestation of the best human traits that touched him —pure gems illumining a nature otherwise so clouded and crude.

Late at night footsteps approached, and the two physicians entered. "I first permitted Dr. Armand to form his own impressions, and since have told him everything," said Dr. Markham, "and he strongly inclines to my view. Realizing the gravity of the case, however, he has consented to remain a day or two longer. We will give you no hasty opinion, and you shall have time on your part to exercise the most deliberate judgment."

Dr. Armand confirmed his associate's words, and added, "We will leave you now to the rest you must need sorely. Let me assure you, however, that I do not by any means consider Mrs. Hilland's case hopeless, and that I am strongly impressed with the belief that her recovery must come through you. A long train of circumstances has given you almost unbounded influence over her, as you enabled me to see this evening. It would be sad to place such a glorious creature in the care of strangers, for it might involve serious risk should she regain her memory and intelligence with no strong, sympathetic friend, acquainted with her past, near her. I am inclined to think that what is now little more than an instinct will again develop into a memory, and that the fact that she was committed to your care will fully

reconcile her to the marriage—indeed, render her most grateful for it, if capable of understanding the reasons which led to
it. If further observation confirms my present impressions,
I and Dr. Markham will plainly state our opinions to her
father and Mrs. Mayburn. As my colleague has said, you
must comprehend the step in all its bearings. It is one that
I would not ask any man to take. I now think that the
probabilities are that it would restore Mrs. Hilland to
health eventually. A year of foreign travel might bring
about a gradual and happy change.''

"Take time to satisfy yourselves, gentlemen, and give
me your decision as requested. Then you have my permission to give your opinions to Major St. John.''

Within a week this was done, and the poor old man
bowed his head on Graham's shoulder and wept aloud in
his gratitude. Mrs. Mayburn also, wiping away her tears,
faltered, "You know, Alford, how I schemed for this marriage years ago; you remember my poor blind strategy on
that June day, do you not? How little I thought it would
take place under circumstances like these! And yet, I've
thought of it of late often, very often. I could not go on
much longer, for I am old and feeble, and it just broke my
heart to think of Grace, our Grace, passing into the hands
of some hired and indifferent stranger or strangers. I believe she will recover and reward your sacrifice.''

"It is no sacrifice on my part, aunt, except she wakens
only to reproach me.''

"Well, devotion, then; and little sense she'd ever have,''
concluded the old lady, after her own brusque fashion, "if
she does not fall on her knees and bless you. You could
now take better care of her than I, for she trusts and obeys
you implicitly. She is docile and gentle with me, but often
strangely inattentive. She would be still more so with a
stranger; and the idea of some strong, unfeeling hands forc-
ing her into the routine of her life!''

Thus almost completely was removed from his mind the
unspeakable dread lest he was taking an unfair advantage

of helplessness. He fully recognized also that the ordeal for himself would be a terrible one—that it would be the fable of Tantalus repeated for weeks, months, perhaps for years, or for life. The unfulfilled promise of happiness would ever be before him. His dark-visaged rivals, Grief and Death, would jeer and mock at him from a face of perfect beauty. In a blind, vindictive way he felt that his experience was the very irony of fate. He could clasp the perfect material form of a woman to his heart, and at the same time his heart be breaking for what could not be seen or touched.

The question, however, was decided irrevocably. He knew that he could not leave helpless Grace Hilland to the care of strangers, and that there was no place for him in the world but at her side; and yet it was with something of the timidity and hesitation of a lover that he asked her, as they paced a shady garden-walk, "Grace, dear Grace, will you marry me?"

His voice was very low and gentle, and yet she turned upon him a startled, inquiring look. "Marry you?" she repeated slowly.

"Yes, let me take care of you always," he replied, smilingly, and yet as pale almost as herself.

The word "care" reassured her, and she gave him her wonted smile of content, as she replied, very slowly, "Yes. I want you to take care of me always. Who else can?"

"That's what I mean by marrying you—taking care of you always," he said, raising her hand to his lips.

"You are always to take care of me," she replied, leaning her head on his shoulder for a moment.

"Mrs. Mayburn is not strong enough to take care of you any longer. She will take care of your father. Will you let me take care of you as she does?"

She smiled contentedly, for the word "care" appeared to make all natural and right.

It was arranged that they should be married in the presence of Dr. Markham, Aunt Sheba, and Jinny, in addition to those so deeply interested. The physician prepared the clergyman for the ceremony, which was exceedingly brief and simple, Grace smiling into Graham's face when he promised to take care of her always, and she signifying her consent and pleasure in the manner that was so mute and sad. Then he told her that he was going to take her away, that she might get perfectly strong and well; and she went at his request without hesitancy, although seeming to wonder slightly at the strong emotion of her father and Mrs. Mayburn when parting from her. Jinny, who had been her nurse in childhood, accompanied her. Dr. Markham also went with them as far as the steamer, and they sailed away into a future as vague and unknown to them as the ocean they were crossing.

The waves seen from the deck of the steamer produced in Grace the same content with which she had gazed at them from the shore during the previous summer; only now there were faint signs of wonder in her expression, and sometimes of perplexity. Her eyes also wandered around the great vessel with something of the interest of a child, but she asked no questions. That Graham was with her and smiled reassuringly seemed sufficient, while the presence of her old colored nurse, who in some dim way was connected with her past, gave also an additional sense of security.

As time elapsed and they began their wanderings abroad, it seemed to Graham that his wife was beginning life over again, as a very little quiet child would observe the strange and unaccountable phenomena about it. Instead of her fixed vacancy of gaze, her eyes began to turn from object to object with a dawning yet uncomprehending interest. He in simplest words sought to explain and she to listen, though it was evident that their impression was slight indeed. Still there was perceptible progress, and when in his tireless experimenting he began to bring before her those things which would naturally interest a child, he was encouraged to note that they won a larger and more pleased attention. A garden full of flowers, a farmyard with its sleek, quiet cattle, a band of music, a broad, funny pantomime, were far more to her than Westminster Abbey or St. Paul's. Later, the variety, color, and movement of a Paris boulevard quite absorbed her attention, and she followed one object after another with much the same expression that might be seen on the face of a little girl scarcely three years old. This infantile expression, in contrast with her silver hair and upon her mature and perfect features, was pathetic to the last degree, and yet Graham rejoiced with exceeding joy. With every conscious glance and inquiring look the dawn of hope brightened. He was no longer left alone in the awful solitude of living death. The beautiful form was no longer like a deserted home. It now had a tenant, even though it seemed but the mind of a little child. The rays of intelligence sent out were feeble indeed, but how much better than the blank darkness that had preceded! Something like happiness began to soften and brighten the husband's face as he took his child-wife here and there. He made the long galleries of the Louvre and of Italy her picture-books, and while recognizing that she was pleased with little more than color, form, and action—that the sublime, equally with the vicious and superstitious meanings of the great masters, were hidden—he was nevertheless cheered and made more hopeful by the fact that she *was* pleased and observant—that she began to single out favorites; and before these he would let her stand as long as she chose, and return to them when so inclined.

She had lost the power of reading a line. She did not know even her letters; and these he began to teach her with unflagging zeal and patience. How the mysterious problem would end he could not tell. It might be that by kindling a little light the whole past would become illumined; it might be that he would have to educate her over again; but be the future what it would, the steadfast principle of devotion to her became more fixed, and to care for her the supreme law of his being.

From the time of his first message to them he had rarely lost an opportunity to send a letter to the anxious ones at home, and their replies abounded in solicitous, grateful words. Dr. Markham often called, and rubbed his hands with increasing self-gratulation over the success of his bold measure, especially as encomiums on his sagacity had been passed by the great Dr. Armand.

Nearly a year had passed, and Graham and his wife, after their saunterings over the Continent, were spending the summer in the Scottish Highlands. They sailed on the lochs, fished from their banks, and climbed the mountain passes on little shaggy ponies that were Scotch in their stubbornness and unflinching endurance. Grace had become even companionable in her growing intelligence, and in the place of her silent, inquiring glances there were sometimes eager, childlike questionings.

Of late, however, Graham noted the beginnings of another change. With growing frequency she passed her hand over her brow, that was contracted in perplexity. Sometimes she would look at him curiously, at Jinny, and at the unfamiliar scenes of her environment, then shake her head as if she could not comprehend it all. Speedily, however, she would return with the zest of a quiet little girl to the pleasures and tasks that he unweariedly provided. But Graham grew haggard and sleepless in his vigilance, for he believed that the time of her awakening was near.

One day, while sailing on a loch, they were overtaken by a heavy storm and compelled to run before it, and thus to land at no little distance from their inn. Grace showed much alarm at the dashing waves and howling tempest. Nor was her fright at the storm wholly that of an unreasoning child. Its fury seemed to arouse and shock her, and while she clung to Graham's hand, she persisted in sitting upright and looking about, as if trying to comprehend it all. After landing they had a long, fatiguing ride in the darkness, and she was unusually silent. On reaching her room she glanced around as if all was unfamiliar and incomprehensible. Graham had a presentiment that the hour was near, and he left her wholly to the care of her old colored nurse, but almost immediately, from excessive weariness, she sank into a deep slumber.

Her lethargy lasted so late in the following day that he was alarmed, fearing lest her old symptoms were returning. With anxious, hollow eyes, he watched and waited, and at last she awoke and looked at him with an expression that he had longed for through many weary months, and yet now it terrified him.

"Alford—Mr. Graham," she began, in deep surprise.

"Hush, dear Grace. You have been very ill."

"Yes, but where am I? What has happened?"

"Very much; but you are better now. Here is Jinny, your old nurse, who took care of you as a child."

The old colored woman came in, and, as instructed, said: "Yes, honey, I'se tooken care ob you since you was a baby, and I'se nebber lef' you."

"Everything looks very strange. Why, Alford, I had a long, sad talk with you but a short time since in the library, and you were so kind and unselfish!"

"Yes, Grace; we spoke frankly to each other, but you have been very ill since then, worse than ever before. At your father's request and Dr. Markham's urgent counsel, I brought you to Europe. It was said to be your only chance."

"But where is Mrs. Mayburn?"

"She is at home taking care of your father. Her old sickness threatened to return. She could take care of you no longer, and you needed constant care."

A slow, deep flush overspread her face and even her neck as she faltered: "And—and—has no one else been with me but Jinny?"

"No one else except myself. Grace, dear Grace, I am your husband. I was married to you in the presence of your father, Mrs. Mayburn, and your family physician."

"Now long since?" she asked, in a constrained voice.

"About a year ago."

"Have we been abroad ever since?"

"Yes, and you have been steadily improving. You were intrusted to my care, and there came a time when I must either be faithful to that trust, or place you in the hands of strangers. You were helpless, dear Grace."

"Evidently," in the same low, constrained tone. "Could —could you not have fulfilled your trust in some other way?"

"Your father, your second mother, and your physician thought not."

"Still—" she began, hesitated, and again came that deep, deep flush.

"For your sake, Grace, I incurred the risk of this awful moment."

She turned, and saw an expression which brought tears to her eyes. "I cannot misjudge you," she said slowly; "the past forbids that. But I cannot understand it, I cannot understand it at all."

"Perhaps you never will, dear Grace; I took that risk also to save your life and mind."

"My mind?"

"Yes, your mind. If, in recalling the past, the memory of which has returned, you can preserve sufficient confidence in me to wait till all is clear and explained, I shall be profoundly grateful. I foresaw the possibility of this hour; I foresaw it as the chief danger and trial of my life; and I took the risk of its consequences for your sake because assured by the highest authority that it was your one chance for escape, not from death, but from a fate worse than death, which also would have removed you from my care—indeed the care of all who loved you. I have prepared myself for this emergency as well as I could. Here are letters from your father, Mrs. Mayburn, Dr. Markham, and Dr. Armand, one of the most eminent authorities in the world on brain diseases. But after all I must be judged by your woman's heart, and so stand or fall. I now have but one request, or entreaty rather, to make—that you do not let all the efforts we have made in your behalf be in vain. Can you not calmly and gradually receive the whole truth? There must be no more relapses, or they will end in black ruin to us all. Now that you can think for yourself, your slightest wish shall be my law. Jinny, remain with your mistress."

He lifted her passive hand to his lips, passed into their little parlor, and closed the door. Grace turned to her nurse, and in low, almost passionate utterance, said: "Now tell me all."

"Lor' bress you, Missy Grace, it 'ud take a right smart time to tell yer all. When de big doctors an' all de folks say you'se got to hab strangers take care ob you or go ter a 'sylum, and arter all you'd git wuss, Mas'r Graham he guv in, and said he'd take care ob you, and dey all bress 'im and tank 'im, and couldn't say 'nuff. Den he took you 'cross de big ocean—golly! how big it be—jes' as de doctor said; an' nebber hab I seed sich lub, sich 'votion in a moder as Mas'r Graham hab had fer you. He had to take care ob you like a little chile, an' he was teachin' you how to read like a little chile when, all on a suddint, you wakes up an' knows ebryting you'se forgotten. But de part you doesn't know is de part mos' wuth knowin'. No woman eber had sich a husban' as Mas'r Graham, an' no chile sich a moder. 'Clar' ter grashus ef I b'lieve he's ebber slep' a wink wid his watchin' an' a-tinkin' what he could do fer you."

"But, Jinny, I'm not ill; I never felt stronger in my life."

"Laws, Missy Grace, dar's been a mirackle. You'se strong 'nuff 'cept your mine's been off wisitin' somewhar. Golly! you jes' git up an' let me dress you, an' I'll show yer de han'somest woman in de worl'. All yer's got ter do now is jes' be sensible like, an' yer won't have yer match."

Grace cast an apprehensive look toward the door of the parlor in which was her husband, and then said hurriedly: "Yes, dress me quick. Oh, heavens! how much I have to think about, to realize!"

"Now, honey dear, you jes' keep cool. Don't go an' fly right off de handle agin, or Mas'r Graham'll blow his brains out. Good Lor', how dat man do look sometimes! An' yet often, when he was pintin' out yer letters ter yer, or showin' yer pearty tings, like as you was a chile, he look so happy and gentle like, dat I say he jes' like a moder."

Grace was touched, and yet deep, deep in her soul she felt that a wrong had been done her, no matter what had been the motives. Jinny had no such fine perceptions, but with a feminine tact which runs down through the lowliest natures, she chose one of Grace's quietest, yet most becoming costumes, and would not let her go to the glass till arrayed to the dusky woman's intense satisfaction. Then she led her mistress to the mirror and said: "Look dar, honey! All de picters you'se eber seen can't beat dat!" and Grace gazed long and fixedly at the lovely creature that gazed back with troubled and bewildered eyes.

"Was—was I like that when—when he married me?"

"Yes, an' no, honey. You only look like a picter of a woman den—a berry pearty picter, but nothin' but a picter arter all. Mas'r Graham hab brought yer ter life."

With another lingering, wondering glance at herself, she turned away and said: "Leave me, now, Jinny; I wish to be alone."

The woman hesitated, and was about to speak, but Grace waved her away imperiously, and sat down to the letters Graham had given her. She read and re-read them. They confirmed his words. She was a wife: her husband awaited her but a few feet away—her *husband*, and she had never dreamed of marrying again. The past now stood out luminous to her, and Warren Hilland was its centre. But another husband awaited her—one whom she had never consciously promised "to love, honor, and obey." As a friend she could worship him, obey him, die for him; but as her *husband*—how could she sustain that mysterious bond which merges one life in another? She was drawn toward him by every impulse of gratitude. She saw that, whether misled or not, he had been governed by the best of motives —nay, more, by the spirit of self-sacrifice in its extreme manifestation—that he had been made to believe that it was her only chance for health and life. Still, in her deepest consciousness he was but Alford Graham, the friend most loved and trusted, whom she had known in her far distant home, yet not her husband. How could she go to him, what could she say to him, in their new relations that seemed so unreal?

She trembled to leave him longer in the agony of suspense; but her limbs refused to support her, and her woman's heart shrank with a strange and hitherto unknown fear.

There was a timid knock at the door.

"Come in, Alford," she said, tremblingly.

H stood before her haggard, pale, and expectant.

"Alford," she said, sadly, "why did you not let me die?"

"I could not," he replied, desperately. "As I told you, there is a limit to every man's strength. I see it all in your face and manner—what I feared, what I warned Dr. Markham against. Listen to me. I shall take you home at once. You are well. You will not require my further care, and you need never see my face again."

"And you, Alford?" she faltered.

"Do not ask about me. Beyond the hour when I place you in your father's arms I know nothing. I have reached my limit. I have made the last sacrifice of which I am capable. If you go back as you are now, you are saved from a fate which it seemed to me you would most shrink from could you know it—the coarse, unfeeling touch and care of strangers who could have treated you in your helplessness as they chose. You might have regained your reason years hence, only to find that those who loved you were broken-hearted, lost, gone. They are now well and waiting for you. Here are their letters, written from week to week and breathing hope and cheer. Here is the last one from your father, written in immediate response to mine. In it he says, 'My hand trembles, but it is more from joy than age.' You were gaining steadily, although only as a child's intelligence develops. He writes, 'I shall have my little Grace once more, and see her mind grow up into her beautiful form.'"

She bent her head low to hide the tears that were falling fast as she faltered: "Was it wholly self-sacrifice when you married me?"

"Yes—in the fear of this hour, the bitterest of my life— yes. It has followed me like a spectre through every waking and sleeping hour. Please make the wide distinction. My care for you, the giving up of my life for you, is nothing. That I should have done in any case, as far as I could. But with my knowledge of your nature and your past, I could not seem to take advantage of your helplessness without an unspeakable dread. When shown by the best human skill that I could thus save you, or at least ensure that you would ever have gentle, sympathetic care, I resolved to risk the last extremity of evil to myself for your sake. Now you have the whole truth."

She rose and came swiftly to him—for he had scarcely entered the room in his wish to show her respect—and put-ting her arm around his neck, while she laid her head upon his breast, said gently and firmly: "The sacrifice shall not be all on your side. I have never consciously promised to be your wife, but now, as far as my poor broken spirit will permit, I do promise it. But be patient with me, Alford. Do not expect what I have not the power to give. I can only promise that all there is left of poor Grace Hilland's heart—if aught—shall be yours."

Then for the first time in his life the strong man gave way. He disengaged her so hastily as to seem almost rough, and fell forward on the couch unconscious. The long strain of years had culminated in the hour he so dreaded, and in the sudden revulsion caused by her words nature gave way.

Almost frantic with terror, Grace summoned her servant, and help from the people of the inn. Fortunately an excellent English physician was stopping at the same house, and he was speedily at work. Graham recovered, only to pass into muttering delirium, and the burden of his one sad refrain was: "If she should never forgive me!"

"Great heavens, madam! what *has* he done?" asked the matter-of-fact Englishman.

What a keen probe that question was to the wife as she sat watching through the long, weary night! In an agony of self-reproach she recalled all that he had done for her and hers in all the years, and now in her turn she entreated *him* to live; but he was as unconscious as she had been in the blank past. No wooing, no pleading, could have been so potent as his unconscious form, his strength broken at last in her service.

"O God!" she cried—forgetting in her anguish that she had no God—"have I been more cruel than all the war? Have I given him the wound that shall prove fatal—him who saved Warren's life, my own, my reason, and everything that a woman holds dear?"

Graham's powerful and unvitiated nature soon rallied, however, and under the skilful treatment the fever within a few days gave place to the first deep happiness he had ever known. Grace was tender, considerate, her own former self, and with something sweeter to him than self-sacrifice in her eyes; and he gave himself up to an unspeakable content.

It was she who wrote the home letters that week, and a wondrous tale they told to the two old people, who subsisted on foreign news even more than on Aunt Sheba's delicate cookery.

Graham was soon out again, but he looked older and more broken than his wife, who seemingly had passed by age into a bloom that could not fade. She decided that for his sake they would pass the winter in Italy, and that he should show her again as a woman what he had tried to inter-

est her in as a child.   Her happiness, although often deeply
shadowed, grew in its quiet depths.   Graham had too much
tact to be an ardent lover.   He was rather her stanch friend,
her genial but most considerate companion.   His powerful
human love at last kindled a quiet flame on the hearth of
her own heart that had so long been cold, and her life was
warmed and revived by it.   He also proved in picture galleries and cathedrals that he had seen much when he was
abroad beyond wild mountain regions and wilder people,
and her mind, seemingly strengthened by its long sleep,
followed his vigorous criticism with daily increasing
zest.

The soft, sun-lighted air of Italy appeared to have a
healing balm for both, and even to poor Grace there came
a serenity which she had not known since the "cloud in the
South" first cast its shadow over her distant hearth.

To Graham at last there had come a respite from pain
and fear, a deep content.   His inner life had been too impoverished, and his nature too chastened by stern and bitter
experience, for him to crave gayety and exuberant sentiment in his wife.   Her quiet face, in which now was the
serenity of rest, and not the tranquillity of death in life,
grew daily more lovely to him; and he was not without his
human pride as he saw the beauty-loving Italians look wonderingly at her.   She in turn was pleased to observe how he
impressed cultivated people with his quiet power, with a
presence that such varied experiences had combined to create.   Among fine minds, men and women are more truly
felt than seen.   We meet people of the plainest appearance
and most unostentatious manner, and yet without effort they
compel us to recognize their superiority, while those who
seek to impress others with their importance are known at
once to be weak and insignificant.

It was also a source of deep gratification to Grace that
now, since her husband had obtained rest of mind, he turned
naturally to healthful business interests.   Her own affairs,
of which he had charge in connection with Hilland's lawyer,

were looked after and explained fully to her; and his solicitude for Henry Anderson's success led to an exchange of
letters with increasing frequency. Much business relating
to the Virginia plantation was transacted on the shores of
the Mediterranean.

Grace sought to quiet her compunctions at leaving her
father and Mrs. Mayburn so long by frequent letters written
in her dear old style, by cases of Italian wines, delicate and
rare; exquisite fabrics of the loom, and articles of *vertu;*
and between the letters and the gifts the old people held
high carnival after their quaint fashion all that winter.

The soft Italian days lapsed one after another, like
bright smiles on the face of nature; but at last there came
one on which Grace leaned her head upon her husband's
shoulder and whispered, "Alford, take me home, please."

Had he cared for her before, when she was as helpless
as a little child? Jinny, in recalling that journey and in
dilating on the wonders of her experience abroad, by which
she invariably struck awe into the souls of Aunt Sheba and
Iss, would roll up her eyes, and turn outward the palms of
her hands, as she exclaimed, "Good Lor', you niggers, how
I make you 'prehen' Mas'r Graham's goin's on from de
night he sez, sez he ter me, 'Pack up, Jinny; we'se a-gwine
straight home.' Iss 'clares dat Mas'r Graham's a ter'ble
soger wid his long, straight sword and pistol, an' dat he's
laid out more 'Federates dan he can shake a stick at. Well,
you'd nebber b'lieve he'd a done wuss dan say, 'How d'ye'
to a 'Federate ef yer'd seen how he 'volved roun' Missy
Grace. He wouldn't let de sun shine on her, nor de win'
blow near her, and eberybody had ter git right up an' git
ef she eben wanted ter sneeze. On de ship he had eberybody, from de cap'n to de cabin-boys, a waitin' on her.
Dey all said we hab a mighty quiet v'yage, but Lor' bress
yer! it was all 'long ob Mas'r Graham. He wouldn't let
no wabes run ter pitch his darlin' roun'. Missy Grace, she
used ter sit an' larf an' larf at 'im—bress her dear heart, how
much good it do me to hear de honey larf like her ole dear

self! Her moder used ter be mighty keerful on her, but 'twan't nothin' 'pared ter Mas'r Graham's goin's on.''

Jinny had never heard of Baron Munchausen, but her accounts of foreign experiences and scenes were much after the type of that famous *raconteur;* and by each repetition her stories seemed to make a portentous growth. There was, however, a residuum of truth in all her marvels. The event which she so vaguely foreshadowed by ever-increasing clouds of words took place. In June, when the nests around the cottage were full of little birds, there was also, in a downy, nestlike cradle, a miniature of sweet Grace Graham; and Jinny thenceforth was the oracle of the kitchen.

CHAPTER XL

RITA ANDERSON

THE belief of children that babies are brought from heaven seems often verified by the experiences that follow their advent. And truly the baby at the St. John cottage was a heavenly gift, even to the crotchety old major, whom it kept awake at night by its unseasonable complaints of the evils which it encountered in spite of Grandma Mayburn, faithful old Aunt Sheba, who pleaded to be its nurse, and the gentle mother, who bent over it with a tenderness new and strange even to her heart.

She could laugh now, and laugh she would, when Graham, with a trepidation never felt in battle, took the tiny morsel of humanity, and paraded up and down the library. Lying back on the sofa in one of her dainty wrappers, she would cry, "Look at him, papa; look at that grim cavalry-man, and think of his leading a charge!"

"Well, Gracie, dear," the old major would reply, chuckling at his well-worn joke, "the colonel was *only* a cavalry-man, you know. He's not up in infantry tactics."

One morning Grandma Mayburn opened a high conclave in regard to the baby's name, and sought to settle the question in advance by saying, "Of course it should be Grace."

"Indeed, madam," differed the major, gallantly, "I think it should be named after its grandmother."

Grace lifted her eyes inquiringly to her husband, who stood regarding what to him was the Madonna and child.

"I have already named her," he said, quietly.

"You, you!" cried his aunt, brusquely. "I'd have you

know that this is an affair for grave and general deliberation.''

"Alford shall have his way," said the mother, with
quiet emphasis, looking down at the child, while pride and
tenderness blended sweetly in her face.

"Her name is Hilda, in memory of the noblest man and
dearest friend I have ever known."

Instantly she raised her eyes, brimming with tears, to
his, and faltered, "Thank you, Alford"; and she clasped
the child almost convulsively to her breast, proving that
there was one love which no other could obliterate.

"That's right, dear Grace. Link her name with the
memory of Warren. She will thus make you happier, and
it's my wish."

The conclave ended at once. The old major took off his
spectacles to wipe his eyes, and Mrs. Mayburn stole away.

From that hour little Hilda pushed sorrow from Grace's
heart with her baby hands, as nothing had ever done before,
and the memory of the lost husband ceased to be a shadow
in the background. The innocent young life was associated
with his, and loved the more intensely.

Graham had spoken from the impulse of a generous
nature, too large to feel the miserable jealousies that infest
some minds; but he had spoken more wisely than he knew.
Thereafter there was a tenderness in Grace's manner toward
him which he had never recognized before. He tasted a
happiness of which he had never dreamed, alloyed only by
the thought that his treasures were mortal and frail. But
as the little one thrived, and his wife bloomed into the most
exquisite beauty seen in this world, that of young and happy
motherhood, he gave himself up to his deep content, believing that fate at last was appeased. The major grew even
hilarious, and had his morning and evening parades, as he
called them, when the baby, in its laces and soft draperies,
was brought for his inspection. Mrs. Mayburn, with all
the accumulated maternal yearnings of her heart satisfied,
would preside at the ceremony. Grace, happy and proud,

would nod and smile over her shoulder at her husband, who made a poor pretence of reading his paper, while the old veteran deliberately adjusted his spectacles and made comments that in their solemn drollery and military jargon were irresistible to the household that could now laugh so easily. The young life that had come had brought a new life to them all, and the dark shadows of the past shrank further and further into the background.

But they were there—all the sad mysteries of evil that had crushed the mother's heart. Once they seemed to rush forward and close around her. Little Hilda was ill and Grace in terror. But Dr. Markham speedily satisfied her that it was a trivial matter, and proved it to be so by his remedies. The impression of danger remained, however, and she clung to her little idol more closely than ever; and this was true of all.

Time sped tranquilly on. Hilda grew in endearing ways, and began to have knowing looks and smiles for each. Her preference for her grandfather with his great frosty eyebrows pleased the old gentleman immensely. It was both droll and touching to observe how one often so irascible would patiently let her take off his spectacles, toy with and often pull his gray locks, and rumple his old-fashioned ruffles, which he persisted in wearing on state occasions. It was also silently noted that the veteran never even verged toward profanity in the presence of the child.

Each new token of intelligence was hailed with a delight of which natures coarse or blunted never know. The Wise Men of old worshipped the Babe in the manger, and sadly defective or perverted in their organizations are those who do not see something divine in a little innocent child.

Henry and Rita Anderson, at the urgent solicitation of Graham and his wife, came on in the autumn to make a visit, and, by a very strange coincidence, Graham's favorite captain, a manly, prosperous fellow, happened to be visiting him at the time. By a still more remarkable conjunction of events, he at once shared in his former colonel's admiration of the dark-eyed Southern girl. She was very shy, distant, and observant at first, for this fortuitous captain was a Northerner. But the atmosphere of the two cottages was not in the least conducive to coolness and reserve. The wood fires that crackled on the hearth, or something else, thawed perceptibly the spirited girl. Moreover, there were walks, drives, horseback excursions, daily; and Iss shone forth in a glory of which he had never dreamed as a plantation hand. There were light steps passing to and fro, light laughter, cheery, hearty voices—in which the baby's crowing and cooing were heard as a low, sweet chord— music and whist to the major's infinite content. The shadows shrank further into the background than ever before. No one thought of or heeded them now; but they were there, cowering and waiting.

Only Aunt Sheba was ill at ease. Crooning her quaint lullabies to the baby, she would often lift her eyes to heaven and sigh, ''De good Lord hab marcy on dem! Dey's all a drinkin' at de little shaller pools dat may dry up any minit. It's all ob de earth; it's all ob tings, nothin' but tings which de eyes can see and de han's can touch. De good Lord lift dar eyes from de earth widout takin' dat mos' dear!''

But no one thought of old Aunt Sheba except as a faithful creature born to serve them in her humble way.

The Northern captain soon proved that he had not a little Southern dash and ardor, and he had already discovered that his accidental visit to Graham was quite providential, as he had been taught to regard events that promised favorably. He very significantly asked Colonel Anderson to take a gallop with him one morning, but they had not galloped far before he halted and plumply asked the brother's permission, as the present representative of her father, to pay his addresses to Rita. Now Captain Windom had made a good impression on the colonel, which Graham, in a very casual way, had been at pains to strengthen; and he came back radiant over one point gained. But he was more afraid of

that little Virginian girl than he had ever been of all her
Southern compatriots. He felt that he must forego his
cavalry tactics and open a regular siege; but she, with one
flash of her mirthful eyes, saw through it all, laughed over
it with Grace, whom from worshipping as a saint she now
loved as a sister. Amid the pauses in their mutual worship
of the baby, they talked the captain over in a way that
would have made his ears tingle could he have heard
them; but Grace, underneath all her good-natured criticism, seconded her husband's efforts with a mature woman's tact. Rita should be made happy in spite of all her
little perversities and Southern prejudices, and yet the
hands that guided and helped her should not be seen.

The captain soon abandoned his siege tactics, in which
he was ill at ease, and resumed his old habit of impetuous
advances in which Graham had trained him. Time was
growing short. His visit and hers would soon be over.
He became so downright and desperately in earnest that
the little girl began to be frightened. It was no laughing
matter now, and Grace looked grave over the affair. Then
Rita began to be very sorry for him, and at last, through
Graham's unwonted awkwardness and inattention to his
guests, the captain and Rita were permitted to take a different road from the others on an equestrian party. When
they appeared the captain looked as if he were returning
from a successful charge, and Rita was as shy and blushing as one of the wild roses of her native hills. She fled to
Grace's room, as if it were the only refuge left in the world,
and her first breathless words were: "I haven't promised
anything—that is, nothing definite. I said he might come
and see me in Virginia and talk to papa about it, and I'd
think it over, and—and— Well, he was so impetuous and
earnest! Good heavens! I thought the Northern people
were cold, but that captain fairly took away my breath.
You never heard a man talk so."

Grace had put down the baby, and now stood with her
arm around her friend, smiling the sweetest encouragement.

"I'll explain it all to you, Miss Rita," began Graham's deep voice, as he advanced from a recess.

"Oh, the powers! are you here?" and she started back and looked at him with dismay.

"Yes," said he, "and I merely wished to explain that my friend Windom was in the cavalry, and from much fighting with your brave, impetuous hard-riders we gradually fell into their habits."

"I half believe that you are laughing at me—that you are in league with him, and have been all along."

"Yes, Rita, noble little woman, truest friend at the time of my bitter need, I am in league with any man worthy of you—that is, as far as a man can be who seeks to make you happy;" and he took her hand and held it warmly.

"Here come my silly tears again," and she dashed them to right and left. Then, looking up at him shyly, she faltered, "I must admit that I'm a little bit happy."

"I vowed you should be, all through that dark ride on which you led me away from cruel enemies; and every flower you have placed on the grave of that noble man that Grace and I both loved has added strength to my vow."

"Oh, Rita, Rita, darling!" cried Grace, clasping her in close embrace; "do you think we ever forget it?"

"Can you think, Rita, that in memory of that never-to-be-forgotten day I would give Captain Windom the opportunities he has enjoyed if I did not think he would make you happy? One cannot live and fight side by side with a man for years and not know his mettle. He was lion-like in battle, but he will ever be gentleness itself toward you. Best of all, he will appreciate you, and I should feel like choking any fellow who didn't."

"But indeed, indeed, I haven't promised anything; I only said—"

"No matter what you said, my dear, so long as the captain knows. We are well assured that your every word and thought and act were true and maidenly. Let Windom visit you and become acquainted with your father.

The more you all see of him the more you will respect him."

"You are wonderfully reassuring," said the young girl, "and I learned to trust you long ago. Indeed, after your course toward Henry, I believe I'd marry any one you told me to. But to tell the truth, I have felt, for the last few hours, as if caught up by a whirlwind and landed I don't know where. No one ever need talk to me any more about cold-blooded Northerners. Well, I must land at the dinner-table before long, and so must go and dress. It's proper to eat under the circumstances, isn't it?"

"I expect to," said Graham, laughing, "and I'm more in love than you are."

"Little wonder!" with a glance of ardent admiration toward Grace, and she whisked out. In a moment she returned and said, "Now, Colonel, I must be honest, especially as I think of your vow in the dark woods. I am very, *very* happy;" and then in a meteoric brilliancy of smiles, tears, and excitement, she vanished.

On the day following Captain Windom marched triumphantly away, and his absence proved to Rita that the question was settled, no matter what she had said when having little breath left to say anything.

She and her brother followed speedily, and Graham accompanied them, to superintend in person the setting up of a beautiful marble column which he and Grace had designed for Hilland's grave.

It was a time of sad, yet chastened, memories to both. In their consciousness Hilland had ceased to exist. He was but a memory, cherished indeed with an indescribable honor and love—still only a memory. There was an immense difference, however, in the thoughts of each as they reverted to his distant grave. Graham felt that he had there *closed* a chapter of his life—a chapter that he would ever recall with the deep melancholy that often broods in the hearts of the happiest of men whose natures are large enough to be truly impressed by life's vicissitudes. Grace knew that her girlhood, her former self, was buried in that grave, and with her early lover had vanished forever. Graham had, in a sense, raised her from the dead. His boundless love and self-sacrifice, his indomitable will, had created for her new life, different from the old, yet full of tranquil joys, new hopes and interests. He had not rent the new from the old, but had bridged with generous acts the existing chasm. He was doing all within his power, not jealously to withdraw her thoughts from that terrible past, but to veil its more cruel and repulsive features with flowers, laurel wreaths, and sculptured marble; and in her heart, which had been dead, but into which his love had breathed a new life, she daily blessed him with a deeper affection.

He soon returned to her from Virginia, and by his vivid descriptions made real to her the scenes he had visited. He told her how Rita and her brother had changed the plot in which slept the National and the Confederate officer into a little garden of blossoming greenery; how he had arranged with Colonel Anderson to place a fitting monument over the young Confederate officer, whose friends had been impoverished by the war; and he kissed away the tears, no longer bitter and despairing, evoked by the memories his words recalled. Then, in lighter vein, he described the sudden advent of the impetuous captain; the consternation of the little housekeeper, who was not expecting him so soon; her efforts to improvise a feast for the man who would blissfully swallow half-baked "pones" if served by her; her shy presentation of her lover to the venerable clergyman, which he and Henry had witnessed on the veranda through the half-closed blinds, and the fond old man's immense surprise that his little Rita should have a lover at all.

" 'My dear sir,' he said, 'this is all very premature. You must wait for the child to grow up before imbuing her mind with thoughts beyond her years.'

" 'My dear Dr. Anderson,' had pleaded the adroit Windom, 'I will wait indefinitely, and submit to any conditions that you and Miss Rita impose. If already she has impressed me so deeply, time can only increase my respect, admiration, and affection, if that were possible. Before making a single effort to win your daughter's regard, I asked permission of her brother, since you were so far away. I have not sought to bind her, but have only revealed the deep feeling which she has inspired, and I now come to ask your sanction also to my addresses.'

" 'Your conduct,' replied the old gentleman, unbending urbanely toward the young man, 'is both honorable and considerate. Of course you know that my child's happiness is my chief solicitude. If, after several years, when Rita's mind has grown more mature, her judgment confirms—'

"Here Rita made a little *moue* which only her red lips could form, and Henry and I took refuge in a silent and precipitate retreat, lest our irreverent mirth should offend the blind old father, to whom Rita is his little Rita still. You know well how many years, months rather, Windom will wait.

"Well, I left the little girl happier than the day was long, for I believe her eyes sparkle all through the night under their long lashes. As for Windom, he is in the seventh heaven. 'My latest campaign in Virginia,' he whispered to me as I was about to ride away; 'good prospects of the best capture yet won from the Confederacy.' "

And so he made the place familiar to her, with its high lights and deep shadows, and its characters real, even down to old Jehu and his son Huey.

CHAPTER XLI

A LITTLE CHILD SHALL LEAD THEM

AUTUMN merged imperceptibly into winter, and the days sped tranquilly on. With the exception of brief absences on business, Graham was mostly at home, for there was no place like his own hearth. His heart, so long denied happiness, was content only at the side of his wife and child. The shadows of the past crouched further away than ever, but even their own health and prosperity, their happiness, and the reflected happiness of others could not banish them wholly. The lights which burned so brightly around them, like the fire on their hearth, had been kindled and were fed by human hands only, and were ever liable to die out. The fuel that kept them burning was the best that earth afforded, but the supply had its inherent limitations. Each new tranquil day increased the habitual sense of security. Graham was busy with plans of a large agricultural enterprise in Virginia. The more he saw of Henry Anderson the more he appreciated his sterling integrity and fine business capabilities, and from being an agent he had become a partner. Grace's writing-desk, at which Graham had cast a wistful glance the first time he had seen it, was often covered with maps of the Virginia plantation, which he proposed to develop into its best capabilities. Grace had a cradle by the library fire as well as in her room. Beside this the adopted grandmother knitted placidly, and the major rustled his paper softly lest he should waken the little sleeper. Grace, who persisted in making all of her little one's dainty plumage herself, would lift her eyes from time to time, full of genuine interest in

his projects and in his plans for a dwelling on the plantation, which should be built according to her taste and constructed for her convenience.

The shadows had never been further away. Even old
Aunt Sheba was lulled into security. Into her bereaved
heart, as into the hearts of all the others, the baby crept;
and she grew so bewitching with her winsome ways, so
absorbing in her many little wants and her need of watching, as with the dawning spirit of curiosity she sought to
explore for herself what was beyond the cradle and the
door, that Aunt Sheba, with the doting mother, thought of
Hilda during all waking hours and dreamed of her in sleep.

At last the inconstant New England spring passed away,
and June came with its ever-new heritage of beauty. The
baby's birthday was to be the grand fête of the year, and
the little creature seemed to enter into the spirit of the occasion. She could now call her parents and grandparents
by name, and talk to them in her pretty though senseless
jargon, which was to them more precious than the wisdom
of Solomon.

It was a day of roses and rose-colors. Roses banked the
mantelpieces, wreathed the cradle, crowned the table at
which Hilda sat in state in her high chair, a fairy form in
gossamer laces, with dark eyes—Grace's eyes—that danced
with the unrestrained delight of a child.

"She looks just like my little Grace of long, long years
ago," said the major, with wistful eyes; "and yet, Colonel,
it seems but yesterday that your wife was the image of that
laughing little witch yonder."

"Well, I can believe," admitted Grandma Mayburn,
"that Grace was as pretty—a tremendous compliment to
you, Grace—but there never was and never will be another
baby as pretty and cunning as our Hilda."

The good old lady never spoke of the child as Grace's
baby. It was always "ours." In Graham, Grace, and
especially Hilda, she had her children about her, and the
mother-need in her heart was satisfied.

"Yes, Hilda darling," said the colonel, with fond eyes, "you have begun well. You could not please me more than by looking like your mother; the next thing is to grow like her."

"Poor blind papa, with the perpetual glamour on his eyes! He will never see his old white-haired wife as she is."

He looked at her almost perfect features with the bloom of health upon them, into her dark eyes with their depths of motherly pride and joy, at her snowy neck and ivory arms bare to the summer heat, and longest at the wavy silver of her hair, that crowned her beauty with an almost supernatural charm.

"Don't I see you as you are, Grace?" he said. "Well, I am often spellbound by what I do see. If Hilda becomes like you, excepting your sorrows, my dearest wish in her behalf will be fulfilled."

Old Aunt Sheba, standing behind the baby's chair, felt a chill at heart as she thought: "Dey'se all a-worshippin' de chile and each oder. I sees it so plain dat I'se all ob a-tremble."

Surely the dark shadows of the past have no place near that birthday feast, but they are coming nearer, closing in, remorseless, relentless as ever, and among them are the gloomy rivals against whom Graham struggled so long. He thought he had vanquished them, but they are stealing upon him again like vindictive, unforgiving savages.

There was a jar of thunder upon the still air, but it was not heeded. The room began to darken, but they thought only of a shower that would banish the sultriness of the day. Darker shadows than those of thunder-clouds were falling upon them, had they known it.

The wine was brought, and the health of the baby drank. Then Graham, ordering all glasses to be filled, said reverently: "To the memory of Warren Hilland! May the child who is named for him ever remind us of his noble life and heroic death."

They drank in silence, then put down the glasses and sat for moments with bowed heads, Grace's tears falling softly. Without, nature seemed equally hushed. Not a breath stirred the sultry air, until at last a heavier and nearer jar of thunder vibrated in the distance.

The unseen shadows are closing around the little Hilda, whose eyelids are heavy with satiety. Aunt Sheba is about to take her from her chair, when a swift gust, cold and spray-laden, rushes through the house, crushing to the doors and whirling all light articles into a carnival of disorder.

The little gossamer-clad girl shivered, and, while others hastily closed windows, Grace ran for a shawl in which to wrap her darling.

The shower passed, bringing welcome coolness. Hilda slept quietly through its turmoil and swishing torrents— slept on into the twilight, until Aunt Sheba seemed a shadow herself. But there were darker shadows brooding over her.

Suddenly, in her sleep, the child gave an ominous barking cough.

"Oh, de good Lor'!" cried Aunt Sheba, springing to her feet. Then with a swiftness in which there was no sign of age, she went to the landing and called, "Mas'r Graham."

Grace was in the room before him. "What is it?" she asked breathlessly.

"Well, Missy Grace, don't be 'larmed, but I tinks Mas'r Graham 'ud better sen' for de doctor, jes' for caution like."

Again came that peculiar cough, terror-inspiring to all mothers.

"Alford, Alford, lose not a moment!" she cried. "It's the croup."

The soldier acted as if his camp were attacked at midnight. There were swift feet, the trampling of a horse; and soon the skill of science, the experience of age, and motherly tenderness confronted the black shadows, but they remained immovable.

The child gasped and struggled for life. Grace, half

frantic, followed the doctor's directions with trembling
hands, seeking to do everything for her idol herself as far
as possible. Mrs. Mayburn, gray, grim, with face of ashen
hue, hovered near and assisted. Aunt Sheba, praying often
audibly, proved by her deft hands that the experience of
her long-past motherhood was of service now. The servants
gathered at the door, eager and impatient to do something
for "de bressed chile." The poor old major thumped rest-
lessly back and forth on his crutches in the hall below, half
swearing, half praying. Dr. Markham, pale with anxiety,
but cool and collected as a veteran general in battle, put
forth his whole skill to baffle the destroyer. Graham, standing in the background with clenched hands, more excited,
more desperate than he had ever been when sitting on his
horse waiting for the bugle to sound the charge, watched
his wife and child with eyes that burned in the intensity of
his feeling.

Time, of which no notice was taken, passed, although
moments seemed like hours. The child still struggled and
gasped, but more and more feebly. At last, in the dawn,
the little Hilda lay still, looked up and smiled. Was it at
her mother's face, or something beyond?

"She is better," cried Grace, turning her imploring eyes
to the physician, who held the little hand.

Alas! it was growing cold in his. He turned quickly
to Graham and whispered: "Support your wife. The end
is near."

He came mechanically and put his arm around her.

"Grace, dear Grace," he faltered, hoarsely, "can you not
bear this sorrow also for my sake?"

"Alford!" she panted with horror in her tones—"Alford!
why, why, her hand is growing cold!"

There was a long low sigh from the little one, and then
she was still.

"Take your wife away," said Dr. Markham, in a low,
authoritative tone.

Graham sought to obey in the same mechanical manner.

She sprang from him and stood aloof. There was a terrible light in her eyes, before which he quailed.

"Take me away!" she cried, in a voice that was hoarse, strained, and unnatural. "Never! Tell me the belief of your heart. Have I lost my child forever? Is that sweet image of my Hilda nothing but clay? Is there nothing further for this idol of my heart but horrible corruption? If this is true, no more learned jargon to me about law and force! If this is true, I am the creation of a fiend who, with all the cruel ingenuity of a fiend, has so made me that he can inflict the utmost degree of torture. If this is true, my motherhood is a lie, and good is punished, not evil. If this is true, there is neither God nor law, but only a devil. But let me have the truth: have I lost that child forever?"

He was dumb, and an awful silence fell upon the chamber of death.

Graham's philosophy failed him at last. His own father-heart could not accept of corruption as the final end of his child. Indeed, it revolted at it with a resistless rebound as something horrible, monstrous, and, as his wife had said, devilish. His old laborious reasoning was scorched away as by lightning in that moment of intense consciousness when *his* soul told him that, if this were true, his nature also was a lie and a cheat. He knew not what he believed, or what was true. He was stunned and speechless.

Despair was turning his wife's face into stone, when old Aunt Sheba, who had been crouching, sobbing and praying at the foot of the little couch, rose with streaming eyes and stretched out her hands toward the desperate mother.

"No, Missy Grace," she cried, in tones that rang through the house; "no, no, no. Your chile am not lost to you; your chile am not dead. She on'y sleeps. Did not de good Lord say: 'Suffer de little chillen ter come unter Me'? An' Hilda, de dear little lamb, hab gone ter Him, an' is in de Good Shepherd's arms. Your little chile am not lost to you, she's safe at home, de dear bressed home ob heben, whar your moder is, Missy Grace. De Hebenly Father say,

'Little Hilda, you needn't walk de long flinty, thorny path
and suffer like you'se dear moder. You kin come home
now, and I'se 'll take keer ob ye till moder comes.' Bress
de little lamb, she smile when de angels come fer her, an'
she's safe, safe for ebermore. No tears fer little Hilda, no
heartbreak in all her 'ternal life. Dear Missy Grace, my
little baby die, too, but I hain't los' it. No, no. De Good
Shepherd is a keepin' it safe fer me, an' I shall hab my
baby again.''

It is impossible to describe the effect of this passionate
utterance of faith as it came warm and direct from the heart
of another bereaved mother, whose lowliness only empha-
sized the universal human need of something more than
negations and theories of law and force. The major heard
it in the hall below, and was awed. Mrs. Mayburn and
the servants sobbed audibly. The stony look went out of
Grace's face; tears welled up into her hot, dry eyes, and
she drew near and bent over her child with an indescribable
yearning in her face. Aunt Sheba ceased, sank down on
the floor, and throwing her apron over her face she rocked
back and forth and prayed as before.

Suddenly Grace threw herself on the unconscious little
form, and cried with a voice that pierced every heart: "O
God, I turn to Thee, then. Is my child lost to me forever,
or is she in Thy keeping? Was my mother's faith true?
Shall I have my baby once more? Jesus, art Thou a Shepherd of the little ones? Hast Thou suffered my Hilda to
come unto Thee? Oh, if Thou art, Thou canst reveal Thy-
self unto me and save a broken-hearted mother from despair.
This child *was* mine. Is it mine still?'' and she clasped her
baby convulsively to her bosom.

'' 'Suffer de little chillen ter come unter me, and forbid
dem not,' '' repeated Aunt Sheba in low tones.

Again a deep, awed silence fell upon them all. Grace
knelt so long with her own face pressed against her child's
that they thought she had fainted. The physician motioned
Graham to lift her up, but he shook his head. He was

crushed and despairing, feeling that in one little hour he had lost the belief of his manhood, the child that had brought into his home a heaven that he at least could understand, and as he heard his wife's bitter cry he felt that her life and reason might soon go also. He recognized again the presence of his bitter rivals, Grief and Death, and felt that at last they had vanquished him. He had not the courage or the will to make another effort.

"Mrs. Graham, for your husband's sake—" began Dr. Markham.

"Ah! forgive me, Alford," she said, rising weakly; "I should not have forgotten you for a moment."

She took an uncertain step toward him, and he caught her in his arms.

Laying her head upon his breast, she said gently, "Alford, our baby is not dead."

"Oh, Grace, darling!" he cried in agony, "don't give way, or we are both lost. I have no strength left. I cannot save you again. Oh! if the awful past should come back!"

"It now can never come back. Alford, we have not lost our child. Aunt Sheba has had a better wisdom than you or I, and from this hour forth my mother's faith is mine. Do not think me wild or wandering. In my very soul has come the answer to my cry. Horrible corruption is not the end of that lovely life. You can't believe it, any more than I. Dear little sleeper, you are still *my* baby. I shall go to you, and you will never suffer as I have suffered. God bless you, Aunt Sheba! your heaven-inspired words have saved me from despair. Alford, dear Alford, do not give way so; I'll live and be your true and faithful wife. I'll teach you the faith that God has taught me."

He drew long, deep breaths. He was like a great ship trying to right itself in a storm. At last he said, in broken tones:

"Grace, you are right. It's not law or force. It's either God, who in some way that I can't understand, will bring

good out of all this evil, or else it's all devilish, fiendish.
If after this night you can be resigned, patient, hopeful,
your faith shall be mine."

The shadows, affrighted, shrank further away than ever
before.

"I take you at your word," she replied, as she drew him
gently away. "Come, let us go and comfort papa."

One after another stole out after them until Mrs. Mayburn was alone with the dead. Long and motionless she
stood, with her eyes fixed on the quiet, lovely face.

"Hilda," at last she moaned, "little Hilda, shall poor
old grandma ever see our baby again?"

At that moment the sun rose high enough to send a ray
through the lattice, and it lighted the baby's face with what
seemed a smile of unearthly sweetness.

A few moments later Aunt Sheba found the aged woman
with her head upon little Hilda's bosom, and there she
received a faith that brought peace.

A few evenings later there was a grassy mound, covered
with roses, under the apple-tree by the rustic seat; and at
the head of the little grave there was placed a block of marble bearing the simple inscription:

"Here sleeps our Baby Hilda."

.   .   .   .

Years have passed. The little monument is now near
another and a stately one in a Virginia cemetery. Fresh
flowers are on it, showing that "Our Baby Hilda" is never
forgotten. Fresh flowers are beneath the stately column,
proving that the gallant soldier sleeping under it is never
forgotten. Fresh flowers are on the young Confederate's
grave, commemorating a manly and heroic devotion to a
cause that was sacred to him. The cause was lost; and had
he lived to green old age he would have thanked God for
it. Not least among the reasons for thankfulness is the
truth that to men and peoples that which their hearts
craved is often denied.

Not far away is a home as unostentatious as the Northern

cottage, but larger, and endowed with every homelike at-
tribute. Sweet Grace Graham is its mistress. Her lovely
features are somewhat marked by time and her deep experiences, but they have gained a beauty and serenity that will
defy time. Sounds of joyous young life again fill the house,
and in a cradle by her side "little Grace" is sleeping.
Grandma Mayburn still knits slowly by the hearth, but
when the days are dry and warm it is her custom to steal
away to the cemetery and remain for hours with "Our
Baby." The major has grown very feeble, but his irritable protest against age and infirmity has given place to a
serene, quiet waiting till he can rest beside the brave soldiers who have forgotten their laurels.

Colonel Anderson, now a prosperous planter, has his
own happy home life, and his aged father shares the best
there is in it. He still preaches in the quaint old church,
repaired but not modernized, and his appearance and life
give eloquence to his faltering words. The event of the
quiet year is the annual visit of Rita and Captain Windom
with their little brood. Then truly the homes abound in
breezy life; but sturdy, blue-eyed Warren Graham is the
natural leader of all the little people's sport. The gallant
black horse Mayburn is still Iss's pride, but he lets no one
mount him except his master. Aunt Sheba presides at the
preparation of state dinners, and sits by the cradle of baby
Grace. She is left, however, most of the time, to her own
devices, and often finds her way also to the cemetery to
"wisit dat dear little lamb, Hilda," murmuring as she
creeps slowly with her cane, "We'se all a-followin' her
now, bress de Lord."

Jinny's stories of what she saw and of her experiences
abroad have become so marvellous that they might be true
of some other planet, but not of ours. Dusky faces gather
round her by the kitchen fire, and absolute faith is expressed
by their awed looks. Old Jehu has all the chickens and
"sass" he wants without working for them, and his son
Huey has settled down into a steady "hand," who satisfies

his former ruling passion with an occasional coon-hunt. Both of the colonels have the tastes of sportsmen, and do all in their power to preserve the game in their vicinity. They have become closer friends with the lapsing years, and from crossing swords they look forward to the time when they can cross their family escutcheons by the marriage of the sturdy Warren with another little Rita, who now romps with him in a child's happy unconsciousness.

There are flecks of gray in Graham's hair and beard, and deep lines on his resolute face, but he maintains his erect, soldierly bearing even when superintending the homely details of the plantation. Every one respects him; the majority are a little afraid of him, for where his will has sway there is law and order, but to the poor and sorrowful he gives increasing reason to bless his name. His wife's faith has become his. She has proved it true by the sweet logic of her life. In their belief, the baby Hilda is only at home before them, and the soldier without fear and without reproach has found the immortality that he longed for in his dying moments. He is no longer a cherished, honored memory only; he is the man they loved, grown more manly, more noble in the perfect conditions of a higher plane of life. The dark mysteries of evil are still dark to them—problems that cannot be solved by human reason. But in the Divine Man, toward whose compassionate face the sorrowful and sinful of all the centuries have turned, they have found One who has mastered the evil that threatened their lives. They are content to leave the mystery of evil to Him who has become in their deepest consciousness Friend and Guide. He stands between them and the shadows of the past and the future.

THE END